INTRUDERS

Wake up, Jace pleaded silently. *Please, wake up.*

He wanted to yell at them, but didn't—in part because he was scared, but also because his brain felt so sluggish and fuzzy.

Then one of the intruders leaned over his mother's chest and did something so awful, Jace took a tentative step forward, thinking he should try to stop it. But as his foot swept across the floor, it connected with a small toy truck, knocking it with a clatter. Convinced the intruders had heard, he ran for his bed. Pulling the covers up over his head, he curled himself into a tight ball.

Frightened and trembling, he huddled beneath the covers. When the sounds finally stopped, he still stayed hidden. It was half an hour before he finally summoned up the courage to peek beyond the covers.

The house was deathly quiet. With as little noise as possible, Jace tiptoed to the door, peeking around the edge. The strange light and the intruders were gone.

But so was his mother.

Praise for

Cold White Fury

"[A] first-rate supernatural thriller . . .
a novel filled with convincing twists . . .
that lead to a knockout ending."

—*Publishers Weekly*

Books by Beth Amos

Cold White Fury
Eyes of Night
Second Sight°

Published by HarperPaperbacks

°coming soon

HarperChoice

EYES OF NIGHT

BETH AMOS

HarperPaperbacks
A Division of HarperCollinsPublishers

HarperPaperbacks
A Division of HarperCollins*Publishers*
10 East 53rd Street, New York, N.Y. 10022-5299

This is a work of fiction. The characters, incidents, and dialogues are products of the author's imagination and are not to be construed as real. Any resemblance to persons, living or dead, is entirely coincidental.

ISBN 0-06-101006-5

HarperCollins®, ®, and HarperPaperbacks™ are trademarks of HarperCollins*Publishers*, Inc.

Cover design by Derek Walls
Cover photo © 1997 Tony Stone Images

First printing: December 1997

Printed in the United States of America

Visit HarperPaperbacks on the World Wide Web at
http://www.harpercollins.com

❖ 10 9 8 7 6 5 4 3 2 1

For Harry Arnston
author, mentor, gentleman, and friend.
Though sorely missed, you live on
in the hearts, minds, and words
of so many.

ACKNOWLEDGMENTS

A special nod of thanks to Ed "Dr. Dirt" Schreiner, Research Biologist and Naturalist for the Olympic National Park; to Dr. Art Kruckeberg, Professor Emeritus with the Department of Botany at the University of Washington; to Barb Masaki, surely the best tour guide Bill Speidel's Underground Tour ever had; and to Ken Dilling, for sharing your vacation, the whales, and most of all, your pictures.

A warmhearted thank you to my good friends: Dr. James T. "Buzzy" May, III, both for helping me to explore the scientific possibilities and for maintaining a level of enthusiasm that often exceeded my own; to Jerilyn Dufresne and Nelson Thurman, my faithful readers and critics; and to all the wonderful, supportive folks on the Prodigy Books and Writing bulletin board.

A big hug of thanks to my parents, Frank and Laura Webb, for their neverending love and support. And to Dad, a special nod for being one of my most reliable sources for information and technical advice. Much love to you both and the rest of my family.

My final thanks go to the two women who helped make it all possible. To my editor, Jessica Lichtenstein, for her support, enthusiasm, and patience; and last, but hardly least, my agent, Linda Hayes. I am forever indebted.

PROLOGUE

Jace Johansen awoke with a suddenness that made him gasp for air. The way his heart bounced inside his chest, he thought he'd had another bad dream. Except he couldn't remember one.

Puzzled, he rolled his head to the side to look for bogeymen who might be hiding in the corners. The movement made him wince as he felt a throbbing ache in his neck. His head hurt, too, and he wondered if he was sick. A few of the kids at school had something called chicken pox, and his mom had said he might get it. He didn't know what chicken pox was exactly, and as he stared into the shifting shadows of his room, he tried to imagine a bunch of huge monster chickens silently creeping up to his bed.

But even in the dark, monster chickens seemed silly, and Jace managed a sleepy smile. He thought about calling out to his mother, but hesitated. She kept telling him he was a big boy now that he was in the first grade, and he really wanted that to be true. *This time I'll be brave*, he thought. Which wasn't terribly difficult, seeing as how he wasn't all that scared in the first place.

He heard a noise—a soft rustling kind of thump.
Mommy.

If she was up anyway, he might as well join her. She would probably just send him back to bed, but maybe she would tuck him in. Or better yet, snuggle up beside him. He loved it when she did that, her breath warm on his hair, her arm soft beneath his shoulders. Sometimes she sang to him or told him stories.

It was the possibility of a story that convinced him. He threw the covers aside, climbed out of bed, and padded across the room, his gait shuffling and sleepy. In the doorway he paused, gazing bleary-eyed down the hall toward his parents' room and steadying himself with one hand on the doorframe.

A strange light shone from the other end of the hall, and puzzled, Jace rubbed a fist in his eye before looking again. He blinked slowly, heavily, tilting his head to one side to ease the ache in his neck, his brow furrowing. Then a shadow moved across the light and Jace's head snapped up, his eyes growing wide. Instinctively, he backed up a step.

Hugging the doorjamb, he peeked around its edge and watched.

There were three of them, and as he thought this the fingers on his right hand ticked off the numbers: one, two, three. The intruders hovered around his parents' bed, and Jace could see his mother lying on her back, almost naked, her nightgown pushed up around her neck. He wondered why she didn't yell at the intruders and tell them to go away. Or why his father didn't. But they both lay still and quiet, sleeping while the intruders moved about the room.

Wake up, Jace pleaded silently. *Please, wake up*.

He thought about yelling to his parents, but didn't—in part because he was scared, but also because his brain felt so sluggish and fuzzy, he wondered if this might not be a bad dream after all.

Then one of the intruders leaned over his mother's chest and did something so awful, Jace took a tentative step forward, thinking he should try to stop it. But as his foot swept across the floor, it connected with a small toy truck, knocking it into the baseboard with a clatter. He pulled back from the door, holding his breath and feeling a shiver of fear race down his spine. Convinced the intruders had heard him and would now come after him, he darted across the room, leaping into his bed. Pulling the covers up over his head, he curled himself into a tight ball and closed his eyes in the naive belief that if he couldn't see the bogeymen, they couldn't see him.

Frightened and trembling, he huddled beneath the covers, listening to the sounds down the hall. He fought the drowsiness that pulled at him, knowing if he went to sleep, the monsters would come and get him for sure. When the sounds finally stopped, he still stayed hidden, fearful the bogeymen were only trying to trick him. It was half an hour before he finally summoned up the courage to peek beyond the covers.

No bogeymen.

The house was deathly quiet. Slowly, and with as little noise as possible, Jace slid out of bed and tiptoed over to the door, peeking around the edge. With relief he saw that both the strange light and the intruders were gone.

But so was his mother.

ONE

Kerri Whitaker pushed through the door of the
Seattle police station and approached the glassed-in
reception area. Behind the bullet-proof barrier sat a
uniformed woman officer, a phone held to one ear, her
back to the window. Kerri tapped on the glass and the
officer spun around, her face lighting with pleasure
and recognition. She held up one finger to indicate
she'd be just a moment, and Kerri waited, her foot
tapping with impatience.

"Dr. Whitaker!" the officer said when she'd finally
hung up the phone. "Long time, no see. How's everything?"

"Fine, Catherine. And you?"

"Can't complain," the woman said with a shrug.
"You're here to see Kevin, right?"

Kerri nodded. "He wanted me to come down and
observe an interrogation he has scheduled for uh . . ."
She paused to make a pointed glance at her watch.
"Five minutes ago."

"Then you best get on back there," Catherine said.
The phone in front of her rang, and with a roll of her
eyes, she jabbed at a button on it with one hand, while
she reached beneath the desk with the other. A buzzer
sounded, and Kerri stepped over to the door on her

left and yanked it open. "Good to see you again," Catherine said. Then, with a little finger wave at Kerri, she snatched up the phone. Kerri returned the wave along with a smile, then headed down the hallway, letting the door clank shut behind her.

The corridor was lined with offices—most of them little more than cubbyholes—and as Kerri worked her way down the hall she saw some familiar faces. A few people hollered out to her as she went by, and it was apparent they would have liked her to stop and chat, but she was late already and kept her greetings perfunctory as she hurried on toward the interrogation rooms.

Rounding the corner at the end of the hall, she immediately recognized Kevin, even though his back was to her. His expanding girth and graying black hair didn't distinguish him all that much from a half-dozen other detectives who worked here, but his height—six six—made him easy to identify. He was leaning against the wall, talking with a baby-faced uniformed officer Kerri didn't recognize. *A rookie,* she thought.

"Kevin?" Kerri said softly.

Kevin spun around, an amazingly graceful gesture given his size. His blue eyes crinkled into a smile. "Kerri! Glad you made it. I was beginning to think you were going to stand me up." He settled one huge, beefy hand on her shoulder.

"I thought about it," Kerri said with a hint of annoyance. She glanced at her watch. "I don't have much time. I have another patient due at the office in just forty-five minutes."

"Well then, let's get to it," Kevin said. He gave the officer a brief "catch you later," then cupped Kerri's elbow in his palm and steered her toward a doorway just a few feet away.

They entered a narrow, darkened room that contained three chairs positioned along the wall opposite the door. In front of the chairs was a window—a two-way mirror, actually, that allowed someone to observe the interrogation room beyond. At the moment, the interrogation room was empty except for a small table scarred with numerous cigarette burns and two equally beat-up chairs. The bleakness of the furnishings was accentuated by gray cinder-block walls, a darker gray concrete floor, and the harsh light of a fluorescent fixture in the ceiling.

Kevin lifted a phone on the wall near the door, and muttered, "We're ready." When he hung up, he turned to Kerri and said, "It'll be just a moment."

Kerri gave him a cursory nod along with a look that clearly communicated her impatience. "I still don't understand all the mystery, Kevin. Why won't you tell me anything about this person you want me to evaluate? It's not like I haven't done this before."

Kevin fumbled in his shirt pocket and extracted a pack of cigarettes. He tapped one out, lit it, and after taking one long satisfied pull, blew out a trail of smoke. His eyes were focused on the other room. "This case is different," he said slowly. "It's not your run-of-the-mill interrogation. The . . . uh . . . person we're questioning isn't a suspect. He's a witness."

"So? I've observed and evaluated witnesses for you before, as well as suspects. What makes this one so different?"

The door in the other room opened, and Kevin gave a quick nod toward the glass. "You'll see."

Kerri turned toward the window and watched as a detective entered the interrogation room. A second later, a woman—a psychologist named Marge Turner, whom Kerri knew vaguely—steered the witness through the door and sat him in one of the chairs.

Kerri's reaction was swift and decisive.

"No way, Kevin," she said, whirling around to confront him. She shook her head vehemently to punctuate the statement, an angry glint in her green eyes. "I've told you I can't do any more kids." She promptly headed for the door, but Kevin made a quick sidestep and blocked her way. Stopping just short of a collision, Kerri rolled her eyes and crossed her arms over her chest. She glared up at him, teeth clenched, lips pursed into a thin line.

"Just wait a minute, okay?" Kevin pleaded. "I know you're probably angry with me for bringing you down here like this, but if I'd told you it was a kid beforehand, you wouldn't have come."

"Damn right, I wouldn't have! How can you do this, Kevin? You know . . . how hard it's been for me." Her voice cracked on the last words and her eyes filled with the liquid sheen of tears. She turned away from him and stared at the wall, the muscles in her jaw twitching.

Kevin gave his cigarette a disgusted look, then dropped it to the floor and snuffed it out with his foot. He, too, crossed his arms over his chest as he let out a heavy sigh and studied Kerri's profile. "Look," he said finally. "I know things have been rough for you lately. But it's been over a year since Mandy's death. Don't you think it's about time you got back into it again?"

Kerri shot him a nasty look. "Who's the psychiatrist here, Kevin? You or me? Don't you think I'm capable of judging when I'm ready?"

"No, I'm not sure you are," Kevin shot back. His eyes narrowed. "How much longer are you going to wallow in this grief of yours?"

Kerri's jaw dropped with disbelief; her arms fell to her sides. She turned to face him head-on, her eyes wide. "Wallow? You think I'm wallowing? Jesus Christ, Kevin! You try losing your six-year-old daughter and your husband all in the period of a few months. You try sitting at the bedside of the one person in the world you love most of all, feeling helpless as you watch her waste away. You try sitting around wishing for some horrendous tragedy to befall someone else's child so that your own might live." Tears coursed down her face, leaving a silvery trail along her cheeks. She sagged momentarily, her anger draining away with the tears. More quietly, her voice wavering as she struggled to maintain control, she said, "You try all that, Kevin. Then talk to me about wallowing." She turned away from him and stared at the wall.

Kevin looked into the other room. "I didn't mean to belittle your feelings," he said heavily. "I wouldn't have asked you to come down here if I wasn't desperate."

He glanced back toward Kerri, his expression softening at the sight of her tear-stained face. "Look," he said, "Marge Turner has tried for the past two days to get the kid to open up. But all he does is sit there like that, staring off into space, rocking back and forth. He's got this hyperactive thing and can't sit still for two minutes." He paused. "The kid needs help, Kerri. And getting him to talk may mean saving someone's life— his mother's to be exact."

Kerri's eyebrows shot up at that, and Kevin, sensing a weakening in her resistance, plunged on.

"Marge is good, but she's not half as good as you. You've always had such a knack with kids. I know you can get through to him. He needs you." Then, more softly he added, "And I think you need him."

Kerri turned and looked at him, her expression a mix of hurt and incredulity. She ran her palms over her cheeks to wipe away the itchy burn of her tears, then looked up toward the ceiling and slowly closed her eyes, letting out a weary sigh.

"Please?" Kevin asked. "At least watch him for a few minutes, and if you decide you don't want to see him, so be it."

Kerri stood perfectly still, her head tilted back, her eyes closed. Then she lowered her head and slowly turned toward the window, looking into the other room.

Marge Turner sat on one side of the table, her arms resting on its surface, her body leaning eagerly toward the boy on the other side. The male detective was gone, apparently having left the room.

With a deep, bracing breath, Kerri let her gaze crawl toward the boy. He was rocking back and forth in his seat, his chest bumping against the table, his hands busy in his lap, wringing the hem of his shirt. His white-blond hair was mussed, sticking up around his head in a series of spikes. His eyes—huge, round, and very blue—stared across the table, just past Marge's shoulder. The T-shirt he wore was far too big for him and hung loosely on his thin, bony shoulders. His feet dangled several inches above the floor as he swung them back and forth, banging his feet against the legs of the chair. Kerri guessed his age to be around five or six.

"What did he see?" Kerri asked in a low voice.

Kevin moved closer, watching the scene in the other room over Kerri's shoulder. "I don't know," he admitted. "That's what we're trying to find out. His mother disappeared rather mysteriously this past weekend. Ever since, the kid's been acting real strange. He's fine until we try to talk to him about his mother. Then he gets that blank look on his face and just stares off into space. I'm sure it's more than the fact that his mother is gone. I think he saw something."

"Is there a father in the picture?" Kerri asked.

"Uh-huh. We convinced him to bring the kid down here so Marge could try to get him to open up. He's waiting outside now. He seems . . . concerned about the changes in his son's behavior."

"What does he say happened?"

"I'd rather leave that for you to ferret out. I don't want to color your opinion."

On the other side of the window, Marge spoke to the boy in a soft, murmuring tone. "Jace? There's no need to be scared. All I want to do is talk to you. Is there something you'd like to talk about? Anything at all?"

The boy gave no indication he'd heard her. He kept rocking, back and forth, back and forth.

"Jace? Please stop rocking," Marge tried.

Amazingly, he did.

"Jace? Can we talk about your mother for a moment?" Marge asked.

Kerri shook her head and blew out a little puff of annoyance. "Come on, Marge," she mumbled. "You can do better than that."

For a moment, the boy sat perfectly still. Then he leaned forward and laid his cheek on the table, his face turned toward the wall just below the window. Kerri cocked her head to one side to better study him. As she watched, he closed his eyes. A second later, fat tears slid over his nose and down his cheek, pooling in a wet blotch on the table beneath his head. Slowly, he began to rock again.

Kerri felt a stab of anguish tear through her heart like a wooden spike. She clasped one hand over her mouth and felt the hot rush of her own tears. Several silent minutes ticked by before she turned around and faced Kevin. "I want to see both him and his father," she said tersely.

Kevin gave her the briefest flicker of a smile. "No problem. I've already spoken to his father about it."

"Can you have them come by first thing tomorrow? Say, eight o'clock?"

"They'll be there."

"Fine." Kerri stepped past him and moved toward the door. As she yanked it open, she paused, turning back toward Kevin. "What are their names?"

"Johansen," Kevin said. "Thad and Jace Johansen."

Kerri nodded, started to leave, then turned back once more. She cocked her head at Kevin. "You knew I'd give in once I saw him, didn't you?"

Kevin shrugged. "I hoped so," he said.

"Sometimes I hate you, Kevin McCallister."

"I know."

After one last glance toward the window, Kerri left the room, letting the door close softly behind her.

TWO

❧❖❧

The morning ferry ride into Seattle was usually Kerri's favorite part of the day: watching the morning sun chase away the gray blanket of early dawn as it nudged its way over the Cascade Mountains, seeing the western slopes come to life in a bath of warm golden-white glow, following the fingers of light as they crept their way through the Seattle skyline. Behind her, the peaks of the Olympic range were slowly revealing themselves in a breathtaking display of pink light and blue shadow, their quiet majesty providing a sense of protection and insulation from the rest of the world. The number of days where the skies were clear and the mountains visible would rapidly dwindle now that September was drawing to a close. But that didn't matter to Kerri. Even when thick clouds in shades from pearly white to charcoal gray embraced the coast, there was a certain mystical beauty to the area.

With the unexpected gift of a clear day, Kerri decided to forgo her usual spot inside the cabin area and climbed instead to the upper deck. She did so hoping the majestic beauty around her might chase away the lingering images from the night before.

But it was not to be. The surrounding beauty went

unnoticed as remembered bits of her nightmare flashed through her brain like a movie trailer.

Sitting in the doctor's office, feeling as if all the air had just been sucked from the room, hearing that awful word for the first time—cancer. . . .

Mandy's sixth birthday, tears rolling down her face as she lay weakened, pale and bald, her beautiful copper-colored hair—so like Kerri's own—lying in lonely clumps on her pillow. . . .

Stroking Mandy's arms—tiny sticks that seemed too fragile to lift even a butterfly—their surface marred by bruises and scars. Her hand frighteningly cold and as weightless as a dead leaf . . .

Staring at Mandy's body, small and scrawny, adrift on a sea of sterile white sheets and surrounded by an armada of tubes and equipment. . . .

It was the same nightmare that had haunted her in the months immediately following Mandy's death—a series of rapid segues, an entire year of tragedy compressed into a few horrifying images. Throughout it, Kerri relived the utter helplessness of those months, felt anew the anguish and frustration of watching her daughter slip away while she stood by, angry and powerless.

But Mandy had survived the first battle. Kerri could still recall the bemused expressions on the doctors' faces as they stood around Mandy's bed, scratching their heads in amazement as they declared her cancer in complete remission. She could still recall the incredible sense of relief and happiness she'd felt, though now it was colored by the knowledge of what was to follow, for that blessed moment of happiness was only a tease, one of life's cruel ironies. Kerri's nightmare never focused on those wonderfully blessed weeks where it seemed Mandy might be healthy and whole again. Instead, it skipped to the final blow, with the doctors again surrounding Mandy's bed, their faces marked with sadness and pity as they explained how the chemotherapy had destroyed Mandy's heart and kidneys along with the cancer.

Mandy's death had been a terrible blow. For months, Kerri stumbled blindly through life, surprised at the depth of her sorrow. She threw herself into her work, discovering quickly how focusing on the problems of her patients made it easier to forget her own. But she'd made one significant change: she no longer saw any children. Though they had been a large part of her psychiatry practice prior to Mandy's illness, their presence became an all-too-painful reminder after Mandy's death. At first Kerri's grief had been like a razor-sharp knife, striking quick and deep, its wounds nearly mortal. But gradually, the edges of her grief had dulled, leaving behind a subdued but constant ache. Oddly enough, the signs of her emotional healing saddened Kerri. She measured the depth of her love for Mandy by the intensity of her grief. Its waning seemed somehow insulting, a mockery of the emotional bond that had existed between them. Yet despite that irrationality, Kerri hadn't mourned the eventual disappearance of her nightmare. Its tortured images had haunted her sleep one too many times. Now, thanks to Kevin, it had returned.

The ferry was nearing the dock, and its horn blasted through the air, making Kerri jump. Grateful for the distraction, she gathered up her briefcase and made her way to the other end of the boat.

As soon as the passenger bridge was in place, Kerri quickly joined the scurrying throng of people as they made their way down the covered gangplank toward the terminal building. By the time she reached Yesler Way and crossed under the viaduct to start the more rigorous uphill part of her walk, the familiarity of the daily routine had calmed her jangled nerves. Despite the fact she was in pretty good shape and made this same trek five days a week, the climb made her legs ache by the time she reached the office. Seattle's streets, with their steep angles and endless hills, were not for the lame and weary.

When she arrived at the office a few minutes before eight, she was not surprised to find Stephen already in; he was more of a morning person than she was. He sat behind his desk, both feet propped up, the morning paper stretched out in front of him, the crew-cut tufts of his shiny black hair barely visible above the paper's upper edge. Hearing the door open, he lowered the paper just enough to peer over it. His warm, Asian eyes smiled at Kerri.

"Good morning, boss lady."

"Hard at work as usual, I see," Kerri teased.

He cocked one black eyebrow at her, folded the paper haphazardly, and tossed it onto the desk. Then he spun around in his chair to face the small credenza along the wall behind him. Lined along its top were a coffee machine with a half-full pot, a bean grinder, and an assortment of one-pound coffee bags. "Ready for your morning brew?" he asked.

"As always." Kerri tossed her briefcase into one of the four chairs along the wall by the door and slipped out of the sweater coat she was wearing. "Let's see. What day is it?" she asked as she hung the sweater on a coat stand in the corner.

"Wednesday."

"Ahh, snickerdoodle day," she said, rubbing her hands together both with anticipation and to warm them. "One of my favorites."

Stephen handed her a steaming cup of coffee in a large white mug with GRADUATE of PSYCHOTIC STATE printed on one side. Kerri grimaced. The saying had seemed funny when she bought the damned thing, but this morning its message was a little too ironic. She wrapped her hands around the ceramic warmth, the symbolism of covering those all-too-meaningful words helping somehow. "Thank you, Stephen," she said, taking a sip of the cinnamon-flavored brew.

Stephen's face turned mockingly solemn as he folded his hands in front of him and bowed his head. "I am here to serve you, master. Your wish is my command."

"Smart-ass." Kerri took another sip, then realized Stephen was staring at her, the Oriental slant of his eyes made even narrower by his squinting assessment.

"You look tired this morning, boss lady," he observed.

Though the term boss lady was a teasing affectation Stephen had adopted years ago, there was nothing teasing in his tone. In the past, Kerri had found Stephen's image of himself as her caretaker somewhat amusing, particularly in light of their history. But this morning it felt oddly intrusive.

"I *am* a little tired," she said, turning away from his scrutiny. "I was up late last night." She shifted her attention to the small assortment of pink phone slips laid out on Stephen's desk. "Any important messages?" she asked, dismissing the subject.

There followed a brief and awkward moment of silence, where Kerri could see Stephen as clearly as if she had eyes in the back of her head. She knew he was weighing her avoidance of the subject, debating whether or not to let her get away with it. Then she heard him puff out a quick sigh between his lips and knew the moment had passed. Still, she avoided looking him in the eye as he walked around the desk and scooped the pink slips up with one sweep of his hand.

"Just the usual," he told her. He dealt the slips to her like a croupier in Las Vegas. "Dr. Landers called to follow up on the bulimic he sent you. Deandra wants to know if you can do lunch this week. Mr. Talman wants you to call him. Something about his medication. And Mrs. Rivers canceled her appointment . . . *again*," he added with a pointed arch of his brows. "I think she's got a secret, and she's afraid you're going to find out."

"Thank you for that medical opinion, Dr. Stephen," Kerri teased.

Stephen shrugged. "Hey, I don't need a medical degree to detect an addict. Not when I've known them up close and personal."

Kerri saw right though Stephen's nonchalance. She wasn't the only one with painful memories. More than once she'd thought it was this common bond of tragedy that had forged their friendship, making their relationship something more than just employer and employee . . . or doctor and patient, though it had ceased to exist on that level some years ago.

Kerri clutched the pink slips in one hand, her coffee cup in the other, and started to head into her office. Stephen darted around the desk, snatched up her briefcase, and met her in the doorway.

"You sure you're ready for this, boss lady?" he asked, riveting her eyes with his own. Though his build was slender, he had managed to maneuver himself between her and the office so her way was blocked. He looked her straight in the eye, their heights, both around five-seven, matching. There was no getting around him this time.

"Ready for what?" she asked meekly. It was a damned pathetic attempt, and they both knew it.

Stephen acknowledged it by rolling his eyes heavenward and shaking his head. "Confucius say man who acts stupid, is stupid."

"Confucius didn't say that."

"Quit avoiding the subject."

"Stephen Sato, you're trying my patience. Now please let me . . ."

Kerri's halfhearted admonition was cut short when the outer door to the office opened and they both turned to look. A very tall, slender man peered in, then gently steered the boy Kerri had seen yesterday through the doorway. The man had the same piercing blue eyes and thick mop of white-blond hair as the boy, though the boy's was longer and lacked the carefully trimmed angles. The noses were a mirror image as well—long and narrow with a small hump just below the bridge. Both pairs of lips were amazingly full, and a matching blush of ruddy color graced both sets of cheeks. Even if Kerri hadn't known she had a father-and-son appointment first thing this morning, there would have been no doubt these two were related.

The resemblance ended with their clothing, however. Where the boy was dressed in faded and tattered blue jeans, topped off by an oversized red T-shirt haphazardly tucked into one side of his pants, the father wore a tailored dress shirt, suit pants with a crease sharp enough to slice tomatoes, and expensive leather loafers.

The man looked at Kerri holding her message slips and coffee, then at Stephen, who was holding Kerri's briefcase. He dropped the hand on his son's shoulder and stuck it out toward Stephen. "Dr. Whitaker, I'm Thad Johansen."

Kerri smiled; Stephen uttered a nervous little cough. "I'm not Dr. Whitaker," Stephen said. "I'm Stephen Sato, her receptionist. That," he gestured toward Kerri with a nod, "is Dr. Whitaker."

The man looked over at Kerri, the crimson in his cheeks spreading across his face. "Oh. I am sorry," he stammered. "I just assumed—".

Kerri set her coffee cup on Stephen's desk and stepped forward, extending her hand. "Don't worry about it, Mr. Johansen. It's a common mistake."

The man gave himself a token slap on one side of his head, then reached out to accept Kerri's proffered hand. "I really am sorry," he repeated. "All that detective gave me was a name and an address. I gather your name is not Cary, C-a-r-y."

"No," she said. "It's K-e-r-r-i." She shook his hand quickly, assessing his grip as she did so. Though she fully embraced the scientific aspects of her field, she was unwilling to dismiss the more archaic indicators of human nature—things like body language, eye movements, gestures and such. She could often tell as much about a person by their handshake as she could after an hour-long session. Thad Johansen, she was delighted to see, had a warm hand and a solid grip, though without the bone-crushing intensity some men felt compelled to demonstrate.

Sucking in a deep breath, Kerri shifted her attention

to the boy. She let her breath back out by slow
degrees, acutely aware of Stephen's eyes watching her.

The boy couldn't have been more oblivious to
Kerri's discomfort. He hovered by the office door, his
gaze darting about the room, his hands wringing the
hem of his shirt, his feet and body shifting restlessly as
if he was doing some new modern dance. His eyes
never focused on any item for long, and as they roved
he chewed on his lower lip as if it was the first meal
he'd had in days.

Thad Johansen walked over to his son and placed a
steadying hand on the boy's shoulder. "Jace, this is Dr.
Whitaker, the psychiatrist I told you about."

The boy briefly looked at Kerri, then just as
quickly dismissed her and resumed his haphazard sur-
vey of his surroundings. His father sighed and looked
at Kerri with a wan, somewhat weary smile, though his
eyes reflected only patience and understanding. "As
you can see, Jace doesn't stay focused very long," he
said.

Kerri was impressed by the lack of apology in the
man's voice. Most parents with hyperactive children
were embarrassed by their child's lack of control, as if
it were a direct reflection of their own inadequacies.
But Thad Johansen's tone was one of calm concern and
acceptance.

Stephen, casting one last checking glance at Kerri,
handed over her briefcase and walked over to the boy.
He squatted down in front of him. "Jace? Wanna see
my dinosaur collection?"

The boy's eyes stopped their ceaseless roving and
focused on Stephen. "What kind of dinosaurs?" he
asked. His voice startled Kerri; it was so little and soft,
not unlike Mandy's had been. She swallowed hard.

"Toy ones, unfortunately," Stephen said. He dropped his voice down to a conspiratorial whisper and gave the room a wary once-over. "But they are way cool. I have a bunch of them in my desk drawer, but the boss lady doesn't know it. When she's not looking I take 'em out and let old T-rex beat the crap out of the brachyosaurus."

"Can I be the T-rex?" Jace asked, his eyes gleaming with the first hint of focused interest Kerri had seen since he entered the office.

"Well . . ." Stephen frowned. "I don't know. I like to be the T-rex. But I suppose for a little while . . ."

Kerri looked over at Mr. Johansen and gestured toward the door to her office with a sweep of her arm. "Why don't you go on in," she suggested. "I'd like to get a little history from you before I spend some time with Jace. Stephen will keep an eye on him until we're ready."

Mr. Johansen's brow furrowed with doubt.

"Jace will be fine, Mr. Johansen. Stephen is trained to handle kids like this and has plenty of experience, I assure you."

Thad Johansen looked from his son to Kerri, then back again to his son, indecision stamped on his face.

Kerri gave a little sideways nod of her head. "Come," she urged gently.

Thad Johansen let out a world-weary sigh, stared at the floor a moment, then gave an almost imperceptible nod. Looking like a man about to go to his own execution, he shuffled his way past Kerri and into her office.

Seeing that Stephen had already opened the dinosaur drawer in his desk, Kerri followed Mr. Johansen with a mirroring weary sigh of her own.

THREE

Located on the third floor of a building bordering
Pioneer Square, Kerri's office was mere blocks from
the waterfront. The room—a much-coveted corner
suite—was open and airy with a high ceiling and windows on two sides. Situated in front of the windows
was a small seating area with two well-stuffed chairs
and a matching love seat separated by a small
mahogany coffee table. The chairs faced a window
overlooking Puget Sound; the window beside the love
seat opened onto a view of Pioneer Square.

"Have a seat anywhere you like, Mr. Johansen,"
Kerri said once she closed the door. Her desk, most of
its surface covered with an assortment of charts,
papers, and journals, sat tucked into the corner beside
the seating area. Kerri set her briefcase on top of the
papers, opened it, and took out her pumps. Then she
settled into her chair and traded her walking shoes for
the dressier ones, waiting for Mr. Johansen to choose
his seat.

Though the shoes offered a handy excuse this
morning, Kerri usually trumped up some sort of delay-
ing tactic when bringing a new patient into her office
for the first time. Observing which seat they chose
gave her a certain amount of insight into their person-

ality. People who were open-minded and unafraid of closeness generally chose the love seat, bypassing the personal space protection offered by the individual chairs. The fact that the love seat's position at the side of a window offered less of a distraction also indicated a willingness to face the therapist head-on, focusing on the issues at hand.

When Thad Johansen chose the love seat without hesitation, Kerri logged the information in a file she kept only in her mind. She shoved her walking shoes beneath the desk, closed her briefcase, and picked up a notepad and pen. Then she walked over and sat in one of the chairs. She was pleased to see her theory apparently supported by Johansen's eager posture. He sat on the edge of the seat, elbows propped on his knees, hands folded together, his gaze intently fixed on Kerri.

"Okay, Mr. Johansen, I would like to start by having you give me a little bit of history—what led to your appointment here today."

Thad Johansen's brow drew down into a puzzled frown. "Didn't that detective tell you?"

Kerri shook her head. "He merely told me Jace is having some trouble, and that he thought I might be able to help. He was intentionally vague, as I prefer to draw my own conclusions without any preconceived notions." Kerri hesitated, thinking back to her conversation with Kevin. She studied Thad Johansen a moment and decided a forthright approach was best. "I do know the police are investigating the disappearance of your wife, and that your son's problems seem to be related. But beyond that, I know nothing. My primary interest here is to help you and Jace. Of course, I'm doing this at the behest of the police, but they have indicated your willingness to participate. Is that correct?"

Thad Johansen nodded. "If it will help them find my wife, or help Jace in any way, I'm willing to try anything."

"Good," Kerri said with a satisfied nod. "You do understand that my conversations with you and your son are privileged, protected by the doctor-patient relationship. Though the police would like me to share my opinions with them, or any information I might uncover, I will not do so without your express approval."

Thad Johansen seemed to weigh the import of her words, then he shrugged. "I have no problem with you sharing information with the police. As I've said, my primary interest is in finding my wife as quickly as possible. The police seem to think Jace knows something about her disappearance, and that's why he's been acting so strangely every time someone mentions Janet. If he does know something, he sure isn't telling. I've asked him myself a few times, and all he does is clam up and start rocking and staring." Thad Johansen gazed off across the room a moment, his eyes unfocused. "He gets this look on his face when he's like that, sort of a frightened, horrified expression." His eyes shifted back toward Kerri. "And he's not sleeping well."

Kerri nodded, scribbling some notes on the pad in her lap. "Tell me about your wife's disappearance," she prompted.

Thad Johansen leaned back, slid his palms along his thighs, and looked around the room. He blew out a long breath and said, "Well, let's see. We went to bed together Saturday night, and when I woke up Sunday morning, she was gone." He fixed his gaze on Kerri and hesitated, as if waiting for her to respond to this information.

She obliged by asking him a question. "Gone from the house, you mean?"

"I mean gone," he said quietly. "Packed a suitcase and everything."

"Were there problems between the two of you?"

Thad shrugged. "Not that I was aware of. I've gone over this in my mind a zillion times and still can't make sense of it."

"Was there another man involved?"

"Not that I was aware of," he repeated.

Kerri placed little stock in his answer. She knew from prior experience that men had a tendency to wear blinders where infidelity was concerned.

"Where did she go?"

"Well . . ." Thad hesitated, once again assuming a perplexed expression. "That's a good question. I have no idea."

Kerri frowned. "Did she leave a note or any other explanation?"

Thad shook his head sadly.

"What about family? Might she be staying with them?"

"She has no family except for a grandmother with Alzheimer's in a nursing home," Thad said. "Just me and Jace." Raw pain was evident in both the flinching expression on his face and the defensive hunch of his shoulders. He looked as if he expected a tremendous physical blow to descend upon him at any second.

Kerri felt a wave of pity for him. "This must be terribly confusing and painful for you," she said softly.

Thad Johansen nodded almost imperceptibly, his eyes brimming with tears.

Kerri gave him a moment to collect himself before she asked her next question.

"How did the police get involved?" she asked.

"I called them. To report that Janet was missing."

"And what did they have to say?"

Johansen's face tightened. "They said it happens all the time. A young woman becomes overwhelmed by the burden of marriage and motherhood and has an identity crisis." It was apparent from the sing-song quality of his voice that he was quoting a speech he had heard once too often. He paused and made a poor attempt to smile. "There were no signs of foul play, no reason to think anything happened to her. They told me, as gently as they could, that she had merely grown tired of me and Jace and needed to get away to find herself."

"And do you believe that?" Kerri asked gently.

Johansen turned away from Kerri, setting his gaze out the window over Pioneer Square. "No," he said flatly. "Our life may not have been perfect, but we were happy. And Jace means the world to Janet. She dotes on that boy. I can't believe she would just walk away from him like that with no parting words, no contact . . . no nothing." His voice faded away as he spoke, so that the last words he uttered were little more than a whisper. His tears took full release and trickled over, weaving two crooked streams, one down each cheek.

Once again Kerri sat silent, allowing him to absorb his emotion. Then she asked, "How is Jace taking all this?"

Thad Johansen swiped a quick hand over each cheek and sucked in a deep breath. He blew it out slowly; his head reared back and he stared at the ceiling.

Kerri waited.

After a few seconds, Thad lowered his head and looked at her. "He's been acting rather strangely, actually," he said.

"How so?"

"Well, he's always suffered from this hyperactivity thing. You experts call it attention deficit disorder."

Kerri nodded.

"He's been taking Ritalin for a few months now, with good results. His schoolwork has improved and he's much more focused. Or at least he was. Ever since Janet disappeared, he's been having these nightmares. He wakes up at all hours screaming and crying for his mother, covered in sweat, shaking, as if he's afraid of something.

"Plus," Thad continued, "he's been having these weird spells where he gets this blank look on his face and stares off at nothing whenever the subject of Janet comes up. He did it with the policemen, and that's when they suggested letting the psychologist down at the police station try to talk to him. I agreed, primarily because it kills me to see him like that. But when that didn't work, Detective McCallister suggested I bring Jace to you. He said you had a good record when it comes to working with kids."

Kerri inwardly winced at that and silently cursed Kevin for the umpteenth time since yesterday afternoon. She felt a tiny stab of pain in her heart, like a too-tight squeeze. Mandy's face flashed through her mind—not sick and dying with tubes sticking out of every inch of her little body, the way she'd last seen her, but healthy, laughing, running, her red curls bouncing in the breeze. Seeing the glimmer of hope in Thad Johansen's eyes, Kerri pushed the image away and said a silent prayer that she was up to this task.

"I have seen and treated a number of children," Kerri told him. "Though not for the past year." She debated telling him why, then decided not to. It wouldn't be fair to burden him with her own troubles; he had enough of his own. Still, he didn't miss what she said, and though his next question was awkward, Kerri was glad to note he was at least paying attention.

"What made you decide to take Jace on?"

Kerri thought hard about her answer before she gave it. Once again, she decided to opt for total honesty. "Actually, it was Kevin's—Detective McCallister's—pleading," she told him. "I've known him for a long time. He and my father used to be partners on the police force. Kevin has referred a number of troubled children to me over the years."

"I see," Johansen said thoughtfully.

Anxious to get him back on the subject at hand, Kerri asked, "What do you do for a living, Mr. Johansen?"

Thad leaned back suddenly and cocked his head to one side. Kerri knew the sudden change of subject had thrown him a little.

"I'm an architect. Why? What does that have to do with anything?"

"Nothing really," Kerri said. She gave him a reassuring smile. "I was just curious. You're obviously an intelligent person, and your level of intelligence will likely reflect in some manner on Jace."

"He is a bright boy, when he can focus his energies properly."

"I'm sure he is. Who cares for him while you are at work?"

"We have a baby-sitter. Though Jace has a fit when we call her that. He insists he is not a baby."

Kerri smiled. "Well that is certainly understandable, considering his age," she said. "Where did you find this baby sitter?"

"She's a neighbor actually—she and her husband live a few doors down from us. Carol and Karl Bohannon. They're our age—that would be late thirties—and have two teenage daughters. Karl and I sometimes work together. Jace has been going there for a little over a year now. Last year, when he started kindergarten, Janet took a part-time job at a little craft shop in Pike Place Market. Whenever Janet has to work, Carol Bohannon meets Jace's bus and takes him to her house."

"I see," Kerri said, noting Johansen's consistent use of the present tense in referring to his wife. "Does Jace like her?"

Johansen shrugged. "I guess so. He's never indicated otherwise."

"What does he do when he's at the Bohannons'?"

"Well, she has a few other kids from the neighborhood she cares for, including a couple who are Jace's age." He paused and turned to gaze out the window, deep in thought. "I guess they just play together," he said finally. "You know, whatever kids that age do."

Kerri nodded. "*How* does Jace play with the other kids, do you know? Does he take part in group games, or does he tend to isolate himself?"

Johansen thought about that. "Carol hasn't mentioned any problems, though if she had, it would have been to Janet. I hardly ever see her. I assume Jace gets along okay, but to be honest, I don't really know." He shot Kerri a guilty look. "I guess I should pay more attention to stuff like this," he said sadly. "But Janet's always been more involved with that end of things."

Kerri set aside her notepad and stood. "Okay, Mr. Johansen. I think I have enough for now. I'd like to bring Jace in here and talk with him alone for a bit, then perhaps we can all talk together."

Thad Johansen nodded mechanically and stood, glancing about the room as if he were momentarily lost. Kerri cupped his elbow in her hand and steered him toward the door, making a mental note to include him, as well as his son, in some therapy. Thad Johansen looked like a man on the edge.

When they opened the door to the reception area, the sound of a guttural growl filled the air. Stephen and Jace were sitting cross-legged on the floor, facing each other, each of them holding a model dinosaur in one hand. Jace whacked the T-rex he held against Stephen's long-necked brachyosaurus and growled in a low voice, "I'm going to eat you up!" Stephen whimpered, dropped his dinosaur on the floor, and let Jace's T-rex swoop down on top of it. Jace ground the head of the T-rex into the other dinosaur's throat, making a guttural chewing noise. Stephen grabbed his own throat with both hands, rolled backwards onto the floor, and acted as if he was being strangled.

"You got me," Stephen gargled.

Jace smiled.

"Okay you two, game's over," Kerri said.

Stephen sat up, scooped up the dinosaurs with one hand, and proceeded to get to his feet. Extending a hand to Jace, he helped the boy up. "Next time, I get to be T-rex," he whispered. Jace frowned, his eyes following the prehistoric figures as Stephen stuffed them back into his desk drawer.

"Jace?" Kerri said. "Why don't you come back here with me so we can talk."

The boy shifted his focus from Stephen's desk drawer to Kerri's face, his frown deepening. His hands, which had been still for a few moments, wrung the hem of his shirt. He glanced briefly at his father and then, with a shrug of resignation, headed for Kerri's office.

Not willing to let the boy choose where to sit given his propensity for distraction, Kerri steered him toward the love seat. "Sit here," she instructed him.

Jace did as he was told, settling in on one end of the small couch and wrapping his arms around its end. His gaze wandered out the window.

Seeing the difficulty she might have in keeping him focused, Kerri sat on the love seat beside him. She hoped it would force him to look at her, rather than out the window.

"Jace?" He didn't look at her, but he did grunt a little by way of an answer.

"Do you know why you're here?"

Jace shrugged, still staring out the window. His feet swung back and forth against the front of the love seat.

"How old are you, Jace?"

He finally turned away from the window but still didn't face Kerri. Instead, he held both hands, fisted, in front of his face. Slowly, starting with the thumb on his left hand, he extended his fingers one at a time. "One, two, three, four, five . . ." He hesitated as his focus switched to the other hand and its thumb popped out. "Six." He shot Kerri a quick glance, then turned away to once again wrap his arms around the end of the couch, staring out the window.

"That's very good, Jace," Kerri said. "You count very well. Did you learn that in school?"

Jace nodded.

"Do you like school, Jace?"

Again he nodded, with a little more vigor this time.

"Jace, can you tell me about your mother?"

The reaction was so swift, Kerri was startled. The boy froze, perfectly still for several moments. Then a tiny shudder ran through his body. His face went slack, totally devoid of any animation or emotion. Though he was still staring out the window, he didn't appear to be focused on anything in particular.

Kerri waited, hoping he was merely trying to summon up his thoughts. When a full two minutes passed without a word, she tried again.

"Your father tells me she left the two of you." Studying him, Kerri thought she saw a twitch in the boy's cheek. But he remained silent. "Think she ran away from home?" Kerri asked.

Finally, the boy pivoted and looked at her, his face turbulent with emotion, though just what emotion, Kerri couldn't tell. His hands began to rub together frantically and his body rocked back and forth, back and forth, as if the love seat were a rocking chair. His face darkened, his eyes narrowed, his lips pursed. Then he turned away from her and stared across the room, once more taking on that unfocused and dazed expression. He continued to rock, faster than before. His hands wrung themselves so hard, Kerri was surprised they weren't raw.

Kerri watched him a moment, then reached over and gave his shoulder a gentle squeeze.

He gave no indication he felt her, not so much as a blink.

With a sigh, Kerri stood and crossed to her desk, grabbing a pad of paper. She tossed the pad onto the table in front of the love seat, then crossed to the far corner of the room. There, she removed a box from a bookshelf and rummaged inside it, pulling out a worn and faded cigar box. She carried it over to the table and set it beside the paper. Though Jace was still rocking, Kerri did note he was focused on her now, instead of just staring off into space.

Watching him from one corner of her eye, she knelt beside the table and opened the cigar box, revealing an assortment of crayons in varying hues and sizes. She ripped off the top sheet of paper on the pad, then pushed the tablet aside. Positioning the single sheet in front of her, she selected a red crayon from the box and began to draw the outline of a house. When that was done, she traded the red crayon for a green one, and added in some grass and a couple of trees.

Jace had stopped rocking, and he watched Kerri with a wary curiosity. After a few more moments, he slid to the edge of the love seat, then stood beside the table. He stared into the cigar box a moment, studying its contents. Then, with an abrupt, awkward motion, one hand darted into the box and came out bearing a fat blue crayon. Holding it aloft, his other hand reached down and turned the notepad ninety degrees to the right. He studied it a moment, then turned it another ninety degrees, so it was upside down. Apparently satisfied, he dropped to his knees beside the table and, gripping the crayon in a clumsy fist hold, began to draw.

Kerri continued with her own picture, adding in some flowers and a curlicue of smoke from the house's chimney. By then, Jace was well into his own drawing, and Kerri set aside her crayon to watch him. She studied his profile, smiling at the way his tongue darted in and out of his mouth, noting the fine white down covering his cheeks. Slowly, almost reluctantly, she shifted her focus to his drawing.

On the pad, Jace had drawn a typically childlike rendition of a person. Kerri guessed from the curly, shoulder-length hair that the figure was a woman, but lest she had any doubts, Jace had drawn what appeared to be two large breasts on the figure's chest, though they more closely resembled side-by-side bulls-eyes. The figure appeared to be lying down, and beside it, Jace had drawn a second figure, this one with an outlandishly large, almost triangular-shaped head. The figure wielded some object—was it a knife?—in one outstretched, sticklike hand, hovering just above the female figure's left breast. For his final touch, Jace drew two large circles in the face of the standing figure—presumably, Kerri thought, eyes. When he was done, Jace set the crayon aside and started up again with his rocking motion, this time on his knees.

Kerri stared at the picture. "Is that your mother?" she asked gently, pointing toward the female figure.

Jace stopped his rocking, frozen still as a picture. He gave a spasmodic nod, then resumed the back-and-forth motion.

"And who is this?" Kerri asked, indicating the other figure.

Jace's rocking sped up, becoming so fast and furious he was bumping the table with each swing, nudging it across the floor inch by inch.

"Jace?" Kerri's voice was firm but not harsh. She reached over and gripped his shoulder. Jace froze, his body angled forward, his chin bare inches from the table's top. He chewed at his lower lip; his hands twisted the cloth of his shirt. His eyes looked wild, frightened.

"Jace, are you afraid of something?"

For a moment, Kerri wondered if he'd even heard her. Then his body slowly straightened to a vertical position. His head swiveled toward her, and his eyes met her own. They were incredibly blue—the color of the sky on a clear, autumn day—and their color deepened as they filled with the sheen of tears. He looked totally terrified as the tears breached his lower lids and trickled down his face, weaving a serpentine trail through the fine blond down of his cheeks.

"Who is this?" Kerri repeated, stabbing a finger at the standing figure in Jace's drawing. "Is it your father?"

Jace shook his head so hard Kerri half expected to hear something rattle or creak. "No," he whispered. Then, with a suddenness that made Kerri jump, he flung himself toward her, wrapping his tiny arms tightly around her neck and nestling his head in the crook of her shoulder. Stunned, Kerri sat there, her arms dangling at her sides. Then slowly, she raised one hand to his back and began a gentle rub. With the other hand, she smoothed his hair. She was struck by the amount of heat radiating through Jace's shirt onto her chest. She had forgotten what little furnaces children's bodies could be.

She felt Jace's tiny body vibrate with his sobs, felt the dampness of his tears on her blouse. The innocent scent of baby shampoo wafted up from his hair as she stroked it, and Kerri felt an aching lump settle in her throat. A fierce surge of maternal protectiveness washed over her—and with it, a feeling of guilt and anguish over her failure to protect her own. "It's okay,

Jace," she murmured. "It's okay. I'll help you." And she meant it with every part of her being.

When Mandy had been stricken with cancer, Kerri had done everything within her power to save her daughter's life. She sought out only the best physicians, researched the latest information available, stayed at her daughter's side to offer hope, love, and encouragement. But that was all she could do. And it hadn't been enough.

Now, with Jace, with this little boy whose emotions seemed as battered and bruised as her own, Kerri saw a chance. Here was a child she could help. She was struck by an almost overwhelming need to atone for her past ineptitude by stepping in as Jace's protector.

Tightening her grip on the boy, Kerri instinctively fell into the routine she had always used when Mandy needed soothing. Slowly, she began to rock him—back and forth, back and forth, back and forth.

FOUR

Feeling totally drained by the time she finished with Jace, Kerri intended to forgo any additional time with the boy and his father, even though there were still ten minutes left in their hour appointment. But when she escorted Jace out to the waiting area, she saw her next patient had already arrived—Margaret Hellman, an obsessive-compulsive whose primary obsession was never to be late. Knowing she couldn't brush Mr. Johansen off without some sort of summary of her time with Jace, and unable to converse with him in private out in the waiting area, Kerri had no choice but to bring the Johansens back into the inner sanctum of her office.

She seated father and son on the love seat and took one of the chairs opposite them. Leaning forward and balancing her elbows on her knees, she twirled her thumbs, staring at them while she decided how best to couch her words. When she finally lifted her head, she found Thad Johansen's eager blue eyes waiting patiently.

"Mr. Johansen, I didn't get Jace to say anything, but I feel encouraged. He seems to be able to express himself through drawing, and today's effort shows some promise. That, in itself, is a very good sign."

Thad Johansen nodded mechanically, and Kerri

was relieved he didn't ask to see the drawing. She wanted some time to analyze it herself first.

"I would like to continue to see Jace as often as possible, if that is agreeable with you," Kerri suggested. "In fact, if possible, I'd like to see him again tomorrow, and Friday. You, of course, are welcome to join us for these sessions," she added. "Though I think letting me spend some portion of each appointment alone with Jace would be beneficial."

"Okay," Thad Johansen said in a quiet monotone. He looked around the room then as if suddenly confused as to his whereabouts. "Okay," he repeated. Then he slid his palms down the length of his thighs and stood. "Come along then, Jace. Let's go home."

Kerri rose with him, watching Jace carefully as he allowed his father to take his hand and lead him toward the door. Unable to twist his shirt enough with just one hand, Jace shifted his focus to his hair, where he twisted one lock of it around his finger over and over again. His eyes avoided looking at anyone or anything in particular; they roved the office instead.

"You can schedule your appointments with Stephen," Kerri said as she opened the door to the waiting area. Shifting her attention to Margaret Hellman, Kerri crooked a finger at her, indicating she should come into the office.

Margaret glanced at her watch, then at the clock on the wall. She stood up and marched imperiously past the Johansens and muttered the words, "You're late," under her breath as she squeaked past Kerri. Another of Margaret's obsessions involved germs, and she had a cleaning routine she went through with each appointment—dusting the chairs, spraying Lysol on the cushions, and laying a white cloth down on her chosen seat. Kerri waited in the doorway, watching as Margaret began her routine. After a moment, she glanced back toward the waiting room. "Stephen? Can we squeeze the Johansens in for the next couple of days?" she asked.

Stephen quickly perused the schedule book, flipping the pages back and forth, then nodded. "We have a couple of slots open," he said to Thad. "Tomorrow we have one at eight in the morning and another at four in the afternoon. Is there a time that's better for you?"

As Thad and Stephen worked out the times, Kerri's eyes drifted toward Jace. The boy stood to one side of the desk, his body amazingly still, his blue eyes watching Kerri with a surprising intensity.

She smiled at him. "See you tomorrow?" she asked quietly.

He didn't answer immediately; he just stared at her. But then he gave her a slow, subtle nod of his head. The gesture seemed so out of character, so mature and sedate coming from a six-year-old kid—much less one with attention deficit disorder—that Kerri felt her heart tug achingly inside her chest. When she had held the boy in her arms and soothed his sobs just a short while ago, he seemed so vulnerable—young, fragile, and helpless. Now there was an air of great solemnity and wisdom about him that gave Kerri a flash picture of the man he would grow to be. It made her feel oddly sad, and she was seized by a sudden urge to gather him up and keep him there with her—maybe even take him home. Though her clinical mind recognized the urge as a misplaced emotion—a remnant of the maternal protectiveness that had been so much a part of her life when Mandy was alive—the knowledge offered her little solace. The child standing before her was not her own, yet the desire to shield him from all of life's hurts was intense and compelling. She felt pinned to the spot by his unblinking and unwavering stare, unable to move until Margaret Hellman's rather loud "harumph" shook her from her reverie. With some difficulty, she dragged her gaze away from Jace's beseeching blue eyes and turned to go into her office.

Jace was still watching her as she slowly closed the door.

When Margaret Hellman's session ended, Kerri found herself with fifteen free minutes before her next scheduled appointment. That was the offsetting advantage to Margaret's fixation with timeliness. Though the woman always arrived early for her appointments out of a need to be on time, she subsequently ended the sessions early for the same reason—so she could get to wherever she was going next in plenty of time. As soon as the woman was gone, Kerri took a few moments to jot down some notes in her chart; then she picked up Jace's drawing and studied it.

The differences between the two figures bothered her. Children Jace's age were generally able to distinguish size relationships well enough to draw fairly realistic pictures. They understood the difference between the size of a house and the size of a person, or the size of an adult and that of a child. They also drew generally proportional human figures. Where the woman figure— Jace's mother—was typical for a child Jace's age, the other figure bore some odd characteristics. The head was disproportionately large, as were the eyes. That alone was not unusual—it could have been nothing more than Jace's style or perception. It was the fact that the two figures differed so dramatically that was bothersome. Whatever a child's perceptions, they were generally consistent. The other difference Kerri found troubling was the lack of facial features—other than eyes—on the standing figure. And then there was the item the standing figure held in its hand. It was slender and drawn to a point at the end, hovering just above the mother's breast. The longer Kerri looked at it, the more convinced she became it was some type of knife.

Kerri knew that before she could make any valid conclusions about the drawing, she would need to have Jace identify the standing figure. Once she knew who the figure was supposed to be, the distinguishing characteristics might make more sense. Maybe tomorrow, she thought hopefully. She stuffed the drawing inside the chart Stephen had created for the Johansens and set it aside.

She then picked up the phone and dialed a number, listening to the ring on the other end six times before she gave up. Just as she was about to set the phone back in the cradle, she heard a male voice say, "McCallister."

She snatched the handset back to her ear. "Kevin? Are you there?"

"How'd it go?"

That was so typical of Kevin—waste no time with greetings, just get directly to the point.

Kerri glanced at her watch and saw she had only a few minutes left before her next appointment. "Any chance we can meet over lunch and talk about it? I'm a bit pressed for time at the moment."

"Sure. Where at?"

"How about the Red Robin? Say about oneish?"

"See you there."

"Thanks, Kevin."

"Say, Kerri?"

"Yes?"

"Are you okay?"

Kerri smiled. "I'm fine. I'm not going to tell you it was easy, because it was far from it. I hardly slept at all last night. This has dredged up some things I think were better left buried." The irony of her words hit Kerri like a punch in the gut, and for one horrifying moment, she actually saw an image of Mandy's decomposing body as it lay in a muddy grave. She sucked in a sharp breath and shook the image off. "I still hate you, if that's what you want to know."

Kevin chuckled. "I'll see you at lunch," he said. And then he was gone.

Kerri arrived at the Red Robin ten minutes late. Kevin was standing by the front door, leaning casually against the wall, chewing on a toothpick. He eyed her closely as she approached.

"Oh, no," Kerri said, seeing the splintered toothpick between Kevin's teeth. "Don't tell me you're trying to quit smoking again."

Kevin pulled the wooden stub from his mouth and gave her a wounded look. "Well, what would you have me do, lass? The lungs need the break, and I can't afford to eat my way out of this." He patted the bulk of his stomach where it hung out over his belt buckle.

"Good point," Kerri said.

Kevin tossed the toothpick aside and opened the door to the restaurant. "After you," he said with a sweep of his hand.

The majority of the lunch crowd had been and

gone, so the hostess offered them their choice of tables. Kerri indicated a corner booth, hoping for some privacy. They had barely settled into the red vinyl seats when their waitress, a perky little blonde with an incredibly large chest, appeared at their side. They placed their orders—Kevin selecting a steak sandwich and fries; Kerri, a chef's salad and a milk-shake.

As soon as the girl was gone, Kevin leaned forward, his arms resting on the table. "So," he said, impaling Kerri with his gaze, "what's your preliminary take on the father?"

"Boy, you don't waste any time, do you?"

Kevin gave her a noncommittal shrug. "I got a funny feeling about this one, and I'm anxious to get your impressions."

"What kind of funny feeling?"

Kevin dismissed her question with an impatient wave of his hand. "I'll tell you later. First tell me what you think."

"Well," Kerri said slowly, thinking back to her time with Thad. "He seems a bit on the edge, but no more so than anyone else whose spouse has just deserted them. I did get the impression he was a little skeptical about the idea his wife simply upped and left. And he seems very forthright and caring. Very concerned about his son."

"Did you get anything out of the kid?"

"A little," Kerri said.

"Such as?"

"Un-uh," Kerri said, shaking her head. "Now it's your turn."

Kevin leaned back and scanned the area nearby. Seeing no one within hearing distance, he leaned forward again, his eyes narrowing. "Just between you and me, I think the husband offed his wife."

Kerri couldn't have been more startled if Kevin had said he thought *she* killed the woman. "You're kidding, right?" she said.

Kevin shook his head.

Kerri thought about the picture Jace had drawn, with the standing figure holding something that looked like a knife over his mother's chest. Then she thought about Thad Johansen, the concern on his face, the confusion in his mind. *No way,* she thought.

"You think the woman's dead, not just missing then?" Kerri asked.

"I do."

"But Thad told me the police believe she left of her own volition."

Kevin sighed heavily. "We did, at first. Figured it was just another one of those wife-goes-crazy deals. But then some things came up that started making the whole scene smell a bit fishy. The husband claims he has no inkling of any problems between the two of them, and he further claims he doesn't have a clue as to how his wife managed to sneak out of the house in the middle of the night without waking him. Kind of odd when you consider she packed up a bunch of clothes and toiletries to take with her."

"Could she have packed them earlier, anticipating her escape once Thad went to sleep?"

"Thought about that, but Johansen swears most of the stuff that's missing was still there when he went to bed the night before."

"Well that's not a very bright thing to say if he's guilty and wants to make it look as if the woman left on her own," Kerri said.

"Unless you're clever enough to anticipate the precise reaction you just gave," Kevin said, giving her a pointed look.

Kerri frowned. Her first meeting with Thad Johansen had not given her the impression he was at all duplicitous. For him to put on that good an act, he would either have to be a very talented sociopath or an extremely vicious and intelligent psychopath. Somehow, neither scenario seemed to fit.

"I assume you've looked into the prospect of another lover?" she asked Kevin.

Now it was his turn to frown. "Of course. And that's what makes this case so puzzling. Everyone we've talked to describes Janet Johansen as the perfect loving housewife and mother. If she did have a lover, she did one hell of a job keeping it a secret."

"Then why would her husband want to kill her?"

Before Kevin could answer, the waitress returned with their food. The woman had barely set Kevin's plate in front of him—the biggest steak sandwich Kerri had ever seen—before Kevin picked it up and ripped off a hefty bite.

"Anything else?" the waitress asked.

Unable to talk with his mouth so full, Kevin merely shook his head. The waitress left.

Shaking her head in silent wonder, Kerri watched Kevin try to chew the food in his mouth while she poked her fork around in her salad. "No wonder you've gained so much weight," she observed.

"It's hell," Kevin said with his mouth still half full. He grabbed his napkin and dabbed at his lips with a daintiness that was almost comical. "I want a cigarette so bad I could scream," he said when he finally swallowed. "And it hasn't even been twenty-four hours yet.

Every time I try to quit, I stuff everything I can find in my mouth, hoping it will take the place of what I really want. But it's never good enough." With that wistful phrase, he picked up the sandwich and ripped off another bite.

Kerri waited until he had eaten most of the sandwich and half of his fries before she again broached the subject of Thad Johansen. "Okay, you've stalled long enough. Now tell me why you think Johansen would want to kill his wife."

Kevin leaned back in his seat, hooked his thumbs in the belt of his pants, and stared up at the ceiling. "I'm not sure yet of the why part. All I know is there are some things that don't make sense."

"Like what?"

"Like the fact the woman packed at least two suitcases of stuff, but left behind her makeup kit and a prescription for some antibiotics she was taking for a bladder infection. Like the fact there was no missing vehicle and there is no public transportation available there. And like the fact the woman had a doctor's appointment scheduled for the next morning and had set her alarm clock."

"So, maybe she just forgot that stuff in her hurry to get away. And maybe someone picked her up. And maybe she set the alarm out of habit, without thinking about it."

Kevin shook his head vehemently and leaned forward again, looking Kerri in the eye. "No. Something doesn't smell right here. It just doesn't make sense."

"What was the appointment for?" Kerri asked.

"Hmm? Oh, you mean the doctor's appointment? It was with her gynecologist. Routine checkup, I imagine."

"She didn't keep the appointment, I presume."

Kevin shook his head.

"So," Kerri said, cocking her head, "the only reason you suspect her husband is because you don't have a clue about anything else. Am I right?"

"Something like that," he admitted. "It's just the instinct. I think there is more to this case than meets the eye. And then there's the kid. Something's bothering him. Something more than just his mother's absence. I got a feeling he knows something. Even if his father isn't involved, I think this woman's disappearance is more sinister than just another frustrated housewife. That's why I wanted you to work with him. If the woman did simply leave, then the very least you can do is help the kid to understand and adjust. If she didn't disappear on her own, maybe she's still out there somewhere. And I got a hunch the kid knows something."

Kerri gazed thoughtfully into space, digesting Kevin's theories. Finally she said, "The subject of his mother is certainly disturbing to him. The change in his demeanor when you mention her is quite startling."

"So what did you get out of him?" Kevin asked. "Anything?"

Kerri shook her head. "Nothing verbal. But I did get him to draw some."

"And?"

Kerri hesitated. She really wanted to take some time to examine the picture Jace had drawn in more detail before rendering any sort of professional opinion. "I don't know," she said. "I need more time. I'm seeing them both again tomorrow and Friday. Maybe I'll get a better feel for things after that."

She could tell Kevin was disappointed, but he didn't push the issue. Instead, he leaned back in his chair, reached into his shirt pocket, and dragged out a fresh toothpick. He shoved it into one corner of his mouth and started to chew.

"Thanks for doing this for me, lass," he said softly. "I know it wasn't easy for you."

The unexpected change of subject, combined with the sympathetic tone in Kevin's voice made Kerri's throat tighten. The whole puzzle of the Johansen thing had been a nice distraction, allowing her to keep her thoughts away from Mandy and last night's return of her nightmare. Now, with this one simple expression of concerned gratitude, Kevin brought it all crashing back in on her. She dropped her gaze to the table, where she picked up her napkin and did a remarkable imitation of Jace Johansen with his shirt hem.

Kevin's hand snaked over and wrapped itself around her arm, giving it a quick comforting squeeze. His brows drew together with compassion and concern. "I know it still hurts," he said softly.

Kerri nodded, then shrugged, a gesture of helplessness. She kept her eyes averted, knowing if she looked at Kevin, she would likely burst into tears. Her throat spasmed and the backs of her eyeballs burned. They sat in silence for a long moment, while Kerri tried desperately to get her emotions in check. But the tears bloomed anyway. Seeing them, Kevin grabbed the napkin from his lap and tossed it on his plate. Sliding out of his seat, he came around and pulled Kerri out of hers, wrapping an arm around her shoulders. "Come on," he said. "Let's take a walk."

Kerri managed to hold herself together long enough for Kevin to pay for their meal and escort her outside. The last thing she saw, before the tears again blurred her vision, was the curious expression of their waitress as she watched them exit through the door.

FIVE

✦━◆━✦

They headed back toward Kerri's office. The day had turned unusually warm, and they hadn't gone far before Kerri shrugged off her sweater coat and draped it over her arm. After several blocks, she was able to get her emotions in check and would have been content to make the entire journey in silence, but Kevin's frequent sidelong glances told her it wasn't likely. So she decided to beat him to it.

"I'm sorry about that outburst, Kevin."

"Outburst?" Kevin harumphed. "I'd hardly call it that."

Kerri managed a grimace of a smile.

"You look tired, lass."

"I am. Didn't get much sleep last night."

"Because of the kid?" Kevin's tone had a tinge of guilt to it.

Kerri nodded.

"Maybe I did push you too hard."

Kerri shrugged. "It's done now," she said. "Besides, seeing him wasn't so bad. It was the anticipation of it. It dredged up a lot of painful memories."

Though Kerri sensed Kevin watching her, she kept her eyes focused on the sidewalk in front of her. It seemed to be the only safe place to look. Seeing the guilt and compassion in Kevin's face would only start her crying again. So she concentrated on putting one foot in front of the other, keeping the plain monotony of the dull gray sidewalk as her only scenery, silently counting off each crack as it passed. She was so caught up in this little mind game it startled her when Kevin said, "Well, here we are."

Kerri looked up to see the entrance to her office building.

"You going to be okay?"

Kerri nodded, the motion coming out as more of a spasm. Her gaze met Kevin's briefly, then dropped down toward her sweater coat, where she proceeded to pick and brush at some invisible spot on the sleeve.

"Call me tomorrow after you've seen the kid, okay?"

Again Kerri nodded. She'd managed to pick loose a long thread of yarn on her sweater. Shoving the string aside impatiently, she glanced at her watch and said, "I have to run. Thanks for lunch." With that, she whirled around and headed inside, leaving Kevin to watch after her with a wistful expression, wishing like hell he had a cigarette.

The rest of the afternoon flew by, and Kerri was grateful she had no appointments scheduled after four o'clock. Her mind kept wandering back to the morning's session with the Johansens, and she was painfully aware that the two patients she saw this afternoon had received less than the full benefit of her professional attention.

When she suggested to Stephen they close shop early, he was more than eager to take her up on it. "I have an exam tonight," he said. "I could use a few extra hours to study. By the way, don't forget that shindig you have at the Weathertons' tonight."

"Oh, hell! I had forgotten about it," Kerri said with a grimace. The "shindig" Stephen was referring to was an informal cocktail party at Dr. Frank Weatherton's home. Though socializing was the last thing Kerri felt like doing, she knew her attendance was a necessary evil. As the chief of staff at King Medical Center—one of the largest hospitals in the Seattle area— Dr. Weatherton's approval was crucial to maintaining her referral base. It wouldn't do to violate the norms established by the good-ole-boy network. Besides, she'd been avoiding the social scene ever since Mandy's death.

Stephen cleared the few items on his desk and hauled his backpack onto his shoulders. "You sure there isn't anything else you want me to do today?"

Kerri waved him on. "I'm sure. You go on and make sure you ace that test. I'll see you in the morning."

With Stephen gone, the place seemed dreadfully quiet and empty. Kerri stood in the doorway between the two offices, her mind once again seeing Jace Johansen's tiny face staring up at her. She recalled the porcelain delicacy of his fair skin, the feel of his soft body against her own, and the terror reflected in his incredibly blue eyes. The image was so strong, she could still smell the scent of shampoo on his hair and feel him trembling in her arms.

She shook the image off and turned into her office. Since the party at the Weathertons' didn't start for another hour and a half—not enough time to be able to go home and then get back to the mainland—she might as well take advantage of the wait to catch up on some things. Settling in at her desk, she began by attacking the ever-growing pile of professional journals stacked on one corner.

Dr. Weatherton's palatial home didn't exactly roll out the welcome mat. A high spiked fence topped with three rows of barbed wire made the place look like a POW camp. Beyond that, myriad trees and shrubs provided a much thicker, and equally impenetrable, inner wall. The only feasible entrance lay at the gate, and it was guarded by no less than three stern-faced, steroid-fed blocks of human flesh. Entry onto the grounds required the offering of identification and one of the invitation cards sent to each guest. After convincing the hulks she was both harmless and invited, Kerri's cab was allowed onto the grounds.

A long, tree-lined drive wound its way uphill, ending in a clearing that held the main house. The place was Victorian to the point of being Gothic, with two capped towers on either end and a dark, menacing look to its stone facade. Despite the daunting appearance on the outside, the interior offered a warm welcome, thanks to the light and contemporary influence of Weatherton's wife, Phyllis. Though there was an abundance of heavy, dark wood trim, the walls and floors were all done in white or beige tones. Most of the furnishings were pastel, and a generous smattering of glass and chrome gave the overall effect of a much more modern home than what the outside would lead one to expect. Large windows on all sides made the interior light and airy.

A doorman took Kerri's sweater coat and directed

her toward the back of the house, where the warm evening had prompted the Weathertons to move their party outside. Kerri stepped out onto a multitiered flagstone patio anchored on all four corners with flower boxes displaying colorful blooms and carefully trimmed shrubs. Beyond the patio lay a sea of well-tended green bordered by a thick ring of woods. An Olympic-size swimming pool held center stage; beyond the pool and off to one side was a tennis court. To the right of the patio, a curving stone pathway led to a large gazebo nestled near the trees.

Though the invitation said six o'clock and it was now half past, only a handful of other people milled about. Kerri spied Frank Weatherton almost immediately. He stood near one corner of the pool talking in his usual animated way, waving his drink-holding hand in a manner that made everyone near him back up a step or two. His audience at the moment consisted of Dr. Fenton—one of the hospital's anesthesiologists— and his very pretty and much younger wife, whose name Kerri couldn't recall.

Weatherton saw Kerri and acknowledged her with a little arch of his eyebrows. Moments later, he excused himself from the Fentons—who Kerri thought looked somewhat relieved to see him go—and in the aggressive long stride that so matched his personality, he moved across the patio. His face broke into what Kerri had heard the nursing staff refer to as his "gonna get ya" smile.

"Kerri! So good of you to come!" Weatherton draped a long, lanky arm over her shoulders and blew martini breath in her face. "I was hoping you would make it. You haven't been out much for a while, have you?"

Weatherton's typical lack of tact was one of the reasons he was now chief of staff. He hadn't so much earned the title as bullied his way into it. With his powerful political connections and his tenure as one of the top cardiac surgeons at the hospital, there weren't many willing to come to odds with the man. After years of having his conceited and bullying ass kissed by nearly every hospital administrator and physician on staff, Weatherton had evolved into a manipulative and calculating monarch, reigning over his hospital kingdom. If it hadn't been for his truly remarkable skill as a surgeon—which had made both him and the hospital nationally renown—Kerri suspected he would have been ousted years ago.

Though she inwardly despised the man, Kerri managed a smile and resisted the urge to come back at him with some cutting remark. Instead, she used the only other ploy she knew was guaranteed to make him back off with lightning speed. Dropping her eyes and batting her lashes, she grabbed his arm and moved her body closer. Summoning up her best flirtatious smile, she simpered, "Why, Frank, have you missed me?"

Frank Weatherton brushed her off his arm as if she was an annoying speck of lint. He backed up so quickly he almost tripped himself. His eyes darted about frantically, settling on his wife, Phyllis, who stood near the vast array of food set out near the house.

"Well, we uh . . . of course, everyone has been worried . . . I mean about how you are doing and all. Can I get you a drink?" he stammered.

Kerri arched her brows at the abrupt change in subject, struggling to control the bubble of laughter threatening to roll out of her. One thing—probably the

only thing—Frank Weatherton feared in this world
was the wrath of his wife. Having been caught in a
short-lived but well-publicized (at least throughout the
hospital grapevine, which Weatherton now referred to
as the gripevine) affair a few years back, Frank
Weatherton's wife made it quite clear he would lose
not only his reputation and standing in the hospital,
but every red cent he owned if she decided to divorce
him. For all Weatherton had when he came to the
marriage was his inborn talent as a surgeon. All the
rest—the family money, the high-powered political
connections, and a controlling interest in the corporation that owned King Medical Center and some sixty
other hospitals throughout the country—came from
Phyllis. Hence, Frank was understandably nervous
whenever he thought his behavior might in any way be
construed by dear Phyllis as flirtatious.

"I would love one of those martinis you've been
sampling," Kerri said in her sweetest voice.

She had the satisfaction of seeing Frank
Weatherton's plastic smile falter for just a moment
before he cleared his throat and said, "Of course."
Anxious to be away from her, he snapped his fingers at
one of the roving butlers, gestured with his glass, and
pointed at Kerri. Once the servant acknowledged the
request, Weatherton gave Kerri a tolerant and slightly
frigid smile before excusing himself to greet other
guests who were arriving.

As Kerri watched the servant fetch her drink from
the bar, she chastised herself for her behavior with
Weatherton. Her whole reason for coming to this thing
in the first place was to ensure the continuation of
future hospital privileges and referrals. Pissing off
Weatherton probably wasn't the wisest move. Yet she

hadn't been able to resist. Her tolerance for Weatherton had always been weak at best; today she seemed to lack the strength and energy necessary to play the game.

The servant carried Kerri's drink over to her, sporting it high above his head on a tray. As he approached, he swept the tray down with a melodramatic flourish, bowing before her. "Your drink, madam," he said stiffly.

Kerri took the drink, mumbled a barely audible "thank you," then turned quickly away in hopes of containing her laughter. Her suppressed glee faded in an instant when she found herself face-to-face with Dr. Nathan Palmer. As she stared up at the startlingly blue eyes, she was struck for the umpteenth time by how truly handsome he was. Even now, after ten years of marriage and a painful divorce, he could still snatch the very breath from her.

"Kerri. It's good to see you." Nathan's eyes, like two gleaming sapphires, roved over her face.

Kerri felt herself start to blush and swallowed hard in an effort to pull herself together. "I wondered if I might see you here."

Nathan smiled and ran a hand through his blond mane, triggering a montage of memories in Kerri's mind—pictures from an easier, happier time. "Is this the first time you've been out since . . ." He didn't finish the sentence; he didn't have to. They were both painfully aware of what should have followed.

"It is," Kerri said with a nervous little smile. Nathan's scrutiny made her uncomfortable, and she averted her gaze, staring at a small group of people gathered around Weatherton over by the pool. "I figured it was time to get back into things."

"How are you doing?"

His voice, as soft and caressing as a summer's breeze, struck a feeling of nostalgia in Kerri that was so strong, it carried with it an almost palpable physical pain. She squeezed her eyes closed and forced up an image of Nathan as she had seen him on their last night together—entwined in the naked limbs of nurse Carolyn Krykovich. Her painful longings for the past were swiftly replaced with a remembered sense of hurt and betrayal.

Her eyes flew open and she turned back to face him, her expression clearly conveying her emotions. Nathan stepped back, his smile slackening into an expression of sorrow and shame.

"I am doing as well as can be expected, Nathan," Kerri said, her tone clipped.

Nathan dropped his gaze and stared at his feet, the muscles in his jaw twitching. "You're still angry with me," he muttered.

"Does that surprise you?"

Nathan raised his eyes momentarily, then looked back at the ground. He let out a weary sigh. "No, I suppose not." The healthy golden tone of his face quickly gave way to a ruddy flush that started at his throat and worked its way toward his hairline. "Forgiveness is obviously not your style," he said with no small amount of sarcasm.

Kerri gaped at him, her eyes sparking. "Jesus, Nathan," she hissed. "It would have been hard enough to forgive you fu—" She bit off the word, sucking in a quick breath and glancing around. Satisfied no one was eavesdropping, she dropped her voice a notch, though she was still seething. "To do what you did was unforgivable enough. To do it only one month after our daughter was in her grave was reprehensible."

With that, Kerri sidled past him into the house. Setting her untouched drink on a table near the door, she hurried outside. On the wide, fan-shaped front steps she hesitated, realizing she had no means of escape without calling for a cab. She debated going back inside, but anger spurred her on and she took off on foot, walking at a furious clip down the long drive. Though her ire found some release through the sheer force of her physical exertion, by the time the gatehouse came into view, she still wanted to get as far away from here as possible. When she saw the guards warily watching her approach, she slowed her pace and wrapped one arm over her stomach. She walked up to the closest guard.

"I'm feeling a little ill," she said weakly. "I thought the walk might help, but now I feel even worse." She flashed the man an apologetic smile. "I'm sorry to inconvenience you, but I just don't think I can make it back to the house. Would you mind calling me a cab?"

The guard's stony expression softened, and he made a little grimace Kerri suspected was meant to be a smile. Without a word, he nodded and disappeared inside the gatehouse. He returned a moment later, lugging a chair behind him. Setting it against the gatehouse wall, he gestured toward it with his hand.

"Thank you," Kerri said, walking over and sitting down.

The guard gave her another cursory nod, then turned his back to her. The three of them stood, rigid and attentive, paying her no attention whatsoever during the five minutes it took for the cab to arrive. Grateful to escape, Kerri settled herself into the back seat and instructed the driver to take her to the Pier 52 ferry landing.

SIX

By the time the ferry left the pier, the sun was low on the horizon, and the Olympic Mountains were the color of a deep bruise. Kerri wished she had brought along something to read—a magazine, some case files, anything—to distract her. She had decided to leave her briefcase in the office rather than lug it along to the Weathertons', and now she was left feeling out of sorts and empty, though she suspected the feeling was due to more than a mere lack of accoutrements. There was a heaviness in her heart, almost as if it were draped in a wet, woolen blanket.

Not until she settled into her car in Winslow did she begin to relax. Her neck felt stiff and achy, and she rolled her head to ease the tension. In an effort to keep her mind off more disturbing thoughts, she planned the meal she would fix for herself once she got home, mentally walking through every detailed step of the process as she made the forty-minute drive. Though she succeeded in distracting herself, some tiny part of her mind was still painfully aware of the night to come, carrying with it the potential for dreams that were disturbingly real.

Night had fully settled by the time she pulled off Route 20. Her driveway was little more than a rutted

dirt track that tunneled through the trees, the overhead canopy blocking out much of the light on the
brightest of days. Now, with the sun long since put to
bed, the car's headlights struggled to penetrate the
gloom, the blackness seeming to swallow up their light.

Though the relative isolation of the house had
never bothered her before—in fact, it had been one of
the selling points of the place—tonight Kerri felt
frightened and wary. A cacophony of screeches,
squeaks, and squawks emanated from the woods, and
she could feel a hundred pairs of eyes watching her
bounce along the road. When she finally emerged into
the clearing where the house stood looking dark and
abandoned, she wished she'd had the forethought to
leave the outside lights on. Though this was hardly a
crime-ridden area, one couldn't be too careful nowa-
days.

She pulled in beside the house, locked the car,
and, stifling the urge to glance fearfully over her shoulder, made her way around to the front porch. As she
climbed the front steps, her fingers fumbled and jug-
gled the many keys on her ring, her eyes straining
through the inky darkness to identify the one for the
house. The incident with Nathan, combined with the
nightmarish and sleepless night before, left her feeling
edgy and vulnerable. She was suddenly anxious to get
inside, to be secured within the protective walls of
what she often thought of as her fortress.

Pausing in front of the door, she tried first one key,
then another in the lock. Her fingers felt numb as she
tried to identify the keys by feel alone, and then she
dropped the whole ring on the floor, where they
landed with a loud clatter that echoed off the nearby
trees. Cursing, she bent down and picked them up,

deciding to start at one end of the ring and work her way through until she found the right one. Her mind was now totally focused on the task at hand, a simple-minded task that was proving to be inexplicably difficult. She flipped through the keys with mounting irritation, shoving first one, then another at the key-hole, too preoccupied to notice the dark shadow creeping across the porch toward her feet. When the shadow reached out and made a grab for her ankle, Kerri let forth with a strangled scream.

"Christ, Shadow!" she hissed breathlessly. Slapping her chest, she looked down and gave her offender a vexing look. "You nearly scared the life out of me!"

In response, the darkness at her feet arched its back and wove a figure eight around her ankles, mewing softly.

"You may have nine lives, but I only have one, you know," she muttered, finally finding the proper key and driving it home. She pushed the door open and stood aside, knowing the cat would dart in ahead of her. True to form, Shadow scampered through the doorway and across the polished wooden floor toward the darkened kitchen. Closing and locking the door behind her, Kerri tossed her purse on the couch, then followed Shadow's trail. Flipping the light switch, she found the cat sitting on the counter beside the sink, twitching his tail with impatience.

"Shadow, you know better than that. Get down!"

After a brief and hesitant look of defiance, Shadow leaped from the counter onto the floor, landing with incredible grace considering his massive size. Apparently deciding affection might be more productive, he promptly made a nuisance of himself winding in and around Kerri's feet.

"You're a real pest sometimes, you know?" Kerri said.

Yellow eyes stared up at her. Shadow's whiskers twitched and his mouth moved, but no sound came out.

"Okay, okay. Get out from under my feet and I'll get your food. Not that you need it, fatso."

Nonplussed by his master's name-calling, Shadow moved away and stood patiently in the corner where his water bowl sat next to an empty food dish. His eyes watched Kerri with hooded composure as she went to the cupboard, took out a can of cat food, and popped the lid. Scraping the contents into Shadow's dish, she wrinkled her nose at the smell, wondering how an animal so fastidious about self-grooming could eat something that smelled so nasty.

With Shadow contentedly chowing down, Kerri got a beer from the fridge, and after twisting the top off she decided to bypass her usual glass and drink it straight from the bottle. Despite the elaborate meal she had planned on the way home, she had no appetite, and Shadow's little scare out on the front porch had drained away the last of her energy. Making her way into the living room, she drew the drapes across the picture window overlooking the bay, still unable to shake the unsettling feeling that hundreds of eyes watched her. She set her beer on the end table beside the recliner, kicked off her shoes, reached up under her skirt and yanked her pantyhose down to knee level. Dropping into the recliner, she took a long pull on the beer, taking a moment to relish the taste of it before she set the bottle aside. Lifting first one leg, then the other, she stripped her hose the rest of the way off and tossed them over the back of the chair. She knew it was a foolish move; the hanging hose would be an open invitation to Shadow. But she was too tired to care.

Leaning back and elevating the foot rest, Kerri grabbed her beer and took another swallow. The effects of the alcohol on her empty stomach were almost immediate, and she welcomed the warm flow of lassitude spreading through her body. Letting her head fall back against the chair, she stared at the ceiling, listening to the creaks and groans of the house—the same noises that had kept her tense and alert when she first moved in, but which were now as familiar to her as the beat of her own heart.

Her thoughts drifted back to the party at the Weathertons'—and Nathan. Seeing him had disturbed her more than she cared to admit. One of the reasons she'd moved into this house when she and Nathan split was to escape the everyday reminders of the happiness they once shared—a happiness that now seemed more of a taunt than anything. Lifting her head, she gazed around the room, realizing just how thoroughly she had eliminated Nathan from her life. Other than the one picture on the mantel of her and Nathan with Mandy—one of her favorite Mandy pictures or she probably would have ditched it along with all the other pictures of Nathan—there was no trace of her ex-husband. And that suited her just fine. If she could have figured out a way to avoid the occasional sightings that occurred whenever she had to venture over to the hospital, she would have done that as well. Every time she saw Nathan it was like a slap in the face, its sting lingering for hours as an aching reminder of the pain he was still capable of inflicting on her already wounded psyche.

She studied the picture on the mantel—a snapshot of their trip to Disneyland—remembering the innocent pleasure and excitement that had radiated from Mandy's face. The picture had captured their happiness well, frozen in time on a five-by-seven piece of paper. Most times she relished the memories triggered by the picture—taken mere weeks before Mandy's initial diagnosis—but tonight they mocked her instead, a scornful reminder of all she had lost in the two short years since.

The effects of the beer may have numbed her body, but her mind ached with an old and familiar pain. As she stared at the snapshot, tears welled in her eyes, blurring the details. But it didn't matter; every curve, every line, every nuance of Mandy's face was forever burned into her memory. God, how she missed her!

That thought carried her back to the present, to the puzzle of Jace Johansen and his mother. How could the woman have simply walked away from her child? The very idea was both repugnant and perplexing. Though Kerri knew women abandoned their children all the time—more often than she wanted to think about—there was something about the Johansen situation that just didn't make sense. Either there was more to the story than Thad Johansen was letting on, or Janet Johansen was an unusually cold-hearted and uncaring woman. Somehow, Kerri didn't think the latter was the case. Despite the fact she had no real knowledge of the woman or what life was like in the Johansen household, her gut told her there was something fishy about the whole scenario. She thought it interesting she and Kevin both had the same impression, though their conclusions were certainly disparate.

Her thoughts were abruptly diverted when Shadow, having finished his disgusting and smelly meal, leaped onto her lap with an unsettling thud that made Kerri grunt. Oblivious to his master's discomfort, the cat settled himself into a bowling ball of fur and, with one last feral glance that dared Kerri to move him, closed his eyes and began to purr. The soothing rhythm of the animal's vibrations, combined with the spreading warmth created by the beer, left Kerri feeling exhausted but relaxed. Mirroring Shadow, she closed her own eyes and breathed a heavy, purging sigh. Ten minutes later, she drifted off into a blessedly dreamless sleep.

When Kerri arrived at the office the following morning, she grabbed her cup of coffee from Stephen, then settled in her office to spend the remaining twenty minutes before the Johansens' arrival to plan out her strategy. The first thing she did was open the chart she'd started the day before to take out the picture Jace had drawn. This morning, while she was showering, she had thought it might be helpful to have Jace continue with the drawing. Maybe he would add something to the picture to offer further clues as to its meaning.

But when she opened the chart, the picture wasn't there. She spent a few moments shuffling the papers on her desk before determining the picture was nowhere to be found. Puzzled, she picked up the phone and buzzed Stephen at the front desk.

"Yes, boss lady?"

"Stephen, did you take anything out of the Johansens' chart this morning?"

"Nope. I haven't even been in your office yet today. Why?"

"I can't find the drawing Jace did yesterday, and I'm sure I stuffed it inside the chart."

"Maybe it slid out. Did you look around on your desk?"

"I did. It's not here."

"Want me to come in and help you look for it?"

"No. Thanks anyway." Kerri hung up the phone, then leaned back and glanced around the room, her expression growing more puzzled. She remembered stuffing the drawing inside the chart and was sure she hadn't taken it back out. So where was it? Maybe it had slid out, as Stephen suggested, and the cleaning crew, failing to recognize its significance, had tossed it in with the rest of the trash. Though she knew it was futile, she scooted her chair back and checked the garbage can beneath her desk. It was empty.

"Damn," she muttered. Reorganizing her thoughts, she decided to try some doll therapy on Jace instead. Getting up from her chair, she walked over to the file cabinet and opened the bottom drawer. There, in the back, were a pair of cloth dolls—one male and one female, both anatomically correct. She had used them in the past when she was working with children who were suspected victims of sexual abuse. After sitting in the drawer for well over a year, they were now dusty and a little faded. She brushed them off and set them on the coffee table between the love seat and chairs. A few minutes later, Stephen buzzed her to let her know the Johansens had arrived.

She decided to spend a few minutes with Thad again before bringing Jace back. As she watched him take his seat, she noted the dark circles rimming his eyes and the slump in his shoulders. Today he was wearing a pullover shirt and khaki pants—more casual than yesterday's dress but still immaculate and wrinkle free. She started him off with some general chitchat about the weather, hoping to relax him a little, then asked how Jace had been since yesterday's appointment.

"About the same, I guess," Thad said, running a hand through his hair. "He didn't sleep much last night. He woke up twice crying. Some nightmare or something. I offered to bring him into bed with me, but he refused. So I ended up sleeping with him."

"Then I'd venture to guess neither of you got much sleep," Kerri said.

Thad didn't answer; he merely gave her a tired smile.

"Did he say what the nightmare was about?"

Thad shook his head sadly. "No. All he would do was cry for his mother." He leaned back and clenched his jaw closed, staring out the window to his right. "This is crazy," he said finally. "It's apparent to me the cops have rethought this whole thing, or they would have left us alone by now." He turned and stared at Kerri. "They think something has happened to her, don't they?"

Kerri returned his stare unblinking. She thought a moment before she answered, recalling Kevin's suspicions from the day before.

"They think there might be something more to it," she admitted. "There are some things that bother them."

Thad slapped his thighs and stood so quickly, it made Kerri flinch. He walked over to the window, stuffed his hands in his pockets, and stared at the scene below. "If they think that, why aren't they out there looking for her?" he said. He looked back over his shoulder at Kerri. "I know my wife. She didn't just walk out of that house on her own." Tears welled in his eyes, and before they could run down his face, he turned back toward the window. Kerri studied him quietly, watching his shoulders heave as he tried to regain control. Finally, he said, "Do you really think Jace knows something?"

"What do you think?"

Thad shrugged. "I know something is wrong with him. He's had nightmares before, but never like this. And twice now I've found him standing in the doorway to his bedroom, staring down the hallway toward our room with this horrified expression on his face."

"Really?" Kerri said, scribbling a note in the chart on her lap. When she was done, she chewed on the end of her pencil while she stared at Johansen's back. After a moment, she tossed the pencil onto the table in front of her and stood. "Why don't we go ahead and bring Jace back here. Let me see if I can get him to open up any today," she suggested.

Thad didn't answer right away. Then, slowly, he nodded. Without a word, he turned away from the window and headed out to the waiting room.

Jace seemed less wary of Kerri today, and she was delighted to see his immediate interest in the dolls on the table. He walked over to them and picked up the female doll, holding it close to his chest. Kerri sat in the chair across from him and smiled.

"Do you like that doll?" she asked him.

He nodded, one hand stroking the doll's head.

"What about the other doll?" Kerri asked.

Jace's eyes moved toward the male doll, still lying face up on the table. He stared at it a moment, then shrugged.

"I really liked the picture you drew for me yesterday," Kerri said.

Jace said nothing; he just kept stroking the doll.

"Does that doll you're holding remind you of your mother?" Kerri tried. She bit her lip and held her breath, waiting for his reaction. Amazingly, all she got was a slow nod.

"Why don't you lay the mommy doll down on the table," Kerri suggested. "Like she was in the picture."

Jace thought about it, then did as she suggested. But not before sweeping the male doll off onto the floor. He cocked his head to one side and studied the female doll, then bent down and retrieved the male doll, laying it alongside the other.

"Is that your dad?" Kerri asked, reaching out and touching the male doll.

Jace nodded.

"Are they sleeping?"

Again, Jace nodded.

"Are they happy?"

Jace screwed his face up as he considered the question, then shook his head.

"Why aren't they happy?" Kerri asked carefully.

Jace stared at the dolls, his expression sad and forlorn. Then he reached across the table and picked up her pencil. Holding it aloft, he brought it down, stabbing it into the left breast of the female doll. Though it left a dent and a lead mark on the doll's clothing, it didn't pierce the material. Instead, the point snapped off, and as Jace let go, the pencil rolled onto the floor. Kerri felt her heart skip a beat and gasped before she could catch herself.

Jace shot a quick, pained glance at her, his lower lip trembling. Then he turned and ran from the room.

SEVEN

Kerri followed Jace out to the waiting room,
where she found him in his father's lap, sobbing quietly, his face buried in Thad's chest. Thad's expression
was one of stunned confusion. Even Stephen looked a
bit surprised.

Kerri walked over and sat beside Thad. She
reached out and rubbed her hand up and down Jace's
back, murmuring to him. When the child had calmed
down some, Kerri looked up at Thad, her face apologetic. "I think he's had enough for today. Why don't
you take him home and bring him back tomorrow."

Thad nodded, an automatic gesture. Without a
word, he scooped Jace up into his arms and carried
him out the door.

"What was that all about?" Stephen asked.

"Believe it or not," Kerri said, staring at the door
with a troubled expression, "I think it was progress."

Throughout the rest of the day, Kerri's mind was more
on Jace Johansen and his puzzling behavior than anything else. When Stephen poked his head into her
office to ask if she wanted some lunch, Kerri dug her
wallet out of her purse and gave him some money.

"Bring me back a sandwich or something," she said, handing him the cash. "Anything is fine." She tossed her wallet onto the desk, then promptly walked over to the bookcase and selected several hefty tomes, which she lugged over to the table in front of the love seat. The next hour flew by as she perused the texts, ate but barely tasted the tuna sandwich Stephen brought her, and read up on case studies in an effort to find anything that might give her a clue as to which direction to move next with Jace. When Stephen buzzed her to announce the arrival of her next patient, Kerri marked several spots in the text and tossed the books atop the growing mountain of paperwork piled on her desk.

Though she tried throughout the afternoon to focus on her patients, more often than not she found herself merely feigning interest in what they were saying. Consequently, by the time she was ready to head home, she was feeling guilty as hell, knowing she'd failed to provide them with the care and attention they needed. She was surprised she hadn't heard from Kevin and thought about calling to fill him in on the morning's events, but she was reluctant to say anything until she'd better analyzed it herself. Besides, she thought one more session with Jace might reveal the answers she was looking for. It could wait until tomorrow, she decided. In an effort to make up for her lack of attentiveness with the rest of the day's patients, she stuffed their charts into her briefcase, intending to focus on them later that evening when she was home.

It wasn't until she arrived at the ferry terminal and went to pay for her fare that she realized she didn't have her wallet. She panicked; then she remembered tossing it onto her desk at lunchtime. No doubt it was still there, buried beneath mountains of paperwork.

Cursing under her breath, she turned around and headed back up the hill.

By the time she reached the office, her self-annoyance had grown considerably. She was muttering, lecturing herself on the need to stay focused and not get so caught up in one particular case. Irritated, she flung the office door open once she had it unlocked and marched across the waiting room, tossing her briefcase and purse onto Stephen's desk as she passed. Opening the door to her own office, she stepped inside and immediately sensed something was wrong. She knew her internal alarm had rung a hairsbreadth too late when she heard a noise behind her—a fleeting rush of air. A split second later, a blinding pain struck the back of her head, quickly spreading down her back and around her neck. A flash of color spun before her eyes in a brief and brilliant display before everything faded to black.

When Kerri opened her eyes, the first thing she focused on was the kindly, wrinkled face of an elderly Chinese man hovering just above her. Gradually, she came to realize she was lying on the floor, and a moment later she recognized the uniform shirt the old man was wearing—that of the office cleaning crew. The name *Charlie* was stitched across the breast pocket.

"You all right?" the little man asked, studying Kerri's face with concern.

Kerri tried to sit up, but the pain in the back of her head throbbed with a nauseating intensity.

"I call police," the old man told her. "They come now."

Kerri blinked hard to clear her head, and as she looked beyond the old man, she saw several other faces hovering nearby, all of them watching her with fearful worry. Then a cold rush of air whispered past her, and Kevin's face replaced the old man's.

"Kerri! What the hell happened?" He knelt beside her, his eyes roving from her head to her toes in a quick assessment.

"I don't know exactly," Kerri said. Kevin helped her sit up, and she winced as a bolt of pain shot down the back of her neck. By now, she recalled the faint whisper of sound and the crashing blow she'd felt just before she blacked out. "Someone was in my office," she said weakly, massaging the back of her head.

Kevin's hand shoved hers aside and gently probed her scalp. "You got whacked a good one," he said. "There's a lump the size of a robin's egg back here. Didn't break the skin though," he added. "You're lucky. What the hell happened?"

Kerri took several deep breaths to clear her mind. "I came back to the office because I forgot my wallet," she explained. "I guess I surprised a burglar or something. One minute I was standing in the doorway, and the next thing I know, I'm looking up at Charlie there." She gestured toward the elderly Chinese man.

Kevin stood and approached the old man. "You, sir," he said. "What did you see?"

The old man's face took on a panicked look and he made a tentative step backward. He began to jabber something in Chinese, and one of the other crew members, a younger fellow, stepped up to explain. "We came in here to do the cleanup and found the door open. She was there, just like that, on the floor."

"Did you see anyone else?" Kevin asked.

The younger man shook his head. The old man continued to babble, and he began pacing back and forth across the office, his hands gesturing wildly. One of his coworkers hauled him aside and tried to calm him down.

Kevin helped Kerri to her feet and settled her in one of the waiting-room chairs. "You need to go to the ER and get checked out," he said.

Kerri started to shake her head, then stopped when the motion made her head squeeze with pain. "I'm fine," she said, massaging her neck. "All I need is a couple of aspirin."

Kevin opened his mouth to argue, but Kerri cut him off. "I just want to go home, Kevin," she said, her voice weary. "I'm fine. Really."

Kevin's face darkened. "Sit there a few minutes and see how you feel. Then we'll decide."

Two uniformed officers had arrived along with Kevin, and one of them had ushered the cleaning crew out into the hallway, where he was questioning them further on the exact sequence of events. The second officer was looking around Kerri's office, trying to determine if anything had been disturbed or taken. Kevin left Kerri's side and went to join him.

As Kerri sat rubbing her neck with her hand, she noticed her purse and briefcase still sitting on Stephen's desk. That struck her as odd. She assumed whoever had broken in had been intent on robbing the place, yet they left her stuff there when they could have easily carried it off. Of course, her wallet, which had all her money and credit cards in it, was not in the purse. The burglar had probably already found it on her desk by the time she came in and interrupted him. Still, she found it curious that anyone would target her office in the first place. Surely there were more lucrative places to rob.

Wondering if her wallet had, in fact, been taken, Kerri stood slowly and made her way into her office. Kevin and the patrolman were standing in the corner by the window, looking down at the street below and conversing in subdued tones. Kerri walked over to her desk, shoved the piles of papers around, and breathed a sigh of relief when she found her wallet buried beneath the mess.

"You shouldn't be up walking around," Kevin said, striding toward her, his face clearly showing his irritation.

"I came in to see if this was still here," Kerri said, holding the wallet aloft. She opened it then, to inspect its contents and see if everything was still there. It was.

"Why would someone break in here?" she asked, still puzzled. "It's not as if they would expect to find a bunch of cash lying around."

"Probably after drugs," the patrolman offered.

"But I don't keep any drugs stocked here."

"But they may not have known that," Kevin said. "What about your prescription pads? Where do you keep those?"

"Top drawer," Kerri answered. Kevin reached over and yanked the drawer open. He grabbed three prescription pads and tossed them onto the desk.

"That's all of them," Kerri said. "Though I suppose a few sheets might have been torn off."

"I think you managed to interrupt things before this guy found what he was after," Kevin said. "You're damned lucky he didn't kill you. I don't suppose you saw anyone?" The tone in his voice suggested he already knew the answer.

Kerri shook her head. "He was behind me. I was over there in the doorway," she turned and pointed, "and I heard a whoosh of air near my ear. Then I was hit. That's all I know." She gave him an apologetic shrug.

"Well, we'll check the place over anyway, though as I said, I think you stopped whatever was about to happen." He turned to the patrolman. "Not much point in dusting the whole place for prints, do ya think? There's bound to be hundreds of them. Maybe check just the doorknobs and the desk here." The patrolman nodded his agreement.

The officer who had been questioning the cleaning crew entered the office. "Looks like the guy got away," he told the others. "The cleaning crew said they saw no one. They found the office door open, saw Dr. Whitaker on the floor, and called 911." He looked at Kerri. "Ma'am, do you remember locking the door to your office when you left? Because there doesn't appear to be any signs of a break-in."

Kerri thought back to when she'd first left the office. "I can't be one hundred percent sure," she said, frowning. "But I must have. It's automatic. And I know it was locked when I came back."

Kevin's eyes burrowed into her own. "That doesn't mean anythin'. Whoever was in here probably locked the door behind him. Were you in a hurry when you left? Or distracted or anything like that, so you might have forgotten?"

Kerri felt herself flush with guilt. "My mind was on other things," she admitted. "But I can't believe I would have walked out of here without locking the door behind me, distracted or not." She saw the three men exchange a look that clearly expressed their doubts. Defeated, Kerri sighed and gave a shrug of acquiescence. "I'll be more careful from now on," she said.

Kevin gave her a look that reminded her so much of her father. That same chastising, you-should-know-better look she had seen throughout her childhood. She half expected him to start lecturing her, the same way her father would have, but instead he said, "How about that trip to the ER?"

Kerri shook her head. "I'm fine, Kevin. I swear. I just want to go home."

Kevin's eyes challenged hers, but she met his gaze without backing down. "Come on then," he said irritably. "I'll drive you to the ferry."

By the time she reached her house, Kerri's headache had grown to astounding proportions. After sidestepping past Shadow, she headed straight for the upstairs bathroom and swallowed three aspirin tablets. Shadow, clearly annoyed with the delay in getting his supper, howled his displeasure from the bottom of the stairs. After shutting the cat up with a can of chicken-and-gravy dinner that made Kerri's stomach lurch threateningly, she settled into the recliner in the living room and closed her eyes, waiting for the aspirin to take effect.

Kevin had asked about today's appointment with the Johansens as they drove to the ferry terminal. Kerri had been intentionally vague, saying only that she was making progress but had nothing definite yet. She was surprised when Kevin left it at that, though she supposed he did so in deference to the incident in her office. He dropped her off, but not without first promising he would call her in a couple of hours to see how she was doing. Kerri started to object but thought better of it. She figured she'd already garnered all the concessions she was going to for one night. When the time for Kevin's call came and went, she found herself feeling inexplicably annoyed. At eleven, she popped three more aspirin and headed for bed.

Though she felt exhausted and drained, she couldn't get to sleep. She tossed and turned, trying to find a comfortable position that didn't make her head throb, her thoughts turning once again to Jace Johansen. His behavior with the dolls disturbed her. Initially, she'd thought it might have been a way for him to express his anger toward his mother for leaving him. But now she wasn't so sure. For him to act out his anger in such a violent way seemed highly unusual. Besides, he didn't really seem angry. Frightened, confused, lonely, abandoned—yes. But not angry.

That left her with Kevin's theory and the possibility Jace had merely been acting out a scene he witnessed between his mother and father. Yet, no matter how hard she tried, she couldn't imagine Thad Johansen murdering his wife. She admitted to herself she really didn't know him all that well, and her belief was based on less than professional criteria. But if Jace had seen his father do something to his mother, would he have run to Thad for solace the way he did this morning? Highly unlikely.

There was also the issue of the supposed crime scene. According to Kevin, there were no signs of foul play, and surely if the woman had been stabbed in the chest there would be some evidence of that. Blood at the very least. She understood why the police had come to the initial conclusion that Janet Johansen simply left the house of her own free will. The only reasons Kevin suspected otherwise were those troubling details he had mentioned yesterday. Her mind continued its endless circling until finally, around one o'clock in the morning, she dropped off to sleep out of sheer mental exhaustion.

She was awakened some time later by the shrill and persistent ring of the phone. Rubbing her eyes, she squinted at the clock beside the bed; it was after two. Who in the hell would be calling her at this hour?

"Hello?"

"Kerri? It's Kevin. Did I wake you?"

"Of course you did," she said irritably. She raked a hand through her hair and sat up, trying to blink away the gritty sensation behind her eyelids. The aspirin she'd taken upon going to bed had worn off, and her headache returned with a vengeance. "It's after two, Kevin. A little late to be calling to check on me."

"I know. I'm sorry. Something came up. Glad to see you're still alive."

"No thanks to you."

"We found Janet Johansen's body."

The words washed over Kerri like a bucket of ice water, eliminating any last vestiges of drowsiness. The hand that had been rubbing her neck dropped into her lap. Instantly, she forgot about her headache. Her mind took off on a whirlwind of thoughts and questions. Seizing the first one she could, she asked, "Where?"

"In Lake Washington near Lakeridge, about ten miles from the Johansens' house."

"Cause of death?" Kerri asked, squeezing her eyes closed as she anticipated the answer. Her stomach started to churn uncomfortably. The aspirin she'd taken earlier felt as if they were now burning a hole in her gut.

"Not sure yet," Kevin said. "The medical examiner's

done a preliminary, but there was nothing obvious. Only thing we know for sure is that she was dead before she hit the water."

Kerri's eyes shot open at that, and she breathed a sigh of relief. If Thad Johansen had stabbed his wife in the chest, it would have been noticeable immediately. "Have you told Thad?"

"Not yet, though we'll have to notify him soon so he can ID the body."

"Then you're not sure it's her?" Kerri asked, jumping on the bone of hope Kevin had unwittingly tossed at her.

"Oh, it's her all right. Fits the description right down to the locket pendant she's wearing and a crescent-shaped birthmark on the back of her neck."

"Shit," Kerri muttered as her hopes flagged. She thought about Jace Johansen's terrified face, those huge blue eyes looking back at her with an appeal for help, for understanding. "Listen, Kevin. Would you do me a favor?"

"What?"

"Will you let me be there when you tell the Johansens?"

There was a stretch of silence on the other end and Kerri could imagine Kevin's brow furrowing with concern and puzzlement. "Now, why do you want to do that, lass?" he asked finally.

"Because I'm very concerned about how Jace is going to take this. And I'm not so sure his father will deal with it all that well either."

"I don't think it will be any big surprise to the husband," Kevin said, the sarcasm in his voice unmistakable. "At least not the fact she's dead, though the fact we found her might not sit too well with him."

"You still think he killed her," Kerri said tiredly.

"Well, somebody sure as hell did. Right now, he's the most likely suspect."

"And what was his motive?" Kerri challenged. "You said there was no evidence of an affair, that the woman was a loving wife and mother by all accounts. So what possible reason could he have for killing her?"

"Well, I was going to tell you this earlier, but with everything that happened, I thought it might be better to wait."

"What?" Kerri said, feeling a blanket of dread descend over her.

"I talked with Janet's doctor today, the gynecologist she was scheduled to see?"

"Yes?"

"Seems she thought she might be pregnant."

Kerri digested the information a moment before saying, "So?"

"So, what if she was pregnant by someone other than Thad?"

"That's ridiculous, Kevin. You said yourself there was no indication of a lover."

"Just because we haven't found one yet, doesn't mean there isn't one."

Kerri tried to think of a comeback, but couldn't. Though she hated to admit it, Kevin might be right.

"Anyway," Kevin continued, "I'm figuring on bringing Johansen down to the morgue to ID her first thing in the morning. No sense dragging him and the boy out of bed in the middle of the night. Want to meet me in the viewing room?"

"How about if I meet you at the Johansens' instead?" Kerri countered. "I want to be there when you tell them."

Kevin let out a weary sigh. "I think it's a dumb idea."

"Your opinion is noted and appreciated, Kevin. But I'm going to be there, whether you agree to it or not."

"Your father was right about you, ya know. You're a stubborn damned lass."

"Runs in the family. How about if I meet you at the Johansens' at seven?"

When she heard Kevin's weighty exhalation on the other end, she knew she'd won. "Okay," he said grudgingly. "But I still think it's a stupid idea."

"Wait and let me get a pen to write down their address," Kerri said, ignoring his protest. "I don't have their file with me." She set the phone down and reached over to flip on the light. Grabbing a pen and notepad from the bedside stand, she leaned back against the headboard and cradled the handset of the phone against her shoulder. "Okay, shoot."

Kevin rattled off the address, then said, "I don't guess you need directions."

"Not hardly." The address was in the same neighborhood where she and Nathan had lived. "I'll see you at seven."

Hanging up the phone, Kerri did a quick mental calculation of how long she would need to get showered and dressed and then catch a ferry that would allow her to get to the Johansens' by seven. Glancing at the clock, she figured she could possibly steal another two hours of sleep, assuming she nodded off right away. But as wide awake as she felt at the moment, she knew it was pointless to even bother. With a sigh of resignation, she threw back the covers and headed for the shower.

EIGHT

The Johansens' house was nestled at the end of a cul-de-sac and bordered on three sides by thick groves of towering pines. It was a quiet neighborhood, filled with spacious lots, expensive homes, and well-manicured lawns. Though the street was deserted this early in the morning, Kerri knew garage doors would soon slide open on well-oiled tracks, triggered by the push of a button on the visor of a Mercedes or Jaguar. It was the type of neighborhood where everyone wore a uniform: the kids, their private school plaids; the husbands, their pinstriped suits and tasteful ties; the wives, expensive stirrup pants and baggy tunic tops designed to look like bargain basement fare.

The Johansens' house was neither the largest nor the stateliest on the street, but its carefully landscaped lawn and shrubs, the tasteful and understated wood tones of its siding, and its location at the end of the cul-de-sac—set out on center stage- -drew one's attention. Yet, despite the obvious care devoted to the house, Kerri thought it looked lonely and empty, its windows staring back somber and vacant. The cold wet blanket of clouds that had descended upon the city during the night didn't help. The pervasive gray dampness drained all color and life from everything it touched. Kerri knew it was more than the weather that made the Johansen house look gloomy and deserted; it was the knowledge of what might have transpired inside—and what was about to.

Seeing Kevin's unmarked car already parked a discreet distance from the house, Kerri pulled in behind him and got out, pulling her coat closed and wrapping her arms around herself for warmth.

Kevin climbed out of his car and walked back toward her. Kerri smiled when she saw he'd replaced his toothpick with a wooden match. "I see you've graduated to a thicker chew toy," she teased.

Kevin leaned back against the fender and glanced at her with a puzzled expression, then dawning spread across his face. "Oh, this you mean," he said, plucking the half-pulpy match from between his lips. He stared at it a moment, as if unsure how it got there. Then he shrugged and stuck it back in place. "Hey, at least it's in the same general family as a cigarette. How's your head?"

"Fine," Kerri lied. In actuality, her headache was now pounding with a new intensity.

Kevin turned away and stared at the Johansen house. "Think he's up yet?" he asked.

"I'm sure he is," Kerri said. "They have an appointment at my office at eight." She eyed Kevin accusingly as the import of his question hit her. "Didn't you call to tell him we were coming?"

Kevin rolled the match from one side of his mouth to the other, then plucked it out. "No, I want to see his reaction when I tell him. Besides, I don't want to give him the chance to run."

"He's not going to run, Kevin," Kerri said impatiently. "I can't believe you're trying to sandbag him like this."

Kevin glanced back at her. "You're tenacious in your beliefs, lass. I'll give ya that."

"Look who's talking," Kerri flared, walking toward the house. "Come on. Let's get this over with."

She heard Kevin grunt as he pushed himself away from the car and followed. He quickly overtook her, strutting officiously toward the house. On any other occasion, Kerri might have risen to the bait and raced him toward their goal. But today she was more than willing to let him take the lead. Ever since his phone call earlier this morning, a feeling of dread had settled over her. Now it felt like a clinging pall drawing tighter with every step, slowly suffocating her. Though a mild surge of anger at Kevin had catapulted her forward, reluctance now strolled by her side, occasionally grabbing at her hand to pull her back. Doing her best to ignore this wayward and uninvited companion, she was nevertheless struck by a sudden impulse to turn tail and run. Instead, she glued her eyes to the scuffed heels of Kevin's loafers and followed him up the five brick stairs to the Johansens' narrow front porch.

Kevin stabbed a finger at the doorbell and Kerri continued to stare at his shoes, using these last few seconds to steel herself for what was coming. When she heard the door open, she finally looked up, expecting the Thad Johansen she had seen for the past two days in her office. But the man standing in the doorway made her blink twice before she was convinced it was the same person.

He was clad in a pair of stained sweat pants and a worn T-shirt. The platinum color of his hair was the same, but this morning it boasted a crop of bed-head spikes. Dark half moons had risen beneath his eyes, making him look years older, and a snowy blanket of day-old beard graced his cheeks and chin.

Johansen's eyes settled on Kevin first, his face registering recognition, then resignation.

"Detective," he said wearily. "What can I do for you this time?" He spared a cursory glance at Kerri, then started to look away. But as recognition hit, his eyes snapped back toward her, his expression changing rapidly to one of puzzlement. "Dr. Whitaker? What are you . . ."

Kerri knew the instant Thad Johansen understood the nature of their visit. His reaction was so sudden, so profound, she could almost hear the faint clink as the puzzle pieces dropped into place. His eyes grew round and wary; his lower jaw dropped open. All traces of color in his ruddy complexion drained away, leaving his face bleached and bloodless. Every muscle in his body flinched and tensed, as if preparing for a tremendous blow. The look of impatient resignation he had worn moments ago quickly transformed into a mask of dawning realization and abject terror.

"Oh my God," he whispered. Licking his lips, he braced himself with a deep, gasping breath. "Something has happened, hasn't it? Something with Janet." His eyes darted back and forth between Kevin and Kerri, waiting.

"Can we come in, Mr. Johansen?" Kevin asked, intentionally ignoring the man's question.

Kerri shot Kevin a scathing glance, irritated at his need to play psychocop by stringing the poor man along. Had his tone not been soothing and solicitous, she would have been tempted to pop him in the ribs with her elbow.

"We'd like to talk to you inside," Kevin urged when he failed to get any response to his first request.

Johansen neither answered nor moved. One hand gripped the doorframe so tightly the knuckles were blanched and taut. In fact, his whole body was so tensed and ready to spring, Kerri wouldn't have been surprised to see him suddenly catapult himself through the door and into the street.

Johansen blinked—a long, slow blink—and swallowed hard. Kerri let her eyes drop toward his throat, finding it too painful to watch his face. As he struggled to speak, his Adam's apple bounced up and down like some crazed, miniature elevator. When the words finally did come out, the voice accompanying them quivered and croaked.

"Please," Johansen begged. "Just tell me. Is she all right?"

Kerri brought her eyes back up reluctantly, relieved to see Johansen's gaze was fixed on Kevin rather than her. Kevin didn't answer immediately; she knew he was gauging the situation, taking advantage of the moment to size up his prey. A wave of anger surged through her. Kevin might suspect Thad Johansen, but Kerri didn't believe for one moment that the pathetic, destroyed figure standing before her was in any way implicated in his wife's death. Her heart went out to the man; his suffering was obvious. He looked like a blown-out eggshell—fragile, pale, and ready to crumble at the first inkling of pressure.

As the moments ticked by, with Kevin merely staring and Johansen crumbling away, Kerri's anger grew. Finally, unable to stand it any longer, she took matters into her own hands. Moving a step closer, she reached over and wrapped her hand around Johansen's free arm. His head pivoted slowly, until he was looking down at her. The muscles in his cheeks twitched and jerked. Except for his eyes, which were glassy with fear, his expression was vacuous.

Swallowing hard, Kerri summoned up her gentlest voice and said, "No, Mr. Johansen, she's not all right. The police found her body last night, in Lake Washington."

Whatever source of strength Thad Johansen had relied on deserted him in an instant. His long, lanky body went into a sliding collapse as if every bone had suddenly turned liquid. Kevin shoved Kerri aside and grabbed the man about the waist, halting his precipitous slide toward the floor. Pulling one of Johansen's arms around his neck, Kevin led him inside, squeezing past a large grandfather clock in the foyer and heading for a couch in the living room straight ahead.

Kerri hurried to Johansen's side, helping Kevin lower him onto the sofa. Despite their efforts, Johansen went down fast, sinking into the plush softness of the cushions. He sat slumped and dejected looking, his hands lying uselessly in his lap, his eyes glazed and without focus. He looked like a dead man.

Kerri knelt down in front of him and looked up into his face. "Mr. Johansen? Thad?"

Getting no response, no indication whatsoever he heard her, Kerri cast a worried glance at Kevin. He looked back at her and shrugged.

Kerri turned back toward Johansen. "Thad, I know this is an awful shock for you, but you need to pull together here." Glancing around the room, she asked, "Where's Jace?"

That seemed to sink in, for his eyes widened and focused on Kerri. Then he moaned, burying his face in his hands. "Oh, God. Jace. How can I tell Jace?" He lifted his head and stared at her. Everything that had been alive and vibrant in the man was gone. Even his eyes appeared drained of life, the normally brilliant blue now faded to an almost transparent gray.

"Jace is upstairs," he said, his voice flat. He raised his head and gazed toward the ceiling, the sheen of tears in his eyes growing thicker. Drops trickled over his lids and hovered amidst the pale white of his lashes like heavy dew. "Getting dressed," he added listlessly. His eyes squeezed shut, and two tiny rivulets channeled their way down his cheeks.

Kerri glanced up at Kevin, prepared to give him one of her "are you satisfied?" looks. But even Kevin's face had softened, touched to some degree by Johansen's obvious emotional turmoil.

She stood and placed a reassuring hand on Thad's shoulder. "I'll tell Jace about his mother if you want me to," she said. The offer was sincere, but it didn't stop her gut from squirming as she uttered the words. It was a task she would not relish.

Johansen leaned back, rolling his eyes toward the ceiling. "No," he said, rolling his lips inward and biting down on them. "I should do it."

Kerri gave him a doubtful look. "Are you sure?" she asked.

Johansen drew a long, quivering breath, then blew it out, locking in his resolve. He pushed himself up from the couch. "I'm sure," he said. "But if you would come along, I'd appreciate it. I don't think he's going to take this well."

"Certainly," Kerri said, craning her neck to look up at him. Even with the depressive slump that rolled his shoulders, he towered over her. Worried that his conviction was greater than his ability, Kerri gestured to Kevin with a sideways nudge of her head, inviting him

to follow along. Then she cupped Johansen's elbow
lightly in her palm and steered him toward the stairs.

Kerri doubted Thad Johansen could have walked
to his own execution with any more reluctance and
fear than he displayed now. With each stair he
climbed, his back became more bowed, and his legs
moved as if they were weighted down with cement.
They were about halfway up, Kerri urging Johansen
with a gentle nudge on his elbow, when she felt him
freeze, his whole body turning rigid as a plank. His
eyes stared at the landing above them, his expression
one of fearful apology.

Kerri knew, even before she followed Johansen's
gaze, that Jace was standing at the top of the stairs.
One of the boy's hands rested on the newel post, the
other twisted at a strand of hair standing out almost
perpendicular from his head. His face was expressionless, but he kept rolling his bottom lip in and scraping
it along his upper teeth. He was dressed except for his
feet, which were bare, the toes curling around the
edge of the top step.

"Jace," Thad said, his voice carrying a timbre that
surprised Kerri with its strength. "You remember Dr.
Whitaker?"

Jace nodded hesitantly, his eyes darting between
Kerri and his father.

Kerri felt Johansen's arm tremble in her palm, and
she gave it a little squeeze. She looked up at his face and
saw his mouth opening and closing as he struggled for
his next words. Once again deciding to take the initiative, she moved past him and ascended the remaining
steps until she was directly in front of Jace. She sidled
her butt onto the landing so she was at eye level with
him.

"Jace," she said softly, "I'm afraid we have some bad news for you."

His eyes were so round and blue and guileless, Kerri felt a pitiable ache tug from somewhere deep inside her chest. But then Jace's stare took on an unsettling intensity and the innocence disappeared. In its place was an expression of wizened acceptance, as if this six-year-old boy had lived through decades of suffering and injustice only to be hardened by life's adversities. Watching this saddening transition take place, Kerri knew her news would come as no surprise to the child.

"It's about your mother," Kerri said slowly. Jace's eyes never left her own. Kerri heard Thad utter a strangled whimper from below.

"I know," Jace said simply. "Is she dead?"

Kerri bit her lip and nodded.

"So she can't ever come home?"

Kerri swallowed down the huge lump crawling up her throat. "No, honey, she can't ever come home."

Jace contemplated that a moment, then his eyes filled with a liquid sheen. "I think I'm going to be sad," he said with great solemnity. His head fell forward and fat tears dropped onto the carpet at his feet, leaving two dark blotches. "Why did they take my mommy?" he asked, his voice hitching painfully.

Hearing that, Kevin leaped past Johansen—who was slumped against the wall, his head hanging in abject misery—and bounded up the remaining stairs. "Who took your mommy, Jace?" Kevin asked brusquely. "Did you see something?"

Kerri flung her arm out between Kevin and Jace, using it to gather the boy to her. "Not now, Kevin," she hissed. "Let's take this a little slower, shall we?" She held Jace protectively against her chest, rubbing her hand over his tiny back. She could feel his heart pounding against her own, feel his ribs heaving with pitiful sobs. Holding him, she was reminded of the tiny, fledgling bird she had rescued some months ago when Shadow had routed the poor thing from its nest. Trembling with fear, the bird had hidden within the safety of her palm while Shadow mewed plaintively for what he obviously thought was his rightful reward. Kerri had stared down the cat's determination then; she gave Kevin the same look now.

"Why don't you two go downstairs and take care of business," she suggested, knowing Kevin wouldn't be satisfied until he'd had his shot at Thad. "Give me a few minutes to help Jace get his shoes and socks on, and then we'll be down."

Kevin met the challenge of her gaze for a moment, but recognizing from past experience that she was unlikely to back down, he finally caved in. "Fine," he said grudgingly.

Kerri didn't give him an opportunity to rethink the situation. Standing up, she hauled Jace into her arms and carried him off down the hall in search of his bedroom.

NINE

By the time Kerri found Jace's bedroom (easy to identify, with toys and clothes strewn everywhere, it was as chaotic as its resident), Jace was starting to settle down. His breathing was steadier, and the trembling had subsided. Kerri lowered him onto the edge of the bed and sat beside him, her hand resting below the nape of his neck.

"You okay?" she asked, leaning forward and peering into his face.

Jace stared at his hands in his lap. The skin on his face was blotchy, his eyes red-rimmed and damp, but the restless fidgeting Kerri had come to associate with him had vanished. At least for the moment. He answered her with a tentative nod.

Kerri gave his neck a gentle squeeze. "Okay then. Where are your shoes?" she asked, looking around at the room's clutter.

"Over there," Jace said, pointing toward a large wooden toy chest that sat, empty, in one corner of the room. In the mountain of toys surrounding it, Kerri spied a grass-stained sneaker peeking from beneath some molded plastic castle thing. She walked over and pulled the shoe out, then, with a little digging around, found its mate.

"Socks?" she asked, carrying the shoes over to the bed.

Jace glanced around the room, then hopped down and dropped to his knees. He reached under his bed, coming up a moment later with a mismatched pair of dusty socks. He handed them to Kerri.

Holding the socks gingerly between her thumb and fingers, Kerri eyed them dubiously. "Don't you have some clean ones somewhere?" she asked.

Jace shrugged. "Dad doesn't do too good with laundry," he said.

Unconvinced, Kerri walked over to the dresser and prowled through the drawers. She managed to come up with two clean socks, both of them white, though the stripes at the top didn't match. "Here," she said, tossing them onto the bed. "Put these on."

Jace obliged, pulling on first the socks, then the shoes. He hopped off the bed and walked over to Kerri, stopping in front of her. He folded his arms over his chest and looked up at her expectantly.

"What?" Kerri asked.

"I don't know how to tie yet."

"Oh." Kerri squatted down and reached for the first foot Jace stuck out for her. The motion was like a ride in an instant time machine, transporting her back to a rainy morning some three years ago. She had been trying to get Mandy dressed and out the door, and they were running late. In her frantic rush, her fingers became clumsy and awkward as they tried to tie the laces in Mandy's shoes.

"Can you teach me how to do that, Mommy?" Mandy had asked, holding one foot in the air, her tiny hand grasping Kerri's shoulder for balance. The expression on her freckled face was imploring.

"Not today, Mandy. We're in a hurry. Some other day, okay?"

Mandy frowned—an adorable but petulant expression that never failed to get her what she wanted from her father. But Kerri was in too big a hurry to be affected by her four-year-old-daughter's attempts at emotional manipulation.

"Alicia knows how to tie her shoes." Mandy pouted. "She says I'm dumb 'cause I can't do it."

"You're not dumb," Kerri said, finishing one shoe and reaching for the other. "You'll learn. Just not right now."

Remembering the incident, Kerri felt a new wave of grief wash over her. Back then, the only thing that had seemed important was time. With grim irony, she realized how true that had been—though not in the way she had thought. She wished now she had taken more pleasure in each precious second of Mandy's existence.

Burning from the memory of those missed moments, Kerri let go of Jace's laces and patted the floor beside her. "Sit down," she said. "I'll show you how to tie them yourself."

Jace dropped down in front of her, both legs bent at the knees, his feet pulled up close to his butt. His chin settled onto one knee as he locked his legs in place by wrapping his arms around them and clasping his hands together. In this huddled position, he studied the dangling strings of his shoes.

Kerri scooted behind him. Snuggling up against his back, she reached her arms around and picked up the laces. "Okay," she said. "First thing we do is take one of the strings in this hand, and the other one in the other hand." She showed Jace what to do, then let him grasp the laces himself. "Cross them over like this." Guiding his tiny hands with her own, she led him through the steps. "Now bring this one under and through. Good! Now pull them tight."

Jace did what she asked, his tongue sticking out the entire time.

"Okay," Kerri said. "Next we take this one and make a bunny ear, like this."

Jace's level of concentration as she walked him through the process was remarkable, and he quickly completed the first bow.

"Great!" Kerri said. "Now, you do the other one."

Jace shifted his focus to the other foot and, with only minimal guidance from Kerri, managed to tie it as well.

"Splendid job!" Kerri told him, ruffling his hair. "You're very bright. Most kids have to try four or five times before they get it right."

Jace twisted his head and beamed at her over his shoulder. "Really?" he asked.

Kerri gazed back at those incredibly blue eyes and felt a pleasant warmth wrap around her heart. "Yes, really," she told him. She sandwiched his face between her palms and planted a quick kiss on his forehead. "Have you had breakfast yet?"

Jace nodded.

"Then what do you say we head downstairs and see what those two big guys are up to?"

"Okay." Jace pushed himself off the floor, waited for Kerri to get up, then followed her to the door.

Kerri was halfway to the stair landing before she realized Jace was no longer beside her. She looked back and saw him standing at the threshold to his room, staring down the hallway with a look of fearful anticipation. She walked back and knelt beside him, studying his face. "Jace? Are you okay?"

He continued to stare—wide-eyed and unblinking.

"Jace? What's wrong?" She set her hands on his shoulders and felt them tremble. Turning him toward her, she tried again. "Jace? What is it?"

He was breathing hard, his little chest heaving with the effort. Kerri could see his pulse jumping in his neck. "What if they come back to take me?" he whispered.

Kerri stared at him a moment before the implication hit her. "What if *who* comes back?" she asked slowly.

"The . . . the . . . things that took Mommy."

Kerri's brow furrowed. *Things?* she thought. What an odd term. She considered her next question very carefully. If Jace was starting to open up, she didn't want to scare him. If he had, in fact, seen someone in the house, it might help prove his father's innocence. She felt her heart pound a little harder, a little faster. "Do you mean people, Jace?" she asked, taking care to keep her voice even. "Men?"

"No," he whispered. "They weren't like . . . people. They were like . . . like . . . They didn't have mouths, or hair, or ears." Kerri instantly recalled how the standing figure in Jace's drawing had lacked any facial features other than eyes. "They were all white . . . and . . . and . . ." He clamped his mouth closed, his chin trembling, his face whiter than his socks.

Kerri reached up and petted his head, smoothing his hair back from his face. "Okay," she said soothingly. "Forget about what they looked like for now. And don't be afraid. They're not here now, and no one is going to hurt you. Okay?"

Jace nodded, but his eyes remained fixed on the room at the end of the hall.

"Jace?" Kerri said softly. "Can you tell me what happened? What did they do?" She knew it was a risky question; he was already so frightened, it might just push him over the edge, making him clam up again. But to her surprise and relief, he answered.

"They stuck something in Mommy's booby." He finally tore his eyes away from the end of the hallway and looked at Kerri, his face frighteningly lifeless. "Then they just took her," he said, his voice as banal as his expression. He made a little half shrug that looked more like a twitch.

Kerri frowned, trying to interpret what Jace was describing. "Where was your father when this happened?" she asked.

"Sleeping. Right next to Mommy."

"He was there? Beside her?" Kerri struggled to hide her skepticism. Though Jace's story was beginning to sound pretty incredulous, there was a disturbing ring of sincerity in his voice. Whatever he saw, or thought he saw, he obviously believed his own interpretation.

Jace dropped his gaze toward the floor, staring at his feet. "He was there," he said. "He didn't help her. He just kept sleeping." Two fat tears rambled down his nose and dropped onto his shoes. His voice had taken on a distinctly immature quality, so that he pronounced the word "didn't" as "did dint."

"I did dint help her, either," he said with great sadness.

Kerri reached over and pulled him to her, wrapping him in her arms. He came willingly, his head nestling in the crook of her shoulder, his small body trembling with his sobs. Kerri stroked his hair and lowered her face to whisper in his ear.

"It's okay, Jace. It's okay. You're just a little boy. You did just what you should have done."

She held him a long time, rocking him back and forth, comforting him, until his sobs abated. When she felt he was calm enough, she gently pushed him away from her and held him at arm's length. "You did real good, Jace," she told him. "Thank you for telling me what happened."

Jace didn't respond; he just stared back at her.

"Ready to go downstairs?" she asked him.

He hesitated, but only for a moment. Slowly, he nodded.

"Okay then, let's do it." Kerri stood and ruffled his hair. Jace gazed up at her, his damp eyes probing her face like the hands of a blind person. There was something different in the way he looked at her—a level of reliance and acceptance that wasn't there before. He reached up tentatively with one hand, his fingers nestling against her palm, his thumb wrapping over her knuckles. His eyes shyly questioned her.

Kerri answered his plea by closing his hand within her own. Together, they headed downstairs, side by side.

They toured the first floor looking for Kevin and Thad, Kerri taking in the decor as they went. The living room walls were covered with pictures of Jace at various stages in his life: one with the characteristically misshapen head and red-marked face of a newborn; one a few months later with Jace on his stomach, raising a head capped with white fuzz and smiling with typical baby delight; another at about two years of age with Jace astride a rocking horse; still another with a frightened and pensive look on Jace's face as he sat in Santa's lap.

Off the living room was a den. One look told Kerri this was Thad's room. Huge tablets of white paper with blue-line drawings of floor plans lay everywhere. A drafting table with a work in progress sat before a window overlooking the side yard; an antique rolltop desk occupied the space by the front window. The far wall boasted a lovely stone fireplace, its hearth cold, dark, and empty.

Having found no sign of the men, they wandered into the kitchen. As they passed the refrigerator, Kerri glanced over at its door. Every square inch of it was covered with Jace's drawings. At the center was a piece of wide-lined paper with large awkwardly printed block letters that read, "I love you mommy." Taped to the bottom of this page was a snapshot of Jace and a woman Kerri assumed was Janet Johansen.

Curious, Kerri studied the photo from the corner of her eye, not wanting to draw Jace's attention to it. The picture had been taken outdoors on a day with plenty of sunlight and brilliantly blue skies. In the background was a sturdy wooden jungle gym and behind that a thick copse of trees. Janet stood beside Jace, one hand resting on his shoulder. Jace obviously took after his father; Janet's hair was dark and curly, her complexion tawny. Her expression as she gazed down at her son was one of love and tenderness. Even with this fleeting perusal, the affection between mother and son was so apparent, Kerri wondered if the police had seen the picture. She thought not, for she didn't see how anyone viewing this captured moment could believe Janet Johansen would run away from home, leaving her son behind.

As it was obvious Kevin and Thad were not in the house, Kerri moved toward the back door and looked out to the yard. A small deck overlooked a gently sloping expanse of grass leading down to the woods' edge. Kerri recognized the setting as the same one from the picture on the refrigerator. Centered in the yard was the jungle gym—a heavy-duty affair constructed with huge bolts and wood beams and boasting two swings, a slide, a pair of hanging rings, and a horizontal ladder along its top. There was a sandbox on one side of the deck, filled with an assortment of Tonka-sized heavy equipment. Parked beside it was a fire-engine-red tricycle, its wheels caked with mud. An umbrellaed patio table was situated off to the left; seated at it were Kevin and Thad.

"Here they are," Kerri said to Jace. She opened the door and led the boy outside. Though the men had been talking in earnest when she first looked out, as soon as they heard the back door open their conversation stopped. Kerri studied their expressions, searching for some clue as to the tone of their discussion. But both faces were impassive and unreadable.

"What's going on?" Kerri asked, wrapping a protective arm over Jace's shoulders.

"Not much," Kevin answered with a shrug. Kerri was relieved to see no trace of the predatory expression that had been on his face earlier. "We were just discussing how to, uh . . . coordinate the, uh . . . the rest of the morning," Kevin added, casting a quick glance at Jace.

Kerri grasped his meaning immediately. Thad Johansen was needed to identify his wife's body at the morgue, an exercise that would be painful enough without Jace coming along—not to mention the effect any additional trauma might have on the boy.

"Why don't I take Jace to the office with me," Kerri suggested. "My appointment schedule this morning is light, and Stephen can stay with him while I'm tied up."

The expression of relief on Thad Johansen's face was both immediate and pitiful. Kerri's heart went out to the man. "That would be a big help, Dr. Whitaker," he said. "If you're sure you don't mind."

"No problem at all," Kerri said. "It would be my pleasure."

"I want to talk to the kid later," Kevin reminded her.

Kerri shot him a look of exasperation. "You know where to find us," she said.

Thad Johansen shoved his chair back and stood. "Well, then," he said, his eyes taking on a haunted look. "Let's get this over with."

Kerri felt Jace stiffen beside her. "Where are you going, Daddy?" he asked, his voice edgy and frightened.

Thad walked over and squatted down in front of his son. "I need to go with the detective here to take care of some business," he said softly. "You go with Dr. Whitaker and I'll come by to get you when I'm done. Okay?"

Jace ruminated a moment before he nodded. "Where's Mommy?"

Thad's lips disappeared into a thin line, and the muscles in his cheeks clenched. Fearing the man was once again on the verge of emotional collapse, Kerri grasped Jace's shoulders and turned him toward her.

"Your mother is in a special kind of hospital, Jace. With special doctors who need to look at her . . . body," she added, hesitating only a moment before deciding frank honesty was the best tactic. "They want to figure out what happened to her ... why she died. So it doesn't happen again."

"Can the doctors make her better?" Jace asked, hope burgeoning for a moment.

Kerri shook her head slowly. "No, Jace. I'm sorry. They can't make her better."

"Oh."

Watching the flame of hope extinguished in the child's eyes was heartbreaking. He started fidgeting with his shirt hem, his body swaying from side to side. His gaze drifted out toward the yard, toward the jungle gym, and Kerri wondered if he was recalling the moment preserved in time on the refrigerator door.

Thad Johansen stood and, with tears welling, pinioned Kerri with his eyes. "Please, take care of my son for me," he whispered. Then he shuffled toward the door. Kevin scrambled to his feet and followed.

When they were gone, Kerri gave Jace a squeeze on his shoulder. "Are there some toys or something you'd like to bring with you?" she asked him.

He gave her a barely perceptible shake of his head, his gaze still fixed on the backyard with that empty, in-another-world look.

"Are you sure?" Kerri persisted. "Stephen loves new toys to play with. Sometimes he gets tired of those old dinosaurs of his."

Much to Kerri's relief, Jace finally shifted his attention back to the present, and to her face. He studied her thoughtfully, then said, "Think he would like to play with my GI Joes?"

Kerri smiled. "I think he would *love* to," she said. "Let's get them."

* * *

Stephen was waiting for them when they arrived at the office. Before leaving her house, Kerri had called in and left a message on the answering machine, explaining she might be a little late getting into the office, and why. She'd also filled him in on the break-in from the night before, though she left out the part about getting conked on the head. As she and Jace walked through the door, Kerri saw Stephen already had the dinosaurs spread out on top of his desk, nestled within a miniature diorama of plastic trees and hills he had confiscated from some other game.

"Uh, oh," Stephen said with an exaggerated grimace. "The boss lady caught me good this time."

Kerri swallowed down a chuckle when Jace rolled his eyes and said, "It's okay. She knows you have 'em." He crossed the room and plopped a brown grocery bag on top of Stephen's desk. "She said it was okay for you to play with these, too," he said. "But just for today, 'kay?"

Stephen reached over, opened the bag, and peered inside. "Cool!" he said. He reached in and pulled out one of the plastic soldiers. "I bet this guy can beat the crap out of ole T-rex. What do you think?"

Jace shrugged and screwed his mouth up in contemplation. "He's pretty good," he admitted. "But so's T-rex."

"Well, we'll just have to see then, won't we?" Stephen said, wiggling his eyebrows.

Kerri shook her head and grinned as she headed into her office. Dropping her purse into a desk drawer, she stood a moment, hugging herself and gazing around the room, remembering the incident from the night before. A tiny shiver coursed through her, and the bump on her head began to throb as an additional reminder. Determined to put the whole thing out of her mind, she shoved aside the pile of stuff on her desk and checked out the day's schedule on her calendar. Her first appointment—other than the Johansens'—wasn't until eleven. Glancing at her watch, she saw it was only nine thirty. It was going to be a long day.

She dug out the charts for today's patients from the file cabinet and settled in to review them. She was reading the last note in Mr. Carren's chart—a depressed widower in his fifties who was making remarkable progress—when she sensed someone watching her. Looking up, she saw Jace standing a few feet from her desk.

Stephen hovered in the doorway, his eyes questioning. He gave her a little shrug. "He wanted to see you," he explained.

Kerri set aside the chart she was reading and dismissed Stephen with a wave of her hand. "It's okay," she said.

Stephen left, closing the door quietly behind him. Kerri sat back and watched Jace as he stood before her, his eyes roving over her desk, his hands, as usual, working his shirt hem into a frenzy.

"Don't you want your toys?" Kerri asked him.

Jace shook his head. His feet began to shift and dance, as if he were swaying to the rhythm of some song only he could hear. Suddenly, he lurched forward and grabbed one of the journals off the pile on her desk. "What's this?" he asked, studying the glossy cover, which featured an art deco rendering of multicolored pills floating around the page.

"That's one of my professional journals," Kerri told him, noting how his constant motion ceased when his attention was fully focused on something.

"What's a perfeshal journey?" Jace asked, his face frowning in puzzlement. He flipped the magazine open, scanning the pages of text.

Kerri laughed. "It's pro-fesh-un-al jern-al," she enunciated for him. "It's a magazine that tells me how to do my job better."

Jace continued flipping through the pages, then dropped the magazine on the floor and reached up to take another one off the pile. He flipped through this one as well.

"Do you have any books or magazines at home?" Kerri asked him.

Jace nodded. "Yeah," he said. "Mommy reads me stuff from *Humpty Dumpty*."

"Ah, *Humpty Dumpty*," Kerri said, feeling a nostalgic tug. It had been one of Mandy's favorites as well. "That's an excellent magazine. Do you have a favorite story?"

Jace didn't answer her, and Kerri was so caught up in her own painful reminiscing, it took her a second to realize something was wrong. The magazine Jace held trembled in his hands; his face had gone chalky white. His eyes were round and fearful and frozen on the page before him.

"Jace?" Kerri said, rising from her chair and coming around the desk toward him. "What's wrong?" She craned her neck to see what had captured his attention. On the right-hand page of the magazine was a drawing of a creature with a large bulbous head and a tall, thin body. Huge black eyes were centered on its face—the only facial features present. Though less crudely drawn, the figure bore a striking resemblance to the one Jace had drawn for her two days before.

"That's one of 'em," Jace said, his voice small and shaky. "That's the thing that took my mommy." He looked up at her trembling, pale, and frightened.

Kerri took the magazine and studied the picture. The caption beneath it read, "Drawing of an alien done by a purported abductee." She flipped back a page to catch the title of the article. The words ALIEN ABDUCTIONS—FACT OR FICTION? stared back at her in big, black type. Glancing back at Jace's terrified, upturned face, Kerri felt icy fingers play an arpeggio along her spine.

"Oh my God," she whispered.

TEN

Kerri stood, stunned and immobile, staring at the picture. Jace wrapped himself around one of her legs, hiding behind it as best he could. "I'm scared," he said in a tiny voice. "Are they gonna take me, too?"

Kerri dropped the magazine and knelt in front of Jace, grabbing him by his shoulders. She looked him straight in the eye and said, "No one is going to hurt you, Jace. I promise."

Jace didn't answer her. Instead, his gaze cast about the room fearfully, as if he expected someone to be lurking in the corners. After the incident last night, it was all Kerri could manage not to do the same.

"Jace? Look at me." He did, but his eyes darted back and forth nervously. "I promise you there is no one here who will hurt you, okay?" Slowly, and with apparent reluctance, Jace managed a nod. "You're perfectly safe here. No one is going to take you anywhere." Kerri kept her voice calm and soothing—not an easy task as her own insides were jumping.

"Why don't we sit down," she suggested, giving him a gentle nudge toward the couch. He went, but his hand gripped hers the entire way. As soon as they were seated, Jace curled himself into a ball and nestled his head in the crook of her shoulder. Kerri held him, rocking gently. After several moments passed, she could tell his fright had eased some, and with her arms still wrapped securely around him, she said, "Jace, I want to ask you some questions about what happened to your mom that night, okay?"

After a long pause, Jace nodded.

"Okay," Kerri said, keeping her tone soft and even. "I want you to tell me what you remember." Still not convinced the child hadn't merely had a very realistic and frightening dream, she asked, "Were you in bed when they came?"

"I was sleeping," Jace said, his voice sounding small and distant. "And then I woke up."

"Why did you wake up? Did you hear something?"

There was another long pause before Jace answered her. "I . . . I don't know. I did dint feel very good."

"What was wrong? Tummy ache?"

"Un-uh. I just . . ." He shrugged, and his hand flopped in his lap like a dying fish. "I just did dint feel good," he went on. "My neck hurt and it was hard to move. I almost fell down," he added, raising his head long enough to give her a very serious look. Then he snuggled back into her shoulder. "And my room was furry."

"Your room was furry?" Kerri repeated, puzzled.

"Yeah, furry. You know, soft and fuzzy."

"You were dizzy," Kerri said, finally grasping his meaning.

"Yeah. That's it."

Kerri wondered if he might have been coming down with some bug on the night in question. Had his mother given him any medicine? That might account for what he thought he'd seen—maybe he'd been hallucinating. She made a mental note to ask Thad about it later on.

"So then what happened?" she prompted.

"I got out of bed to find my mommy. And then I saw that funny light."

Kerri felt him tense and gave him a little squeeze to try and comfort him. "What funny light?" she asked gently.

"It was a funny color," Jace said. "Like Barney."

Kerri was quite familiar with the large dinosaur who had been a mainstay of children's TV for some time. "You mean the light was purple?" she asked.

"Yeah," Jace said, a little calmer now. "It was purple."

"Where was this purple light?"

"In Mommy's room."

"Did you go to your mommy's room?"

Jace shook his head, and Kerri felt him tense. "Un-uh," he said, his voice a little breathless. "I looked at my mommy's room and that's when I saw . . . them."

"Tell me what you saw."

Jace sucked in a deep breath and clenched his teeth, letting the air hiss out between them. "They were like that picture," he said, shifting his eyes toward the magazine on the floor. "Big, and white . . . and their heads were big, too. And their eyes were black and shiny, like my teddy bear's." He paused, gazing off at a scene only he could see. "And . . . and . . . they had lines everywhere," he added, becoming more agitated as the picture grew clearer in his mind. "Dark lines, all over."

"You mean in their clothing?"

Jace mentally and—judging from the constant motion of his mouth—literally chewed on the question at hand before looking up at Kerri with something akin to dawning. "No," he said, his blue eyes huge. "They did dint have any clothes. Just skin. The lines were on their skin."

Kerri was more confused than ever. She had no idea what these lines were. And the fact that Jace perceived the intruders to be naked was certainly odd. "What did they do?" she asked him.

"They looked at Mommy in her bed." His face wrinkled in disgust. "Then they stuck that thing in her boobies."

"What did the thing look like? Was it a knife?"

Jace shook his head, slowly and thoughtfully. "It was like one of Daddy's special pencils," he said. "The ones he turns to make 'em write." He pulled away from her a bit so he could better see her face. "That's the only kind of pencil Daddy uses. I'm not allowed to touch them." His eyes dropped to his lap, then he peered up at Kerri with a guilty expression. "But I did one time when he wasn't home," he said with a tiny grimace.

Kerri smiled at him. "I don't think your dad would mind," she assured him. "At least not that one time." Then, to get him back on track, she said, "Did this thing they poked in your mom look exactly like your dad's special pencils?"

"Kinda," Jace said, looking away, his brow furrowed in thought. "Except it had a light on it. A red light."

"What did you do next, Jace?"

"I got scared and got back in my bed. They started making a funny noise and moving more in the room." He paused, staring off into space. His eyes grew round as saucers; his pupils dilated with remembered fear. "I thought they were gonna come and get me," he added, his voice wavering.

Kerri reached up to gently knead the back of his neck. "Remember, there is nothing here to be afraid of. Okay?"

"Okay," Jace said, but he moved a few inches closer.

"All right. You said they were making a funny noise. Can you tell me what kind of noise?"

Jace idly twisted a strand of his hair as he thought. "Kinda like the radio does when the music isn't coming out," he said.

"Static," Kerri said, more to herself than to him. "What happened after you got back in bed?"

"I pretended I was asleep."

"So you didn't see anything else?"

"Un-uh. But I could hear 'em. They were banging stuff in the room. Kinda loud, but not really." He gave her a questioning look, to see if she understood what he meant.

Kerri smiled at him and said, "Okay. That's good. What did they do next?"

Jace gave her a spastic little shrug. "Then they left," he said.

Kerri sighed. Jace's memories from that night were certainly vivid—probably too vivid to have been a mere dream. She wasn't sure exactly *what* he saw that night, but she was quickly becoming convinced he saw something. Still, she was puzzled by Jace's description of all the noise the intruders made, and his claim that his father was sleeping right beside his mother. Why didn't the noise arouse Thad?

"Jace, you said your dad was sleeping in the bed next to your mother?"

Jace nodded.

"And he didn't wake up at all?"

His face fell, and he shook his head. He grabbed the bottom of his shirt and started twisting it back and forth, his eyes focused on his hands.

Since that topic obviously upset him, Kerri decided to try a different tack. "How many men were there?" she asked.

Jace's head shot up, his eyes confronting hers. "They weren't men," he protested. "They were . . . things."

"Okay, okay." Kerri paused, taking a deep breath. She stared at him, one eyebrow cocked in challenge. But he never wavered. He stared right back at her, his expression one of solid belief. "Okay, you win," she said with a sigh. "How many *things* were there?"

Jace hesitated, his eyes roving over her face, as if assessing the sincerity of her deferment. "One, two, three," he answered finally, flipping a finger up with each number.

Kerri thought, trying to decide where to go next. "Do you know how to tell time, Jace?" she asked.

"I know how to tell what the numbers are."

"Do you know what the numbers were when the men—I mean, the things—came?"

Jace started to shake his head but then sat up straighter, his eyes bright. "The gong thing downstairs went off one, two times," he said. "Right after I got back in bed. I remember 'cause it scared me."

At first his answer confused Kerri. Then she remembered the grandfather clock in the Johansens' foyer. "That's great, Jace. That means it was two o'clock in the morning." She bestowed him with a smile, though inwardly she was growing more and more concerned.

The fact that he recalled the chiming of the clock made her even more convinced his memories were based on reality.

Jace fairly glowed beneath her praise, and she decided now would be a good time to quit, while his mood was lighter. "Okay," she said, rising from the couch. "You did very, very well. Thank you." She leaned over and gave him a quick peck on his forehead. "How about doing me a favor?" she asked him.

"Okay."

His quick acquiescence, without so much as a moment's hesitation, made her realize just how far they had come. He trusted her, she realized. And to some degree, he had come to depend on her as well. The thought both warmed and frightened her.

"I want you to go out front and keep an eye on Stephen for a while," she said. "I have some work to do, but if I know Stephen, he's got his toys out, playing with them."

Jace looked over toward the door to the waiting area. "Yeah," he said. "I'll bet he's eating my GI Joes with those dinosaurs." He rolled his eyes and pushed himself off the couch.

Kerri laughed, uttering a silent prayer of thanks for the amazing resilience of kids. "You're probably right," she said, walking him to the door. "Those GI Joes are going to need some backup."

After delivering Jace to Stephen and the dinosaurs, Kerri went back into her office, closing the door behind her. Walking back to her desk, she bent over and picked up the magazine from the floor—still open to the article that had upset Jace. She glanced at her watch and, seeing she still had about half an hour before her first patient was due, settled in to read.

The article was written by a psychiatrist—a Dr. Mike Bender—and summarized many of the observations he'd made while interviewing patients who claimed to be victims of alien abductions. Though some of the information bordered on the ridiculous, a disturbing number of details were common to all the patients involved: unexplained marks on their bodies, fragmented memories of odd-looking creatures, visions of experimental probes, and a strange-colored light.

While reading one patient's description of the creatures who supposedly kidnapped her, Kerri felt an icy tingle race down her spine:

> The creatures were tall, and their heads were large and bulbous. The eyes were almond shaped and huge . . . black as night and glassy looking. Their bodies were all white, and the skin was almost transparent . . . I could see veins beneath their skin, crisscrossing like a bunch of dark lines. . . .

Kerri again studied the picture accompanying the article, remembering how Jace had said the "things" he saw in his mother's room that night had lines all over their bodies—a detail not evident in the drawn sketch. Yet his description matched that of the quoted patient almost perfectly. She finished the rest of the article, keenly aware of how Jace's other descriptions—the "things'" overall appearance and the color of the light in his mother's room—also matched those of the patients interviewed by this Dr. Bender. At the end of the article was a brief author bio, and to Kerri's surprise, Dr. Bender was located in Bellingham, Washington—an hour-and-a-half drive north of Seattle.

She set the magazine aside and leaned back in her chair to think. Surely this alien abduction stuff was some form of mass hysteria, or a unique brand of psychosis. Yet Jace didn't strike her as being vulnerable to the first, nor did he show any signs of mental illness. Though the psychiatrist who wrote the article had been careful not to position himself definitively on any one theory, the tone of the article suggested he gave a certain credence to his patients' experiences. Whatever the explanation, Kerri couldn't ignore the uncanny number of similarities between Jace's experience and those of Dr. Bender's patients. *What could it hurt to talk to the man?* she thought. Picking up her phone, she dialed information and asked for a listing for Dr. Mike Bender in Bellingham. After jotting down the number, she pressed the switch hook, took in a deep breath, and then started to dial again.

The intercom beeped, and Stephen's voice echoed into the room before she had punched in the first three numbers.

"Dr. Whitaker? Mr. Carren is here for his appointment."

Kerri hung up the phone and tossed the magazine article aside. Punching the intercom button, she said, "Send him in, Stephen."

To Kerri's chagrin, Thad and Kevin came by during her session with Mr. Carren and left before she was through, taking Jace with them. She suspected Kevin was anxious to grill the boy and was worried about Jace's ability to deal with it, particularly after his reaction to the picture in the magazine. Angry she had been left out so matter-of-factly, she tried calling Kevin at the police station, only to be told he wasn't in. Next she tried the Johansen house, but no one answered. Knowing she had a patient waiting outside, Kerri's frustration grew as she played her last card and dialed Kevin's beeper number. Foot and fingers tapping with impatience, she waited a full five minutes before giving up and calling out to Stephen for the next patient.

By the time that patient left, Kevin still hadn't answered Kerri's page, and she was now beyond angry with him—she was furious. She picked up her phone and punched in the number of the police station again, jabbing at the key pad with such viciousness, the number 8 key stuck in the down position and she had to pry it loose with her thumbnail and start over. She forced herself to sit back and take a few deep breaths, trying to calm down before she made another attempt at dialing. This time, her efforts were successful in all regards—not only did she get through, but Kevin answered.

"Kevin McCallister, where in the hell have you been?"

"Well, I've been—"

"And why didn't you answer my page, dammit?"

"Page? Oh, hell, lass. The damned battery's dead. Sorry."

Kerri could hear him unclipping the beeper from his belt. "So," Kevin went on with infuriating calm, "what the devil has blown yer skirt up?"

"You know damned well what! Why did you come and get Jace without checking with me first?"

"You were with a patient and Stephen said—"

"I don't care what Stephen said! You know damned well I wanted to be there when you questioned Jace, but you went ahead and did it anyway, didn't you?"

"I did. But believe me, you didn't miss anythin'. Besides, he said he'd already told you all of it."

That made Kerri pause. "What did he tell you?"

"Bunch of damned gibberish about some creatures or something who poked his mother's boobs and then took her away. Seems to me the kid has a pretty vivid imagination."

"Then you don't believe him?" Kerri asked guardedly.

"Believe him? Hell, no! I think he's just struggling with his mother's death and has concocted some story to explain it. Or maybe he saw his father do something so awful his mind has conjured up this monster story instead, so he doesn't have to face the truth."

"You aren't still considering Thad Johansen as a suspect, are you?" Kerri asked, incredulous. "Christ, Kevin! The man couldn't look any more devastated by all this."

"That doesn't mean he didn't do it. Believe me, I've seen my share of cold-hearted psychopaths who put on a good act for the public, but were pretty sick sons a bitches on the inside. So have you, for that matter."

Kerri couldn't deny there was some truth to his statement. Still, Thad Johansen wasn't acting. She'd stake her reputation on it.

"What kind of shape was Jace in when you finished with him?"

"Shit, lass. You make it sound like I'm some kind of monster myself."

"Well, you do tend to be a bit overbearing when you're . . . uh . . . interviewing someone."

"The kid was fine," Kevin said, his tone sounding both hurt and annoyed. "I dropped them off at their house about half an hour ago. Go by and check on them if you doubt me," he said irritably.

Kerri sighed. "Sorry, Kevin. I didn't mean to be so short with you. I'm just worried about Jace. That's all."

There was a long silence on the other end. "You know," Kevin said finally, "maybe you were right. Maybe it was too soon for you to get back into the kid scene."

"Why do you say that?"

"Well, it just seems like you're getting a mite over-involved here."

"I'm fine, Kevin. I'm just concerned for one of my patients."

"Uh-huh."

Kerri ignored his skepticism. "So, what did you get out of Thad?" she asked, anxious to change the subject.

"Not a hell of a lot," Kevin admitted. "He certainly seems upset by all this. Though it may be just that we found her so soon. And by the way, Janet Johansen was pregnant."

Kerri winced. "Thad's?" she asked, dreading the answer.

"Won't know for sure until the DNA tests come back. And that will take a while."

"Does Thad know?"

"You mean did I tell him? No. But I'd wager he knows all right."

Kerri blew out a breath of exasperation. "God, you're stubborn," she muttered.

"It's the Irish in me, lass. That, and my cop's nose, which says something smells pretty fishy in all this."

"Did they determine the cause of death yet?"

"No, but it's obvious she was murdered."

"Obvious? How?"

"Well, for one thing, she wasn't your typical floater. She was at the bottom of the lake, weighted down with some rope and a cinder block. A couple of student divers from the U of Dub found her," he said, using the local shortened term for the University of Washington.

Kerri squeezed her eyes closed. She pictured the smiling brown-haired woman from the photo on the Johansens' refrigerator anchored in the murky depths of the lake, her face swollen and white, the eye sockets empty, the hair swirling about like some ghostly shroud. It made her shudder.

"Look," Kevin said. "I've got to run. I'll keep you posted, okay?"

"Okay," Kerri said. "Thanks."

"One more thing."

"Yeah?"

"Your head okay?"

Kerri smiled despite her lingering annoyance over Kevin's obstinate belief in Thad Johansen's guilt. "It's fine, Kevin. Thanks for asking."

She hung up the phone and sat back in her chair, staring across the room, trying to shut out the image of Janet Johansen's bloated face. Failing miserably, she was glad when her office door opened and Stephen poked his head in.

"Hey, boss lady," he said. "You want to go to lunch?"

Her appetite had died long before the image of Janet Johansen. "No, thanks, Stephen. You go on ahead. I think I'll stay here and finish up some charts."

"Want me to bring you back something?"

"No. I'm fine. But thanks for the offer."

"Okay. I'll be back in an hour. You only have two

appointments this afternoon—one at two and one at three."

"Good," Kerri said. "Maybe we can get out of here early today."

Stephen studied her from the doorway, his head cocked to one side, the overhead lights giving his hair a bluish sheen. "You look tired, boss lady," he observed.

"I am a little," Kerri said.

"You sure you don't want me to bring you something? Might perk you up a little."

"Tell you what," Kerri said. "Why don't you pick me up a double latte on your way back."

Stephen snapped a quick salute. "Gotcha! One double, leaded latte coming up." With that, his head pulled back from the doorway, like a turtle retreating into its shell.

"Stephen?" Kerri yelled after him.

His head popped back into the room. "Yeah?"

"I appreciate all you did to help Jace Johansen this morning, having the dinosaurs all set up and everything."

"No problem," Stephen said. "He's a good kid."

"I'm curious," Kerri said, leaning forward and resting her elbows on the desk. "How did you know I'd be bringing him back here to the office?"

Stephen shrugged. "I know you got a thing for kids in trouble. It hasn't been that long since I was the one you hauled in here with you."

"It's been three years, Stephen."

"Yeah, but to me it seems like yesterday," he said with a faint tone of wistfulness.

"Do you still miss your family a lot?"

"Some days more than others. I don't think about them as much as I used to." His gaze shifted off to

Kerri's right, and he stared out the window lost in memory. Then, as if he'd been prodded, his eyes shot back to her. "Watching Jace, with his mother gone and all, sort of strikes home, you know?"

Kerri saw raw pain in Stephen's eyes—a pain she hadn't seen for a long time.

"Anyway," Stephen said, clearing his throat, "I best get going before my lunch hour turns into a lunch minute. Sure you don't want some food?"

"No, just the latte. Need any money?"

"I got it covered," Stephen said, his head again disappearing behind the doorframe. "Just remember this when it comes time for my next raise," he said, his voice fading as he moved away.

Kerri heard the outside door close and she leaned back in her chair, letting her head fall back so she was staring at the ceiling. An old leak had left a water stain just to her right, the shape of its browned edges bearing a striking resemblance to the shape of the head in the magazine drawing. Raising up, she reached forward and rummaged around on her desk until she found the slip of paper with Dr. Bender's phone number scribbled on it. She held it a moment, staring at it and pulling thoughtfully on her lip.

"What the hell," she said finally, and picking up the phone, she punched in the numbers.

ELEVEN

After listening to the phone on the other end ring several times and anticipating either an answering machine or a receptionist to answer, Kerri was caught off guard when a male voice picked up and said, "Dr. Bender."

"Uh . . . is this *the* Dr. Bender?"

A deep and delightful chuckle followed. "The one and only," he said. "And might I ask who this is?"

"My name is Dr. Whitaker. Kerri Whitaker. I'm a psychiatrist practicing in Seattle."

"I see. Glad to make your acquaintance, Dr. Whitaker." In contrast to his initial greeting, this came out in a tone of barely contained civility. "What can I do for you?" he asked tiredly.

"I'm sorry," Kerri said, puzzled by the abrupt change. "Did I catch you at a bad time?"

"No. What do you need?"

The question came out clipped and curt, and Kerri's puzzlement shifted toward irritation. She chewed on the inside of her cheek, debating whether she should ignore his rudeness and move on, or just hang up. Before she could reach a decision, he made it for her.

"Look," he said, "I'm sure you're a very nice lady

and all that, but I really don't have the time or the
patience for all you quack hunters. So, if you will
excuse me, I have patients I need to attend to." There
followed a faint clicking sound and the electronic hiss
of an open but empty line.

"Hello?" Kerri said, refusing to believe what had
happened. "Hello?"

When the whine of the dial tone provided the only
answer she was going to get, she held the phone out
and stared at it in disbelief. "Shit!" She dropped the
phone back into the cradle and sat stunned, replaying
the brief conversation in her mind, trying to understand what had happened. The more she thought
about it, the more confused she became. Confused and
angry.

For the second time, she picked up the phone and
stabbed viciously at the numbers with her finger. She
listened as the connection went through, and by the
time she heard the phone ringing at the other hand,
her fingers were drumming on the desktop while her
foot tapped impatiently on the floor.

"Dr. Bender."

This time the voice sounded more resigned than
anything else. "Dr. Bender, this is Dr. Whitaker again.
Look, I don't know what your problem is, but I'd
appreciate it if you would refrain from exercising your
anger on me."

She half expected him to hang up again, and the
heavy, hissing silence of the line left her thinking that
was precisely what had happened. But then she heard
the exhalation of a weighty sigh on the other end.

"What do you want, Dr. Whitaker?" he asked heavily.

"I want to discuss your recent article in *Psychology*

News—the one on . . . alien abductions." She suspected that no matter how many times she said those words—alien abduction—they would never sound normal to her ears.

"What about it?"

His voice was still curt, but Kerri thought she detected a note of cautious curiosity there. She made a conscious effort to control her temper and keep her own voice even.

"Well, I have a patient, a six-year-old boy, who claims to have seen something the night his mother disappeared—under rather mysterious circumstances, I might add—and his description of what went on bears a striking resemblance to the descriptions in your article."

"Such as?"

Kerri took in a deep breath and plunged on. "Well, for one thing, he claims his mother was taken away by these . . . intruders, for lack of a better word. Intruders he insists on calling things rather than men or people. And his description of these things matches those of your patients in the article. In fact, when he saw the drawing in the magazine, he became very frightened, pointed to it, and said, 'That's one of 'em.'"

"You say this is a six-year-old kid?"

"That's right."

There were another few seconds of weighted silence before he spoke again. "This is for real, isn't it? I mean, if you're one of those quack-hunter types . . ."

"Look, Dr. Bender," Kerri snapped, her anger sparked again, "I'm trying to get some professional input from a colleague for one of my patients. If that's asking too much from you, please tell me now and we can put an end to this torture."

This time the silence crackled with tension. "Sorry," Bender said finally, letting loose with yet another world-weary sigh. "It's just that I've been plagued by crank calls and letters for years because of my interest in this subject. And ever since that article came out, the numbers have increased tenfold, many of them from my colleagues, as you call them. I've had two already today. So I'm a little touchy. It seems the subject of alien abduction is considered by many to be a topic for quacks only."

"Well, I guess I can understand that," Kerri said. "I'm not so convinced myself. But I'm beginning to believe this kid has seen something. And that something—whether it be aliens or whatever else—seems to be the same thing your patients saw. Frankly, I'm at a bit of a loss here."

"Understandable," Bender said. "And again, I apologize."

"Apology accepted. So tell me, have you worked with any children who have had this abduction experience, or are they all adults?"

"I haven't treated any children myself," Bender admitted, "although some others around the country have. However, if I understood you correctly, your patient isn't claiming he was abducted, but rather that he saw someone else abducted."

"True. It was his mother he saw."

"And you say she's missing?"

"Well, not anymore," Kerri said with a grimace. "Her body turned up early this morning in Lake Washington."

"Oh," Bender said thoughtfully. "Any signs of foul play?"

"Well, someone tried pretty hard to hide the body.

Weighted it down with rope and cinder block. But they haven't determined the cause of death yet. And her son, my patient, claims he saw these men—or things as he calls them—stab something into his mother's chest."

"Think you can get a summary of the autopsy findings?"

"Well, yes," Kerri said, puzzled. "But why?"

"Most of the abductees I've worked with have certain characteristics in common," Bender explained. "Specific body markings and such. It would be interesting to know whether or not this woman had any of those markings."

"I'll see what I can find out," Kerri told him, making a mental note to check back with Kevin later.

"One other thing," Bender added. "I assume the police have investigated this case?"

"They have."

"I'm curious to know whether or not they found any blood at the scene of the abduction. Where was the woman when it occurred?"

"According to her son, she was asleep in her bed. And I'm sure there was no blood at the scene, or the cops would have suspected foul play sooner."

"You mean, they didn't?"

"Not right away. They thought she'd simply left on her own."

"Interesting," Bender said. Kerri waited for him to elaborate, but instead he said, "See if you can find out if there was a trace of blood anywhere. Most likely on the bed or her clothing. It would be small—pinpoint size—and therefore considered insignificant by the police. If there wasn't any, it doesn't rule out an abduction," Bender said. "But if it was there, it would lend more credence to the abduction theory."

Kerri frowned as she listened to the solid tone of belief in Dr. Bender's voice. "Tell me something," she asked him. "Do you really believe these people were abducted by aliens?"

He didn't answer immediately, and Kerri found herself relieved by his hesitation.

"I believe *something* has happened to these people," Bender said finally. "I'm not sure what, but there is something real here. These people are not your average run-of-the-mill spaceman fanatics. The patients in my group are all highly intelligent down-to-earth people, who are having as much trouble buying into this as any skeptic."

"Down to earth, huh? Was that a pun?" Kerri teased.

Bender laughed, and Kerri was again struck by what a pleasant sound it was. "No, it wasn't intended to be a pun, though I wish I'd thought of it."

Kerri found herself warming up to the man. She was still wary of this whole alien-abduction idea, but Bender's thoughtful and reasonable response to her questions eased her doubts about his professional standing. Had he given her a definite yes, she would have cut the conversation off right there. But his equivocation was to be expected, particularly if the affected patients were as normal in all other regards as he claimed. Treating something like this—whether it be delusional, real, or something in between—required a balance of skepticism and open-mindedness. It was obvious, based on Bender's initial reaction to her call, that he had been the subject of some ridicule from others in the profession. While a certain amount of ostracism was understandable—given the unusual and rather sensational focus of his work—Kerri couldn't completely discount the possibility the good doctor was as looney as his patients. Yet he didn't strike her as such.

"Look," Bender said, interrupting Kerri's train of thought, "I hate to put you off, given the bad start we had here, but I have a patient due any moment. And I suspect you and I will need to discuss some things at length."

"I understand, " Kerri said. "Perhaps you can suggest a time when I might call back? Or you can call me."

"Actually, I have a different idea. I was wondering if I might be able to entice you to come up here this evening for a group session I'm having. I have seven of these abduction patients who meet on a biweekly basis to discuss their experiences and I think you might find it . . . well, let's just say it will be intriguing. If all these people who think I'm a quack would sit in on just one of these sessions, I think they would see things differently."

"Oh, I don't think that's necessary," Kerri said quickly.

Though the suggestion made a certain amount of clinical sense. It would give her an opportunity to assess the quality of the both the patients' claims and the doctor treating them. Still . . .

"I assure you, merely listening in does not make you a believer," Dr. Bender said, his voice gently teasing.

"It would disrupt the dynamics of the group," Kerri said, grasping at the first reasonable excuse she could think of.

"Actually, I think it would do them some good— and me, too, for that matter. They could use a skeptic in their midst, to keep them from getting too wrapped up in their own beliefs."

"I don't know," Kerri said. "It's a bit unorthodox."

"I don't think so. Besides, how important is unorthodox when you're treating people who believe they've been abducted by aliens?"

"Good point," Kerri said with a smile.

"I could certainly use the opinion of another professional," Bender said hopefully.

"Well . . ." Kerri was wavering; she knew it and Bender knew it.

"Please," Bender persisted.

What could it hurt? At the very least, it would be an intriguing glimpse into a mental aberration she had yet to encounter. At the most, she might be able to arm herself with some needed help and insight into Jace's problem. Still, something made her hold back. "Where and when is this session held?" she asked, stalling.

"Here at my office in Bellingham. Seven o'clock." There was a certain breathless anticipation to his voice.

Kerri glanced at her watch, bit her lip, and made her decision. "Okay," she said. "You win. Give me directions to your office. She scribbled down his instructions and stuffed them in her purse. "I should be there around six-thirty. Is that okay?"

"That's fine. If you get tied up in traffic or something, don't worry. We'll wait for you."

That made her nervous. Once she hung up and thought this through, she might decide it was a huge mistake. She didn't want to feel responsible for the group's schedule. She started to tell him it was unnecessary for them to wait on her, but before she could utter so much as a syllable, Bender spit out a quick "see you then" and hung up.

Kerri held the phone out, staring at it as if it had bitten her. Frowning, she dropped it back into the cradle, wondering what the hell she had gotten herself into.

After her last scheduled patient for the day left at four o'clock and she had bidden Stephen good night, Kerri picked up the phone to call Kevin. Once again she was told he was unavailable, so she hung up and dialed his beeper number. This time he called her back a few minutes later.

"Where are you?" Kerri asked him.

"At the ME's office."

"Perfect!" Kerri said, and in her mind she could see Kevin's eyebrows shoot up with cynical humor. "Have you found out anything more?"

"Well, not much actually. There is no sign of any overt trauma, though the body isn't in the best condition. Tox tests won't be available for a while, of course."

"Kevin, tell me something. When you examined the Johansens' bedroom, did you find any blood anywhere? Even tiny amounts?"

"Now, why are you asking that, lass?"

"Just curious."

"The only blood we found was one tiny spot on a nightgown on the bathroom floor. Johansen said it was the same one Janet was wearing when they went to bed that night. The blood was her type, and we didn't think it was significant."

"Just one spot?" Kerri asked, feeling her pulse start to race.

"Yeah, a small one. Pin size," Kevin said, and Kerri

felt her heart leap. "Probably nothing more than a splatter from a nose bleed, or a scratch, maybe even from brushing her teeth. Why so curious?"

"Just wondering why you seem so convinced Thad Johansen did something to his wife," Kerri said, trying to keep the excitement out of her voice.

"No blood doesn't mean a thing," Kevin argued. "He could have poisoned her or suffocated her, ya know."

"I know, Kevin. But I'm telling you, you're barking up the wrong tree on this one." A quick glance at her watch told her she needed to get moving if she was going to make it to Bellingham on time. "Kevin, I'd like to talk some more about this, but I have to run or I'll be late for an appointment."

"An appointment?"

Kerri winced. Somehow she knew Kevin wouldn't approve of her agenda for the evening, and she thought fast to come up with a plausible explanation. "I'm meeting someone for dinner," she said. "Remember Kathy Marlin? My old college chum? Well, she's in town and called me today, so I'm getting together with her tonight." Kerri was glad they were conversing by phone so Kevin couldn't see her. He'd always had an uncanny ability to tell when she was lying.

"Sounds like fun."

"I'm sure it will be, but if I don't get moving she'll be yelling at me about being late. You know, Kathy always was a stickler for timeliness," Kerri added, rather pleased with herself for recalling the one quirk of Kathy's that would add credence to her lie.

"Call me tomorrow then?"

"I will, Kevin. Bye."

Kerri replaced the phone and grabbed her purse to leave, trying hard to ignore the guilt she felt over lying to Kevin. Their relationship was built on trust and a genuine shared affection. Deceiving him, even about something this trivial, needled her. She wasn't sure what it was that so convinced her he would disapprove of her plans, but she felt sure he would.

Perhaps it was her own lingering doubts about what she was doing that bothered her. Though her mind was committed to going through with this evening, a tiny voice inside her head warned she might come to regret it.

TWELVE

By the time Kerri left the office and walked the three blocks to the parking garage, the oppressive cloud cover that had lingered most of the day had moved off to the east and now hovered over the Cascades. The temperature had warmed up into the high sixties, with clear skies and sunshine above and to the west. The Olympic range was in view, and Kerri could see a first dusting of snow atop the highest peaks.

Seattle was building up for the rush hour crunch, and despite Dr. Bender's assurance he would wait, Kerri worried she would be late. Traffic in the city was heavy; on the interstate it slowed nearly to a crawl. But once she got up around the Edmonds area it thinned out, and she slid the car up to sixty-five. She passed the time trying to picture Dr. Bender in her mind. He hadn't sounded very old on the phone—she guessed mid-thirties or so—and was probably one of those studious, pseudointellectual types who always seemed so attracted to the more supernatural end of science: short, kind of frumpy, with thick glasses and a nest of wayward hair.

Following Bender's directions, she found her way to the street where his office was located, surprised to see it was a primarily residential area. Scanning the numbers as best she could in the waning light, she finally found the right one and pulled into a driveway beside a single-story building that obviously had once been someone's home. At the back of the house, in place of a yard, was a small black-topped parking lot. Kerri parked and climbed out, making her way back around to the street side of the building.

A narrow porch led to the front door, and a tasteful brass plaque hung on the wall beside it. In the light of dusk, Kerri could just make out the lettering:

MIKE BENDER, MD
FAMILY COUNSELING SERVICES

Kerri hesitated, unsure if she should ring the bell or just walk in. Then she reminded herself that, despite its outward appearance, the house was really an office. She tested the knob and, finding it unlocked, pushed the door open and stepped inside.

The door opened onto a roomy living area with a large stone fireplace and a half-dozen mismatched comfortable-looking chairs. Warm beige carpet covered the floor, and an assortment of framed watercolors hung from the walls. A hallway ran off from the middle of the room, and to its immediate left was a small alcove with a sliding glass window—obviously the reception area. Though it was lit, there was no one in sight.

"Hello?" Kerri hollered, hearing her voice echo down the hallway. "Anybody here?"

A door at the opposite end of the hallway opened and out stepped a man who was as far from Kerri's imagined description as he could get—tall, slender but muscular, with broad shoulders tapering down to very narrow hips, eyes so brown they almost looked black, and an angular face topped by a head of short, but thick, brown hair. He strode toward her with the air of someone very comfortable with the workings of his own body. His lips were almost pouty looking—the word *sensual* flitted through Kerri's mind, and she just as quickly chased it away. He was dressed in a pair of worn blue jeans, a blue-and-black flannel shirt, and a pair of grass-stained sneakers. Kerri, in her Liz Claiborne suit, suddenly felt very overdressed.

"Dr. Whitaker, I presume," he said, smiling and extending his hand.

Kerri nodded as he gave her a quick but firm handshake. She could still feel the heat of his hand on hers long after he pulled it away.

"You made good time."

"The traffic wasn't bad," Kerri mumbled.

His eyes gave her a rapid once-over. "You don't look anything like I expected," he said.

"Nor do you," Kerri admitted.

"Well, I hope your surprise was as pleasant as mine."

Kerri felt her ears grow hot and knew she was blushing. Bender saved her from the embarrassment of an answer by saying, "Since we have a few minutes before folks start arriving, can I give you a tour?"

Kerri nodded numbly, and as Dr. Bender turned to head back down the hallway, she fell into step behind him.

The first room on the right off the hallway was an eat-in kitchen furnished with a complete set of appliances: stove, refrigerator, dishwasher, microwave— even a toaster oven on one counter.

"This is the kitchen," Bender explained unnecessarily. "My patients are welcome to help themselves to snacks, soft drinks, coffee, tea . . . whatever they can find."

"Geez," Kerri said. "All I offer my patients are cookies. Though I do spring for those fancy Pepperidge Farm ones."

Bender laughed: deep, rich, resonant. "This room," he said, moving past the kitchen, "is where we hold the group sessions."

He stood aside and let Kerri peek around the corner. She guessed the area had probably served as a dining room at one time. Now it held an assortment of chairs arranged in a loosely shaped circle, a deacon's bench against the left wall, and a narrow table at the back, covered with a variety of pamphlets. A dazzling array of healthy plants—some of them rather exotic looking—sat on the floor or hung from the ceiling. To the right was a pass-through counter with a sliding wood panel that opened into the kitchen.

"Nice," Kerri said. "Are you the one with the green thumb?"

Bender shrugged. "I dabble," he said. Then he turned and crossed the hall, opening another door. "This is the room where I see most of my patients," he explained.

Kerri stepped across the threshold, taking in the golden pine paneling, a polished hardwood floor partially covered by a cream-and-blue-colored rug, and a small seating area comprised of a large corduroy recliner, a full-sized couch, and a straight-backed armchair. Recessed lights in the ceiling gave the room a warm, homey feel, and Kerri noticed a dimmer switch that would allow Bender to adjust the mood to suit his—or his patients'—needs. Another dozen or so plants were centered around the room's single window in the opposite wall.

"This is quite nice," Kerri said. "Good atmosphere."

"Thanks. Come on and I'll show you my office."

Kerri followed him to the door at the end of the hall. They were about to enter when the front door opened, and both she and Bender turned to look.

A blond-haired man stepped inside, closed the door behind him, and strode down the hallway. He stopped near the entrance to the kitchen, an expression of surprise marking his face.

"Why, Dr. Whitaker! Fancy meeting you here." As he extended his hand, Kerri numbly offered hers in return, allowing him to pump her arm vigorously.

"Tom Frederick," Kerri said, the shock in her voice matching the expression on her face. "What a . . . pleasant surprise."

Bender gave Kerri, then Tom, a curious look. "You two know each other," he said, more of an observation than a question.

"We do," Tom answered. "I worked with Dr. Whitaker on a case a few years back."

"Stephen Sato," Kerri offered with a quick glance at Bender. "My receptionist."

"How is Stephen doing?" Tom asked.

"Quite well, actually," Kerri told him. "He's enrolled at the University of Washington, majoring in psychology. He'll be graduating in two years."

"That's great," Tom said with a fleeting smile. "So what brings you here? Don't tell me you're one of us?"

"One of you?"

Tom hesitated, looking toward Bender for help.

"Dr. Whitaker is visiting our group tonight," Bender explained. "She has a patient who has experienced some similar things, and I thought the group might be able to help her out."

"Why didn't you just bring the victim to group?" Tom asked, looking at Kerri.

She didn't miss his choice of words—*victim* as opposed to *patient.*

"He's only six years old," Bender answered, "and his experience is a little bit different."

"How so?" Tom asked. Both his tone and expression reflected an intelligent curiosity. It struck Kerri that he was acting like a typical lawyer, gently probing, trying to get at the truth. For some reason, his questioning made her uncomfortable.

Perhaps having sensed her discomfort, Bender grabbed Kerri's elbow and turned her toward his office. "We'll get to that," he said to Tom. "Would you do me a favor and set up the coffee? I need to discuss some things with Dr. Whitaker before we get started."

"Sure," Tom said with a shrug. He turned and walked into the kitchen.

Bender steered Kerri into his office and closed the door. A huge mahogany desk occupied the center of the room, and Kerri was impressed by how clear it was of clutter—she hadn't seen the top of hers in years. Behind the desk was a brown leather chair, its high back shiny from frequent use. Windows in three walls would let in plenty of sunlight during the day, and there was another plethora of plants to take advantage of it. Now, venetian blinds were drawn against the fading light of dusk, and the primary source of light came from recessed lamps in the ceiling.

Two corners of the room were covered with

floor-to-ceiling bookcases. A quick perusal of the titles showed Kerri the subject matter was varied and eclectic—everything from psychology texts to fiction paperbacks. Some of them, she couldn't help but note, had to do with UFOs and similar phenomena. Curious, Kerri moved closer.

Bender walked over to his desk and hiked one hip up on the corner. "Look," he said, "I didn't think you would know anybody from the group. If it makes you uncomfortable . . ."

Kerri turned toward him and dismissed his objection with a wave of her hand. "No, I'm fine. It was just something of a surprise to see someone I knew—particularly Tom." She shook her head in wonderment. "He's the last person I expected to find here."

"Why is that?" Bender folded his arms over his chest and cocked his head to one side, giving her a quizzical look.

"Well," Kerri said, "I've seen the man in action. He's a high-priced well-known defense lawyer with a reputation for being one of the sharpest and brightest legal minds anywhere in the area. He's got a no-nonsense personality and cuts quickly to the core of any matter. A bit of a workaholic perhaps, but he always struck me as being pretty well balanced. Not the kind of person I pictured attending a group of this nature."

Bender smiled; it was sly, but not spiteful. "Well, I hate to say I told you so, but I *did* tell you these people are not your run-of-the-mill spaceman types."

"I do think I should ask Tom if he's okay with me being here, however."

"I doubt he'll object," Bender mused, "but you're right. I'll ask the entire group if they have any objections to you sitting in. How is it you know Tom again?"

"I hired him several years ago," Kerri explained, "to defend a patient of mine."

Bender's eyebrows arched in surprise. "You hire lawyers for your patients?"

"Not usually, but this one Stephen . . . he was special."

"How so?"

Coming from anyone else, Kerri might have found the persistent questioning intrusive and rude. But Bender's interest seemed earnest and sincere. She leaned back against the corner of the bookcase, her arms crossed over her chest, mimicking Bender's own posture.

"I met Stephen about four years ago when he was seventeen. A friend of mine—actually he's more like family—is a detective on the Seattle police force. He brought Stephen in for some counseling after they picked him up on a shoplifting charge. His mother and sixteen-year-old sister had both been raped and murdered a few months earlier. Turns out Stephen's older brother, Samuel, had been dealing drugs with some not-too-savory types. Apparently, he tried to scam them. They found out and, as punishment, went after the family."

"Ouch," Bender said, grimacing.

"Yeah, it wasn't a pretty scene. Stephen's father had died the year before—he was a long-standing alcoholic—and it left the family in financial straits with Samuel trying to be the man of the house. When he found out how much money he could make with the drug scene, the temptation was simply too much for him."

"So how did Tom figure in?"

"Well, during the time I was counseling Stephen,

the police finally figured out what had happened to his mother and sister . . . and why. Stephen got wind of it and confronted his brother. They ended up coming to blows, and some neighbors who heard the commotion called the cops. By the time the police got there, things had quieted down, though I understand the apartment was pretty torn up—it must have been a nasty fight. Both boys were banged up pretty good—cuts, bruises, split lips, and black eyes . . . that sort of thing—but they both refused medical attention. So the cops gave them a standard brotherly love lecture and left.

"Once they were gone, Stephen was still angry. So, using a suggestion I had given him, he decided to take a walk, to distance himself from his brother and give himself time to calm down. He returned an hour later, and when he walked into the apartment, someone knocked him over the head. Near as we could figure, he was out for a half hour or so, and when he came to, his brother was lying dead on the couch from a bullet wound to the head. The gun was on the floor beside the body.

"Thinking his brother had committed suicide, Stephen called the police. But when the forensics team turned up the fact that there were no powder burns on Samuel's hands, and that the angle of the entry wound ruled out the possibility it was self-inflicted, their attention turned to Stephen. The crowning blow was when the only fingerprints on the murder weapon turned out to be Stephen's. The gun was subsequently traced to two other murders, and Stephen was arrested and charged.

"Stephen claimed he'd been set up. And I believed him. By this time, I knew him pretty well. Though he was certainly having some problems dealing with all that had happened, he wasn't the killing kind. And even though his brother was a total screw-up and was partially responsible for the deaths of their mother and sister, Stephen had a strong sense of family obligation and devotion. He wanted to help his brother. Besides, if he had done it, he was certainly smart enough not to leave such blatant evidence for the police to find. His IQ tested out at one forty-five."

Kerri took in a deep breath and let it out in a long sigh. "So . . . after asking Kevin—that's my detective friend—for the name of a good defense lawyer, I found Tom. Between the police records that proved Stephen's brother hung out with the wrong crowd, my testimony as to Stephen's character, and Tom Frederick's brilliant description of how easily the whole thing could have been staged, there was sufficient evidence to raise reasonable doubt. The jury acquitted him."

"And you paid for the lawyer?" Bender asked, his voice skeptical.

Kerri shrugged. "I felt sorry for the kid. He was a basically good person with a bright mind. There he was with no family, no job, nothing. I couldn't bear to see his life go to waste. Shortly after the trial, my receptionist turned in her resignation, so I offered Stephen the job.

"Since then, he's done remarkably well. He enrolled at the U of Dub when he was eighteen, and between night and summer classes he's managed to keep a busy school schedule, hold down a full-time job, and pull down straight A's."

"Wow," Bender said, scratching his head. "That's quite the story."

Kerri shrugged. "No big deal. It worked out well

on all sides. Stephen got another chance at life, and I got a crackerjack office receptionist who has my coffee waiting for me in the mornings."

"Still, that's a little above and beyond, don't you think?"

Kerri shrugged. "I've always had a soft spot for kids. Especially kids in trouble. For a while, almost half my practice was with kids."

"Have any of your own?"

Kerri should have seen the question coming; it was a natural evolution of their conversation. But it blindsided her. She jerked, as if she'd been slapped. She stared at Bender, her eyes blinking with the sudden sting of unshed tears.

Bender pushed himself away from the desk and walked toward her, confused and concerned. "Are you okay?" he asked. His hands settled on her shoulders. They felt warm, comforting, and reassuring—the last thing Kerri wanted. Kindness was one of her tears' greatest triggers. She twisted away, ducking from beneath his touch.

"I'm sorry," she said, staring at the wall. "You caught me off guard, is all."

She thought he might drop the subject and move on to something else. Instead, he used one of psychiatry's most valuable tools: silence. It took only a few indeterminate seconds of it before Kerri succumbed.

"I had a daughter, but she died a little over a year ago. Cancer."

"I'm sorry."

Bender's voice came from close behind her, closer than she thought he was. Suddenly, she was afraid he would place his hands on her shoulders again, and she knew the gesture would break down the last of her feeble defenses. She made a hurried, darting movement toward the office door.

"Thank you," she said, blinking hard and swallowing down the lump in her throat. She raked a hand through her hair and tried to sound as nonchalant as possible. "It was a difficult time, but life does go on. Shall we go out and meet the rest of the group?"

With her hand on the doorknob, she risked a look back at Bender. The compassion and concern on his face nearly did her in. She blinked again and felt the muscles in her jaw clench and twist. "Please?" she whispered through gritted teeth.

Bender's warm brown eyes held hers for a long moment. Then he jerked into action. "Certainly," he said, clearing his throat and marching toward the door. "After you."

THIRTEEN

※━◆━※

Seven people had gathered in the room next to the kitchen, occupying all but two of the chairs in the circle. Kerri quickly scanned the group; there were three women and four men, including Tom Frederick. They were all busily chatting, and fragments of their conversations drifted toward Kerri—mundane topics such as kids, jobs, and the latest world events. A couple of faces turned toward her and Bender as they entered, but just as quickly turned back to their conversing partners. One of them, a well-dressed woman who looked to be in her late thirties or early forties, said, "Good evening, Mike."

"Good evening, Nancy. Looks like everyone is here, so let me get our guest some coffee and we'll get started."

On the shelf below the pass-through window to the kitchen sat a carafe, some coffee cups, saucers, sugar, cream, and a plate of vanilla sandwich cookies. The coffee smelled wonderful, its fragrance permeating the room. Kerri's stomach growled and she eyed the cookies greedily.

Bender steered her toward the two empty chairs and gestured for her to have a seat. "Coffee?"

"Yes, please," Kerri answered. "And a handful of

those cookies, if you don't mind. I haven't eaten any-thing since breakfast."

Bender leaned closer, and in a low voice said, "I have some sandwich stuff in the kitchen. Want me to fix you something?"

"No, no," Kerri said, shaking her head. "Don't go to all that trouble. The cookies will be fine."

"You sure? It will only take a minute."

"I'm sure. Thanks for the offer though."

"Okay," Bender said, making it clear from his tone that he disapproved of her choice. "What do you take in your coffee?"

"Just cream, thanks."

Bender took off toward the pass-through window and Kerri settled into one of the empty chairs, taking advantage of the moment to further study the group's members. To her left, next to the other empty chair, sat Tom Frederick. Beside him was a woman who looked to be in her mid-thirties, with a very pretty face, black hair that was cut short and curled around her face, and large brown doe eyes. Beside her was the woman Bender had called Nancy; next to her sat a young man who couldn't have been much older than Stephen. He wore round wire-rimmed glasses, and his dirty-blond hair was pulled back into a shoulder-length ponytail. He was wearing a pair of torn, worn blue jeans and a faded blue polo-type shirt. His feet were encased in a pair of scuffed hiking boots that looked to be about two sizes too big.

To Kerri's right was a short, balding man, dressed in an expensive suit, a brown leather briefcase at his feet. He was explaining his son's choice of college majors to a large-boned woman with distinctively Scandinavian fea-tures: high cheek bones, long light-blond hair, and big blue eyes. Kerri tried to guess at her age but ended up with a range that included everything from twenty-five to forty, though she suspected from the tiny laugh wrinkles at the corners of her eyes that forty might be closer to the mark.

Leaning toward the Scandinavian woman, and listening in on the conversation between her and the bald man, was a young, attractive fellow—his long lanky legs suggesting he was well over six feet tall. He had a head of curly dark hair, thick-lashed green eyes, and a facial structure reminiscent of the aquiline lines found on ancient Greek sculptures. Curious, Kerri glanced at his hands. No wedding ring. If he was, in fact, single, Kerri suspected he led a number of hopeful women on a very merry chase.

Bender reappeared carrying two mugs of coffee, a saucer carefully balanced atop one of them and piled high with cookies. He handed her one of the cups, then settled himself in the chair beside her. Setting the plate of cookies in her lap, he leaned over and whispered in her ear. "Sorry, these are cheap cookies."

Kerri smiled. "I'll survive," she whispered back.

Bender cleared his throat and turned his attention to the rest of the group. "Okay, folks, let's get started. We have a guest with us tonight."

Seven pairs of eyes turned toward Kerri.

"This is Dr. Kerri Whitaker," Bender went on. "She's a psychiatrist from Seattle, and she's here to listen to your stories in hopes of finding something helpful she can use for a patient of hers who's had a similar experience. Dr. Whitaker is a psychiatrist, like myself, and anything you say here in this group will be kept strictly confidential. But if anyone feels uncomfortable with this arrangement, please say so."

Bender paused a moment; when no one spoke up he continued.

"Okay, what I would like to do is have each of you give a brief introduction, tell a little about yourselves, and then relate the experiences that brought you to this group." Bender looked toward Tom Frederick. "Tom, why don't you start?"

Tom Frederick reached down and set his coffee cup on the floor beside his chair. Instead of leaning back, he hunched forward: elbows on his knees, hands clasped in front of him, eyes staring at his feet.

"Well," he began with some hesitation, "I'm the newest member of the group here. This is only my third visit."

Kerri saw a few of the others nod in agreement.

"My name is Tom Frederick . . ." He looked over at Kerri. "But then, you know that," he said.

Kerri was aware of a few curious glances her way. Having just bitten off a large chunk of cookie, her jaws froze in midchew and she tried to flash the group what she hoped would pass for a professional, but friendly, smile. She was relieved when Tom Frederick continued his tale and everyone's attention turned back toward him.

"I found out about the group from Fiona . . . she's my lady friend and a friend of Maria's," he added with a sideways nod toward the doe-eyed woman sitting beside him. He paused, studying the floor. After drawing in a slow, deep breath, he continued. "It started a little over a month ago when I was staying at my house on Lopez Island. I was there, alone, waiting for Fiona to arrive the following day for a week of vacation. I was tired—it had been a busy week at work—but even though my mind was exhausted, I felt physically charged in anticipation of the week to come.

"I was standing in front of my bedroom window, looking out over the cliff, thinking what a beautiful night it was. Full moon, a brisk breeze . . . I remember hearing the cry of an eagle, and after that, the blast of a ferry horn."

Kerri noted his voice sounded dreamy and faraway. He fell quiet for a moment, and as Kerri took another bite of cookie, the crunch sounded unusually loud in the almost perfect silence.

"The next thing I remember clearly," Tom continued, "is waking up the following morning. I was in my bed, but I'll be damned if I can recall ever getting into it. That in itself was no big deal, but I found myself feeling oddly out of sorts. There were these images in my mind. . . ."

He leaned back and switched his gaze to the ceiling. His eyes squeezed closed. "The images were of these . . . creatures, for lack of a better word. Tall, ghostly looking things that came into my bedroom and started . . . doing things to me."

Kerri sat holding the mug of cooling coffee in one hand, the plate of cookies in her lap momentarily forgotten as she listened with rapt attention to Tom Frederick's story.

"And then," Tom continued, "I wasn't in my bedroom anymore. I was in some kind of laboratory, or surgical suite, or something. It was very plain—gray walls, a white ceiling with a huge light above me, no furniture other than what I was lying on, and some surgical trays covered with these . . ." Tom grimaced and took a deep bracing breath. "Instruments, I guess you would call them. There was very little noise, just a low-pitched humming sound in the background."

"You were on their spaceship," the woman next to Tom interjected softly.

Tom lowered his head, but his eyes remained closed. His face took on a pained expression. "These things, these creatures, poked and prodded my body . . . they stuck something into my belly . . ." Tom's hand fluttered toward the right side of his abdomen and rubbed a spot just below his rib cage. "They were talking . . ." He frowned. "No, communicating is probably a better word because I could make no sense of anything they said. It was just noise, almost like static."

Kerri suppressed a tiny shudder when she heard Tom's reference to static, recalling Jace's similar description.

"And then they were just gone," Tom said with an almost wistful tone. He opened his eyes and fixed his gaze on Kerri. "At first I thought it was nothing more than a dream. That is, until I found the physical evidence. A small, triangular-shaped reddened area . . . here." He again massaged his abdomen. "And a peculiar bruise on my neck along with some tiny, pin-sized blood drops on the sheet and my pajama top."

He paused, studying Kerri's face for a reaction. She concentrated on keeping her expression carefully neutral.

After a moment, Tom continued. "There was also a vague sense of unease, as if I were being watched or something. I thought it would go away with the light of day, but it only grew worse. I tried to shrug it off, but when Fiona arrived she could tell something was bothering me. Of course I denied it in the beginning, chalking it up to fatigue. But the images grew more and more vivid with each passing day, and I was seized by a sense of melancholy, or perhaps fright would be a better term."

Kerri studied him as he spoke, searching for some sign of deception. Both the innocent and focused set of his eyes and the open language of his body—turned slightly toward Kerri without any crossing of his legs and arms—relayed honesty. Nor was there any hint in his tone that he was playing the braggadocio. Though carefully measured, his words rang sincere. Either the man was telling the truth or he was one hell of a liar. Still, Kerri reminded herself, Frederick was a lawyer. And lawyers—particularly the good ones—were known for their acting ability.

"Anyway," Tom continued, finally letting his eyes rove the faces of the others, "Fiona pestered me into telling her what was wrong. She was the one who made me realize what had happened, that my body had been somehow procured by these creatures—aliens, she called them—and used for testing or sampling of some sort."

Kerri noticed some of the other group members nod in agreement.

"I thought sure Fiona would think I was crazy, but she believed every word of what I told her. She brought me books and articles about other people who'd had strikingly similar experiences. And then she told me about Maria."

Tom turned toward the woman at his side. "I can't tell you what a relief it was to let everything out in the open and know I wasn't crazy. Though I haven't been too eager to share my tale with others," he added, turning his focus back to Kerri. "From what I've heard, most people's reactions to stories like mine are precisely what I feared most: laughter and ridicule."

Kerri felt her blood grow hot under Tom's stare. Feeling guilty because her own reaction to his story was the very skepticism he feared, she nervously snatched a cookie from the plate in her lap and stuffed it into her mouth. When Tom finally looked away, it was all she could do not to breathe a sigh of relief.

"Maria brought me here, and the rest, as they say, is history," Tom concluded.

"Thank you, Tom," Bender said. "As we told you last week, you're not alone." Bender looked over at Kerri. "Any questions?" he asked her.

Her mouth full of cookie crumbs, Kerri gave a spastic shake of her head and sipped some coffee in hopes of making the pulpy mass in her mouth easier to swallow.

"All right then," Bender said. "Maria, why don't you go next?"

Kerri listened, once again enthralled, as the woman named Maria told a tale that varied little from Tom Frederick's. Except Maria's red triangular marking was above the flank area of her right hip. Her descriptions of the creatures and the spaceship—as she called it—were identical to Tom's, and she even claimed to have had the same strange bruising on her neck. But in one regard, Maria's story did vary some.

"I didn't place a lot of emphasis on the bruise at first," she explained to Kerri, "because my husband had a similar one. Yet he had none of the other symptoms."

Kerri was startled to learn Maria was a high school chemistry teacher working toward her Ph.D. She was beginning to see what Bender meant about his patients' backgrounds. The point was brought home even stronger when she discovered the balding man was a stockbroker, the blond woman with the Scandinavian features was a nurse, the ponytailed young man was a computer software designer, and the Grecian god was a cop! Only Nancy, who defined herself as an artist, had an occupation that might possibly be construed as dramatic. All of them seemed—on the surface anyway—to be people with soundly grounded minds and lives. It wasn't difficult to understand why Bender believed something real had happened to these people. But Kerri was still having trouble buying into this alien scenario. There had to be another explanation.

By the time the members of the group finished their stories, Kerri was startled to see by her watch that it was almost eight thirty. Bender brought the session to a close, thanking the members for allowing Kerri to sit in. Somewhat stymied by all she had heard, Kerri felt as if she should say something to the group. But everything she could think of sounded trite and patronizing. In the end, she merely echoed Bender's thanks for allowing her to attend.

As the group broke up, milling about the room and chatting as they made another run on the coffee and cookies, Bender pulled Kerri out into the hall.

"So, what do you think?" he asked her, leaning against the wall with his arms folded over his chest, his dark eyes penetrating her own.

Kerri shrugged. "I'm not sure," she mused. "Have you considered some form of mass hysteria?"

Bender nodded. "With the exception of Tom Frederick and Maria, none of these people had ever met before they came to the group. Their lifestyles and paths are totally disparate. And they don't strike me as the type prone toward any type of public hysteria."

"They do seem to be rational and intelligent people," Kerri admitted. "And, at least on the surface, I detect no signs of anything organically wrong with any of them. This thing about the aches and bruises on their necks bears some resemblance to what my patient told me. He remembers not feeling well when he was awakened that night, claiming his neck was sore."

"Well, if this kid of yours did, in fact, see something, it would be a hell of a breakthrough. Did you find out whether there was any blood at the scene?"

Kerri nodded. "You hit that nail on the head. They found one spot, a small, pin-sized drop on her night-gown—supposedly the one she was wearing the night she disappeared. It was her own blood, and the police didn't think it was significant."

"Interesting," Bender mused, pulling on his chin. "I would love to know more about what this kid of yours saw. It could provide some valuable insight. Even though these people know something unusual and frightening has happened to them, most of them are still struggling with this whole alien concept. It goes against everything they've ever learned or believed."

"Understandable," Kerri said. "I'm having a little trouble with it myself. I assume you've done the standard tests on them—MMPI and such?"

Bender nodded. "I have, except for Frederick. He hasn't been here that long. Nothing unusual showed up in anyone's tests." He bent and moved his face right next to Kerri's ear. "Although I did discover some interesting sexual tendencies in young Adonis over there."

The warmth of his breath on her neck made Kerri

shiver—not an altogether uncomfortable feeling. "Well," she said, clearing her throat and stepping away, keenly aware of the proximity of Bender's lips to her neck, "I guess I better be going."

Bender reached out and gently brushed at the corner of her mouth with his thumb. "You're wearing your cookies," he said.

Kerri made a self-conscious swipe across her face with the back of her hand.

"I don't suppose you'd consider having dinner with me tomorrow?" Bender asked.

Kerri stared at him, her mouth agape. "Dinner? Tomorrow?"

"Yeah," Bender said with a little chuckle. "You know, where you go to a restaurant and order food and eat it? You obviously don't follow a very sensible diet when left to your own devices."

"Umm . . ." Kerri's mind scrambled for an excuse but came up empty. And besides, the group had her curiosity more than a little piqued. She wouldn't mind having an opportunity to discuss them further. "Okay," she said with little enthusiasm. "What the hell."

"Geez," Bender said, slapping a hand over his heart. "You sure know how to make a guy feel welcome."

"Sorry," Kerri said, amused by his theatrics. "You just took me by surprise."

"Isn't that what we shrinks are supposed to do?"

"I suppose so."

"You like Mexican food?"

"Sure."

"Good. There's a great little Mexican restaurant on San Juan Island in Friday Harbor."

"Wait," Kerri said, holding up her hand. "San Juan Island? That means a ferry trip. And I don't know how late the ferries run the return trip to Anacortes." She opened her purse and dug around for a ferry schedule.

Bender reached over and gently pushed her hand down. "No need to worry about the ferry," he said. "I'll fly us over and back."

"*You'll* fly us? You fly?"

"Sure. I just flap my wings like this . . ." He held his arms out to his sides and pumped them up and down in a flying motion. Kerri stared at him, trying to decide if he was teasing her or if he really was crazy.

Seeing she wasn't amused, Bender dropped his arms to his sides. "Okay. Serious. I'm a pilot. I own a plane."

"Really?"

"Really."

"How long have you been flying?" she asked suspiciously.

"Since I was sixteen. Let's see, that would be almost twenty years now."

"Are you good?"

"The best."

"Why San Juan?" Kerri asked, still not convinced. "There must be plenty of good Mexican restaurants on the mainland."

"Not as good as this one," Bender said. "Besides, I'm kind of partial to San Juan. I live there."

"You live on San Juan Island?"

"Yup."

"So you commute back and forth every day?"

"In the plane. Fly myself over and back five days a week. Haven't crashed yet, so I think you'll be safe."

"I don't know," Kerri hesitated.

"Aw, come on. I swear I don't fly a saucer or anything," he said, lowering his voice.

Kerri grinned. The man definitely had charm. "I guess," she said, caving in with a shrug.

"Great!" Bender clapped his hands. "Where do you live? I can pick you up at your house." Kerri frowned. "Or if you prefer," Bender quickly added, "we could meet at an airport nearby."

"I live on the peninsula," Kerri said. "Near Port Townsend, though I'm kind of in the sticks. Perhaps an airport on the mainland somewhere would be better."

"How about the one in Anacortes?" Bender suggested. "That's the main jumping off spot for the islands anyway."

"That sounds fine," Kerri said.

"Great! Four o'clock okay?"

"Four will be fine."

Bender gave her directions to the airport, and tipping an imaginary hat, he said, "I'll see you tomorrow then. I'm looking forward to it." With that, he turned and went back into the room to mingle with the group, leaving a slightly stunned and bewildered Kerri to find her own way out.

FOURTEEN

The journey home was a long one. After checking the ferry schedules, Kerri drove a little over an hour and a half down the interstate to Route 20, through Anacortes, and into Keystone. There she waited forty-five minutes for the eleven o'clock ferry—the last one of the day—to make the half-hour shuttle to Port Townsend. Then another fifteen minutes for the drive to her house. Throughout the trip, Kerri's mind was occupied with the evening's events.

She thought the group had been fascinating, and grudgingly admitted Mike Bender had intrigued her, too. She felt a certain level of attraction to the man—an attraction involving more than just his physical attributes. Part of it was the amazing level of poise and self-assurance he possessed. In some people, that level of confidence came across as egotistical or pompous. But Mike Bender struck Kerri as being none of those things. Instead, he seemed to be a man who was simply and innately comfortable with both himself and the world around him. This trait alone, she realized, would make him quite effective as a therapist. Eliminating a client's fear of judgment was the first, and often the hardest, test of a doctor-patient relationship.

Contrary to her earlier fears, she now had no

regrets whatsoever about attending the group session. She had garnered some valuable information to use in her treatment of Jace. And though she tried to argue with herself that tomorrow evening's liaison with Bender would be nothing more than an opportunity to explore this phenomenon further, she couldn't deny she was looking forward to it.

It was around midnight when she finally reached her driveway. As she bumped and bounced her way down the tunnel of trees and into the clearing, she was consumed by a mental and physical exhaustion that left her yawning widely. Yet, when her eyes settled on the gray Mercedes parked beside the house, her heart did a little flip-flop inside her chest and she felt instantly wide awake.

As she pulled up beside the car, its lone occupant opened the door and stepped out. The spotlights mounted on the side of the house shone down, making his blond hair shimmer. Kerri squinted in the glare, trying to see his face and gauge his mind-set, but the same light that made his hair shine like spun gold left his face hidden behind a curtain of angular shadows. Turning off the engine, she sat there, eyes averted, steeling herself for what was to come. Though she couldn't see her visitor, she felt his eyes upon her.

Finally, she pushed the door open and climbed out. "Nathan," she said, not bothering to disguise the irritation in her voice or on her face. "What are you doing here?"

If she hoped to rile her ex with this cold greeting, she was disappointed. Nathan merely gave her a sheepish look—the same one that had worked so well on her when they were married. It's effect on her now was nil.

"I can remember a time when you were glad to see me," Nathan pouted.

"That was before, Nathan. This is now. Things change." Kerri moved past him toward the front door, keys in hand, leaving him scramble along behind her. "It's almost midnight, Nathan," she said over her shoulder. "A little late for a social call, don't you think?"

"I brought you something," Nathan said, clomping up the steps at her heels. "You left it at the Weathertons'."

Kerri turned and saw him holding out the sweater jacket she had left behind during her hasty exit from the party. As if echoing her thoughts, Nathan said, "You left in quite a flurry. I was worried about you. Is everything okay?"

The solicitous and gentle tone of his voice, combined with that puppy-dog look she remembered so well, struck a deeply buried chord somewhere in Kerri's memories. For one brief instant, she felt a flush of the old feelings, the way it had been when things were so good between her and Nathan. But just as quickly, the image of Nathan in the arms of another woman flitted through her mind, and the warming nostalgia faded, leaving behind the same hurt and anger that had dogged her for the past year.

"You lost your right to care about me or my feelings a long time ago, Nathan," she snapped, turning away from him. She jammed the key home and pushed the front door open. The thought of closing it in his face flitted through her mind, but Shadow appeared from seemingly nowhere, darting past her feet and over the threshold. Nathan, never one to pass up an opportunity, pushed his way in as well. Fuming, Kerri followed him into the house, flipping on the living room light and dropping her purse into a chair near the door. She leaned on the open door and gave Nathan a look of weary impatience.

"Look, Nathan, I'm very tired. It's been a long day. If you don't mind, I'd like to get ready for bed."

"Where have you been?" he asked her, his face sullen. "I've been waiting for almost three hours."

"Where I have been is none of your business." She snatched her sweater coat from his hands and tossed it on top of her purse. "I didn't ask you to come." Crossing her arms over her chest, she stood before him, challenging.

Nathan hung his head. "Look," he said softly, staring at his feet, "I know I ruined things between us. I really fucked up. I made a stupid, terrible mistake and I understand your anger." His eyes peered up at her imploringly. "But I still love you, Kerri." He shrugged helplessly. "I can't change the way I feel and I can't change the things I've done. But I want you to understand it had nothing to do with you."

Kerri's jaw dropped open and she gaped at him. "Nothing to do with me?" she scoffed. "Jesus Christ, Nathan! You slept with another woman! How can you say that has nothing to do with me?" She spun on her heel and stomped toward the kitchen, sidestepping Shadow's overtures of affection. The sound of the front door closing came from behind her, and she wondered if Nathan had left. But she resisted the urge to look back; if he was still there, she'd be damned if she'd give him the satisfaction.

Instead she opened one of the cupboards and busied herself popping the top off a can of cat food as Shadow wove himself around her feet. As the seconds ticked by, she became fairly certain Nathan was still

there—she could feel his presence. All doubt was eliminated a moment later when he spoke.

"I know what I did hurt you, Kerri," he said.
"And I'm not going to try and justify it. It was wrong,
it was stupid . . . but I never meant to hurt you. I
wasn't in my right mind then. Mandy's death made
me crazy."

The mention of their daughter made Kerri's throat
tighten. Trying to ignore it, she yanked open the silver-
ware drawer, the metallic rattle of its contents sounding terribly loud. She grabbed a spoon and jabbed it
into the can of cat food.

"The pain was so awful, so unbearable," Nathan
continued, his voice little more than a whisper. "And
you were so distant."

Kerri heard the hitch in his throat, and felt her
own turn into a vice. Grabbing the edge of the counter
with her free hand, she stared out the window over the
sink, seeing Nathan's ghostly image reflected on the
inky blackness beyond.

Swallowing down the lump in her throat, she
turned slowly and faced Nathan, leaning against the
counter and holding the open can of cat food in her
hand. Shadow twirled around her feet, mewing plaintively.

"I was hurting, too," she said. "But I didn't try to
find solace in someone else's arms." Though her words
were accusing, there was no blame in her voice. She
was too tired, too drained, to fight this battle anymore.
"What happened, happened. It's done. *We* are done,
Nathan."

She walked over and squatted beside Shadow's
bowl, scraping out the contents of the can. Shadow
started in on the stuff with a vengeance, making an

odd vibrating noise somewhere between a growl and a purr.

Kerri paused to stroke Shadow's soft, thick fur. She didn't want to get into an emotional tug of war with Nathan. She knew she had to distance herself from this whole discussion or risk opening wounds that had barely scabbed over. *Look at things clinically, not personally,* she told herself. It had worked for her before; she prayed it would again.

"You know," she said over her shoulder, slipping into her professional persona, "even if you hadn't slept with what's-her-name, there's a good possibility our marriage would have fallen apart anyway. It's a well-proven statistic that the death of a child is one of the toughest things to overcome in any relationship."

She banged the spoon on the side of the bowl to knock off the clinging clump that remained, then stood and walked back to the sink. She tossed the can into the trash, wrinkling her nose at the smell, then flipped the faucet on and thrust her hands beneath the water to wash away the lingering scent of oily fish parts.

"So I don't place all the blame on you," she continued. "I know I wasn't easy to live with during that period either." Pushing the faucet off, she shook the water from her hands and reached for the towel on the refrigerator door handle. She took much longer than was necessary to dry, and when she was done she replaced the towel with great care, adjusting it until the two sides hung evenly. Finally she turned and, once again, faced Nathan.

He was leaning against the doorjamb, hands in his pockets, his blond hair falling haphazardly over one side of his forehead. His eyes narrowed as he studied her face; his brow furrowed with concern and affection. A half smile flitted across his lips.

"We had some good times together, though, didn't we?" he said.

Kerri returned the smile with a fleeting one of her own. "We did," she admitted. She felt her emotional barrier start to crumble, and, panicked, she forced it back into place. "But they are in the past. The best we can hope for now is to put that past behind us."

Nathan pushed himself away from the door and crossed the room toward her, his gaze never once leaving her face. "Why, Kerri?" he asked. He was standing only inches away, and Kerri's nose filled with the familiar scent of his aftershave. When he reached out and sandwiched her hands between his own, she felt herself start to tremble. "Why do we have to put it all behind us?" he implored. "Can't we learn from it? Can't we try for a future together?" His eyes roved over her face, and he reached up to tenderly brush an errant lock of hair back from her forehead. "I still love you," Nathan whispered. "And I know you must have feelings left for me. You can't erase all those years we shared together that easily."

For one brief moment, Kerri succumbed to his charm, to the arousal of old feelings and shared moments. But then she remembered his betrayal—and the awful pain. Snatching her hands away, she ducked around him and moved to the opposite side of the room. In the doorway she stopped, looking back at him. Her face and voice were amazingly calm, considering the turmoil going on inside her head.

"The main thing I feel toward you these days, Nathan, is indifference. And that is progress. Take it and move on. Now please go. I'm tired."

Nathan crossed the room and stood in front of her, his face clearly displaying the hurt she'd just inflicted. "Is there someone else?" he asked, the muscles in his cheeks twitching.

The image of Mike Bender flashed through Kerri's mind: his warm brown eyes, those full lips, the feel of his hands on her shoulders. She shoved the image aside. "No, there is no one else, Nathan. Not that it's any of your business."

"Then where were you tonight?" he asked, his anger starting to show through.

"As I said before, that is also none of your business," Kerri said, her weariness replaced with impatience. "But since you insist, I was doing some follow-up work on one of my patients."

"Bullshit," Nathan said. "I went by your office and you weren't there. I called the house and you weren't here, either. Then I ran into Kevin at the hospital. He told me you were meeting Kathy Marlin for dinner."

Kerri's eyes flashed with anger. "You have no right to know where I am or what I am doing, Nathan. My life is no longer any of your concern." She wanted nothing more than to run away from him, but she forced herself to stand her ground, her eyes narrowed down to an angry glint as she met his accusing stare.

Nathan took the challenge. "It just so happens I talked to Kathy Marlin's husband yesterday," he sneered. "And he told me Kathy is in England visiting with her mother."

Kerri felt her face go hot.

"So," Nathan continued, shifting his weight from one foot to the other and folding his arms over his chest. "You lied to Kevin. Why would you lie to Kevin, Kerri?"

Kerri spun away from him and stomped toward the front door. She flung it open so hard it hit the wall, leaving a dent in the sheet rock. "Get out!" she seethed.

Nathan sighed. He moved toward her, his hands held out in supplication. "Look, I'm sorry, I just—"

"I said, get out!"

Nathan paused, gauging the depth of her anger. Kerri's jaw was grimly set; her eyes flashed fire. Her breathing was harsh and ragged, her chest heaving.

Nathan bowed his head in acquiescence. "Okay," he said to the floor. "I'll go." He looked up at her one last time, his eyes hound-dog sad. "But I want you to understand that I came by tonight because I'm worried about you. And because I miss you. I miss us."

Kerri's face didn't waver. Nathan suffered beneath her icy stare a few seconds longer before slumping his way out the door. He hesitated on the porch, turned, and opened his mouth to say something more. Kerri slammed the door in his face and threw the dead bolt. Storming into the kitchen, she paced from one side of the room to the other, her lips moving in a silent soliloquy. Shadow, sitting in the corner beside his bowl washing his face with a frequently licked paw, stopped to stare at her, his yellow eyes reflecting a sleepy curiosity.

Kerri continued pacing until she heard Nathan's car start up, followed by the fading sound of its engine. She stopped, frozen in the middle of the room. Her eyes stared off into nothingness, her chin trembled. Two tracks of tears meandered down her cheeks. Her eyes focused on Shadow as she swiped at the tears running down her neck.

"Life sucks," she said.

The cat meowed his agreement, licked his paw, and continued washing his face.

FIFTEEN

~~~~~

Kerri awoke Saturday morning with a pounding headache that refused to subside even after three cups of coffee and a handful of aspirin. As a last-ditch effort, she stretched out on the couch a little before noon with a heating pad beneath her neck and the shades drawn against the bright sunlight outside. Thirty minutes later, the headache was just starting to fade when the shrill ring of the phone shattered the silence, making the pain surge back with a vengeance. Kerri sat up with a groan and snatched the offending device off the coffee table.

"Hello," she mumbled, massaging one temple with her fingers.

"Hey, lass. Top o' the day to ya."

"Hmmm," Kerri muttered back.

"Uh-oh, what's the matter?"

"Just a headache," Kerri said, switching the phone to her other hand and giving the left temple some attention. "What's up with you, Kevin?"

"Well, I don't know if I should be telling ya this, but I thought you'd want to know."

Kerri's hand dropped to her lap, her attention fully focused. "What is it?" she asked.

"We got a search warrant for Johansen's house and went in there this morning."

"And?"

"And, we found a coil of rope in the garage that looks like the same kind we found tied around Janet Johansen's body."

"Oh, God," Kerri moaned. "Does Thad know?"

"He knows we found it, yeah. We're waiting on the lab guys to give us a report once they've analyzed it."

"So you don't know for sure it's the same rope?"

"Not for sure," Kevin admitted. "But my money's on a match."

Kerri wrapped her palm over the back of her neck and rolled her head on her shoulders to ease the tension. "What did Thad say when you showed him the rope?" she asked.

"Claimed he'd never seen it before," Kevin said with a scoff. "Don't they all?"

"It doesn't make sense," Kerri muttered.

"What do you mean?"

"I mean Thad Johansen is a college-educated man and obviously not stupid. If he killed his wife and dumped her body in the lake, do you really think he'd be dumb enough to keep the rope he used?"

"You're thinking of Stephen," Kevin mused. "Does everyone you know have to be the victim of a setup?"

"That's not fair, Kevin."

"You're right. I'm sorry."

"You're forgiven."

"There's more," Kevin said. "An update on the autopsy findings."

Kerri grimaced.

"Seems Janet Johansen died of heart failure brought on by some type of trauma to the heart muscle. They found some tiny hemorrhagic spots on one of the heart muscle walls."

"Hemorrhagic spots? From what?"

"They're not sure," Kevin said.

"What about markings on the skin surface near the heart?" Kerri asked.

"You're thinking about the kid's claim that someone poked his mother with something in the chest area?"

"Well, it is rather coincidental, don't you think? Did they find anything?"

"Unfortunately, the skin in that area was too . . . uh . . . damaged to offer anything conclusive," Kevin said. "Though they did find some scarring on the inside of one elbow. Scarring from old needle marks."

"Needle marks? Was there any history of drug abuse?" Kerri asked. "Or perhaps some past medical history that would account for multiple needle punctures?"

"Turns out she was a frequent blood donor," Kevin explained. "Kind of blew my theory all to hell."

"What theory?"

"Well, my first thought when we found the needle marks, even though they appeared to be old, was that perhaps Th—, er, someone had injected something into her, but the tox tests came back negative. Though there was one interesting thing."

"What's that?"

"She had an unusually high level of carbon monoxide in her body. Not enough to be fatal, but it was there."

"Have you checked out the Johansens' heating system?" Kerri asked. "Maybe there was a build-up of carbon monoxide in the house."

"We're looking into it," Kevin said.

"You need to let Thad know," Kerri said. "If there is a carbon monoxide leak in the house, he and Jace could be in danger."

"Yeah," Kevin said noncommittally.

"Kevin, promise me you'll tell him."

"I'll tell him. But I don't think he's going to be there long enough for it to matter."

"What do you mean?"

"I mean that once the report on that rope comes back, I suspect we'll be placing Thad Johansen under arrest."

Kerri shuddered. "You don't even know for sure how she died, Kevin."

"Doesn't matter," he said. "If the rope we found in his garage matches the rope on Janet's body, that ties him to the crime."

Kerri closed her eyes, massaging both temples now with her thumb and fingers. "Do me a favor, Kevin?"

"What's that?"

"As soon as you know the test results on the rope, will you page me?"

"Page you? You going somewhere?"

Kerri dropped her hand and her eyes widened as she remembered her conversation with Nathan the night before—and the fact that Nathan had uncovered her lie to Kevin. Did Kevin know?

"I have an appointment to meet with another psychiatrist this evening to discuss a case we have in common," she said, feeling somewhat better with the half-truth.

"I see," Kevin said. "By the way, I ran into Nathan last night at the hospital. He was looking for you."

Kerri winced, and she quickly replayed Kevin's

words in her mind, analyzing his tone, trying to discern whether he knew something. She couldn't tell, and decided to gamble. "He found me," she said, taking the noncommittal route. "Came out here to the house and waited until I got home."

"You two thinking about giving things another try?"

"Why would you think that?" Kerri said, a little surprised.

"I got the impression from Nathan he might be interested," Kevin answered. "His voice had that lost and lonely tone to it."

Kerri felt a flicker of guilt. Had she been too harsh with Nathan? After all, a decade of marriage should count for something. Maybe she should consider trying to bury the past—all of it. But her gut told her it was still too soon.

"I think Nathan is interested," Kerri answered vaguely.

There was a long, thoughtful silence before Kevin asked, "Are you?"

"I don't know, Kev." She sighed. "On the one hand, I feel as if our history warrants some consideration before it's all tossed aside. But on the other hand, I can't get past what happened. What Nathan did to me hurt too much. Particularly coming when it did."

There was another long silence, and Kerri knew Kevin was debating whether or not to push her. "Well, uh, if you need an ear to bend, you know where to find me."

Kerri smiled with both affection and relief. "Okay," she said.

"I should know something more on this rope in a few hours. I'll give you a beep when it comes through."

"Thanks, Kevin."

"You're welcome, lass. Later."

Kerri heard Kevin hang up, but as she was about to set her own phone back in its cradle, she thought she heard a clicking noise and snatched it back to her ear. "Kevin? You there?" She heard the sound again, like a faint clacking of castanets. But nothing else. With a shrug, she hung up the phone.

Checking the ferry schedule, Kerri saw she would have to catch a two forty-five ferry out of Port Townsend if she hoped to make it to Anacortes by four o'clock. She hoped Kevin's call would come before she left, but when it didn't, she clipped her beeper onto the waist of her slacks and headed out the door.

The day was sunny with a smattering of billowy clouds floating overhead, though yesterday's cloud cover still hovered over the Cascades, obscuring the mountains from view. The temperature had dropped into the fifties, and Kerri grabbed her sweater coat from where it still lay on the chair. But when she caught a whiff of Nathan's cologne on it, she tossed it aside and grabbed a lightweight jacket instead. She left the house a few minutes before two thirty, arriving at the Port Townsend ferry terminal just in time to see the big boat dock. Forty minutes later, she was driving along Route 20 through Whidbey Island on her way to Anacortes.

The Anacortes airport was at the top of a hill just off Route 20, overlooking a bay and a marina. It was a two-building affair with a single runway and a handful of small planes parked on the surrounding Tarmac. The largest of the buildings—apparently a hangar—sat behind the smaller one, which was little more than a bungalow. Near the right end of the bungalow was a door with a faded sign that read TERMINAL. Beside the door, two finger-printed, rain-splattered windows wrapped around the corner. In front of the bungalow was a parking lot that held some twenty or thirty cars. Kerri pulled into an empty space near the building, climbed out, and headed inside.

The terminal was small—about twenty feet by thirty feet—and boasted a counter, four molded-plastic chairs lined up in front of the windows, and two vending machines tucked into one corner. Behind the counter stood a man of indeterminate age. Though he appeared fit and agile, his hair was a thick cap of snow white, and his browned face bore the leathery creases of someone who has spent a good portion of his life outdoors.

"Good afternoon," the man said in greeting. "May I help you?"

"I'm supposed to meet someone here," Kerri explained. "A Dr. Bender?"

"Ah," the man said. "Dr. Mindbender."

"Pardon me?"

The man laughed good-naturedly. "That's what we call him around here. He's not a real doctor, you know. He's one of them shrinks. So we call him Dr. Mindbender." The man let out a hearty guffaw over his own joke.

"I see," Kerri said, resisting the urge to defend Dr. Bender, or at the very least, their shared profession. "Is he here?"

"He landed a few minutes ago," the man said, nodding toward the runway outside. "Should be here in just a moment. Have a seat and I'll tell him you're waiting," he said, gesturing toward one of the chairs as he headed out the door.

After a cursory inspection of the chairs, which bore a variety of stains and a smattering of brown melted cigarette burns, Kerri decided to remain standing. Sighing, she wandered over and surveyed the contents of the vending machines.

Moments later, she heard laughter behind her and turned to see the white-haired man strolling toward the terminal, accompanied by Bender. Today, wearing jeans, a red plaid flannel shirt, and a denim jacket, Bender was no more formally dressed than yesterday. In fact, if anything, his blue jeans were even more worn than those he'd had on the day before.

"Kerri, glad you made it," he greeted as he pushed the door open. "Jim, this is Dr. Kerri Whitaker, a shrink like myself."

The white-haired man gave her a small bow. "Now, if all shrinks were this pretty, I think I'd have to declare myself crazy," he said.

"Thank you," Kerri said, running a self-conscious hand over her hair.

"So," Bender piped up, "are you ready to go? I best get you away from old Jim here before he steals my date."

"Sure."

"This way," Bender said, holding the terminal door open and waving her through with a sweep of his hand.

"It was nice to meet you, Jim," Kerri said as she headed outside.

"Likewise."

Kerri followed Bender across the Tarmac toward a small twin-engine plane—white with a blue racing stripe down each side. Bender ducked beneath the wing and opened the pilot's door. "After you," he said.

Kerri glanced inside and saw the plane held room

for five passengers and the pilot: two seats in the very back of the plane, two in the middle, and two in the front. There was only one other door—on the opposite side of the plane near the very back. To get to the seat Bender had indicated—one of the front ones—she would have to climb over the pilot's seat, scooting between it and a high dashboard that held a dizzying array of knobs, dials, and indicators. The area was cramped at best, and there was a fairly high step just to get into the plane. Slinging her purse over one shoulder, she grabbed the inside frame of the door, stepped up, and hoisted herself into the pilot's seat. From there she moved over to the passenger side and immediately fastened her seat belt across her hips.

Bender hopped up into his own seat with an easy grace, and after closing the plane door and adjusting a few knobs, he started the engine. The propeller at the front of the plane whirred quietly at first, then began to rattle loudly as it picked up speed. Kerri noticed two foot pedals on her side of the plane as well as Bender's. Fearful of accidentally hitting something she shouldn't, she tucked her feet back toward the seat. There were also matching orange three-quarter steering wheels on both sides, and as Bender pulled his out toward him, Kerri's moved as well, brushing against the purse she held in her lap. She hugged the purse closer to her chest, trying to make herself as small as possible.

Bender laughed. "Don't worry, you're fine. Just relax and enjoy the view."

Bender positioned a set of head phones on his ears and revved up the engine. Inside the small cockpit, the noise was nearly deafening, and Kerri's seat began to vibrate. Bender eased the plane across the Tarmac and taxied to one end of the runway, where he turned the plane 180 degrees, lining it up along a yellow line that ran the length of the strip—a length that looked awfully short to Kerri. At the opposite end was an abrupt drop of a few hundred feet to the water below. Bender revved the engine even higher, and suddenly they were hurtling down the runway. Just as Kerri became convinced they would plummet to their deaths on the rock-strewn coast below, the craft lifted into the air, floating out over the marina. It banked to the right and within seconds they were flying over the Strait of Juan de Fuca.

The sun hung low in the sky and the water below them shone in the early evening light, its aquamarine color making it glimmer like a gigantic jewel.

"That's Cypress Island over there," Bender said pointing out his side window, his voice loud above the roar of the plane's engines. "And that is Guemes to the right, Lopez up ahead."

Because the dashboard in front of her was so high, Kerri was forced to look through the side window. The islands, blanketed with thick groves of evergreens, stretched out before them like giant stepping stones. Here and there she spied cozy little coves backed by rocky granite cliffs, their beaches dotted with drift-wood.

The plane dipped sharply to the right and Kerri felt her muscles tense. She shot Bender a panicked look.

"Don't worry," Bender said, giving her knee a reassuring pat. "I'm just circling around. There's something I want to show you."

The plane dropped down into a narrow channel between two islands. As the water loomed closer, Kerri felt her panic rise a notch.

"Look there," Bender said, reaching past her and pointing out her window. "About fifty feet out from shore."

Kerri looked where he had indicated, at first seeing nothing but the glimmering waves. Then she saw two spots of dark color in the water up ahead. As the plane drew closer, she realized what they were.

"Orcas?" she shouted, looking back at Bender.

Bender nodded and she turned back toward the window. The whales, with their characteristic black-and-white markings, swam side by side, one of them about half the size of the other. Though they were still several feet beneath the surface, they were rising and easily visible through the clear water. Hurtling along like determined torpedoes, they broke the surface in tandem—the big one first, followed an instant later by the smaller one—and the spray from their blowholes glittered like diamonds in the air above their heads. They arched back into the water, swam a short distance, then surfaced again before diving down far enough that they finally disappeared from view.

The plane flew past them and Kerri craned her neck around, hoping for another glimpse. She gave up when she felt the plane start to climb again.

"Beautiful creatures, aren't they?" Bender shouted.

Kerri nodded.

"It's a shame the clouds are hanging over the Cascades," Bender yelled. "On a clear day, you can see Mount Baker to your right and the Canadian Rockies off in that direction." Again he reached over and pointed toward the front of Kerri's wing, his arm briefly brushing against her own. Kerri was instantly and acutely aware of the contact, and found that it wasn't all together unpleasant. She shook her head to gather her senses.

Seeing the motion, Bender's brow furrowed in concern. "You're not getting sick, are you?" he yelled.

"I'm fine. Just a little overwhelmed."

"We'll be landing in a moment," Bender said. "There's the San Juan airstrip over there." Bender brought the plane around in a wide circle over the tiny airport, gradually descending. "Oh, hell!" he yelled, making Kerri start.

"What? What's wrong?" She felt her heart skip a beat and stiffened against her seat. She cast a frantic glance toward the dashboard, her eyes running over the dials and indicators as if she actually understood what they meant. Her hands tightened their grip on her pocketbook until her fingernails carved little half moons in the leather.

"Sorry," Bender said. "I didn't mean to startle you. Just some deer on the runway. Happens all the time. But it means I'll have to buzz them."

"Buzz them?" Kerri said, little more than a whimper.

Bender merely nodded, and a second later the plane dipped down toward the runway, getting within a hundred feet of the ground. It roared over the concrete and then began a steep climb, making Kerri swear her stomach was still behind her, hovering a few feet above the runway. Looking down through her window toward the back of the plane, she saw a small herd of deer standing in the middle of the runway—one of them a huge buck with an impressive rack on his head. As she watched, the herd broke up, all but the buck scattering into the woods surrounding the strip.

"I know this guy," Bender said. "He's a stubborn

old coot. Doesn't move until he's good and ready." There was a glimmer of challenge in Bender's eyes that made Kerri's stomach knot painfully. She held her breath as the plane circled again, once more dropping down toward the runway, lower this time. As they buzzed past the buck, Kerri thought she could reach out and grab the thing by its antlers, it looked so close. She felt a huge sense of relief as she looked back and saw the animal finally move away, sauntering off into the bordering woods.

"He let us off easy," Bender said, bringing the plane around for yet another approach. This time their descent was slower, and moments later the wheels touched the ground with all the impact of a falling feather. Kerri thought concrete had never looked so good.

Bender taxied the plane near the small terminal building, shut off the engines, and removed his headset. He glanced over at Kerri. "You look a little pale."

"I'm fine," Kerri said, trying to keep her limbs from trembling. "It was just a little hair-raising."

"How can you think that's hair-raising," Bender said, opening his door and hopping out, "when you've met my patients?"

Getting out of Bender's plane proved almost as difficult as getting in. Kerri worked her way across the seats, swung her feet outside, and dropped to the ground, bumping the crown of her head on the upper part of the doorway in the process.

"Ouch!" she said, reaching up with her hand to massage the injured area, which was mere inches from the still-tender spot where she'd been hit a few nights before.

Bender reached out and put a steadying grip on

her arm. "Are you okay?" He peered at her head, his hand gently routing around through her hair. Something, either the impact or the touch of his fingers, made Kerri's scalp tingle.

"Didn't break the skin or anything," Bender told her. His fingers combed through the strands. "I love the color of your hair. It looks like polished copper." He looked down at her face, those dark eyes probing her own. He was tall enough and standing so close Kerri had to crane her neck to meet his gaze. For the briefest of moments their eyes locked and Kerri felt her heart speed up a notch. A second later her beeper went off.

Feeling the hot burn of a blush creep up her neck and spread over her face, Kerri reached down to silence her beeper. Bender muttered something unintelligible, then said, "Are you on call or something?"

Kerri shook her head. "Not exactly," she told him, reading the display. "It's Kevin, my detective friend. He was going to call me on something to do with the case I told you about." Kerri looked around, her eyes settling on the small terminal building. "Is there a phone in there I can use?"

"Sure," Bender said, leading off in that direction.

Inside the small building, Bender steered Kerri toward a pay phone mounted on the wall. Kerri punched in the number, following it with the number for her calling card. Kevin picked up on the first ring.

"Kev? It's Kerri. What did you find?"

Bender stepped a few feet away to offer her some privacy. But when he heard Kerri gasp and saw her hand clamp over her mouth, he moved back toward her, his eyebrows raised in question.

Kerri looked up at him, pale and obviously shaken.

"Can you hold on a second, Kevin?" she asked. She cupped her hand over the mouthpiece and stared at Bender.

"What is it?" Bender asked. "What's wrong?"

Kerri swallowed hard, licked her lips, and sucked in a deep shuddering breath. "My patient . . . the little boy I told you about whose mother was killed?"

Bender nodded. "The one who saw the creatures."

"Yes. Well, his father just killed himself. I need to be there. For the boy. I don't suppose you could fly me back to Seattle?"

"Absolutely," Bender said without hesitation. "I'll make the arrangements right now." With that, he strode off toward a small office at the other end of the building.

Kerri lifted the phone back to her ear and made arrangements with Kevin for someone to meet her at the airport and drive her to the Johansens' house. Then she went looking for Bender, massaging her temples with both hands along the way.

SIXTEEN

Bender grilled Kerri for details during the half-hour flight to Sea-Tac. "So your policeman friend thinks the kid's father killed his wife?" he asked, again shouting to be heard above the roar of the plane's engines.

"He does," Kerri said with a nod. "But I don't. It just doesn't fit."

"Does he know the kid's version of what happened that night?"

"He's talked to Jace but doesn't put much stock in his story. Let's face it, the whole thing does sound rather bizarre."

"I suppose it does," Bender said thoughtfully. They flew in silence awhile, the loud hum of the engine combined with the gentle vibrations of the plane making Kerri feel sleepy.

"Listen," Bender yelled, his voice cutting through the noisy silence. "Would you mind if I tagged along with you to the house? You've got my curiosity roused with this story, and besides, you're going to need to get back to your car somehow. Once we get things settled, I could fly you back to Anacortes."

"That would be great," Kerri said, grateful to have even this one minor detail taken care of. She felt so overwhelmed with all that had happened. "I appreciate it."

"No problem," Bender said. "Glad to help. Though I've got to tell you, this is turning out to be one hell of a first date."

Kerri flashed him a weak, apologetic smile.

When they landed at Sea-Tac, Kerri was met by Bill Myers, an officer she knew from the police force. Bill led her and Bender outside to his patrol car and whisked them off toward Seattle. Twenty minutes later, they pulled up in front of the Johansen house. Five squad cars—two of them with their bubble lights still running—filled the cul-de-sac. A half-dozen other vehicles were parked every which way. Kerri recognized two of them: Kevin's and the coroner's.

Kerri climbed out of the patrol car and headed for the house. The neighbors, incited with curiosity, watched from nearby yards and porches, gathered in little groups that muttered and whispered back and forth, spreading the bits of news they were able to glean from the many police and other personnel at the site. One of them, a balding man with the gleam of titillation in his eyes, shouted at Kerri and Bender as they walked by.

"Hey! Can you tell us what happened?"

Kerri ignored him and made her way past the officers guarding the front door, stopping only long enough to assure them Bender was with her. As they entered the house, Kerri's attention turned toward the commotion going on inside the den that served as Thad's office. Several officers and a team of forensic specialists were milling about the room. Through the sea of activity, she caught a glimpse of Thad. He was seated at his draft table, his head lying face down on its top, his arms dangling at his sides. At first glance, it appeared as though he had fallen asleep. But the sea of dark blood dripping off the table's lower end and draping Thad's thighs like some macabre lap robe quickly dispelled that image. Sickened and full of despair, Kerri wanted to turn away. But some inexorable pull made her enter the den instead, her eyes fixed with morbid incredulity on Thad's body. She was still several feet away when she saw the gun lying on the floor at Thad's feet, nestled in a pool of congealing blood.

This is all wrong, Kerri thought, staring at the scene in horror. Thad Johansen wouldn't do this. How could he desert his son this way? Had she been wrong all along? Had Thad Johansen actually killed his wife? Kerri's head moved slowly from side to side, partly in disbelief of the dreadful scene before her, partly in answer to her own questions.

"Excuse me, Dr. Whitaker."

Kerri turned her stunned gaze toward the man who addressed her. It was one of the detectives.

"I'm sorry, but this is a restricted area. You'll have to leave until we finish our investigation," he said.

Kerri nodded numbly and turned away, heading out of the den at a near run. She ran into Bender at the door and he grabbed her shoulders, staring down at her with grave concern.

"Kerri?"

She stared up at him, tears brimming in her eyes. "Where's Kevin?" she asked. "I need to find Kevin." She pushed her way past Bender, searching the faces around her until she found Kevin in the kitchen, chatting with two other detectives.

As soon as he saw her, Kevin excused himself from the discussion at hand and hurried toward her. He draped an arm over her shoulders and steered her to one corner of the room, near the table, giving Bender a curious sideways glance in the process. The other two detectives took their cue and left the kitchen, joining another enclave in the living room. Bender stayed near the doorway, watching Kerri but keeping his distance.

"This is all wrong," Kerri said as Kevin pulled out a chair for her. She ignored the invitation to sit, shrugging Kevin's arm off. "Thad wouldn't do this. He wouldn't do this to Jace." Her eyes gazed up at him, fierce in their denial, moist with barely contained tears.

"I know you don't want to believe it, lass. But the evidence is obvious. The rope was a match."

Kerri's face fell. "An exact match?" she asked, her voice weak.

Kevin nodded, his face somber.

Kerri closed her eyes and turned away, wrapping her arms about her waist and taking in a deep shuddering breath. "How did you find him?" she asked.

"I had an arrest warrant. When I came by the house, no one answered the door. I walked around, peering in through the windows, and that's when I saw him in the den."

"Where is Jace?"

"Don't know," Kevin said carefully. "To tell you the truth, I half expected to find the kid dead as well. But he's not here."

"Then where the hell is he?" Kerri said, turning back to confront Kevin, her voice edged with worried impatience. "You've got to find him, Kevin."

"We're looking."

Kerri started to pace back and forth between the

wall and the sink. "There's a baby-sitter," she said, her brow furrowing as she tried to recall her session with Thad. "A neighbor, I believe."

Kevin nodded, watching her closely. "Okay, I'll have some of the guys question the neighbors. See what we can find out." He turned and looked over toward the kitchen doorway, his eyes narrowing as they settled on Bender. "Who are you?" he asked gruffly.

Bender moved toward them, his mouth opened to answer, but Kerri halted her stride long enough to beat him to it. "This is Dr. Mike Bender," she explained to Kevin. "He's a psychiatrist from Bellingham who's been working on some cases similar to Jace's. I was . . . consulting him about Jace when you called."

Kevin stuck his hand out to Bender, his blue eyes scrutinizing the man in a quick head-to-toe assessment Kerri knew wouldn't miss much. "Nice to meet you, Doc," he said with little enthusiasm.

"Likewise," Bender said. He took Kevin's proffered hand and shook it heartily, the two of them maintaining contact a little longer than Kerri thought was necessary. She watched as the two men sized each other up, their eyes narrowed with some unspoken challenge. Annoyed by their battle of testosterone, Kerri asked, "Did Thad leave any kind of note or anything?"

The distraction worked as the two men immediately broke contact. Kevin looked over at her and nodded. "Not much to it." He reached into his pocket and pulled out a plastic baggie. Inside it was a single yellow Post-it note. He tossed the Baggie onto the table, and Kerri leaned over to read it. It didn't take her long. There were only two words on the paper, written in broad, heavy pencil strokes that formed neat block letters similar to the ones Kerri had seen on the architectural drawings in Thad's den: I'M SORRY.

Kerri turned away, facing the wall and staring up at the ceiling. She let out a dispirited sigh. "Jesus," she said, raking her fingers through her hair. "How am I going to tell Jace he's not only lost his mother, but now his father as well?" She folded her arms over her chest and gave herself a brief, shuddering hug. "Does he have any other family in the area?" she asked over her shoulder.

Kevin grimaced. "Well, that's another problem. Seems Thad has no family, and all there is on Janet's side is a grandmother who's in a nursing home."

Kerri gave him a weary nod. "I know," she muttered. "Alzheimer's."

"Right," Kevin said.

"There is no one on Thad's side? No one at all?"

Kevin shook his head. "Both Janet and her husband are only children. There are no aunts, no uncles . . . nothing."

"You mean to tell me that after all this kid's been through he's going to end up a ward of the state?"

Kevin chewed the inside of one cheek. "Looks that way, lass. Sorry."

Kerri shook her head in disbelief and walked over to the back door to stare out the window, her hands steepled together and tapping against her chin. "Go find him, Kevin," she said to his reflection. "Please."

Kevin stared at the rigid wall of her back a moment, looking pensive and indecisive, before he finally turned and strode from the room.

When he was gone, Bender ambled his way over to her, placing his hands gently on her shoulders. "You okay?" he asked softly.

Kerri nodded, the motion jerky.

Bender kneaded her shoulders, his thumbs massaging the base of her neck, saying nothing. Kerri stood rigid and tense beneath his hands for the space of a few heartbeats, then ducked away from him and lunged toward the door.

"I need some air," she said, her voice tight. She grabbed at the door, then, realizing it was locked, fumbled impatiently with the button on the knob until she managed to turn it. Throwing the door open, she marched out onto the deck, pausing when she reached its edge. Her eyes settled on the jungle gym sitting a few yards away. The image of Janet Johansen's loving face filled her mind so thoroughly, Kerri swore she could see the woman standing there, just as she had in the picture on the refrigerator door. Only this time, the woman's face turned woeful and her hand raised up toward Kerri, beseeching.

And just as quickly the image disappeared, leaving Kerri with a heavy cloak of sadness, its weight wrapping around her like a water-soaked blanket. A sense of loneliness and desolation penetrated down to her very soul, and in a last, desperate attempt to squelch her tears, she squeezed her eyes shut and pinched the bridge of her nose.

The gesture was futile. The tears pushed their way past her pathetic barriers, carrying with them emotions she'd kept locked up since Mandy's death. They flowed into her eyes and down her cheeks, burning a trail that quickly cooled in the evening breeze. They were surprisingly cleansing tears, and moments later she felt an odd sense of relief, as if by releasing them she had rid herself of some huge, hulking mass that pressed painfully against her soul.

She blinked hard, sending another roll of wetness down each side of her face, but clearing the blur from her vision. Seeing Jace's sandbox off to her right, she drifted toward it, staring down at the collection of miniature trucks and bulldozers scattered across its sandy landscape. A moment later, she knew Bender had followed her. She had neither seen nor heard him, but could sense him behind her. Though she was normally embarrassed for anyone to see her crying—to her it had always been an intensely private and personal thing—she felt oddly comforted by his presence and was grateful he was there.

"What's going to happen to Jace?" she asked in a low, quavery voice.

Bender didn't answer her right away, and Kerri thought he was probably unsure whether she was addressing him or just talking out loud to no one in particular.

"You've become quite attached to him, haven't you?" he said finally.

Kerri glanced over her shoulder and gave him a humorless smile. "Yeah, I guess I have. Broke one of the main rules of the profession, right?" She looked out toward the yard again, swiping at the tears on her cheeks with her palms.

"It's a well-meaning rule," Bender said, stepping up beside her. "But the truth of it is, we all break it at some time or another. How can you be human and not?"

"Do you really believe that?"

"I do."

He stood beside her, not touching, but close enough she could feel the heat radiating off his body like some force field. Kerri marveled at how comfortable she felt with him, a total stranger she had known for less than twenty-four hours. Somehow she knew if she made the first move and stepped closer, he would pull her into him, wrapping his arms around her. The thought was appealing, and for a brief moment she imagined just how warm and comforting those arms would feel.

But she wasn't ready for that. Not yet. Instead, she turned and made her way back into the kitchen. She walked over to the table and stared down at Thad's final words, so carefully drawn. Her mind tried to picture him sitting over the pathetic scrap of paper, his shoulders sagging beneath his hopelessness, his face haggard, pencil poised as he prepared to scratch out his final apology.

But the image wouldn't come. Something, some niggling thought, nagged at her mind. At first she thought it was her disbelief over the whole thing. She would have been willing to stake her professional reputation on the fact that Thad Johansen hadn't murdered his wife—or taken his own life—despite the fact the evidence seemed to indicate otherwise. Yet it was more than this simple paradox bothering her. Something about the note. She stared at it, trying to figure out what it was, but nothing came to her. She turned back toward the door, wanting to talk it all through some more with Bender. Thinking he was still outside on the deck, she was surprised to find him standing in the doorway. He was holding something in his hand, staring at it with a puzzled expression. Curious, Kerri moved closer. "What is it?" she asked.

Bender held the item out on his palm. It was a plant, or part of one, no more than an inch or two long. The stem was thick, green, and globular, its surface marked by a series of tiny bumps with coarse, white, woolly-looking bristles sprouting from them. Several barbed spikes sprung out from some of the bumps.

"It looks like some type of cactus," Kerri observed.

Bender nodded. "It is. Unless I miss my guess, it's a prickly pear."

Kerri stared at the plant, trying to understand its importance to Bender. Then she remembered all the greenery she'd seen in his office. "What did you do? Pluck it out of the yard?"

Bender shook his head. "No, I found it. Here," he said, pointing at the floor beside the door.

"So?" Kerri knew she sounded harsh, but she was beginning to feel inexplicably irritable. This was hardly the time for a lesson in horticulture. Couldn't the man indulge his hobby some other time?

"Kerri?"

She whirled around to see Kevin striding back into the kitchen. "We found Jace. You were right. He's at the baby-sitter's house. It's just around the corner."

"Thank God," Kerri said, squeezing her eyes closed with relief. Then she opened them again, staring at Kevin with a horrified expression. "Does he know?"

Kevin shook his head.

"I want to be the one to tell him," she said, squaring her shoulders. "Will you take me to him?"

Kevin nodded, though the expression on his face made it clear he doubted the wisdom of the idea.

"And," Kerri added quickly, "I want to take him home with me tonight. None of that foster care crap. Please make the necessary arrangements."

Kevin's eyebrows shot up and he opened his mouth to protest.

"I don't want to argue about this, Kevin. Please."

Kevin snapped his mouth closed, his face a mass of thunderclouds. He glared at Kerri a moment, then spun on his heel and marched into the living room. Kerri heard him ask—no, demand a cigarette from one of his cronies.

Kerri turned around to find Bender watching her with a narrow-eyed scrutiny. He wrapped the tiny piece of plant in a handkerchief and stuffed it in his pocket before he spoke to her. "Are you sure you want to do this?" he asked her. "Emotionally involved is one thing, but this . . ." He gave her a little shrug.

Kerri considered the question a moment, weighing what she was about to do. She thought about Janet Johansen's love for her son, and about her own love for Mandy. She thought about Jace—the way his hair stuck up with a life of its own, the way he'd looked at her with fear in those huge blue eyes, the way those stubby little fingers could wear out a shirt hem or master a shoelace. She remembered how he'd felt with his arms around her neck, his body shuddering with the strength of his sobs—a tiny, frightened, and vulnerable little boy, who by a cruel twist of fate was now all alone in the world. And she remembered her own desire—or perhaps it was more of a need?—to make a difference.

"I'm sure," she said, swallowing down her resolve.

Bender nodded slowly, his eyes scanning her face for any sign of doubt. "If it will help, I'd be happy to go with you," he said.

Kerri gave him a grateful smile. "I'd like that," she said.

Bender reached up and wiped a lingering trail of tears from her cheek with his thumb. "Okay." He braced himself with a deep breath. "I'm ready when you are."

"Let's do it," she said. And with little enthusiasm, she turned and headed out of the kitchen.

Kevin was busy talking on the phone, and Bender excused himself to head upstairs and use the bathroom. While Kerri waited in the living room, she once more felt herself drawn to the den. She walked over and stood in the doorway, steeling herself for another glimpse inside.

Several men crowded around Thad's body, blocking him from her view. *Just as well,* Kerri thought. Her eyes wandered over the rest of the room, her mind trying to imagine what life was like in the Johansen household before tragedy struck. Just inside the door, butted up against the wall, was Thad's desk. She walked over to it, staring at the large drawing pad that lay on top, a series of floor plans sketched out on the page. A ruler and compass lay beside the pad; a wooden pencil, its surface marred by teeth marks, lay atop it. A soup-sized can, decorated with colored paper cutouts of dinosaurs and with the word DAD scrawled on it in red crayon, stood at one corner of the desk, filled with mechanical pencils. On the wall above the desk hung a piece of paper with a crude pencil drawing of a house surrounded by trees and water. Beneath the house, in Jace's childish scrawl, were the words, HAPPY FATHER'S DAY.

The sight of it made Kerri's heart squeeze with anguish. Sadly, and once again fighting back her tears, she reached over to pick up the can of pencils.

"Please don't touch that, ma'am," a male voice said behind her. Kerri looked up to find a uniformed police officer standing beside her. "We still have to dust this area for prints," the officer explained. "That's where we found the suicide note."

Kerri withdrew her hand, tucking it and the other beneath her arms. "Sorry," she said to the officer. She stared down at the desk, trying to imagine Thad Johansen sitting there, so overcome with despair that death seemed to be the only option left. She wondered if he had looked at the pencil can or the drawing on the wall and thought about Jace in those final moments.

Hard as she tried, she couldn't make sense of any of it. The whole thing was wrong. Terribly wrong. How could Thad have done this to Jace? How could he desert his son this way? A surge of anger toward the dead man washed over her, and some clinical part of her brain knew she was being unfair and a bit irrational. But the emotional part of her was overwhelmed—devastated and hurt. With a final, agonizing glance toward the crowd surrounding Thad's body, Kerri turned and fled the room.

SEVENTEEN

❧❖❧

Kerri could tell by the scowl on Kevin's face that he wasn't pleased with Bender's presence. She suspected he wanted some time alone with her to talk things out, and was, therefore, grateful for Bender's inhibiting presence. Kevin could be very persuasive at times, and she feared he might yet be able to sway her from her resolve. If Bender was aware of Kevin's animosity, he didn't show it.

In order to avoid the attention of the growing crowd outside, which had expanded to include two news vans and their accompanying crews, Kevin drove them completely out of the neighborhood. When he was sure no one had followed them, he turned the car around and drove back slowly, pulling up in the street outside the baby-sitter's house.

Kerri climbed out of the car with mixed emotions. She felt Jace needed her and was determined to stand by the child. No doubt he had sensed by now that something was wrong and the tension alone could trigger an emotional overload. Her desire to forestall that very possibility urged her on.

Yet, she felt wretched about the task before her, knowing the news she would utter from her lips could make or break Jace's already fragile mental health. Her mind whirred crazily, rehearsing the scene, trying to anticipate the boy's reaction as well as her own. She knew she would have to weigh every word, every nuance very carefully.

Bender stuck close at her heels, his hand even cupping her elbow and giving a little squeeze for moral support as they stood on the porch and waited for the baby-sitter to answer their knock. Kevin, perhaps sensing his presence would only complicate things, opted to wait in the car.

The baby-sitter, Carol Bohannon, was a cherub-faced woman with rosy cheeks, a slightly rotund build, and a mass of curly dark hair doing its best to escape the bun at her neck. It was obvious from the blotches on her face and the hang-dog, red-rimmed look of her eyes that she was shocked and upset by the news of Thad Johansen's demise. From the look of her, she'd been crying buckets.

"Mrs. Bohannon," Kerri said. "I'm Dr. Whitaker and this is Dr. Bender. I'm a psychiatrist, and I've been counseling Jace and his father. I'd like to see Jace."

"I know who you are," Carol Bohannon said, her voice shaky. "Thad told me about you. Said he thought you would be able to do wonders with Jace—have already, in fact." She stepped aside and swept her hand in front of her. "Please come in," she said.

Kerri stepped into a small foyer. A coat closet was to her right, the stairs to the upper level on her left. Bender squeezed in behind her, closing the door to the chilly outside air. The house felt invitingly warm, and the scents of butter, cinnamon, and vanilla wafted through the air, making Kerri's stomach growl. Despite the homey atmosphere, Carol Bohannon made no attempt to invite them into the rest of the house. Instead, she gave a furtive glance toward the stairs before leaning toward Kerri and speaking in a low, whispery voice.

"Jace is upstairs with the girls," she said, her eyes looking lost and frightened. "He knows something is up. I'm afraid it didn't take much in the way of perceptive skills for him to figure out I'm pretty upset. My daughters don't know either, though they can tell something is wrong. I wanted to wait for Karl to come home before I told them anything."

"When is your husband expected?" Kerri asked her.

Carol Bohannon glanced at her watch, prompting Kerri to do the same. It was almost six thirty. "He should be back any time now," she said. "He went out to check on a building site. He's a contractor, you know. In fact, that's how we met the Johansens. Karl and Thad have worked on some projects together, including their current one." She glanced up at Kerri, wringing her hands and nibbling on her lower lip. "I thought that's what Thad was doing today. I thought that was why he brought Jace by, so he could get some work done. If I'd only known." Her voice cracked at the end, and her shoulders slumped, as if the weight of her guilt was simply too much to bear.

Bender reached over and laid a hand on her shoulder. "It's not your fault," he said gently, giving her shoulder a squeeze.

Carol Bohannon looked up at him with tear-filled eyes.

"How old are your daughters?" Bender asked. Carol Bohannon glanced up the stairs, then took in a deep, shuddering breath.

"Sherri—the oldest one—is fourteen. Nicki is

thirteen. They're both good kids, and bright, too." A smile flickered across her lips, then her face turned somber again. She leaned even closer and dropped her voice to a conspiratorial whisper. "One of their classmates—a fourteen-year-old boy—committed suicide a little over a month ago. It upset them pretty badly. I'm worried about how they're going to take this. They're at a vulnerable age." Her eyes shifted from Kerri to Bender and back again. "I . . . well, I thought maybe I should tell the girls Thad died some other way." She gave a pathetic little shrug. "You know, I've read how kids their age can get fixated on the whole idea of suicide."

"It's true teenagers are a particularly vulnerable group when it comes to suicide," Bender said. "But I would advise against lying to your daughters about what happened. There is bound to be gossip, and there are even a few news crews parked outside the Johansens' house as we speak. Your daughters will discover the truth eventually. You don't want them thinking you lied to them. That will only arouse their curiosity even more. The best thing you can do is discuss what has happened openly and honestly."

Carol pondered his advice a moment, then shot a glance at Kerri, who nodded her agreement.

Carol's shoulders sagged. "But what *has* happened?" she asked, her eyes wide. "Why did Thad do this? Did he kill Janet?"

"No," Kerri answered, a little too quickly. "At least I don't believe he did. But the investigation is still going on."

Carol raised her eyes toward the ceiling. "That poor kid," she said, shaking her head. "What's going to happen to him?" She looked back at Kerri. "Where is he going to go? I know there isn't any family around."

"For now, he's going to stay with me," Kerri said. "Then, of course, the family court will decide where he goes."

"Well, I'm glad you're going to be there for him," Carol said. "At least for now. I'm sure he's going to be devastated by all this." Suddenly, her eyes grew wide with fear. "Are you going to tell him what happened? Here, I mean?" she asked, glancing toward the upstairs landing.

"I'm not sure," Kerri said. "I need to see him first."

Carol nodded, raked her teeth over her lip once for good measure, then let out a dispirited sigh. "Well then," she said. "I guess I best go get him." She wiped her hands on her skirt as if they were covered with something gross and slimy and, with a fretful little smile, headed up the stairs. A moment later, she reappeared with Jace in tow.

One look at Jace's face and Kerri knew she was right to be worried. As soon as he saw her waiting at the bottom of the stairs, his eyes grew wide, his face lost all its color, and he began to rock back and forth where he stood on the landing. Kerri had a flash of déjà vu; this was almost identical to the scene from yesterday morning at the Johansen house: Jace at the top of the stairs, Kerri waiting below. That time, Jace had learned of his mother's death. No doubt the similarities had struck him as well, and he was now anticipating more bad news. Kerri gave herself a mental kick for failing to anticipate this.

Carol Bohannon took Jace's hand and led him down the stairs. The boy's eyes stayed fixed on Kerri's face throughout his descent, and Kerri struggled to keep her expression impassive.

"Hi," she said, when he was almost at the bottom. "Hope you don't mind me picking you up."

He stared at her, his blue eyes round and fearful. His breathing was rapid and shallow, his chest heaving with each breath like a panting dog. He stood on the bottom stair, shifting back and forth from one foot to the other, his free hand wringing the life out of his shirt.

Kerri reached out and gently tugged his hand away from the shirt. She forced herself to meet his gaze, feeling it was important to establish and maintain a connection. "Ready to go?" she asked, trying to keep her own hands from shaking.

Jace glanced over at Bender, then back at Kerri. "Are you taking me home?" he asked, his voice sounding tinny and small.

Kerri swallowed hard. "No, Jace. Not just now. I need to talk to you first."

"Where's Daddy?" His eyes darted back and forth between Kerri and Bender, his breathing growing more rapid with each passing second. His rocking motion picked up both speed and momentum.

"Your daddy's at home," Kerri said, inwardly grimacing at this stretching of the truth.

Jace digested this, his eyes still bouncing back and forth between Kerri and Bender. Suddenly he focused in on Bender. For a brief second, his rocking stopped. "Who are you?" he asked.

Bender squatted down so he was almost at eye level with Jace. "My name is Mike," he said. "I'm a friend of Dr. Whitaker's."

"Do you know my daddy?" The rocking started again, and Kerri felt his hand start to pull away from hers. She tightened her grip some—more of a gentle squeeze than anything. In response, Jace pulled his other hand free from Carol's and used it to twist and wring his hem.

Bender reached out and tousled Jace's hair. "No, I don't know your daddy," he said. "But I feel like I know you, from all the things Dr. Whitaker has told me about you."

Jace glanced at Kerri, then back at Bender. "I want to see my daddy," he said, the pitch of his voice rising to a whine. "Can you take me to my daddy?"

Kerri's heart gave a painful squeeze and she struggled hard to keep from crying. She knelt beside Bender. "Jace?" she said softly.

From the corner of her eye, Kerri saw Carol Bohannon clasp a hand over her mouth and back herself against the wall.

Jace looked away from Bender, but his eyes stared off into the space between him and Kerri. His face took on a glazed expression. His tongue pushed against first one cheek, then the other. Kerri reached up, gently gripped his chin, and turned his face toward her. "Jace? Look at me."

Jace allowed her to move his head, but his eyes remained unfocused.

"Jace? Look at me." A little sterner this time.

Jace finally responded, his eyes shifting toward Kerri's. But the tongue kept patrolling the inside of his mouth, his breathing remained machine-gun rapid, and the endless rocking motion continued.

Kerri thought quickly and made her decision.

"Jace, something has happened to your father. There's been an accident."

Jace froze, the sudden cessation of all that movement startling Kerri so much she rocked back on her feet and nearly lost her balance. From beside her, Kerri heard Carol Bohannon utter a muffled-sounding whimper.

Kerri plunged onward. "I'm so sorry about this,

Jace. Your daddy is gone. He died. He's gone up to heaven to be with your mommy."

Kerri anticipated any number of reactions: an emotional outburst, a scream of denial, calm questioning, even quiet sobs. What she didn't anticipate was the reaction she got. Jace's eyes rolled up in his head, his rocking started again with a ferocity that did make Kerri lose her balance and fall backward toward the floor. Then Jace's face went suddenly and totally slack, his body quickly following as he descended toward the floor. Carol Bohannon let out a small yelp; Kerri struggled to get back on her feet. Bender, who was closest to the boy, grabbed Jace and eased him onto the floor.

Kerri crawled over to Jace, panic and tears both rushing up her throat. One hand pushed back his hair, while the other one reached for his neck, feeling for a pulse. To her relief, she found one, but it was faint and racing. For a second she thought he'd stopped breathing, but then his chest rose and fell with the same shallow, rapid respirations he'd had just moments before.

"Jace! Can you hear me? Jace?" Kerri struggled to maintain her composure. Her mind raced through the steps necessary to assess the boy, but her hands seemed paralyzed.

Bender reached over and peeled Jace's upper eyelids back. Then his hands slid over the boy's arms and legs. "I think he's catatonic," he said. He looked at Kerri, his eyes full of concern and urgency. "I think we ought to take him to a hospital. Now."

At that moment, a young, female voice drifted down from the top of the stairs. "Mom? Is everything all right?"

Kerri looked up and saw a young, dark-haired girl, her eyes wide with concern as she stared at Jace's prostrate form on the floor. Carol Bohannon's head whipped around and settled on her daughter with a look of pure horror. But the expression faded quickly, to be replaced by a semblance of composure and authority. Kerri was impressed by the woman's control, even more so when she heard Carol Bohannon speak in a voice that was urgent, but calm.

"Jace is sick, Sherri. But these folks are doctors and they're going to take care of him. Now go back to your room and wait there with your sister. I'll be right up."

The girl frowned and opened her mouth to say something more. But a stern look from her mother seemed to change her mind. With a little puff of exasperation, she did as she was told. Carol turned and gave Kerri a pleading look.

"Go on," Kerri said with a nudge of her head toward the stairs.

Carol Bohannon cast one more concerned glance at Jace. "Will you let me know how he's doing?" she asked.

"Of course," Kerri said. "Right now, we need to get him some medical attention. You've done everything you can for him. Now your daughters need you."

"Thank you," Carol said, a look of gratitude on her face. With that, she turned and fled up the stairs.

Kerri looked down at Jace, then at Bender, her eyes laced with guilt. "I shouldn't have told him," she said.

"Don't beat yourself up over this," Bender said. "He was likely to have this reaction no matter how or when you told him. The kid's been through enough to do damage to the best of psyches. Let's get him to a hospital."

Bender reached over and scooped Jace into his arms. "Can you catch the door?"

Kerri held the door as Bender maneuvered past her, then closed it and rushed ahead to open the car's door as well. Scrambling into the back seat, she scooted over to the far side and helped Bender lay Jace inside, his head nestled in her lap. Once he had Jace situated, Bender closed the door and climbed into the front seat next to a startled-looking Kevin.

"Take us to King County," Kerri instructed. "And hurry."

Kevin, bless him, asked no questions. He started the car, leaned over, opened the glove box in front of Bender and grabbed a blue bubble light. Flipping it on, he reached up and stuck it on the roof. Slipping the car into gear, he whipped around in a U-turn and headed for the hospital.

EIGHTEEN

❖

It was a Saturday night and a full moon, so the emergency room at the hospital was hopping. Though she'd been here on occasion to see patients who were referred to her, the only staff person Kerri recognized tonight was one of the physicians—Jim Kraus. Jim and Nathan had done their surgical rotations together in med school, and remained friends even when they went their separate ways with differing residencies. Jim was one of the few people she and Nathan shared in common who hadn't felt it necessary to choose sides during the divorce. To this day, he remained friendly with both of them. So when he saw Kerri come through the doors generally reserved for the ambulance crews, he hurried over to greet her.

"Kerri! Good to see you." He grabbed her hands and gave them a quick, welcoming squeeze. Glancing over at Bender, Jim rapidly discerned he and the apparently unconscious child in his arms were with Kerri. He dropped Kerri's hands and approached the child, doing a quick, visual assessment. "What happened?" he asked.

"He's catatonic," Kerri explained, breathless and shaky from the adrenaline speeding through her veins. "He just lost both his parents. Yesterday he found out his mother is dead, and today his father committed sui-cide. When I told him, he slipped into this catatonic state. He's totally unresponsive." The worry in her voice was apparent, and Jim Kraus gave her a concerned once-over before turning back to Jace.

"Bring him back here," he said after a cursory exam. Kerri and Bender followed him past the many full cubicles—tonight's injured and dying—to one of the few private exam rooms.

Bender carried Jace into the room and gently laid him on the examining table. The boy's limbs flopped lifelessly and Kerri felt the trip-hammer beat of her heart step up a notch.

"Who's the family doctor? Do you know?" Jim asked.

"Dr. Mitchell, I believe," Kerri said, trying to picture the intake sheet on the Johansens' chart in her office. Positioning herself at Jace's head, she smoothed his hair back from his forehead. "He has a history of ADD with some recent episodes of withdrawal—ever since his mother's disappearance several days ago."

Jim grabbed an ophthalmoscope and examined both of Jace's eyes. Then he switched adapters on the instrument and checked out ears, nose, and mouth. Finally, he used his stethoscope to listen to the boy's chest, assessing his heart and lungs.

"Any other physical problems?" he asked, grabbing a reflex hammer from a nearby counter and tapping it on first Jace's arms, then his knees. He pulled off the boy's shoes and socks and ran the handle of the hammer up the bottom of each foot, then he reached up and rubbed his knuckles over Jace's sternum, a frown creasing his face.

"Not that I'm aware of," Kerri said, chewing her

lip. "But Mitchell could probably tell you better than I can. I haven't known him that long."

A nurse scurried into the room and glanced at Jim. "You get vitals?" she asked him.

Jim shook his head and the nurse proceeded to get a blood pressure cuff from a drawer and wrap it around Jace's arm.

"There are no signs of any neuro deficits," Jim said, pulling at his chin. "I'll call Mitchell to come in and take a look at him."

"Pressure is ninety over sixty," the nurse called out. She scribbled the numbers on the sheet covering the stretcher, then listened to Jace's heart with her stethoscope. "Pulse one-fifty and regular. Respirations forty and shallow."

"Let's put him on some oxygen," Jim said. "Two liters with a face mask. And let's get a chem panel, a CBC, and check his gases."

The nurse nodded, then moved toward the oxygen outlet on the wall, turning a knob until the faint hiss of escaping gas could be heard. She opened another drawer and removed some tubing and a small pediatric-sized face mask. After connecting the tubing to the wall outlet, she slipped the mask over Jace's face, securing the elastic strap behind his head.

"He seems stable," Jim said, pulling his stethoscope from around his neck and draping it over his shoulders. "But you're right. He's totally unresponsive to pain. Curious." His brow furrowed in thought. He looked up at Bender. "Are you family?"

"No," Kerri said quickly. "This is Dr. Mike Bender. He's a psychiatrist from Bellingham. I've been consulting with him on Jace's case." She gazed down at the boy's face, most of it hidden beneath the plastic green of the oxygen mask. "Jace has no family," she added miserably. "Just a grandmother who's in a nursing home somewhere."

Jim eyed Bender a moment, one eyebrow arched inquisitively. Then he extended a hand, which Bender shook. "Nice to meet you," he said.

"Likewise," Bender returned with professional politeness.

Jim turned his attention to the nurse. "Amy, better get a social service consult, too. The kid will need to have a guardian appointed."

The nurse nodded, scribbling out his directions on a paper towel.

"I want to be his guardian," Kerri piped up.

All three faces turned to stare at her. Had she been able, she would have stared at herself. For a long moment, no one stirred. Then Jim gave a casual shrug, and the gesture seemed to set the nurse in motion. She scurried from the room, paper towel in hand. "I'll call Mitchell," Jim said. "As luck would have it, he's on call for their group. In fact, I think he's here in the hospital. You going to stay with him?" he asked, looking at Kerri.

She nodded.

"Okay. I'll be outside here if you need anything."

"Thanks, Jim."

"No problem," he said over his shoulder as he walked out of the room, leaving Kerri and Bender alone with only the hissing of the oxygen to mar the silence. Bender walked over and placed a hand on Kerri's shoulder, giving it a little squeeze.

"You're not still blaming yourself for this, are you?" he asked.

Kerri looked up at him and started to answer, but stopped when the door to the room opened. Kevin strode in, glanced at Jace lying on the exam table, and then at Kerri. All the blood drained from his face.

"I'm sorry, lass," he said.

Kerri merely nodded. Seeing the devastation on Kevin's face caused the lump in her throat to double in size, making it impossible for her to speak.

"What's wrong with him?" Kevin asked, eyeing Jace's inert form fearfully.

When Kerri didn't answer, Bender piped up, his hand slipping away from Kerri's shoulder. "So far, there's nothing physically obvious," he explained. "I suspect he's catatonic. Something we call a conversion reaction. It's a physical response to a psychological overload, somewhat uncommon, but certainly not unheard of. The fact that the boy has a history of attention deficit disorder makes him even more vulnerable. It's not unlike autism, though at the moment, he's in an acute phase of the syndrome."

"Will he be all right?" Kevin asked.

Bender shrugged. "Physically? More than likely. But it's too soon to tell what's going to happen with his mental status."

Kevin stared at the boy, misery stamped on his face. He shifted his gaze to Kerri. She avoided looking at him, her eyes fixed on Jace's head, her hand petting Jace's hair. Kevin moved toward her, settling one hand on her shoulder. He bent down and spoke at a near whisper in her ear.

"You thinking of Mandy, lass?" he asked gently.

Kerri nodded, and the tears she'd been struggling to keep in abeyance flowed freely. They coursed down her face, dripping onto the sheet above Jace's head.

Kevin frowned. "Why don't you go home and get some rest?"

Kerri shook her head vehemently. "No," she managed. "I'm not leaving him."

Kevin sighed, his frown deepening. He glanced around the room helplessly a moment, then his eyes settled on Bender, drawing down to a steely glint.

Bender met his gaze head-on, refusing to yield.

Finally, Kevin looked away, the frustration he felt clear in the clenched set of his jaw. "Suit yourself," he said with some irritation. "If you need me, you know where to find me." With that he spun on his heel and left, slamming the door in his wake.

"I don't think he likes me much," Bender said.

Kerri looked up at him, her face stained with tears. "He means well," she said, plowing her fingers through her hair. "He's used to watching after me. I've known him since I was a little girl. My father was with the Seattle police. He and Kevin used to be partners."

Bender nodded slowly. "That explains a lot."

The door to the exam room opened again and Kerri breathed a sigh of relief when she saw Dr. Mitchell's friendly, wizened face.

"Kerri," he acknowledged with a little nod. He quickly perused the clipboard he carried in his hands, then set it on the counter beside him. After a quick glance at Jace, the man shifted his gaze to Bender, his eyebrows arched questioningly.

Bender took the initiative and stepped forward, his hand extended. "Mike Bender," he said. "I'm a psychiatrist. I've been helping Kerri with Jace's case."

"I see," Mitchell said, shaking Bender's hand. "I'm Brian Mitchell, the boy's physician." Mitchell released Bender's hand and shifted his attention back to Kerri. "I just heard about what happened to Thad Johansen," he said, shaking his head sadly. "Terrible, terrible tragedy." He walked over to Jace and, after a rather perfunctory exam, stepped back, arms crossed over his chest.

"We need to admit him," he said. "Run some tests. But I suspect he's having a hysterical reaction to the death of his parents." He glanced up at Kerri, then at Bender. "Do you two concur?"

Bender nodded. Kerri didn't answer.

"I hear you want to be appointed as his guardian," Mitchell said, eyeing Kerri closely. "Do you think that's wise?"

This time, Kerri did acknowledge him. Her head shot up; her eyes flared. "What is it with all of you? Just because I lost my own daughter, doesn't mean I'm not capable of handling another child," she snapped.

Mitchell threw his hands up in surrender. "I didn't mean to imply you weren't capable," he objected. "I just thought . . ."

"I'm quite capable of handling this, Brian. And I intend to."

"Fine, Kerri. I'll get things rolling." He reached into his shirt pocket, pulled out a pen, twisted it to make the point extrude, and started to write a note on Jace's chart.

Kerri stared transfixed at the pen, her mind whirling. "That's it," she muttered a moment later. Her eyes shot toward Bender. "Oh, my God! That's it! I knew there was something wrong." She shoved back the stool she was sitting on and stood.

"What are you talking about?" Bender asked, eyeing her curiously.

Kerri opened her mouth to explain, but paused, shaking her head and grabbing at the edge of the stretcher.

Bender stared at her. "Kerri? What is it? Are you okay?"

Kerri gazed up at him, her eyes sleepy looking. "I don't know," she said, blinking hard. "I feel a little funny." She placed her palm against her forehead, held it there a moment, then pushed her hair back off her forehead. She exhaled slowly through pursed lips. Then her eyes grew wide and she reached out toward Bender.

"Uh-oh," she said.

Bender made a grab for her, but was a split second too late. With a tiny exhalation of air, Kerri collapsed to the floor.

Kerri opened her eyes and blinked, trying to clear away the haze. Though she was aware of lying on her back, she knew little else about where she was or how she had come to be there. A muted light shone from somewhere behind her head, casting miniature shadows along the hundreds of tiny holes peppering the ceiling tiles above. Myriad pains gradually made themselves known: an ache in her right elbow, a throbbing across the back of her head, a soreness in her right hip, a stiffness in her neck. Closing her eyes, she carefully tested her joints one at a time, raising first one leg, then the other, finally moving on to her arms. When she went to raise the left one, she was surprised by how cold it felt, and then something tugged painfully along the back of her hand. She opened her eyes and blinked hard to bring the hand into focus. A clear plastic tube snaked its way along her arm, disappearing beneath a bandage covering the back of her hand. Her eyes followed the tubing up toward the head of the bed, where she saw a plastic bag hanging from a pole. An IV. *Why do I have an IV?* she wondered. She struggled to remember, but her mind was a darkened void. Frustrated, she dropped her arm heavily onto the bed and squeezed her eyes closed.

For several moments she concentrated, trying to recall what had happened, but to no avail. Curious, she rolled her head to the left and slowly reopened her eyes, risking another look around. There was a large window about ten feet away, its curtains drawn fully open. Outside, she could see mountaintops in the distance, their peaks dressed with pink light and purple shadow, and she instantly recognized the view as that of the Olympics being touched by the first light of morning. She glanced at her watch— still on her right arm—and saw it was nearly seven. Idly, she thought how nice it was the day would be a clear one. Then she remembered she had no idea where she was. With a tiny moan, she forced herself into a sitting position.

She recognized the room immediately: one of the patient rooms at King Medical Center. And she was in a patient bed. With a quick, puzzled glance down at her chest, she was dismayed to find she was wearing one of those ugly blue-and-white patient gowns. Her mind racing, she stared in wonderment at the gown until a faint rumbling sound reached her ears from somewhere off to her right. Turning her head, her eyes settled on a sleeping male figure slumped sideways in a chair beside the bed. Brown hair stood up in spikes on his head, his stubble-covered chin and cheek were propped against the palm of his hand. A soft snore accompanied each breath, gently vibrating a pair of full lips.

Bender.

She recognized him immediately, and as if that minor mental exercise had stimulated her tired brain, other memories came flooding back—Jace, his father, the ER, Dr. Mitchell ... but beyond that, there was nothing.

Frowning, she sighed heavily and rolled her head on her shoulders. Bender's head snapped up suddenly, his eyes blinking almost spastically as he tried to focus in on her.

"Hey," he said in a voice laced with sleepiness. "Welcome back." He stretched, then pushed himself out of the chair. Bracing himself with his hands on the side rail of her bed, he studied her face closely. "How do you feel?"

"Dopey," Kerri said. The words came out in a parched croak, and she gave a little cough to try to clear her throat.

Bender reached over and poured a glass of water from a pitcher sitting on the stand beside her bed. "Here," he said, handing it to her.

Kerri took the glass and drank greedily. The water was deliciously cold and soothing as it flowed down her throat. After she had drained its contents, she handed the empty glass back to Bender.

"More?" he asked.

Kerri shook her head, and he set the glass back on the stand.

"Why am I here?" she asked him, gazing around the room in confusion.

"Don't you remember anything?"

"I remember Jace, and the ER, but after that ... nothing."

"Well," Bender explained, "you fainted dead away in the ER."

"I fainted?" The astonishment was evident in both her face and her voice.

Bender nodded. "When was the last time you ate anything?"

Kerri's brow drew down in thought as she tried to remember. "I'm not sure," she said slowly. "I had a headache this morning . . . or I guess that was yesterday morning," she added with a pointed look toward the window. "So I didn't eat anything. And then I went to meet you for dinner."

"And we obviously didn't get around to that."

"I guess the last thing I ate was those cookies you had at your session," Kerri surmised.

Bender scowled at her. "No wonder," he said. "You need to take better care of yourself. You were hypoglycemic. Your blood sugar was only forty-five."

"Oh," Kerri said, staring down at the bedspread. "I guess that explains the IV." She looked up at Bender. "Where is Jace?"

"He was admitted down on Peds. I checked on him an hour or so ago. He's still unchanged. Stable, but unresponsive."

"Damn," Kerri said, punching the mattress beside her.

Bender reached over and placed his hand over her fist. "Hey," he said, leaning down to look her in the eye. "This is not your fault."

"How can you say that? I obviously miscalculated his ability to deal with all of this. If I hadn't told him about his father . . ."

"If you hadn't, someone else would have. He had to know sooner or later. Besides, he already knew something was wrong."

Kerri shook her head. "I don't know," she said

sullenly. "I think it would have been better if I'd waited. Maybe he would have—"

She was interrupted when the door to her room banged open and a blur wearing a lab coat flew into the room. The blur stopped at the foot of her bed and stared at her a moment, then cast a decidedly unfriendly eye toward Bender. "Who the hell are you?"

Kerri once more beat Bender to the punch, her voice weary and strained. "Mike Bender, meet Dr. Nathan Palmer, my ex-husband."

NINETEEN

~~❖~~

Kerri thought Bender handled Nathan's confrontational greeting well. He stuck a hand out and introduced himself. "Dr. Mike Bender. I'm a psychiatrist with a practice up in Bellingham. I've been working with Kerri on a case."

Kerri grimaced when she heard Bender use her given name, as opposed to calling her Dr. Whitaker. She knew Nathan hadn't missed the innuendo either when he glanced at Bender's proffered hand as if it were something repulsive. Bender let his hand hang in the air for a long awkward moment before he finally withdrew it, stuffing it into his pocket.

"What does this case have to do with my wife's illness?" Nathan challenged, his blue eyes sparking.

"I was with her when she collapsed," Bender explained, a touch of impatience filtering into his tone. "I just wanted to make sure she was all right."

"Well, that's my job," Nathan said nastily. "You can feel free to leave."

Kerri gave Nathan a pleading glance. "Please," she said. "Let's not . . ."

Nathan dismissed her objection with a wave of his hand. "I'm here now," he said, his eyes still glued to Bender. "There is no need for you to stay."

Bender stared back at him, looking as if he were prepared to do battle, then apparently thought better of it. He looked over at Kerri.

"It's all right. I've got something I want to take care of anyway. I'll check back with you later." With that, he spun on his heel and left the room.

Kerri fixed a menacing look on Nathan. "What the hell is wrong with you?" she hissed. "You have no right to come charging in here like that and treat a friend of mine so rudely."

"A friend?" Nathan scoffed. "Is that what he is? The nurse out there told me he hasn't left your bedside all night. Sounds like more than a friend to me."

Kerri's face relaxed, not because her anger at Nathan had abated any, but because the thought of Bender standing vigil struck a soft spot in her heart.

Misinterpreting the change in her expression, Nathan's demeanor immediately mellowed as well. "Look," he said, practicing his little-boy-lost look on her. "I'm sorry if I upset you. It's just that I was worried sick. They said you passed out in the ER. I looked at your chart. Christ, Kerri, your glucose had dropped to forty-five."

Kerri felt a surge of anger rocket through her at the thought of Nathan looking through her chart, but she checked it and tried to keep her expression complacent. She was too tired and too worried about Jace to get into another argument with Nathan.

Nathan walked around and hiked one hip up on the bed beside her. His hand reached up and brushed a lock of hair from her forehead; his eyes roved over her face.

"You know I still care about you, Kerri," he said softly.

For one brief moment, Nathan's touch, the gentle timbre of his voice, and the concern in his eyes triggered an almost painful twinge of nostalgia in Kerri, a yearning for the way things had been so very long ago.

"I know I screwed things up between us," Nathan continued. "But I am begging you for one more chance. Can't you find it in your heart to forgive me?"

Had he not made reference to his past sins, Kerri might have succumbed. But his words brought to mind the image of him and that nurse in bed together. Turning away from him, Kerri reached for the call bell. With an almost savage gesture, she punched the button that would summon a nurse.

"I want to go home," she said.

Nathan sighed and stood up. "That should be no problem," he said, his voice betraying the frustration he felt. "The IV fluids have perked you right up. But you need to take it easy for a while. And take better care of yourself."

"I will, Nathan. I promise," she added, her tone softening some as she realized Nathan's influence might just expedite her discharge. She wished she could simply snap her fingers and be home, avoiding the long ride on the ferry. That led her to thoughts of Bender and his plane. And then she remembered her car.

She turned back to Nathan. "I don't have my car," she told him. Wanting to avoid any further provocation, she quickly added, "It's in the shop and Kevin drove me over here. Do you think you could give me a ride back to the house?"

"Why don't you come and stay with me?" Nathan offered, his voice rising in concert with his hopes. "That way I can be sure you're properly cared for."

Kerri shook her head. "No, I can't. I need to get home and feed Shadow," she explained, thankful to the cat for providing a reasonable excuse.

"I'll go by and feed him," Nathan offered. "Or better yet, I'll bring him to my house."

Again, Kerri shook her head. "You know he doesn't like you," she reminded him. "Please, just take me home."

Nathan stared at her, debating her request. "All right," he said, his voice heavy with resignation. "Let me go make the arrangements."

He leaned over and kissed her on the forehead, then stood up. For a moment, he just stood there, staring down at her. "I love you, Kerri," he said finally, his voice catching slightly.

Kerri felt her heart lurch painfully. She knew he wanted her to make a similar claim, but she couldn't. Instead she said, "I still care for you, Nathan. But right now, things are too muddled in my head to say any more than that."

Nathan seemed satisfied, even brightened by her answer. "It will be okay. You'll see. It's not too late. I know we can work things out." And with that, he turned and left the room.

Even with the advantage of Nathan's influence, Kerri's discharge wasn't finalized until almost noon. When her breakfast arrived—dried scrambled eggs and limp toast—she found she was ravenous and scarfed up every bite. She considered asking for seconds, but her stomach churned and gurgled to digest what she already had, so she decided it might be more prudent to wait and go at it a little more slowly. A nurse came in and removed her IV, and Kerri took advantage of her freedom to take a long, hot shower.

The spray revived her, washing away the lingering effects of the night before.

Kevin popped in around ten, managing to look both sheepish and angry at the same time. "I just heard what happened, lass. Why didn't ya call me, dammit?"

Though Kerri knew he meant well, his tirade only irritated her. She was less than cordial to him, not so much because he angered her but because she wanted him to leave before he and Nathan ran into each other and started comparing notes again. She finally convinced him to go by pleading exhaustion. For once, she wasn't lying. Despite the boost she got from breakfast and the shower, she did feel drained and exhausted. And a small part of her was still angry with Kevin, feeling his dogged pursuit of Thad Johansen had somehow contributed to the man's suicide.

As she watched Kevin trudge his way out the door—a tad angry himself—the thought of Thad's suicide spurred something in her mind, something she needed to remember. She rubbed her temples with her fingers, as if she could massage the memory loose. But it eluded her, and she gave up, frustrated.

By the time Nathan came to take her home, she was actually cheered to see him. She was embarrassed over this whole fainting episode and anxious to escape the wary stares of the hospital staff.

"You ready to go?" Nathan asked.

"Very," Kerri said. "I like this place much better when I'm on the other side of the bed."

"Let's do it then." Nathan draped an arm over her shoulders and steered her into the hallway.

At the elevator, Kerri said, "I need to make a stop on Peds before we go. I want to check on a patient of mine, the one who was admitted last night."

"The Johansen kid," Nathan said.

Kerri looked up at him, puzzled. "Yes, how did you know?"

Nathan shrugged. "Brian Mitchell filled me in on what happened," he explained. "Don't you think your involvement with this kid is going a bit overboard?"

"How can you say that, Nathan? He just lost both his parents. He has no one to turn to right now. He needs me."

"Counseling him is one thing. Mitchell told me you want to be appointed as his guardian. Isn't that a bit much?" He saw the fiery glint in Kerri's eyes and raised a hand to forestall her objection. "All I'm saying is I don't want you to overdo it here. You need to go home and get some rest."

"I'm fine, Nathan," Kerri said, stepping into the elevator as the doors slid open. She turned and challenged him with her eyes. "Please don't coddle me. I need to see him—I'm going to see him, so you might as well just accept it."

Pouting like a child, Nathan stepped into the elevator behind her and they rode in silence to the pediatric unit on the fourth floor. Kerri was glad when he opted to wait at the nurse's station while she went into Jace's room.

Seeing Jace lying there, looking lost in the midst of the bed and the moat of equipment surrounding it, made Kerri's heart ache. He was flat on his back, his eyes half closed, only the whites showing. His breathing was more normal now, but he was still unresponsive. An IV line snaked its way into his hand; a tube through his nose fed him from a bag filled with a whitish-gray liquid. Kerri sat beside the bed, holding the tiny hand that felt so cold, murmuring words of encouragement. Images of Mandy's final days, in a room not unlike this one and with even more tubes violating her body, filled her mind. Yet instead of feeling the painful ache in her chest that had always accompanied these memories in the past, Kerri felt calm and at peace. For a brief moment, she thought she could feel Mandy's presence in the room, standing beside her, offering reassurance the boy in the bed would be okay. Rather than frightening Kerri, the thought of Mandy being able to somehow transcend death left her with a feeling of contentment. So vivid was the image, Kerri actually heard Mandy's voice—so childlike, yet so grown-up at the same time.

It's okay, Momma. He's going to be fine. It's not his time yet. And he needs you.

Tears filled Kerri's eyes, but they weren't tears of sadness. Instead, she was imbued with a feeling of gratitude.

When she finally left to hook back up with Nathan, she took a moment to confer with one of the nurses on Jace's case. She left both her phone number and her beeper number at the desk with instructions to be called at the first sign of any change in his condition. And she checked to be sure the necessary steps had been initiated to make her Jace's legal guardian, ignoring Nathan's raised brow as she did so.

When they were finally settled in Nathan's car, headed for the ferry pier, Nathan again broached the subject. "Why would you want guardianship of this kid?" he asked, his tone more curious than condemning.

"I told you. He's all alone. His only surviving family member is a grandmother who is holed up in a nursing home somewhere." Kerri gazed out the window a moment, gathering her thoughts. "And there's something about him," she said finally. "Something that tugs at me. I can't just abandon him to the system, Nathan." She turned and looked at him, her eyes pleading for understanding.

Nathan reached over and gave her thigh a reassuring squeeze. "I just don't want to see you get hurt," he said. He was silent a moment, then said, "Does he make you think of Mandy?"

Kerri hesitated before she answered. "Sometimes. But it's different. I feel the same sense of hopelessness I felt when Mandy was so sick, wanting to protect him the same way I wanted to protect her." She gave a haphazard shrug. "I don't know. Maybe it's a form of atonement, a second chance. I couldn't save Mandy, but maybe I can save Jace."

Nathan gave her a curious look. "That's a pretty big load to carry, isn't it?"

"Doesn't feel like it. It's something I want to do."

Nathan pulled up to the ticket booth and paid for their passage on the ferry, then parked behind the other cars waiting in line for loading. He turned off the engine and leaned back against the head rest, his eyes closed. "Have you ever thought about trying again?" he asked. "For another child, I mean."

Kerri looked over at him, studying his profile, remembering the delight they had shared when Mandy was born. Suddenly she was tired of all the fighting and animosity. She didn't want to hurt him anymore.

"I don't know," she said. "There are times when I wonder what it would have been like if we'd gone ahead and had another child after Mandy—someone to care for, to be strong for . . . to live for after Mandy's death." She looked down at her hands where they lay in her lap, her thumbnail lazily tracing the lines of one palm.

Nathan raised his head and looked over at her. He reached out and stroked her cheek with the back of his hand, then fingered a strand of her hair. "I'm sorry I added to your hurt, Kerri. If there is one thing in life I wish I could take back—no, make that two things—it would be Mandy's death, and my betrayal of you. I know you're tired of hearing my apologies, but you have to understand how Mandy's death tore me up inside. It made me crazy. I wasn't thinking straight. You can understand that, can't you?"

Kerri heard a hitch in his voice and looked up at him, seeing the sheen of tears in his eyes. They surprised her; as best she could recall, she'd never seen Nathan cry over Mandy. With a searing flash of memory, she remembered how devastated he had looked at Mandy's funeral, how his hand had trembled as he held her own. But never did he shed a tear. At the time, she'd given it little thought—she was so wrapped inside the cocoon of her own misery, she'd failed to see the depth of his pain. He had tried to comfort her, tried to be strong for her. And what had she done for him? Nothing. She'd remained withdrawn and isolated, pulled into herself. Was that what drove him into the arms of another woman? His own need to be comforted?

She reached over and laid her hand atop his. "I guess we were both a little crazy back then," she said softly. "I hurt you, too. I couldn't see it then, but I can now. What's done is done. Why don't we try to put the past behind us and move on?"

Nathan gave her a tremulous smile. "Does that

mean you'll consider giving me ... giving us another chance?"

A tiny nub of panic pulsed in Kerri's chest. The image of Bender rose in her mind, unbidden—his dark eyes, those pouty lips, the warmth of his hand on her shoulder. "Let's take things slowly, okay?" she said. "Forgiving what happened is one thing. Trying to regain what we once had is something else all together."

Nathan was unable to hide his hurt; his face sagged and his eyes drooped with the weight of it.

"I'm not saying it's impossible," Kerri added hastily, wanting to make this easier for him—and for herself. "I'm just in too much of a state of flux right now to be able to promise anything."

"There is someone else, isn't there?" Nathan asked sullenly. "That guy that was in your room this morning. Are you dating him?"

Kerri debated her answer. Technically speaking, she had yet to officially date Bender, though there was no denying that had been the intent of their outing yesterday. Still, it was too early to commit to calling their relationship anything but mutual curiosity. She knew admitting her interest in the man would only antagonize Nathan, and she didn't want any more arguments. Nor did she want to wound him. That alone, she found rather startling. Just a short time ago, wounding Nathan in retribution for the grave injuries he'd inflicted on her had been her main goal in life. Now, all she wanted was peace—peace of mind and peace of life.

"I'm not involved with anyone, Nathan," she said finally, arguing to herself that it was only a stretching of the truth, not an out-and-out lie. "I'm still trying to figure myself out. I don't think I have the energy to work on an 'us.' It's all I can do some days just to work on me."

"I understand," Nathan said, still wearing a disconsolate look. "I just want you to know I'm here if you want me. Okay?"

"Okay," Kerri said. Then she added, "Thank you, Nathan," and was rewarded for her efforts with a smile.

The ferry ride across the sound was uneventful, and Kerri was grateful Nathan didn't try to engage her in any more conversation. The day was clear but cold, the temperature hovering somewhere in the low fifties. At first Kerri thought a walk around the upper deck would do her some good; the fresh air felt invigorating. But as the ferry chugged its way into the sound, the wind became a cold salacious hand that snaked its fingers beneath her clothes, chilling first her skin, then her bones. She retreated to the lower deck and, after Nathan treated her to a steaming-hot cup of Starbucks, settled into one of the seats with him and watched the scenery pass by.

By the time they made it back to her house, Shadow was furious. He wound in and out of Kerri's feet, mewing plaintively, as if chastising her for her prolonged absence. When Nathan tried to scoop the cat up, Shadow proved true to his reputation and hissed at him, squirming in Nathan's grasp until he was forced to put the animal down.

"Geez, that beast weighs a ton," Nathan observed, scowling at Shadow. The cat scowled right back.

"Yeah." Kerri laughed. "I wasn't exactly worried about him starving to death. In fact, he often visits the Logans next door and they feed him all the time. Sort of his adopted parents, I guess."

Kerri unlocked the front door and was nearly knocked over as Shadow burst between her legs and dashed into the kitchen. His mewing grew in volume, so that Kerri could hear him clearly even though she was still on the front porch. Ignoring him for the moment, she turned to Nathan.

"Look, I know you want to come in and make sure I'm okay, but I assure you I'm fine. And all I want right now is some peace and quiet. I'm going to fix a sandwich, maybe even have a beer, and then I'm going to take a nap." She saw Nathan open his mouth to object, and quickly continued. "You've been a great help, Nathan. I appreciate it. How about if I call you later this afternoon, just so you know I'm okay?" Having tossed him this conciliatory bone, Kerri waited, hoping it would be enough.

Nathan sighed, shifting his weight from one leg to the other and gazing out over the bay. He chewed the inside of his cheek. "What about your car?" he asked, seizing upon the first excuse he could think of.

The reminder made Kerri frown, but she quickly recovered. "I'll arrange for the garage to bring it out to me," she said. "They've done it before." She bit her lip and said a silent prayer, asking God to forgive all the lies she had told. If worse came to worse, she wouldn't have to get the car back until sometime tomorrow. Monday was a catch-up day for her at the office—no scheduled patients, just paperwork. Perhaps she could track Bender down and get him to help her. Besides, it would give her an excuse to see him again.

"Okay," Nathan said finally, grudging in his defeat.

Kerri realized she had been holding her breath in anticipation of his answer and let it out slowly, by small degrees. "Thank you, Nathan." She leaned over and kissed him on the cheek, the smell of his aftershave triggering a minimatinee of flashing images from the past. Before he, or for that matter, she, could have a change of mind, she stepped inside and quietly closed the door.

She kept her word to Nathan and fixed herself a sandwich, though she decided to forgo the beer. After sating both her own appetite and Shadow's, she kicked off her shoes and headed upstairs for a nap. She'd been dozing for a couple of hours when the peal of the doorbell awakened her. Feeling groggy, she shuffled out of bed and peeked out the window to the driveway below, hoping to identify her visitor by whatever car was parked there. To her surprise, there were two cars: one an old-looking Jeep with a dulled finish and a couple of conspicuous dents; the other was her own.

Her heart leaped when she realized it might be Bender, and she hurried downstairs to open the door.

"Well, hello," Bender greeted. "Looks like you've recovered."

Kerri gazed up at him, surprised at how glad she was to see him, and only dimly aware of the second man who stood beside him on the porch. "I have," she said. "You brought my car back."

"I did." He gave her a little bow. "Bender's car retrieval company at your service."

Kerri smiled at him. "Thank you."

"My pleasure. Besides, I wanted to see how you were doing. I called the hospital and they told me you'd been discharged. When I explained what I needed, one of the nurses gave me your address, though I have to admit it took us a while to find your house. Fortunately, a policeman in Port Townsend took pity on us and gave us directions."

Kerri finally turned her attention to the second man. He was shorter than Bender; in fact, he was no taller than Kerri herself. His dark hair was longish, curling around the collar of his jacket. A full beard covered much of his face; blue eyes gazed back at her from beneath bushy brows.

"This is Ted Saunders," Bender said, making the introductions.

"Nice to meet you, Mr. Saunders," Kerri said, offering her hand for a shake.

"Actually," Bender said, "it's Dr. Saunders. He's a botany professor at the U of Dub and a naturalist for the Olympic National Park."

"Oh," Kerri said apologetically. "Then it's nice to meet you, *Dr.* Saunders." She gave his hand an extra pump, then released it.

"If you don't mind," Saunders said, "I'd just as soon you call me Ted. I'm not as hung up on titles as old Mindbender here."

Kerri laughed. "That's the second time I've heard that nickname," she said, giving Bender a suspicious look. "I'm beginning to wonder just what it is you've done in the past to earn it."

Bender rubbed his hands together and gave her his best lecherous grin. "Heh-heh-heh," he chuckled. "Look into my eyes."

"You're incorrigible," Kerri said, shaking her head. "Can I invite you two in for a beer? I've got a six pack of Coors in the fridge."

Bender turned suddenly serious. "I'll pass on the beer," he said, "but we would like to come in for a moment. I've got something interesting to tell you."

"What about?" Kerri asked, looking back and forth between the two men.

"Remember that plant I found in the Johansens' house by the back door?" Bender asked.

Kerri thought back to the night of Thad's suicide— *no, not a suicide,* her brain argued. She shook the thought off and recalled the tiny plant Bender had held in his hand. "It was some kind of cactus or something, wasn't it?" she asked.

"Yes," Bender said. "It was indeed. And an important little cactus at that. I'm not so sure Thad Johansen committed suicide. At the very least, I don't think he was alone in the house. And that plant I found may be able to tell us who was there with him."

TWENTY

Kerri ushered the two men into her living room and told them to have a seat. After Ted Saunders took her up on the offer of a beer, Bender changed his mind and decided to have one, too. Kerri fetched three of them from the kitchen and, after handing them around, curled up on the couch waiting for Bender to elaborate on his startling statement. Shadow appeared from upstairs, sauntered into the living room, and promptly leaped onto Bender's lap, where he settled down with all the grace of a tumbling boulder.

Bender let out an "oomph" of air as the cat landed.

"Shadow!" Kerri chastised. "Get down!"

The cat eyed her as if to say, "Make me."

Bender stroked Shadow's fur and said, "Leave him be. I like cats." Shadow closed his eyes and purred like a Harley.

Kerri watched the two of them with an expression of amazement. "That's so odd," she told Bender. "He hates strangers. I've never seen him take so well to someone he's just met."

"He obviously has poor taste in humans," Ted Saunders teased.

"Good taste, you mean," Bender countered. He

shifted his lap slightly. "Good grief, what do you feed this creature? Ball bearings?"

Kerri laughed. "Not exactly a lightweight, is he?"

"That's an understatement."

"So tell me about this plant," Kerri said, unable to stand the suspense any longer.

"I think I'll turn it over to Ted," Bender said with a nod toward the other man. "He's the expert."

Ted Saunders leaned forward, setting his beer on the table beside him. He reached into his shirt pocket and pulled out a plastic bag, which held the plant piece inside. "This specimen Mindbender brought me is a piece of *Opuntia fragilis*, more commonly known as a prickly pear. It's a cactus, and a fairly ordinary plant. Not one to catch the eye—except for one thing."

Kerri waited, hanging on the man's every word. "Yes?" she prompted.

"If I understand correctly, this was found inside someone's house."

Kerri nodded, shifting impatiently. She wished the man would get on with it.

"Well," Ted continued, his voice quiet and contemplative, "this particular species is not common in this area of the state. In fact, with two notable exceptions, it can't be found growing anywhere west of the Cascades."

"Meaning?" Kerri said.

Ted Saunders raised a hand. "Patience. I'm getting to that. You have to understand how this particular piece of plant came to be where it was found. Because it isn't indigenous to the Seattle area, it had to have been carried there somehow, tracked by someone. They attach themselves quite easily to clothing. The ends of these spines are barbed. And the plant itself is segmented, a series of these little bulbous pieces. They break apart easily."

Bender piped up at this point. "I went back to the Johansens' house this morning and walked around it on the off chance a stray patch of this stuff might be growing somewhere nearby. It wasn't. I also toured a few of the other yards in the neighborhood—damned near got my ass chewed off by some obnoxious mutt—but no prickly pears. And remember the other night at the house when I said I needed to use the bathroom?"

Kerri nodded.

"That was just an excuse to scout out the house, to see if there were any potted specimens anywhere. There weren't."

"So," Ted Saunders chimed in, "that means our plant likely came from some other outside source. On the eastern side of the state it can be found growing wild in any number of places, but here on the western side there are only two."

"One is on a tiny island in the San Juans," Bender said. "We flew over the spot earlier today and there is nothing there. The island is completely uninhabited."

"The second spot," Saunders explained, "is an isolated patch in a small area along the northern shore of the peninsula here, about ten miles outside of Sequim."

"Sequim?" Kerri asked. "That's not far from here. About a half-hour drive."

Bender nodded.

Kerri chewed her lip a moment, her face furrowed in thought. "So you're thinking someone tracked this plant to the Johansens' house?"

Bender nodded. "Exactly."

"As I said before," Saunders added, "the barbs on

the spines would make it relatively easy for a piece to stick to someone's clothing or shoe and be carried elsewhere."

Kerri thought about it some more, then asked, "Isn't it possible Thad himself tracked the thing there? How do we know it came from some outside source?"

"We don't," Saunders answered. "But it should be easy enough to check. The only place he could have picked it up would be in one of the two spots we mentioned. It's not as if you would run across it on an average outing."

"What about all the cops that were there?" Kerri asked. "Couldn't one of them have tracked it in?"

"I thought of that," Bender said. "If you recall, the back door to the house was locked. While you were waiting outside, I asked Kevin if he, or any of the other men had been back there. He told me that when he saw Thad Johansen through the den window, he went around to the front door and found it unlocked. That was how he got in. No one had been anywhere near the back door. They had no reason to."

"So you think someone else might have been there?" Kerri asked, her eyes wide. Once more, something tickled her brain, some thought she couldn't quite grasp about Thad and his suicide.

"It's certainly a possibility," Bender said. "Ted and I thought we might go and check out the site near Sequim, as long as we're here. We'd like to get there before it gets dark, but I wanted to stop by here first to return your car and see if you'd like to come along. That is, if you're feeling up to it."

"Absolutely," Kerri said, pushing herself up from the couch. "But first I want to call the hospital and check on Jace." She picked up the phone and dialed the number for the pediatric unit at the hospital. After a short conversation, she hung the phone up and looked at Bender with a sad expression.

"No change?" he asked. Kerri shook her head.

"Give him time," Bender said. Kerri nodded, but with little enthusiasm.

"You ready to go?" Again she nodded. "Okay." Bender scooped Shadow's hefty weight off his lap and dropped him onto the floor. The cat landed with a resounding thud and sat there staring up at his offender with an unappreciative eye.

Kerri went upstairs to run a brush through her hair, then came down and slipped on her shoes and a jacket.

Ted Saunders said, "If it's okay with you, I'd prefer we take your car. I'm afraid the Jeep doesn't hold three adults too comfortably. Plus, the heater doesn't work, and it isn't exactly airtight. It can be a chilly ride."

"That's fine," Kerri said. She dug around in her purse and came up with her keys. Then it hit her. She turned and looked at Bender. "How did you manage to drive my car back here without the keys?" she asked.

Bender's face turned red and he gave her a sheepish look. "I hot-wired it," he said.

"You did what?" Kerri said, gaping at him. "How the hell do you know how to do that?"

"Let's just say it's a vestige left over from my misspent youth," he said cryptically.

Kerri frowned at him. "Don't tell me you have a criminal past," she said.

"No," Bender said. Then his face split into a wide grin. "But only because I never got caught."

Ted Saunders chuckled. "Don't worry. I've known him since we were both ten years old. He's turned around. I swear, he's led a clean life for the past twenty years."

"Great," Kerri muttered, rolling her eyes at Bender. "You thought Kevin disliked you before, you better hope he never finds out about your checkered past."

"I won't tell him if you won't," Bender said.

Kerri studied the mischievous twinkle in his eye and the sardonic twist of his lips. She shook her head in amusement. "Let's go," she said. "Before I wise up and change my mind."

After a brief argument about who would drive, they piled into Kerri's car, Bender behind the wheel, Kerri beside him, Ted Saunders in back. When they were a few miles outside of Sequim, Saunders directed Bender to turn down a small dirt road that disappeared into a thick grove of trees. Bender drove slowly, bouncing along the rutted furrows left behind from whoever had preceded them. It was close to dusk, and the bits of sunlight filtering through the trees from the west created a strobe effect that left Kerri feeling slightly dizzy. Grudgingly she admitted to herself it had probably been wise to let Bender drive. Eventually the road emerged into a clearing and ended at the base of a small hill.

Bender pulled up to the road's end and shifted the car into park. Kerri leaned forward and stared out the windshield. "So where are the plants?" she asked.

Ted Saunders opened the rear door and climbed out. "We've got to hike a little ways. Follow me."

He took off on foot, climbing to the top of the small hill, while Kerri and Bender followed. Kerri heard the sound of waves breaking along the beach and was, therefore, not surprised when they reached

the crest and saw the shore a few hundred yards away.
She scanned the area: to her right she could see Port
Townsend glimmering off in the distance, to her left,
the Strait of Juan de Fuca wound its way toward the
Pacific. Across the water she could see Vancouver
Island—its shores dotted with specks of color that
denoted buildings, its mountains rising up into a thin
mist off in the distance. The stretch of land where they
stood had woods crowding the shore to the east, but to
the west a large section of trees had been cut away. In
the midst of this clearing, about a quarter mile away,
sat a large concrete building: five stories high with
tinted windows marking each level, its northernmost
wall only about a hundred feet from the water's edge.
Circling the clearing's perimeter was a high chain-link
fence topped with razor wire.

"What is that place?" Kerri asked Ted, pointing
toward the structure.

"That's the Coleman Institute," he said. "They're a
research facility owned by some drug company—I forget who right off the top of my head. They've been
studying various types of marine life in hopes of discovering new pharmaceutical possibilities."

"Interesting," Kerri said, studying the building. "I
never knew the place was here."

"They run a low-key operation," Saunders
explained. "Pretty tight security and all that. I understand there is a lot of competition and espionage in the
world of pharmaceutical research."

"There is," Kerri acknowledged. "Drug research
costs millions of dollars. With all the testing and
restrictions imposed by the FDA, it can take years
before a new drug ever makes it to market. And then a
company is limited as to how long it can maintain

exclusive rights over its production. But if you hit on the right drug, you stand to make those millions back tenfold."

"So where are our prickly pears?" Bender asked, shifting his weight back and forth impatiently.

"Over there, toward the Coleman Institute," Saunders said, pointing in the general direction. "Grows right along their fence line. In fact, a small part of it grows on their property." He headed off in that direction, and Kerri and Bender fell into step behind him. When they were a few yards from the fence, Saunders stopped and crouched down. "Here," he said, waving his hand over a patch of growth that extended away from him and to his right.

Kerri surveyed the area—about fifty feet square, mostly grass interspersed with clusters of cacti that, in some places, spread out like a spiny mat. The plants varied in height from four to eight inches; their stems were a series of jointed, bulbous segments, each one mirroring the specimen they had found in the Johansens' house.

Most of the plants were on the outside of the fence, but Kerri noted some of them had managed to spring up in a strip of grass that ran in a ten-foot-wide border along the inside, as well. The grass strip edged a parking lot, and Kerri was surprised to see the lot was relatively full, despite the fact it was Sunday.

Her eyes drifted up toward the building, and she stared at the darkened windows, suddenly certain their presence here had not gone unnoticed. She had the eerie feeling they were being watched. She clutched her jacket closer around her.

"Kind of a letdown, I suppose," Saunders said, looking back along the shoreline. "Other than the

Coleman Institute, there isn't much along this stretch. And as you may have noticed, it's not that easy to get here."

"But this is the only spot where this stuff grows, other than this patch on the island you mentioned?" Kerri asked.

Saunders nodded. "They are the only places this side of the Cascades." He stood and gazed out at the ocean. Kerri stared up at the Coleman Institute, her face in thoughtful repose. The wind blowing in off the shore was brisk, and Kerri shivered, though she wasn't sure it was solely from the chill.

"We better get you back," Bender said loudly over the roar of wind and surf.

Kerri ignored him, still staring at the building.

"Kerri?"

She finally turned away.

"Let's get you home," Bender said. "You look like you could use a cup of hot tea."

Kerri nodded, and headed back across the field toward the car, Saunders and Bender following. She struggled the entire way to keep from looking back over her shoulder toward the Coleman Institute, nagged by the persistent feeling they were being watched.

As Bender drove them back to her house, they discussed the significance of their finding.

"I don't think it's mere coincidence you found that plant in Thad's house and then we find it growing here," Kerri surmised. "We need to find out more about this Coleman Institute."

"It wouldn't hurt, I suppose," Saunders said. "Though I doubt you'll find anything of much interest. The Coleman Institute has been here for almost ten years. They have a pretty solid reputation in the community. And corporate espionage aside, marine research isn't exactly sinister."

"But they have ties to a pharmaceutical company you said. Right?" Kerri asked.

"Right," Saunders agreed. "Is that significant?"

Kerri shrugged, her mind busily exploring the beginnings of an idea. At first her thoughts sounded crazy, even paranoid—maybe she'd watched one too many episodes of *The X-Files*. But the more she thought about it, the more it made her wonder. She was anxious to bounce the idea off Bender, to see if he would even consider it. He seemed to have a fairly open mind. If anyone was willing to entertain her idea, she thought, he was the most likely candidate. She hesitated, unsure of posing her theory in front of Ted Saunders. When they pulled into the clearing beside the house it became a moot point.

"Oh, shit," she muttered. Nathan's car was there, parked next to Ted Saunders's Jeep. And Nathan himself, his face a thundercloud of emotion, stood beside it.

"Who's that?" Ted asked.

"My husband . . . ex-husband," Kerri clarified. She could sense Bender tensing beside her. From the corner of her eye she could see his hands clenching and unclenching on the steering wheel. As he parked the car, Kerri put on her best smile and climbed out to face Nathan.

"Where were you?" Nathan asked, trying unsuccessfully to keep his voice even. Kerri saw him shoot a scathing glance at Bender before he turned back to her, awaiting her answer.

"We went for a ride, to look at something," Kerri explained. Behind her, Ted and Bender had climbed out of her car and were about to get into the Jeep. She turned toward them. "Ted Saunders, this is Nathan Palmer," she said, trying to keep things on a lighter, social level.

Though he looked decidedly uncomfortable about doing it, Ted Saunders turned back and approached Nathan, his hand extended. Apparently, he had picked up on the tension between the two men.

"Nice to meet you," Saunders said, giving Nathan's hand a quick pump. To Nathan's credit, he returned the greeting with a tone of reasonable civility, his face even relaxing some.

"Ted is a friend of Mike's," Kerri explained, her heart pounding while she tried to keep her face and voice from betraying the tautness in her nerves. "Ted is a botanist from the U of Dub. He came by to help me with some landscaping ideas. That's where we were. We rode out to look at some other houses so he could show me some of the plants he's been suggesting."

Kerri saw both Ted and Bender flash her a puzzled expression, though thankfully they recovered quickly. She hoped Nathan hadn't caught it.

"Thank you for your help, Ted." she said. "I'll get back to you later this week on my choices. Will that be okay?"

Both Ted and Bender were smart enough to know they were being dismissed. Kerri was grateful for Ted's presence, because Bender looked like a pressure cooker ready to blow. Ted gave him a not-too-subtle nudge toward the Jeep.

"That will be fine," Ted said. "If you have any questions in the meantime, just give me a call." He climbed in behind the wheel of the Jeep, and after making sure Bender was in as well, he started the engine. Rolling down his window, he leaned out and looked at Nathan.

"Pleasure to meet you," he said with a little salute.

"Likewise," Nathan said. Kerri detected a faint tone of suspicion still lingering in his voice, and her heart thumped harder.

Ted shifted the Jeep into reverse, backed it around, and headed out. Watching the vehicle as it disappeared around a bend in the driveway and into the woods, Kerri felt a strong urge to go running after it. Instead, she sucked in a deep breath and turned to face Nathan.

"So what brings you back out here?" she asked as sweetly as she could muster.

"I was worried as hell," Nathan said, the thunderclouds returning to his face. "You said you would call me. When you didn't, I tried to call you. When I got no answer, I was afraid something might have happened."

"Well," Kerri said, turning and heading toward the front door, "as you can see, I am just fine. I was going to call you."

She could hear Nathan's footsteps behind her and wondered how long he intended to stay. Despite her earlier decision to try and forget old animosities, Nathan was beginning to wear on her nerves. She didn't think she could maintain this forced civility very long. Climbing the front steps, she froze. Her front door was open, the window beside it smashed and broken.

"What the hell?" she muttered.

"Sorry," Nathan said sheepishly from behind her. "I didn't recognize the car parked out there and when you didn't answer the door, I thought you might be in trouble."

Kerri turned around and confronted Nathan with an exasperated sigh. "So you broke into my house?"

Nathan shrugged. "I'll pay for the damage," he said.

"It's not the cost that's the point," Kerri said irritably. "This is my house, Nathan. You had no right to come barging in like that."

"I thought you were in trouble, Kerri. Otherwise I never would have done it."

His tone was conciliatory, his expression sincere, and Kerri felt her anger ebb. "Okay," she said, squeezing her eyes closed in defeat. "Just don't do it again. All right?"

Nathan held up three fingers. "Scout's honor."

Kerri glanced around at the surrounding woods. "Look, Nathan, I'm fine. Really I am. But I am a little tired. So if you don't mind . . ."

"No problem," Nathan said, backing down a step. "I don't want to wear out my welcome. As I said, I just wanted to make sure you were okay. I can't help worrying about you, Kerri."

Kerri was taken aback by his quick acquiescence. Feeling guilty and more than a little confused by her emotions, she softened her expression and stepped over to plant a quick kiss on Nathan's cheek. "I appreciate you looking out for me," she said. "I'll call you tomorrow, okay?"

"Okay," Nathan said, seemingly placated by the gesture. He turned and descended the rest of the steps. When he reached the sidewalk, he looked back at her. "You'll call me if you need anything?" he asked.

"I will, Nathan. I promise."

With a little nod, Nathan turned and headed down the sidewalk. When he got to the driveway, he stopped and stared at Kerri's car, a thoughtful expression on his face. Then he turned back toward the porch. Kerri realized he was going to ask her how she had managed to get her car back already. To forestall him, she waved and hollered at him. "Thanks again, Nathan. I'll call you tomorrow." Then she disappeared inside the house. She hurried over to the window and watched as Nathan stood there, indecision stamped on his face. He shrugged and climbed into his own car.

Kerri waited until his Mercedes disappeared into the woods. With a sigh and a shake of her head, she went to find a board and some nails to cover the broken window.

TWENTY-ONE

The following morning, Kerri once again took her car into the city so she could drive to the medical center and check on Jace.

The pediatric unit was bustling with the early morning shift change. A dozen or so nurses crowded around the main station chatting among themselves, while physicians eager to finish their morning rounds competed for their attention. Kerri walked over and pulled Jace's chart from the rack and flipped it open. She scanned the nurse's notes, dismayed to see there was little change in the boy's condition. With a heavy heart, she made her way to his room.

He looked no different than the last time she'd seen him. Lying so still she had to stare at his chest to detect his breathing, he might have been sleeping if it weren't for the many tubes protruding from his body and the dark sunken look of his eyes. Kerri walked over and stroked his hair back from his forehead.

"I'm going to get to the bottom of all this, Jace," she whispered. "I'll find out what happened to your parents. I'll do my part if you do yours and get better for me, okay?" She reached over and picked up his hand, sandwiching it between her palms, somewhat heartened by the fact it didn't feel as cold and dead as it had yesterday. For several moments she stood there, watching him, studying his face for any sign of life. Seeing nothing, she laid his hand gently on the sheet and sighed. "Try, Jace. Please try," she whispered. Then she bent over, kissed him on the forehead, and left the room.

When she got to the office, it was locked and empty. They never scheduled any regular appointments on Mondays, and because he had morning classes, Stephen generally took the day off. After flipping on some lights, checking the answering machine for messages, and brewing up some coffee, she settled in at her desk and stared at the pile of charts in the corner still awaiting her attention. But her thoughts had little to do with the office or the charts. Instead, she sipped her coffee, leaning back in her chair and staring out the window at the people bustling by in Pioneer Square below, toying with the idea that had begun to form in her mind yesterday afternoon.

She wanted to talk to Bender. Part of it was her need to bounce this crazy idea of hers off him. But another part—a part she chose not to dwell on— simply wanted to hear his voice. Finally, she gave in to the urge. Shuffling some papers around until she found Bender's phone number, she dialed.

"Good morning? Dr. Bender's office. This is Kristen. May I help you?"

The voice sounded young, chipper, and decidedly feminine. Kerri felt a twinge of something bordering on jealousy and was surprised at herself. "Is Dr. Bender in?" she asked, trying to sound as professional as possible.

"Yes, he is," answered Miss Chipper. "But he's with a patient right now. May I take a message?"

Kerri toyed with the idea of simply hanging up. This whole idea of hers was foolish anyway, and she knew it wasn't her only motivation for calling. But she couldn't make herself do it. "Yes, please. Ask him to call Dr. Whitaker." Kerri gave the woman her number and hung up. She leaned back in the chair once more, again staring out the window, her fingers steepled together and tapping idly against her chin. When the phone rang a few moments later she found herself feeling annoyed. No doubt it was a patient, or perhaps Nathan, and she didn't have the motivation to deal with either one. Reluctantly, she picked up the phone.

"Dr. Whitaker," she said.

"Is this *the* Dr. Whitaker? In person?"

Kerri recognized the voice immediately and laughed. "You're not going to let me live that one down, are you?" she asked Bender.

"Not if I can help it."

"I didn't expect to hear from you so soon."

"I was hoping you would call," Bender said, his voice dropping a notch and stirring something deep in Kerri's gut. "I wasn't sure if I should."

Kerri knew he was referring to Nathan, and she suddenly felt awkward and embarrassed. "I called," she said quickly, "to bounce an idea off you. Something that occurred to me yesterday when we were out at the Coleman Institute."

"Okay," Bender said, and Kerri wasn't sure if she heard a note of disappointment in his voice.

"Well, I got to thinking about this cactus you found in the Johansens' house. Maybe it's just a coincidence. But maybe not."

"Or," Bender threw in, "like you pointed out, maybe Thad himself carried it there."

"Highly unlikely, but I'm going to ask Kevin if he knows Thad's movements over the past few days. Still, I don't think we can ignore the fact it's growing by this research facility."

"I agree it's a pretty strong coincidence," Bender said. "But what would a marine research facility have to do with Thad Johansen?"

"Don't forget, they're tied to a pharmaceutical company."

"So? I still don't see the connection to Thad."

"Maybe not so much Thad, as Janet," Kerri suggested.

"What do you mean?"

Kerri quickly ran the idea through her mind one more time. It was beginning to sound more farfetched to her by the minute. But surely Bender, as open-minded as he was, wouldn't think she was totally loony just because of this. Would he? She took in a deep breath and plunged in.

"Well, consider this," she said. "Pharmaceutical research costs millions of dollars. There's development and testing, then animal trials, and finally human trials. That whole process can take years. The FDA requirements are rigorous and costly. So what if a company discovered a new drug, something really groundbreaking, like a cure for AIDS or cancer or something? And what if they didn't want to wait all those years and spend all that money trying to get to the market stage of development? What if they wanted to test it on humans early?"

There was a long silence and Kerri bit her lip, waiting for Bender's reaction.

"I see where you're going with this," he said finally. "Interesting theory. But don't they test things on people now? Volunteers, I mean. You see ads in the paper all the time, particularly on campuses, offering money to people who are willing to serve as human guinea pigs."

True," Kerri said. "But even that level of testing is allowed only after years of research and FDA approval. Think of all the money they could save if they bypassed all that. And what if they wanted to test out a drug for a specific disorder or disease? Volunteers wouldn't be much help unless they have the specific disease the researchers are hoping to treat. In order for the results to be valid, you need to test in a good-sized population. If the disease isn't all that common, the chance of getting enough volunteers is slim."

"Point made," Bender said thoughtfully. "But are you suggesting the people in my group might all have some disease in common? Along with Janet Johansen?"

Kerri frowned. When Bender put it like that, it did sound rather unlikely. "Probably not," she admitted. "But you never know. It can't hurt to check it out. You could ask the people in your group, and I'll talk to Janet Johansen's physician, to see if there was anything she might have had."

"Even if your theory is right, wouldn't there have to be some sort of follow-up?" Bender asked. "I mean, if you're suggesting these alien abductions are some sort of staged scenario used to administer a test drug to the victims, wouldn't the drug company have to do some kind of follow-up to determine if the drug was working?"

"You're right," Kerri said, deflated. "I hadn't thought of that."

Bender added, "There are reports of repeated abductions among some of the victims, but to my knowledge, not among the members of my group."

"Maybe it just hasn't happened yet," Kerri suggested. "They all had their experiences fairly recently, didn't they?"

"Most of them," Bender agreed. "I suppose it's possible." He didn't sound very convinced.

"In the meantime," Kerri said, "I wish there was a way to visit the Coleman Institute and take a look around. I still think it's too much of a coincidence this cactus showed up in the Johansens' house."

"I agree," Bender said. "And it just so happens I have an idea about how we can do just that. When would you be free to go? The latter part of the week is pretty heavy for me, but I have some free time this afternoon, and again tomorrow afternoon."

"Today would be better for me," Kerri said. "I don't have any patients scheduled." The thought of seeing Bender again as soon as this afternoon made that something in her gut stir again.

"Today it is then."

"Great. How soon can you get there?"

"Well, let's see. I have an eleven-o'clock appointment, but I can leave here after that. Why don't I drive down to Seattle and meet you there at your office, and we can go over together. How long will it take?"

Kerri whipped open a desk drawer and dragged out a ferry schedule. "If you can get here by one thirty or so, we should be able to catch the two-ten ferry over to Bainbridge. Figure thirty-five minutes to cross, and an hour or so of driving time. Should put us there around a quarter to four."

"Sounds good to me," Bender said. "Give me directions to your office."

Kerri gave him directions to the nearest parking garage, and from there, to her office.

"Sounds like we have us a date," Bender said, "as long as you agree to let me take you out somewhere for dinner afterwards, to make up for the other night. And, of course, to make sure you don't keel over on me again."

Kerri felt herself blush. "I am sorry about that," she mumbled.

"Don't be," Bender said. "Having fair damsels fall into my arms has always been a fantasy of mine."

Kerri's blush deepened.

"Except, it would be nice if you'd wait until my arms are ready next time," Bender teased.

"Just let me know when they're ready," Kerri said, her voice barely more than a whisper. She heard a sharp intake of breath at the other end of the line.

"That," Bender said a bit breathlessly, "is a deal. See you this afternoon."

Once she had hung up the phone, Kerri wasted a few minutes picturing Bender's handsome face—those full lips, that crooked smile, those incredibly dark eyes—eyes with a way of looking at her that made her feel sexy, protected, and appreciated all at once. With a wistful sigh, she pushed the image away and forced her mind to focus on her work.

Kevin called around ten to see how she was doing. She asked him to find out more about Janet Johansen's medical history.

"What for?" Kevin asked, his voice suspicious.

"Just something I'm curious about," Kerri answered vaguely. "I know you didn't find any major surgeries or hospitalizations in her past, but I'd like to know if there were any other, more minor problems."

Kevin badgered her a little longer before finally giving up and agreeing to see what he could find.

"One other thing, Kevin. Do you know if Thad spent any time on the peninsula or in the San Juan Islands during the days before his death?"

"Now why do ya want to know that, lass?" Kevin asked, impatience creeping into his voice.

Kerri thought quickly. She didn't want to irritate him too much, or he might refuse to help her. On the other hand, she wasn't ready to tell him about her crazy theory yet either. "The doctors found some type of insect bite on Jace," she said. "They're worried it might be some bug that's only found on the peninsula and in the San Juans. I thought if you knew whether or not Thad had been there, it might help to rule this out." She chewed her lip, waiting, while Kevin weighed her answer.

"As far as we know, the only places Thad went were the usual—his office, the grocery store, that sort of thing. Though he worked out of his home a lot, he occasionally went in to the company's main office. It's out near the university campus. Sometimes, according to his boss and coworkers, he visited building sites he'd designed, but all the current ones are here in the city."

"Thanks, Kev. You've been a big help." By the time Kerri hung up, she was surprised to discover she felt no guilt over her lies to Kevin. She pondered that oddity a few moments, then shrugged it off.

Though the rest of the morning passed by quickly enough, Kerri found herself anxiously awaiting Bender's arrival. At first she planned to work straight through lunch, but then, remembering the episode at the hospital the other night, she forced herself to run out to a nearby deli and grab a sandwich. She ate at her desk, trying to concentrate on the charts in front of her, while her eyes kept straying toward her watch every five minutes. When one thirty came and went, she felt the first twinges of anxiety. By one forty-five, she was pacing in the front office. When the phone rang five minutes later, her heart sank, knowing it must be Bender calling to say he would be unable to make it. She snatched up the phone on Stephen's desk.

"Hello?" she answered, trying to hide the disappointment she felt. But instead of Bender's deeply resonant voice, it was Nathan's that sounded from the other end.

"Kerri? What's wrong?" he asked.

So much for her ability to mask her emotions, Kerri thought. "Nothing, Nathan. I'm fine."

"You sure?"

"Yes, Nathan, I'm sure."

"Good. I know you said you were going to call me today, but I have a surgery scheduled this afternoon that will tie me up, probably into the evening sometime. So I thought I'd call you first."

"No problem," Kerri said, making another anxious glance toward her watch. It was now five minutes to two. *Where the hell is Bender?*

"I just wanted to touch base and make sure everything is okay."

"Everything is okay, Nathan. Honest."

"Are you eating? I don't want you to get sick again, Kerri. You need to take care of yourself."

"I feel great, Nathan. And yes, I'm eating."

The door to the office opened then, and Kerri whirled around. Bender walked in, looking somewhat harried but wearing a dark gray Armani suit that fit him like it had been sewn together on his body. After a startled but pleased appraisal, Kerri waved him in.

"How about having dinner with me tomorrow

night," Nathan offered. "I'll cook even. Make those broiled scallops you like so much."

Kerri's eyes remained fixed on Bender. She held up one finger, to indicate she would only be a moment. "I can't," she said to the phone. "I already have other plans. Maybe another night?"

She could almost see Nathan's pout at the other end. She prayed he wouldn't ask what her other plans were.

"Okay," Nathan said sullenly. "I'll call you later." Then, to Kerri's surprise, he hung up the phone. No good-bye, no nothing. She held the phone away from her and stared at it a moment. Then, with a shrug, she hung it up and turned toward Bender.

"You had me worried," she said. "If we're going to make that ferry, we need to hustle." She ran into her office, grabbed her purse, and hurried back out. "I'd give you the nickel tour," she said, grabbing her coat and slinging it on, "but under the circumstances . . ."

"No problem," Bender said. "I'm sorry I'm late. The traffic was a bear."

Once they hit the sidewalk outside, Bender turned one way, Kerri another. They stopped, stared at each other, then laughed.

"My car is just three blocks from here and only one block from the ferry," Kerri said.

"Okay, we'll take your car, but I'm driving," Bender said.

Kerri opened her mouth to argue the point, then decided against it. Time was of the essence. They headed downhill, toward the waterfront, at a half run. By the time they got to the ferry landing, all the other cars had been loaded. They had barely parked inside the ferry's belly when the big boat shuddered and got underway.

"Phew!" Kerri said, leaning back in her seat. "That was close." She rolled her head along the head rest and looked over at Bender. His hair was windblown and hung down over his forehead, just above his right eye. She had an almost irresistible urge to finger-comb it back into place, but decided she liked it better the way it was.

"You look nice," she told him. "For once you have me feeling underdressed rather than overdressed."

"Thanks," he said. "I just happened to have the suit in the office. The dry cleaners delivered it this morning."

"You mean you changed into it before coming down here?"

"I did. I'll tell you why in a minute. Was that your husband on the phone back there?"

Kerri's head jerked back. He couldn't have surprised her more if he had reached out and slapped her.

"Sorry," Bender said. He looked away and gazed out the windshield at the rows of cars stretched out before them. "It's none of my business."

"Then why did you ask?"

Bender turned back to her. "Is there still something between you two?" he asked. The muscles in his cheeks twitched as he awaited her answer.

Kerri thought about the question a moment before she answered. "I don't know, Bender," she said finally. This time she was the one to look away. "We were married for over ten years. And we had a daughter together. That's an awful lot of emotional baggage to just sweep under the carpet."

Bender made no comment, but Kerri could feel his eyes upon her. She resisted the urge to turn and look at him. After a few moments of that pensive silence, Bender pushed a little more. "Why did you break up?"

Kerri grimaced.

"You don't have to tell me, if you don't want to," he added quickly.

"No, it's okay," Kerri said. "It's not so much that I mind your question, it's just painful to remember."

"Did it have to do with your daughter's death?"

"Indirectly, I suppose," Kerri said, her mind suddenly filled with images of Mandy. "Our grief drove us apart to some extent. But the real clincher was when Nathan had an affair." Kerri finally risked looking at Bender. "I came home early one day and found him in bed with someone else. Just a month after Mandy's death." She half expected Bender to react to her revelation with some damning cut of Nathan. But to her surprise, he offered up a defense instead.

"He was probably seeking solace for his hurt. Happens a lot with men. They think sex with a woman can heal anything. Temporary insanity, no doubt."

Kerri's eyes flashed at him. "Whose side are you on, anyway?"

"Sorry," he said. "That's the shrink in me. I only say the man suffered from temporary insanity because I can't imagine a sane man passing you up for the arms of anyone else."

His eyes probed hers. Kerri felt as if someone had just snatched her breath away. Her heart started doing double time and she wanted to look away from him, but his eyes held hers prisoner. Bender finally broke the spell by saying, "Tell me about Mandy."

Kerri pulled her gaze away—slowly, reluctantly, but with a modicum of relief as well. Her head fell back against the head rest and she closed her eyes. "Mandy," she said. "Where do I begin?"

Bender said nothing; he merely waited.

"She was so bright," Kerri began. "She could count to a hundred and read by the time she was four. There was such an energy about her. Everything in life fascinated her."

"What did she look like?" Bender prodded gently.

"She had my color hair," Kerri said, and Bender's eyes roved over her head. "But it was all loose curls, not straight like mine. She had my eyes, too. And freckles everywhere." She let out a little laugh. "God, how she hated her freckles. Called them her ugly spots. I used to tease her about them, chasing after her with a felt-tipped pen, saying I knew there was a picture on her body if she would just let me connect the dots. She would run all through the house, squealing and laughing, trying to get away from me."

Bender smiled as he watched Kerri's face delight with the memories. But then she turned grim and serious.

"She was five when she first got sick," Kerri said in a dead monotone. Her eyes flew open, as if the images in her mind had suddenly become too painful. "It all started with a tummy ache. At first I thought it was just a stomach flu, but when it persisted for several days, Nathan examined her. He felt a mass in her belly. Two days later we had the diagnosis: Wilm's tumor.

"They started her on chemotherapy right away, and removed as much as they could with surgery. At first, things looked pretty hopeless; the chemo didn't seem to be working. But then something kicked in and the tumor started shrinking. One year later, it was completely gone."

Bender looked confused. "It grew back?"

"No," Kerri said with a heavy sigh. "It never did. But the chemo doses they gave her were so high it damaged her heart and her kidneys. First the kidneys failed, and we had to start her on dialysis. When her heart went, the clock started ticking. The only thing that might have saved her was a transplant. But we didn't get one in time." Kerri looked over at Bender. "She died two days before her seventh birthday."

Bender's eyes, full of warmth and tenderness, caressed her face. "I can't even begin to imagine how that must have been for you," he said softly. "Though it does explain some things."

Kerri's brow drew down in puzzlement. "Such as?"

"Well, it explains your interest in Jace, why you're so caught up in his case."

At the mention of Jace, Kerri's face fell and her head once more tipped back against the seat, her eyes staring at the car's ceiling. "A lot of good I've done him," she muttered. "He's still unresponsive."

"I know."

Kerri rolled her head and looked at him. "You know? How?"

"I called the hospital this morning and checked on him," Bender explained.

His revelation touched Kerri, and she reached over and laid a hand on his arm, giving it a squeeze. "You know, you're not such a bad guy after all, Mindbender."

"Don't pass judgment too quickly," he cautioned. "You don't know the half of it."

TWENTY-TWO

By the time they off-loaded in Winslow and drove as far as the Hood Canal Bridge on their way to Route 101, Bender had outlined his strategy for approaching the Coleman Institute, which also explained his attire.

"Let me get this straight," Kerri said, shaking her head in wonderment. "You're passing yourself off as some rich corporate executive looking to invest your millions?"

"You got it."

"What millions?" Kerri scoffed. "What if they try to do a credit or financial check of your background?"

Bender ignored the question. "It seems like the surest way to get a tour of the place. But it will require some bluffing. When we get there, you just stand beside me and look ravishing. Leave the rest up to me."

"That's a rather chauvinistic plan, don't you think?"

Bender shook his head and winked at her. "I don't *think* it's chauvinistic, I know it is."

Kerri frowned. "I think I'm beginning to understand why you cautioned me about your character."

"You ain't seen nothing yet," Bender said. "By the way, I was able to reach five of my group patients after I talked to you this morning and, I'm afraid to say, I came up empty. Nancy has a mild case of arthritis but, other than that, they're all fit as a fiddle. In fact, about the only thing they have in common medically is their good health. That, and the fact four of them donate blood on a regular basis."

Kerri gaped at him. "Oh, my God," she mumbled. "That could be it."

"What could be it?"

"They donate blood. Janet Johansen was a regular donor, too. Wouldn't that give them a way to do follow-up studies? If my theory is correct, that is."

Bender shrugged. "Seems a bit iffy to me. I mean there's no guarantee they'll donate on any kind of regular schedule."

"Still," Kerri said, "it's the only common bond we've found. If the two patients you didn't reach also turn out to be donors, don't you think that's significant?"

"Could be," Bender admitted. "I'll try to reach them tomorrow to see what I can find out. Though I doubt they're all donors." He chewed his lip thoughtfully a moment. "You know, this doesn't necessarily rule out the other explanation."

"What other explanation?"

"That they are victims of exactly what they claim."

"What?" Kerri asked, askance. "That they were abducted by aliens? Do you actually believe that?"

Bender shrugged. "I'm not ruling it out," he said.

"If it was aliens," Kerri said, "why would they dump Janet Johansen's body in the lake, taking the time to weigh it down with a cinder block? Why wouldn't they just take her away? On their spaceship, or whatever."

"You have a point," Bender admitted. "But we'll

have to debate it later." He pointed out the window. "There's the turnoff to the Coleman Institute."

The place was more accessible than they expected. They found a rolling gate built into the chain-link fence, but it was open, allowing them to drive unhindered onto the property. They parked in a space marked VISITOR and headed for the main entrance—which also happened to be the only visible entrance on this side of the building.

"By the way," Bender said, adjusting his tie as they walked, "if anyone asks, you're my wife."

Kerri gave him a dubious glance and considered a protest, but thought better of it. Instead, she rolled her eyes and muttered under her breath as they entered the covered walkway leading to the entrance. When they reached the door, the Coleman Institute's easy accessibility ended.

"Looks like you need a key card of some sort," Kerri said, studying the mechanism beside the glass door. She tried to peer inside, but the glass was heavily tinted, and all she could see was the parking lot and trees behind them reflected in the smoky surface. She stepped back and looked around.

"There's a camera," she said, pointing above their heads toward the ceiling of the small alcove.

"And here's a button," Bender said, staring at the wall beside the door. He jabbed it with a finger, holding it in for a few seconds, then releasing it. A moment later, a sultry female voice came from the wall.

"May I help you?"

"Yes," Bender said, staring up at the camera. "My name is Michael Bender. I have an appointment with Mr. Cavanaugh."

Kerri shot him a startled look, then remembered

the camera and stared at her feet instead. She was even more surprised when the woman's voice echoed through the alcove again, saying, "Please open the door when you hear the buzzer, Mr. Bender. And welcome to the Coleman Institute."

Kerri glanced up at Bender with grudging admiration. When the buzzer sounded, he pulled the door open and waved Kerri in ahead of him.

The lobby of the building was small, most of it occupied by a security area with a long counter, a wall of TV monitors, three telephones, and a display of buttons and flashing lights. A couple of chairs, separated by a small end table, sat beneath the window on the left side of the room. Behind the security desk two elevators sat side by side in the back wall, a third was situated off to the left, perpendicular to the first two.

Bender strode toward the security desk with an air of confidence Kerri had to admire. Trying to hide her own nervousness, she followed meekly behind him.

A female receptionist—no doubt the voice they'd heard outside—sat at the desk, chatting into a phone. Behind her stood two men wearing security uniforms. One of them—tall, bald, and granite faced—stared at Kerri and Bender as they approached. The second man, who was shorter but with a solid, thick-built torso, studied the monitor displays.

The bald man flashed an obviously perfunctory smile. "You are Mr. Bender," he stated, his tone businesslike.

"I am," Bender said. He reached back and draped an arm over Kerri's shoulders, pulling her forward. "And this is my wife, Kerri."

Kerri didn't dare look at Bender. She fought an urge to explode with nervous laughter.

"Here are your security passes," the bald guard said, handing each of them a laminated clip-on card with the words *Coleman Institute* emblazoned across them in big, red letters. Kerri clipped hers on her collar, glad to have something to do with her nervous hands. "You can take the elevators to the third floor," the guard told them. "Mr. Cavanaugh's assistant, Ms. Miller, will meet you there."

"Thank you," Bender said. His hand settled in at the small of Kerri's back, and he nudged her toward the elevators.

The bald guard led the way, slipping a card into a slot beside one of the elevators against the back wall. With a quiet whoosh, the door slid open. A ten-digit keypad was built into the wall beside each of the elevators, and the guard punched in a series of numbers before waving Kerri and Bender inside.

"The elevators open on both sides above this floor," the guard explained. "I've programmed this one so only the north door will open when you get to the third floor. Ms. Miller will be waiting for you there."

"You have quite the security system here," Bender observed.

The guard nodded. "All access is controlled by key cards, and every entry is recorded in a computer log, so we can tell who has been where, and when. There is a fair amount of espionage in drug research, so one can't be too careful. Now, if you don't mind . . ." He gestured toward the interior of the elevator.

Kerri followed Bender inside and watched as the door slid closed, gradually blocking out the guard's steely face.

As soon as she felt the car start to move, Kerri looked up at Bender and rolled her eyes. She was anxious to ask him how he had managed to gain an appointment with this Mr. Cavanaugh, whoever he was. But before she could utter a single word, Bender's hand gave her shoulder a warning squeeze, and he said, "Well, at least we can feel confident the security here is adequate."

Kerri followed his gaze to a video camera tucked in one corner of the car near the ceiling. A tiny red light glowed at its base.

Bender looked down at her and winked.

The elevator slid to a smooth stop, and the doors opened onto a narrow hallway that dead-ended to the left. Directly ahead was a row of tinted windows offering a breathtaking view of the strait and Vancouver Island. Standing in front of the windows, haloed by the golden afternoon light, was a tall, slender woman with sleek, black hair pulled back into a neatly coifed chignon. Her eyes were blue, her skin flawless. She was wearing a well-tailored suit that revealed a waist that looked to Kerri to be about as big around as a pencil.

"Hi, I'm Letitia Miller," she said. Her eyes gave Kerri a cursory look, then slid toward Bender. "We spoke on the phone, Mr. Bender. Welcome to the Coleman Institute. If you'll follow me, Mr. Cavanaugh is waiting for you."

With that, she turned and headed down the narrow hallway toward a glass door. Kerri followed, marveling at the thickness of the carpet beneath their feet. It seemed that pharmaceutical research might be more lucrative than she realized. Letitia pushed open the door and held it for them as they entered, then took the lead once again. They passed through a main reception area filled with desks, all of them peopled with efficient-looking women who tapped away at computer terminals or chatted amicably on the phone. The far back corner of the room opened onto another hallway, this one marked by a series of doors down either side, each one bearing a gold colored plaque engraved with the occupant's name. Kerri read them as they passed—CARL BOOKER, CHIEF FINANCIAL OFFICER; MERIDAN CROUCH, MARKETING DIRECTOR; STANLEY DELBERT, VICE PRESIDENT. When they came to the door at the left end of the hallway marked ARTHUR CAVANAUGH, PRESIDENT, Letitia gave a quick little knock and pushed the door open.

"Mr. and Mrs. Bender to see you, Arthur." She stepped aside and waved Kerri and Bender through the doorway.

Kerri went in first, the thick carpet beneath her feet making her feel unsteady. It was a typical executive suite—large, airy, furnished in leather and mahogany, a wet bar positioned against one wall, a conference table and chairs near another. Yet, Kerri was struck by how impersonal the room felt. The walls were bare with the exception of a large framed poster bearing the Coleman company name and logo, and there was a noticeable lack of personal accoutrements—no family photos, no knickknacks, nothing to offer up any clues as to the personality or lifestyle of its main occupant.

Behind the desk sat a small man with thinning blond hair and a face as plain and featureless as the room. He pushed his chair back and stood, then moved around to greet his guests.

"Ah, Mr. Bender," he said with a voice that was smooth and cultured. He extended a hand and gave Bender a hearty handshake. Then his eyes shifted to

Kerri and he gave her a subtle perusal, one eyebrow arching with approval. "And Mrs. Bender," he murmured. Kerri offered her hand for a shake as well, but to her surprise, Arthur Cavanaugh bowed down and brushed his lips over the back of it.

"Please," Cavanaugh said, rising back up and giving Kerri's hand an almost imperceptible squeeze before he released it, "let's have a seat over here." He turned and strode toward the conference table, sliding out one of the chairs near the end for Kerri. She took the seat, then stuffed her hands down between her knees to hide their trembling. Bender took the seat directly across from her; Cavanaugh, the one at the table's head.

"Well, now," Cavanaugh said, folding his hands together on the table in front of him and leaning toward Bender. "I understand you are interested in investing in our company."

"Possibly," Bender said, leaning back in his chair and lacing his hands together over his stomach. "I've been looking around for some time now, trying to find an appropriate investment opportunity."

Cavanaugh smiled—a smile Kerri thought looked both phony and predatory. "Why us, Mr. Bender?" Cavanaugh asked.

Bender pursed his lips and squinted toward the ceiling. "I understand your company has discovered a new drug that might provide a remarkable breakthrough in the treatment of Alzheimer's disease. That, and some of your other research makes me think you're the type of aggressive and far-thinking company I would like to be a part of."

"I see," Cavanaugh said with a curious frown. "May I ask how you became privy to this information?"

Yes, Kerri thought, trying not to gawk at Bender. *How did you uncover this information?*

Bender gave Cavanaugh a cryptic grin. "Wouldn't want to give away all my trade secrets," he said. "Suffice it to say I have plenty of contacts in the business world."

Cavanaugh digested this answer a moment, then apparently decided to accept it. He leaned back in his chair, one elbow propped on the arm, two fingers tapping his cheek. "So tell me, Mr. Bender. How much are you looking to invest?"

"My company has done quite well," Bender explained. "The wife and I are certainly comfortable. But the future is always full of surprises. I'm looking to diversify my holdings more, to ensure our future years," Bender said.

Kerri realized the two men were playing a game of cat and mouse. Though her nerves had been frazzled when they first arrived here, after watching Bender in action, she was beginning to relax and actually enjoy this little riposte. But the next words out of Cavanaugh's mouth sent her heart to tripping again.

"Yes," Cavanaugh said with a little nod. "I took the liberty, after our conversation on the phone this morning, of checking with some business contacts of my own."

Oh, shit! Kerri thought. *That's it. The jig is up.* The man had uncovered their little masquerade, and now they would be escorted from the building and grounds. Oh, God! What if Cavanaugh called the police? Were they breaking any laws? Kevin would kill her if she got arrested.

Kerri tensed, waiting for the climax she knew was mere moments away. She stared at Bender, willing him to look her way. How could the man remain so composed and calm?

"Your company certainly does have an outstanding record," Cavanaugh continued. "You've done quite well."

Kerri dropped her eyes to her lap, afraid of giving away the shock she knew must be visible on her face. Had she heard Cavanaugh right? What the hell was going on?

"Thank you," she heard Bender say. "But before I make any decisions here, I was wondering if we might impose on you for a tour of the facility. I like to see where my money is going, and how it's being spent."

"Of course," Cavanaugh said. "I would do it myself, but unfortunately I have another appointment scheduled here shortly. If you'll excuse me a moment, I'll get Ms. Miller to show you around."

"That would be fine," Bender said.

Cavanaugh stood and moved across the room toward his desk. There, he punched a button on his phone. "Letitia? Could you come in here please?"

While Cavanaugh was across the room, Kerri risked a peek at Bender, questioning him with an arch of her brows.

Bender leaned across the table toward her. "Just go with it," he whispered. "I'll explain later."

The door to Cavanaugh's office opened and Letitia Miller entered, looking as smooth and composed as before. She approached Cavanaugh's desk. "Yes?" she asked him.

"I'd like you to give the Benders a tour of our facility, please. Mr. Bender is very interested in seeing how we operate before he commits himself to investing in our future."

"I'd be delighted," Letitia crooned. Kerri decided then that she did not like this woman; she was much too slick and smooth for Kerri's taste. Besides, she didn't much care for the way the woman had eyed Bender earlier. "If you two will follow me," Letitia said, "we'll get started."

Bender looked at Kerri, his eyes bright with mischief. "Shall we, honey?" he said, standing and coming around to pull her chair out for her.

Kerri bit her lip. She wanted nothing more than to give Bender a hard punch at the moment. Instead, she stood and faced him with a grittingly sweet smile. She would play the game for now, but later, when she had him alone again, Dr. Michael Bender was going to have some serious explaining to do.

TWENTY-THREE

Letitia Miller led Kerri and Bender back out to the elevators. "We'll start with the fourth floor and work our way down," she explained, inserting her ID card into the slot. "The fourth floor is where we do most of our animal research."

"What about the fifth floor?" Bender asked as they stepped into the elevator.

Letitia pushed the button for the fourth floor, then turned to give Bender a congratulatory look. "You are very observant, Mr. Bender," she said. "The fifth floor is restricted. No visitors are allowed there, and only certain employees have access. As you might imagine, we deal with some very hazardous materials at times . . . viruses, bacteria, and such. Those are all contained on the fifth floor and require the utmost biohazard precautions. You can't even get to that floor from the two main elevators. We have a separate elevator that runs only between the first and fifth floors."

Kerri recalled the lone elevator set in the wall perpendicular to the other two in the lobby downstairs. She also noted that, just as Letitia had pointed out, the elevator they were in had buttons for floors one through four only.

The elevator slid to a halt and they stepped into a

hallway mirroring the one below, except this one required a card to access the door at the end. It opened into a small foyer with a loud whoosh of air. Bender and Kerri followed Letitia into the tiny room and waited as the door behind them closed and the one at the other end of the foyer opened with another rush of cool air.

"Air lock," Letitia explained as they stepped into a huge laboratory area with workstations positioned at various points. "To minimize contaminants here in the lab." She walked over to a row of coat hooks and took down a pair of lab coats, handing them over to Kerri and Bender. Then she took one for herself. "If you don't mind," she said, slipping hers on. "These also help to prevent contaminants from getting into our samples." Bender and Kerri dutifully slipped on the coats and buttoned them up. They then followed Letitia into the main room.

A row of lab tables ran down the center, each one covered with a collection of scientific equipment: beakers, pipettes, Bunsen burners, electronic scales, and any number of bottles filled with reagents, chemicals, and such. A dozen or so employees, outfitted in knee-length white lab coats with COLEMAN emblazoned across the breast pockets, scurried about looking studious and preoccupied. No one paid the visiting trio the least bit of attention.

As they moved farther into the room, Kerri saw there were smaller, individual labs bordering the room's periphery. Enclosed behind glass partitions, most were outfitted in the same manner as the main lab except for the large laminar-flow hoods extending out over the worktables.

"This," Letitia said, making a wide sweeping

gesture with her arm, "is our main compounding area. Most of the drugs we use in our animal trials are prepared here. Of course, we maintain rigorous controls over the prep areas and techniques, to be sure to avoid any contamination that might adversely affect the results of the tests."

"What about human trials?" Kerri asked.

Letitia gave her a look of patient tolerance. "We do not conduct any human trials here, of course," she said, as if she was talking to a dumb two-year-old. "Those are handled on the outside. We do coordinate things from our offices, shipping the drugs to outside participants, tracking what goes where, that sort of thing. Most of our studies are double-blinds, using placebos along with the real drug. The labeling is carefully coded so none of the participants can tell which is the real drug and which is the placebo. There are records kept, of course, noting which is which, but they are maintained by an outside agency and guarded with tight security so only a limited number of people have access to the information. That way, we can ensure our study results are legitimate, and not influenced by the researchers, the physicians, or the patients."

"I assume you use blood work in some of these tests?" Kerri asked.

"We do," Letitia answered, looking a little perplexed.

"Who handles your blood work?" Kerri asked.

"Depends," Letitia told her. "We have a number of independent laboratories who run tests for us. Sometimes, the blood is shipped directly to us and the studies are done here. Why do you ask?"

"Just curious," Kerri said with a shrug. "I've always wondered how that sort of thing is handled."

"I see," Letitia said in a way that suggested just the opposite. She turned away from Kerri and flashed a quixotic smile at Bender. Kerri felt as if she had been summarily dismissed.

"Would you be interested in seeing our animal storage area?" Letitia asked Bender. "I'll understand if you'd rather not. Some people are disturbed by the sight of all those caged animals."

Kerri suspected Letitia's last words were directed at her as sort of a challenge. She wasn't about to let this woman get the best of her. "I'd like to see it," she piped up.

Letitia turned toward Kerri with a startled expression. "Well," she said in a tone of voice that clearly communicated her doubt, "follow me." She spun on her heel and sashayed to the far right corner of the main laboratory area. From there, she went through another air lock and headed down a long hallway.

As soon as the door slid shut behind them, Kerri heard the distant chatter of monkeys from somewhere down the hall. A faint scent of disinfectant hung in the air, mingling with an animal smell that reminded Kerri of a trip she, Nathan, and Mandy had taken to the Sydney Zoo in Vancouver some years back.

Letitia halted in front of a door marked ANIMAL HABITAT—AUTHORIZED PERSONNEL ONLY, and again used her card to gain access. The monkey chatter increased several decibels as soon as the door swung open.

The room they entered resembled a long, narrow warehouse: concrete floors and walls extended back a few hundred feet, rows of fluorescent lighting hung from the ceiling. Down the middle of the room was a series of stainless steel tables. The right wall was lined with various-sized cages, stacked one on top of another, looking like some bizarre urban housing complex for animals. Most of the cages were occupied—those nearest the door with rabbits and mice, and farther down, larger cages with furry humanlike fingers poking through the mesh doors. From the incredible screeching chatter arising from that area, Kerri guessed most of those cages held monkeys.

At one of the center tables, a blond female attendant wearing one of the ubiquitous white lab coats stood with her back to them. On the table sat a small spider monkey, his chest shaved bare and covered with a large white bandage. Even from a distance, Kerri could see the animal looked subdued and glassy eyed as the attendant listened to its chest with a stethoscope.

A faint bubbling sound drew Kerri's attention toward the left side of the room. There, built into the wall, was a series of large aquarium tanks. Intrigued, Kerri moved closer, studying their contents. Each one contained a minibiosphere of marine life: plants of all types and colors, starfish, sea horses, anemones, tube worms, squid, urchins, and a variety of fish in varying shapes, sizes, and colors.

Seeing the direction of Kerri's attention, Letitia said, "As you may know, much of our focus here is on the discovery of chemicals and enzymes that might be harvested from marine flora and fauna to use in the production of new drugs."

"Fascinating," Bender said, moving toward the aquariums and studying each one in turn. "These are salt water I presume?"

Letitia maneuvered herself between Bender and Kerri—close enough to Bender that their shoulders touched. Kerri scowled. "They are," Letitia said. "We have technicians who monitor them around the clock to be sure the water content, light, and temperature are maintained as close to real oceanic conditions as possible."

Hearing a chattering whimper, Korri turned back toward the table with the spider monkey. "What is wrong with him?" she asked, genuinely curious but also hoping to divert Letitia's attention away from Bender. Though interested in the monkey, Kerri also studied the back of the blond attendant working on the animal. Something about her seemed familiar.

"He's one of our test subjects for a new cardiac drug," Letitia explained. "We had to perform some surgery on him in order to ascertain the efficacy of the drug on his heart muscle."

"Fascinating," Bender said again.

Letitia leaned closer to him. "We house most of our test animals here, monitoring their reactions to the various drugs under study. The cardiac drug we've used on Horatio over there is one of the more promising items on our menu. It actually regenerates damaged heart muscle and might someday make heart surgery a thing of the past."

"Horatio?" Bender said, amused.

"We treat our animals as humanely as possible. Naming them is just one of the many things we do to personalize their care, to keep them from becoming just another experiment."

Kerri's eyes swept over the nearby cages, studying the faces of the monkeys inside. Several of them, she saw, had bandages covering portions of their bodies, as if they had been subject to some recent surgical procedure. A few of them sat subdued and dejected looking, their brown eyes peering through the mesh with listless apathy. Others clamored about, reaching through the cage doors with their furry fingers, screeching at the visitors and leaping about for attention.

Letitia turned toward the wall of tanks behind them. "Of course," she said, "not all of our treatments are successful and at times the animals must be sacrificed. Behind these walls is our main pathology and surgery area where we perform the animal autopsies and vivisections." She punctuated this last sentence with a cute little wrinkle of her nose. Glancing pointedly at Kerri, she added, "As I said before, not everything about this work is pleasant."

As soon as Letitia turned back toward Bender, Kerri rolled her eyes. Coming here had been a bad idea, she decided. She was wracking her brain for an excuse to leave when providence provided one for her. The insouciant chirping of her beeper echoed through the air.

Bender shot her a startled, almost panicky look. This was obviously one contingency he hadn't planned for. But he recovered quickly. "Oh, dammit, darling," he cooed. "Can't your patients leave you be for a few hours?" With that he turned and gave Letitia an apologetic shrug. "My wife is a psychiatrist," he explained. "She insists on maintaining her practice." He rolled his eyes in a "go figure" manner, making Kerri want to hit him.

Kerri glanced at the beeper, intending to ignore it until she saw the phone number for the pediatric unit at the hospital displayed. Jace! Her heart did a little leap inside her chest. Looking at Bender, she did her best imitation of Letitia's eyelash batting, and said, "Sorry dear, but you know how much my work means to me. Particularly the children."

Bender gave her a small nod to indicate he understood. Kerri turned toward Letitia. "Is there a phone nearby I might use?"

"Certainly," Letitia said with an eagerness suggesting she would be more than glad to get rid of Kerri for a few moments. "Right this way."

Kerri followed her toward the back of the room, past poor Horatio, who glanced up at them with pleading brown eyes. Letitia led Kerri into a small office with three cluttered desks, a couple of filing cabinets, and a coffeemaker that looked as if it had seen better days. "You'll need to dial a nine first," Letitia said, pointing toward one of the phones. "Your husband and I will be waiting for you." With that, she swished her way back down the long room toward Bender.

Letting loose with a volley of tiny eye daggers into Letitia's back, Kerri picked up the phone, punched in the number for the pediatric unit, and waited impatiently while the phone rang several times. Her eyes drifted back toward the woman attendant. Now that she was at this end of the room, she could see the woman's face and recognized it at once—Jeri Sandston—a patient Kerri had treated several years ago. As if on cue, Jeri Sandston's gaze caught Kerri's, and she gave her an almost imperceptible nod of acknowledgment before returning her focus to her simian patient. Kerri was not surprised; her patients often ignored her when they met in public. Even in today's society, where such things were certainly more accepted than they used to be, a surprising number of people didn't want their friends or coworkers to know they suffered from any type of mental health problems. Kerri was willing to play along with the facade, in the interest of her patient's privacy.

"Pediatrics."

Kerri's attention turned to the voice on the other end of the phone. "This is Dr. Whitaker," she said. "You paged me?"

"Yes, Dr. Whitaker. You wanted us to let you know if there was any change in the Johansen boy."

"That's right," Kerri said, barely able to breathe as she awaited whatever news the nurse had to share.

"Well, he has come around," the nurse said. "And he is asking for you."

Kerri's heart somersaulted and she shut her eyes with relief. When she opened them again, she saw Jeri Sandston staring at her. "That is great news," Kerri said, her voice almost breaking with emotion. "Please tell him I will be there as soon as I can. I'm on the peninsula now." She raised her arm and glanced at her watch, doing some quick calculations. "Tell him I'll be there around seven," she said finally.

"I'll do that," the nurse said. "I think he'll be glad to see you."

"Thank you for calling me."

"No problem, Dr. Whitaker. See you later."

Kerri set the phone down and looked for Bender. He and Letitia were chatting amicably near the door at the other end of the room. She made her way toward them, taking her cue from Jeri Sandston's downturned gaze and ignoring the woman as she passed. Resisting the urge to push her way between Letitia and Bender, she settled for hooking Bender's elbow with her arm and pressing herself against his side.

"I'm afraid we need to go, dear," she said with sickening sweetness. She could tell from the glint in Bender's eye that her sarcasm hadn't gone unnoticed.

"Oh, I am so sorry," Letitia said, her eyes focused

solely on Bender. "Perhaps you would like to schedule another visit, so you can see the rest of our facility?"

"Thank you," Bender said more warmly than Kerri liked, though his next words heartened her some. "But I don't think it will be necessary. You may tell Mr. Cavanaugh I will be in touch."

"Wonderful!" Letitia said, clapping her hands together. "I hope that means you will be joining the Coleman family soon."

"That is certainly a possibility," Bender said.

"I'll see you out," Letitia offered, swaying her narrow hips and walking to the door. "I'm very glad I had the opportunity to meet you, and look forward to working together in the future." Almost as an afterthought, she turned and looked at Kerri. "Both of you," she added with saccharine sweetness.

As they ventured back down the hallway to the main lab area, they passed a restroom. "I need to use the ladies' room," Kerri said to Bender. "It's a long drive back."

Letitia stopped, flashed another of her syrupy smiles, and said, "No problem. While you take care of business, I'll introduce your husband to some of our technicians. We'll meet you out in the main lab area?"

Though worded as a question, Kerri knew her answer was neither desired nor necessary. When Letitia hooked her arm through Bender's and steered him toward the main lab, Kerri shoved open the bathroom door and stomped inside. Fuming, she entered one of the stalls, slamming the door so hard it bounced back and hit her in the hip.

"Dammit," she muttered.

Once she was finished, she exited the stall and gave her hands a quick rinse beneath the faucet. As she turned to pull out a paper towel, the bathroom door opened and Jeri Sandston entered.

"Well, hello," Kerri greeted warmly. "It's good to see you. How's everything going?"

Jeri Sandston looked back over her shoulder as if she feared someone might be standing behind her. *Geez,* Kerri thought. *This woman is more paranoid than most about having her little problem discovered.*

Jeri Sandston turned a pale and decidedly nervous face toward Kerri. "Dr. Whitaker, I heard what your husband was discussing with Miss Miller," she said in a low voice.

Kerri started to explain that Bender wasn't her husband, then thought better of it.

"If you are truly interested in investing in this place, I think you ought to know there is something very strange going on here."

"What do you mean?"

"I don't want to go into it here," Jeri said, making another backward glance. "But someone ought to know. It isn't right."

Suddenly, Kerri's ire over Letitia Miller coming onto Bender vanished, and she remembered the reason they had come here in the first place. "Tell me what you mean, Jeri," she urged.

Jeri Sandston shook her head. "Someone might come in here," she said anxiously. "Can you meet with me sometime tomorrow?"

"Sure. Why don't you come to my office? I'll fit you in between patients."

Again, Jeri shook her head. "No, not there. That's too obvious."

"Okay," Kerri said with some confusion. "I'm open to suggestions." She thought back to earlier in the day, when she had scanned the appointment book for the next few days. "I believe my last patient tomorrow is at four. Perhaps we could meet somewhere after that?"

"Are you familiar with the Red Robin Restaurant on Fourth Avenue?" Jeri asked.

"Very," Kerri answered. "In fact, I go there quite often."

"How about if I meet you there? Say, around five thirty?"

"Sure," Kerri said with a shrug. She frowned at Jeri. "Can't you give me some clue as to what this is all about?"

"Tomorrow," Jeri said, chewing on her thumbnail. "I've been here too long already." She moved toward the door, pulled it open, then paused to glance back at Kerri. "Thank you," she mouthed. And then she was gone.

Kerri managed to extricate Bender from Letitia Miller's swooning grasp, but not until they had returned to the main lobby.

"Hope to see you again soon," Letitia cooed, her eyes focused solely on Bender.

"Likewise," Bender said, and Kerri had to resist an urge to yank his arm toward the door. As they were leaving the building, Kerri gave one last glance over her shoulder, half-expecting to see Letitia Miller gazing longingly at Bender's back. But the woman was not watching them at all. Instead, she was busy chatting with the two security guards behind the desk.

Once they were safely ensconced inside the car, Kerri turned toward Bender with an irritated expression. "Okay, Mindbender, you've got some explaining to do."

Bender ignored her and asked instead, "Where are we going? The hospital, I presume?"

"Yes," Kerri said, her curiosity momentarily set aside as thoughts of Jace filled her mind. "Jace has come around, and he's asking for me."

"That's wonderful!" Bender said.

"It is," Kerri agreed, "but it doesn't let you off the hook. Would you mind explaining to me how you managed to pull off that charade in there?"

"I'm a man of many talents," Bender said, casting her a sidelong glance.

"Dammit, Bender! Quit stringing me along."

"Okay, okay." He held one hand up in surrender. "The Bender Corporation really exists. My father started it many years ago, and when he died, ownership passed on to my brother and me. David—that's my brother—is president and CEO. I don't really have much to do with the place, though I own half the stock. We manufacture parts for planes and do some work for NASA as well."

"Wait a minute," Kerri said, studying Bender's profile with a puzzled expression. "The Bender Corporation. You're talking about *the* Bender Corporation?"

Bender shrugged and nodded. "There is only one, I believe."

"Are you telling me you're rich?"

Bender shrugged. "I suppose I am," he said. "Does that lower your opinion of me?"

Kerri let out a snicker of disbelief. "When I found out you hot-wired my car, I was afraid you had some sort of criminal record or something. Now I find out you're a wealthy business magnate. No wonder people call you Mindbender." She shook her head in amazement. "Why do you continue with your practice?"

"Because I love it," Bender answered. "I enjoy the

people, and I enjoy helping them. I guess the fact I don't have to do it makes it even more appealing. Wouldn't you continue with your practice, even if you didn't need to to make a living?"

Kerri pondered the question a moment, then said, "I honestly don't know."

"So," Bender said, "if we were to marry, you'd be willing to stay barefoot and pregnant."

Kerri gaped at him. "Married? What could possibly make you think I'd want to marry a lying, sneaky scoundrel like you? And, no, I wouldn't stay barefoot and pregnant."

"Does that mean yes?"

"Does what mean yes?"

"That you'll marry me."

Kerri studied him, slack jawed. "Are you serious?" she asked.

Bender looked over at her, a teasing glint in his eye. "Why do you think I passed you off as my wife back there? I wanted to give you a taste of how wonderful it could be."

"Wonderful? How could it be wonderful watching that Miller woman hang all over you like an oversized coat?"

Bender grinned broadly. "You were jealous," he teased.

"No, I wasn't jealous," Kerri said, turning away and staring out the side window. "I just didn't want you to lose sight of why we were there."

"Admit it," Bender said. "You were jealous."

"I was not," Kerri said to the window.

"Okay," Bender said with a regretful little shake of his head. "You'll come around soon enough. Though if you could have seen the moves that Miller woman put on me while you were in the bathroom, you'd be worried as hell by now."

"That reminds me," Kerri said, snapping her fingers and turning back toward Bender. "Remember the lab assistant who was working on that monkey?"

Bender nodded.

"Her name is Jeri Sandston, and she's an ex-patient of mine. She met me in the bathroom for an interesting tête-à-tête. Said there's something strange going on at the Coleman Institute and she wants to tell me about it."

"Strange as in what?" Bender asked.

"She wouldn't say. She kept looking over her shoulder as if she was nervous about someone coming into the bathroom and seeing her. I'm supposed to meet her at the Red Robin on Fourth tomorrow at five thirty to find out what this is all about."

"Interesting," Bender said thoughtfully. "Think it would be possible for me to tag along?"

"I don't know," Kerri said hesitantly. "She seemed pretty spooked and I don't want to scare her off."

"It's up to you," Bender said. "She's your patient. You know her better than I. But I would like to hear what she has to say."

Kerri considered it a moment, then said, "What the hell. I don't think she'll mind. As it is, she thinks you're my husband. But I'd like to give her the choice. Why don't you plan on meeting us there and I'll ask her if you can stay. But if she says no, you'll have to go."

"Fair enough," Bender said. Then he added, "But I'm sure she'll let me stay. The Bender charm is hard to resist. Just ask Letitia Miller."

TWENTY-FOUR

Kerri listened to her last patient of the day—Calvin Korb, a recovering alcoholic—with only half an ear. It had been that way most of the day, her mind preoccupied with thoughts of meeting Jeri Sandston this evening, and seeing Jace last night.

Stephen noticed something was bothering her as soon as she walked in the door. As she filled him in on the events of the weekend—Thad Johansen's suicide and Jace's subsequent collapse—she saw his face turn pale and grim. She knew that Stephen, like herself, had grown attached to Jace in the short time they'd spent together. No doubt he identified with the boy's losses on a deeply personal level. Seeing how bothered Stephen was by the latest traumas in Jace's life, Kerri opted not to tell him about her own adventures over the weekend. He looked troubled enough.

Jace's recovery was not as great as she had hoped. Last night, after Bender had graciously offered to let her out of her dinner commitment (though he did insist they stop at a fast food place for burgers, to be sure she ate something), she dropped him off at the parking garage where he'd left his car and drove to the hospital with great anticipation. But when she entered Jace's room, she saw that even though the boy had, indeed, come out of his catatonic state, there was still an air of listless apathy about him. She was briefly heartened by the tiny spark of interest she saw in his dull blue eyes when she first came into the room, but the spark quickly faded, leaving behind an expressionless mask she knew hid the wounds beneath.

Fearful of triggering yet another emotional overload, she carefully avoided any mention of Thad or Janet, figuring the boy would broach the topic himself when he was ready. Instead, she snuggled into the bed beside him and held him against her chest, while she read him stories from some books the nurses brought in to her. Jace drifted off to sleep in her arms, the gentle rhythm of his breathing and the warmth of his body curled against her own stirring maternal longings she thought had died long ago. After easing Jace down onto the bed and tucking the covers in around his bony shoulders, she reluctantly tiptoed out, leaving instructions with the nurses to tell him she would be back in the morning. On the drive home she nearly cried when she thought about all the pain and suffering Jace had experienced at such a tender age. Like Mandy, he had been burdened with trials far too overwhelming for his tiny mind and body. And as she did with Mandy, Kerri once again questioned a God who could make life such misery for the most innocent of his lambs. Though she may not have been able to save Mandy, she was determined to help Jace. Her promise had only strengthened when she visited Jace again the next morning and saw little change in his condition.

Though a good portion of her thoughts throughout the day were focused on Jace, Kerri also wondered about Jeri Sandston and her mysterious invitation. During her brief lunch break, she dragged out Jeri's old chart and reviewed the notes. Jeri Sandston was a well-educated and highly intelligent woman—a scientist who based all of her beliefs and thoughts on visible, tangible proof. She wasn't given to flights of fancy, nor did she have a particularly vivid imagination. So whatever information she might have would certainly be worth listening to. Kerri wondered what it could be. Was it possible the Coleman Institute was somehow involved with what had happened to the Johansens? Could her theory be right? It seemed almost too easy to have stumbled onto something this quickly, but she was a firm believer in fate, and perhaps fate had decided to smile kindly on her for a change.

When Mr. Korb finally left, Kerri asked Stephen to close up the office and headed out. Hiking the mostly uphill blocks to the Red Robin, she arrived flushed and breathless a few minutes before five thirty. Seeing no sign of either Jeri Sandston or Bender anywhere outside the restaurant, Kerri pulled the door open to head inside. But a sudden, startling, and blood-curdling scream echoed through the air, making her pause. Kerri let go of the restaurant's door and quickly backed to the edge of the sidewalk, glancing to her left where the noise had come from. She saw nothing odd at first, just the usual rush hour crowd of vehicles and pedestrians pushing their way along the streets and sidewalks. On the far corner, a gaggle of teenage girls hovered near the entrance to a coffee shop, and Kerri thought the scream had probably emanated from them. But then her eyes fell on a middle-aged woman standing on the corner opposite the girls. Dressed in a long worn-looking trench coat with a flimsy, floral-patterned scarf wrapped around her head, the woman was staring in the direction of the vacant lot that filled the block between the Red Robin and the corner. The woman had one hand clamped over her mouth, and her eyes were wide and startled looking.

And then she started to shriek—a strange, wheezy sound laced with panic and fear. The hand covering her mouth shot out, one finger pointing toward the back of the empty lot.

Kerri scanned the lot—a sea of mud with knee-high weeds and grass growing in sporadic clumps. It was strewn with litter—everything from fast food containers and discarded newspapers to an old tire and the remnants of what appeared to be a bicycle frame. Backing it all was a seven-story parking garage, its sheer cement wall rising upward and decorated with spots of graffiti. It was near the base of this wall, in the direction the woman on the corner was pointing, that Kerri finally saw something. At first it looked to be nothing more than a large pile of junk—perhaps discarded clothing?—but something about it bothered her. Kerri moved closer, her brain slowly assembling the pieces.

She was still fifty feet away when she realized the lump was a person. Kerri quickened her pace, thinking the person had perhaps collapsed or been wounded. A few seconds later, she could tell from the clothing it was a woman.

The lady in the trench coat on the corner was still shrieking, and now she was hopping up and down in a panicked dance. A small group of bystanders gathered nearby, some of them trying to calm her, others straining their necks in an effort to see what it was that had her so upset.

Kerri knelt down beside the fallen woman, who was lying on her left side, facing away from Kerri, her long blond hair draped over her face. One leg was folded back beneath her, and Kerri grimaced when she saw the bloody white shard of bone that had pushed itself through the woman's thigh just below the hem of her skirt. A growing pool of blood seeped through the grass, looking like bubbling crude oil where it mixed with the dirt. The woman's neck was bent at an impossible angle, so her chin was butted up against her right shoulder. One arm was hidden beneath the body; the other lay draped over her abdomen. Kerri stared at the draped arm a moment, looking for any sign of movement, some indication the woman was breathing. But there was none. Reaching over, Kerri gently slid two fingers along the woman's throat, feeling for a pulse. A shadow fell over her, and Kerri glanced up to see a young man dressed in a suit and carrying a briefcase.

"Is she dead?" the man asked, his eyes wide as he stared down at the crumpled form.

Kerri nodded.

"That woman over there said she jumped," the young man said. "Jumped right off the top of the garage here." He tore his eyes away from the woman's broken body and gazed up at the concrete wall.

"Christ," Kerri muttered. "Someone needs to call 911," she said, sitting back on her haunches and staring up the wall of the parking garage.

"Someone did," the man told her, his eyes once again riveted on the woman. As if to confirm this, Kerri heard the distant whine of a siren.

"What a horrible way to go," the man said with a shudder.

Kerri said nothing. She turned her attention back to the lifeless form before her, wondering what possible torment could have caused the woman to take such desperate measures. Curious, she reached over and gently brushed the woman's hair back from her face.

"Oh, my God!" Kerri whimpered, her hand clamping over her mouth.

"What?" the man said, looking frantically back and forth from Kerri's face to that of the dead woman.

Kerri gaped up at him, her eyes wide with disbelief. Then she looked back down at the woman, staring into the dead eyes of Jeri Sandston.

Catapulting herself from the ground, Kerri backed away from Jeri Sandston's body as fast as her legs could carry her, while the young man watched her with an expression of wary concern. Then she turned and ran back toward the Red Robin, her mind in a state of wild panic. She saw a police car hurl itself around the corner and skid to a stop beside the vacant lot. Right behind it was an ambulance, its red lights flashing in rhythm with the frenzied pounding of Kerri's heart. Realizing she was on the verge of a full-blown panic, Kerri forced herself to slow down. Turning, she glanced back at the ever-growing crowd of people standing on the corner and along the edges of the lot. She watched as policemen tried to secure the scene, forcing the more aggressive rubberneckers back to the sidewalk bordering the lot.

Kerri's mind replayed the words of the young man. *That woman over there said she jumped . . . jumped right off the top of the garage here.* Kerri's mind whirled. Her chest heaved with frenzied breaths. Her heart pounded like a bass drum. Though the air outside was cool, a sheen of sweat broke out over her body, making her shiver.

Gradually, her brain slowed its endless spinning and she tried to think. And it scared the hell out of her.

She glanced back toward the shrieking woman, who had calmed down to a controlled hysteria. What, exactly, had the woman seen? Had anyone else seen anything? Kerri scanned the other faces in the crowd, stopping when she saw a man standing across the street from her. Something about him was familiar. Of medium height with a stocky build, his face bore a stolid expression as he stared at the shrieking woman. Kerri studied him, convinced she had seen him before, and suddenly feeling it was desperately important to remember where. Her mind cranked through a few dizzying gyrations, but hard as she tried, she couldn't place him.

He turned and looked at her, holding her gaze for a long moment and making something in Kerri's brain, some internal alarm system, start to clamor. For a split second, recognition flashed before her mind, and she reached out for it. But it had all the consistency of the morning mist, and it was gone before she could grasp it. The man abruptly lowered his eyes and moved swiftly away, melting into the growing crowd on the far corner.

"Kerri?"

Kerri let out a startled yelp and whirled around to find herself face-to-face with Bender.

"Oh, God, Bender!" She closed her eyes with relief. Then they flew open again, wide with horror. "Oh, God," she repeated, and she buried her face in his chest.

Bender's hand fluttered tentatively along her back before finally pulling her into him. "What is it?" he asked. "What's wrong?"

Kerri didn't answer him right away. It felt so good to hide her face in the sturdy warmth of his chest, blocking out the horror surrounding her. She wished she could stay here forever, protected by the strength of his arms, drawing comfort from the rhythmic thrum of his heart. Finally, she lifted her tear-stained face toward his and saw he was watching the melee behind her with an expression of mild curiosity.

"What happened?" Bender asked, his hand gently rubbing up and down her spine. "Was there an accident of some sort?"

Kerri opened her mouth to answer him and felt her heart crawl up into her throat. "They said she jumped," she choked out.

Bender glanced down at her with a puzzled frown, then back toward the lot and the growing crowd of people at the base of the garage wall. Realization dawned on his face, and his gaze lurched up toward the roof of the garage. "Somebody jumped?" he asked with a grimace. "A suicide?"

Kerri nodded, then quickly erased that with a vigorous shake of her head. Her throat felt tight and drawn. Her heart pounded so hard she thought Bender must be able to feel it hammering beneath her breast.

Bender placed his hands on Kerri's shoulders and gently pushed her away from him, holding her at arm's length. He looked down at her with warmth and concern. "Did you see it happen? Is that why you're so upset?"

Again, Kerri shook her head. She sucked in a gasping, strangled lungful of air. "It's Jeri," she managed, her voice little more than a whisper. "Jeri Sandston. The woman we were supposed to meet."

"You mean your patient?" Bender asked, his face taking on a sad expression. "No wonder you're upset."

"No, Bender, you don't understand," Kerri said, her eyes wild looking.

"Then it wasn't the woman we're supposed to meet?" Bender asked, clearly bewildered.

"No . . . I mean yes, it is her," Kerri said. "But she didn't jump off that building."

"Then what happened to her?"

Kerri's thoughts began to solidify with horrifying clarity. She didn't want to voice the idea churning through her brain—saying it would make it real.

She turned and looked back at the mayhem behind her. The crowd had now grown to well over fifty people, and there were three police cars and two ambulances on the scene. Kerri saw they had draped a white sheet over Jeri Sandston's body, and the sight of it, with its edges fluttering slightly in the breeze, slammed the reality home. This was no dream. It was real. Terrifyingly, unbelievably real. She began to tremble. Forcing her gaze away from Jeri Sandston's shrouded body, Kerri glanced back toward the shrieking woman. A police officer was talking with her, and she looked shaken and terrified and ready to bolt.

"That woman over there," Kerri said, pointing with a shaking finger. "The one talking with that policeman. She said she saw Jeri jump from the building."

"Then she did jump," Bender said, his confusion giving way to frustration.

"No!" Kerri said, turning back toward him, her eyes ablaze.

"Look, Kerri," Bender said soothingly. "I know this woman used to be a patient of yours. And I know it's hard when you lose a patient like this. But they can fool the best of us."

Kerri punched Bender's arm. "No, dammit! You

don't understand. Yes, Jeri was my patient. And yes, I treated her for over a year. But not for depression or anything like that. Bender, Jeri Sandston's problem was an extreme case of acrophobia. She was so afraid of heights she couldn't look out the second-story windows of her house."

Bender's brow drew down into a puzzled frown. "What are you saying?" he asked cautiously.

Kerri could see the disbelief—no, more of a reluctance to believe—in his face. Carefully, slowly, she gave life to her thoughts. "I'm saying Jeri Sandston not only wouldn't have jumped off that building, she never would have parked in it. Bender, the woman avoided heights like the plague. The reason she came to see me in the first place was because she was having panic attacks just from working on the upper floors of her office. I managed to teach her some biofeedback techniques that helped her to control it. But her control was limited to enclosed areas. Out in the open, she became immobilized with fear if she was more than ten feet off the ground."

Bender's eyes bored into her own. Kerri knew he understood exactly what she was saying. But she plunged on anyway, voicing the dreaded thoughts that haunted her.

"There is no way Jeri Sandston jumped off that building," Kerri said with a heavy voice. "Jeri Sandston didn't commit suicide, Bender. She was murdered."

TWENTY-FIVE

Bender seized Kerri by the arm and dragged her back toward the Red Robin. He stopped beside the front door and stared at her. "Do you realize what you're implying?"

"All too well," Kerri said weakly. "And I don't think it's a coincidence Jeri Sandston was killed just as she was about to reveal something to me about the Coleman Institute."

"But we're talking murder here, Kerri," Bender said, raking his fingers through his hair. "That's a pretty desperate and drastic measure, don't you think?"

"Not when you've already done it," Kerri said, trying to keep her voice carefully measured. She felt as if she was about to start shrieking like the woman on the corner had.

"What do you mean?"

"I mean Janet Johansen," Kerri said. "We know she was murdered, and I, for one, don't think her husband had anything to do with it. But whoever did wouldn't hesitate to kill again, to protect their interests."

"Shit," Bender said. He turned and paced the few feet to the corner, then back. "Let's get out of here." He grabbed Kerri's arm and tried to haul her along beside him.

Kerri held back. "Wait a minute," she said, her

eyes wide and frantic looking. "I think we need to get some help with this thing, Bender. I think we should talk to Kevin. If what I suspect is correct, then we're in danger. And," she added with a hint of panic in her voice, "so is Jace."

"Jace? How?"

"Think about it, Bender. Jace saw something the night his mother disappeared, though I'll grant you his description is a bit strange. Then we find this plant of yours in the Johansens' house, and discover it only could have come from one of two places. One of those is an isolated, uninhabited island. The other just happens to be bordering the Coleman Institute. We tour the facility to see if anything looks out of whack. Nothing does, but there was a lot we didn't see. And then Jeri Sandston corners me in the bathroom with some cryptic warning about funny stuff that's going on there. She arranges to meet me here tonight, and before we can talk, she ends up dead. Murdered, Bender . . . I'm sure of it. You saw the security in that place. Don't you think it's possible someone at the Coleman Institute knew Jeri was planning to meet me here tonight? And they didn't want that to happen?"

Bender didn't answer her. Instead, he scratched his head and stared at the sidewalk, thinking.

"And," Kerri added, the panic in her voice rising a notch, "if they're that worried about Jeri Sandston, what are they going to do to Jace if they think he saw something he shouldn't have?"

Kerri's eyes grew wide with dawning. "Oh my God," she mumbled, her gaze drifting off somewhere over Bender's shoulder. She turned back to look at him, her face even more terrified. "The picture," she said.

"What picture?"

"Jace's picture. During his first visit with me he drew a picture of one of these things he said took his mother. I stuffed the drawing in his chart, but the next day I couldn't find it. It simply disappeared. And right after that, someone broke into my office, only they didn't take anything from what I could determine. What if they were trying to read Jace's chart to see what, if anything, he knew?"

"I hate to admit it," Bender said, "but you're making sense. Maybe you're right. Maybe we need to talk to Kevin, see if he can find out what might be going on at the Coleman Institute."

"First," Kerri said, her eyes haunted, "I want to go and see Jace. To make sure he's okay."

"Let's go," Bender said, sealing the decision with a definitive nod. "Where is your car?"

"Parked down under the viaduct," Kerri answered. "About ten blocks from here."

"Mine is just a couple of blocks away," Bender said. "Mind if I drive?"

"Not at all," Kerri said. "The quicker we get to Jace, the better I'll feel."

By the time they arrived at the hospital, Kerri's panic had transformed itself into an unsettling sense of foreboding. She half walked, half ran, through the hallways, spurred on by her concern for Jace's welfare, Bender close on her heels. Not bothering to stop at the nurse's station, they hurried into Jace's room. There, Kerri halted just inside the door and squeezed her eyes shut with relief. Jace was sitting up in bed with the TV on, watching Bugs Bunny cartoons. The IV still snaked into his arm, but there was a dinner tray sitting on the overbed table in front of him, though its contents appeared untouched.

"Hey, sport," Kerri said, forcing herself to act calm. She walked over and stroked his head. "I see you've graduated to real food."

Jace didn't answer her. Instead, his head fell back against the pillow and he closed his eyes, seeming to take comfort in Kerri's touch.

A nurse entered the room and greeted Kerri with a smile. "Hello, Dr. Whitaker. Glad you're here. Jace has been asking about you."

"How is he doing?" Kerri asked, her eyes roving over Jace with concern.

"Somewhat better," the nurse said, "though he's refusing to eat. If he doesn't take something soon, we may have to reinsert the feeding tube. I hoped you might be able to coax him."

"I'll see what I can do," Kerri promised. "Thanks."

The nurse left and Kerri sidled one hip onto the bed beside Jace, while Bender positioned himself at the foot. "Honey? How about trying to eat a little something for me," Kerri urged.

Jace opened his eyes and looked at Bender a moment before shifting his gaze toward Kerri. "I'm not hungry," he said.

"I understand that," Kerri said. "But you need to eat anyway. So you can get better and stronger." She looked at the tray on the table. "Would you like something else? If you don't like the macaroni and cheese, I'm sure we can get you something different. How about a peanut butter sandwich?" she suggested, recalling one of Mandy's old favorites.

Jace closed his eyes and gave a slow shake of his head.

Kerri stared at him, her face marked with worry. With a heavy sigh, she stood and motioned Bender over to the door. "I should try to reach Kevin," she said in a low whisper. "I'll scout down to the doctor's lounge and call him from there, so Jace doesn't overhear anything. Want to try your hand with him?" she asked with a sideways nod of her head.

"Sure," Bender answered.

"Are you leaving?" came a tiny, weak voice from the bed.

Kerri's heart tightened when she saw the lackluster look in Jace's eyes. "Just for a moment," she assured him. "I'll be right back. I promise."

Seeming to be satisfied with that response, Jace again closed his eyes.

With one last pained glance at Bender, Kerri left the room. She climbed into the elevator and pushed the button for the ground floor, which was where the doctor's lounge was located. As the car carried her down, her eyes stared unfocused at the speckled pattern in the linoleum covering the floor, while her mind busied itself with a whirlwind of thoughts. She was so preoccupied that when the elevator door opened on the first floor, she headed out without looking and bumped into someone trying to get on. Kerri looked up to apologize.

"Kevin!"

"Hey, lass. I was just coming to see if I could find you. I thought you might be here with the boy."

"I am. Oh, Kevin, I am so glad to see you!" Kerri flung herself at him, wrapping her arms around his bulky warmth.

Looking puzzled, Kevin returned the hug. "What's gotten into you? Is something wrong?"

Kerri released him and stood back, looking up into his blue eyes. "Something is very wrong, Kevin. I really need your help." With a wary glance at the people bustling by them in the hallway, she grabbed Kevin's arm. "Let's find someplace quiet where we can talk," she said, pulling him down the hall in the direction of the cafeteria.

Though it was going on seven o'clock there was still a good-sized dinner crowd in the dining area, and after buying two cups of coffee, Kerri led Kevin to an isolated table near the back of the room. Once they were settled, Kerri filled him in on the latest events: the plant Bender found in the Johansens' house, their tour of the Coleman facility, and Jeri Sandston's horrifying death. After a moment's hesitation, she even told Kevin about her theory. "I don't know if I'm right, Kev," Kerri said, watching his face in earnest. "But something is screwy here."

Kevin listened without interruption. When she was through, his eyes narrowed at her and he scowled. "That plant was evidence, lass. Your friend should have turned it over to us."

"I know, Kev. But at the time, he wasn't sure of its significance. What's done is done. Now we need to figure out what to do next."

Kevin leaned back, his eyes never leaving her face, though his expression did soften some. He reached into his shirt pocket and withdrew a toothpick, shoving it into one corner of his mouth. Kerri's eyes followed his every move, and something in her mind slipped loose. Then, like a bolt of lightning, she remembered the night in the ER, watching Brian Mitchell pull a pen from his shirt pocket and twist it so it would write. Her eyes grew wide, and her mouth dropped open.

"That's it," she hissed. "Oh, God, Kevin! That's what bothered me." She punctuated the statement by pounding her fist on the table.

Kevin gave her a puzzled look. "I don't follow ya."

Kerri hunched forward, dropping her voice to a whisper. "Kevin, I don't think Thad Johansen committed suicide. I think he was murdered, and someone tried to make it look like a suicide."

Kevin lunged back toward the table. "Now hold on, lass. I'm willing to consider your theory that he didn't kill the wife, but it's pretty obvious he did himself in. His prints were all over the gun, he left a note—"

"But that's the key, Kevin!" Kerri said excitedly. "The suicide note. I knew something about it bothered me at the time. I just didn't realize what it was."

"Explain," Kevin said, resting his elbows on the table and leaning closer.

"The words on that paper, the letters, they were heavy, with broad strokes, like a regular pencil would make."

"If you're suggesting Thad didn't write it, we compared it to other samples of his writing and it matched."

"That doesn't mean anything," Kerri argued. "Thad, like most architects, didn't write, he printed. Big block letters. Easy as hell to copy."

"But we found his prints on the pencil . . ."

"What pencil?" Kerri asked. "The one that was lying on his sketch pad on the desk? The wooden pencil with the teeth marks in it?"

"That's right," Kevin said, frowning.

"But Thad wouldn't have used that pencil, Kevin! I remember Jace telling me how his dad only used mechanical pencils. They were his special pencils and Jace wasn't allowed to touch them. That can on his desk, the one with all the pencils in it? They were all mechanical pencils, Kevin. Why would a man who is so distraught he feels he must take his own life, suddenly break a life-long habit and use a pencil other than the ones he's used to, just to write a two-word suicide note? I'll bet those teeth marks in the pencil are Jace's, not Thad's."

"They were," Kevin said, his frown now a full-blown scowl.

"I knew Thad wouldn't do that to Jace," Kerri said, slapping her hand on the table. "You had me doubting myself there for a while, but I should have trusted my instincts."

"But why would someone kill Thad Johansen?" Kevin asked her.

"If that same someone killed Janet, then stashed her body where they never expected it to be found, wouldn't they be concerned when the body does show up? What better way to divert suspicion than to make it look like her husband did it? And with you playing right into their hands by suspecting Thad, what better way to close the whole case than by having it appear as if the husband did do it, and then killed himself over the guilt?"

Kevin's face turned red, and he chewed the toothpick in his mouth like some mongrel dog who had just found a soup bone. "Are you suggesting I was a pawn in someone else's grand scheme?" he asked, his eyes dark with anger.

Kerri reached over and placed her hand on top of his. She didn't say a word. She just waited, letting him sort it out for himself.

Kevin plucked the toothpick from his mouth and tossed it onto the table. He folded his arms over his chest and his eyes narrowed thoughtfully. After several moments had gone by without a word, Kerri said, "Kevin?"

He looked at her, and her heart ached when she saw the pain in his eyes. "It's not your fault, Kevin," she said.

He reached into his pocket and dragged out another toothpick, holding one end while he gnawed on the other. "So you think this Coleman Institute has something to do with all this?" he asked Kerri finally.

"I don't know for sure, Kev. But don't you think it's awfully coincidental this plant we found at the house is growing there?"

Kevin nodded slowly. "Still," he said, "it's something of a long shot. He sipped his coffee, managing to do so with the toothpick still in place. "You're sure this Sandston woman didn't just jump?" he said, setting the cup down.

"I'd bet my life on it," Kerri said, and then she grimaced at the irony of those words.

Kevin studied Kerri's face, his eyes drawn down in a contemplative squint.

"Well?" Kerri asked him when she could stand the silence no longer.

"Well," Kevin said, plucking the toothpick from his mouth and studying the frayed end of it a moment, "I'll grant you it might be worth looking into this Coleman Institute a little further."

Kerri shook her head. "No, Kevin. I want more than just somebody looking into it. I want a policeman posted outside Jace's room."

This time it was Kevin who shook his head. "I can't do that, lass. There isn't enough hard evidence to

warrant it. The chief would never approve it. All we
have so far is supposition. The evidence strongly suggests Thad Johansen killed his wife, then himself. You
don't think he wrote that suicide note, but there's no
proof. Even if we had this damned plant of yours—like
we should have," he added in a chastising tone, "all it
suggests is someone else was in the house at some
point. We don't know who or why they were there.
Hell, it could have been some friend of Thad's who
works out at that place."

"Dammit, Kevin! I know it isn't concrete, but what
if I'm right? What if something happens to that little
boy?" Tears blossomed in Kerri's eyes and she stared at
Kevin, trying not to blink, knowing if she did, they
would cascade down her face. She didn't want Kevin to
think she was reacting on pure emotion.

Kevin gnawed on the toothpick for a few more seconds before tossing it onto the table beside its companion. "Tell you what," he said, leaning across the
table and wrapping a hand over her arm. "I've got
some friends on the force who moonlight on stuff like
this. I'll ask a couple of them to help out."

Kerri rolled her eyes with relief. "Thank you,
Kevin. And I'll be happy to pay them, whatever it
costs."

"Slow down, lass. I'm not promising anything yet. I
don't even know if any of them are available."

"Can you check?" Kerri pleaded. "I don't want
Jace to be alone."

Kevin sighed. "I'll see what I can do." He studied
Kerri's face a moment. "What about you? Where are
you planning on staying tonight?"

"For now, I'm staying here," she said. "With Jace.
Until you find someone."

Kevin frowned at her. "I figured that's what you'd say. Look, I don't think it's wise for you to go home. If what you say is true, you're in danger as well. But staying here all night won't do you or the boy any good."

"I don't want to leave him alone, Kevin."

"How about if I stay with him? And you stay at my place. So I know where you are."

"No," Kerri said with an adamant shake of her head. "I suppose you're right about my not going home, but I want to stay close to Jace." Seeing the determination in Kevin's eyes, and knowing how stubborn he could be, she quickly offered up a compromise. "Tell you what," she said. "How about if I get a room at the Holiday Inn across the street? No one would know to look for me there, and I'll feel a lot better if I'm close to the hospital." A flicker of vacillation crossed Kevin's face, and Kerri chewed on her lip while she waited for his answer.

"Okay," Kevin said finally, shaking his head in defeat. He reached into his pocket and popped another toothpick.

"Thank you, Kev." Kerri stood and walked around the table. She sandwiched his face between her palms and kissed him on the forehead. "I owe you one."

Kevin's face turned blood red, and he muttered something unintelligible under his breath before pushing back from the table. He was still muttering as Kerri followed him out of the cafeteria and back toward the elevators.

As they rode up to Pediatrics, Kerri glanced at her watch and realized she'd been gone for nearly an hour. She was seized by a sudden worry Jace would be upset over her absence, and a vision of him distraught and crying while Bender tried desperately to calm him filled her mind. Thus, she was more than a little surprised when they entered Jace's room and found the boy sitting up, eating his macaroni and cheese, while Bender sat on the edge of the bed beside him, the two of them laughing.

"Hi," Jace said when he saw Kerri come in. His face rapidly turned to a scowl when he saw Kevin standing behind her.

"Well, hi yourself," Kerri said. She cast a questioning glance at Bender, who, after a brief acknowledging nod toward Kevin, said, "Did you know Jace here fancies himself something of a pilot?"

"No, I didn't," Kerri said, walking over and standing beside the bed.

"Yup," Bender said, and Jace nodded his agreement, chewing on a mouthful of noodles, though he continued to frown at Kevin. "I promised I'd take him up in my plane and let him have a run at the controls if he ate his supper," Bender added.

"I see," Kerri said. She gave Bender a look of admiration.

"Wouldn't that be cool?" Jace said, finally dragging his eyes away from Kevin and scooping some more noodles onto his fork. "Mike says sometimes deer stand on the runway when he tries to land," he added.

"Well, that's true enough," Kerri said. "I've seen them myself."

Jace turned toward Bender. "When do you think we can go?"

"Just as soon as you get well enough to get out of here," Bender said. "I'm ready anytime."

To Kerri's amazement, Jace continued to eat the food on his tray, while he and Bender talked more about the thrills and adventures of flying. In the meantime, Kerri and Kevin convened in the hallway outside.

"It's obvious the boy doesn't think much of me," Kevin said, looking somewhat wounded.

"Well, under the circumstances . . ." Kerri let the sentence hang and shrugged.

"I'll stay out here," Kevin offered. "So I don't upset him. Besides," he added with a furtive glance toward the nurse's station, "I've got my eye on this little brunette."

"Really?" Kerri said, an amused expression on her face.

"Yes, really," Kevin answered. "What? You don't think an old overweight flatfoot like myself can still turn a lassie's eye?"

"Not at all, Kevin. You'd be a fine catch for any woman."

Kevin's face flushed a brilliant red, and he let out a "harumph" before saying, "Get yourself a room for the night. I'm going to call the station and see if I can find out which detective was assigned to this suicide of yours, see what I can dig up." He looked over toward the nurse's station and his eyebrows arched with interest. Kerri followed the direction of his gaze and saw a tall brunette nurse standing at the desk, talking on the phone.

"I'll use the phone at the nurse's station," Kevin said, his blush deepening. "Be back shortly."

Kerri watched after him fondly for a moment before heading back into Jace's room. She was delighted to see he had finished his dinner—every last crumb of it. His face was flushed with healthy color, his eyes gleamed with excitement, and he was more animated than Kerri had ever seen him. Yet, despite his excitement, he drifted off to sleep a scant five minutes later.

"I'm impressed," Kerri said to Bender.

Bender shrugged. "No big deal. It was just a matter of finding out what he was interested in and trying to get him to talk about it. Planes are easy. There aren't many little boys who don't fantasize about flying."

"Don't sell yourself short," Kerri said. "What you did here was just short of amazing."

Bender shrugged again, then asked her, "So what did Kevin suggest?"

Kerri motioned Bender over to the door and filled him in on their discussion—including her revelations about Thad's supposed suicide note—in a low whisper so Jace wouldn't overhear anything. "Kevin's pretty miffed we didn't turn the plant over to him. He wants it."

"Understandable," Bender said. "I'll give Ted a call and have him turn it in."

"Well," Kerri said with a sigh, glancing over at Jace's sleeping form, "I guess I better call the Holiday Inn across the way and see if they have a room." She headed for the phone on the stand beside Jace's bed. After calling information for the number, she dialed and, a few moments later, had a room booked for the night. "Well, that's that," she said, hanging up and looking back at Bender. Their eyes held for a long moment. "What about you?" she asked.

"Me?"

"Yes. What are your plans for the night?" She held her breath, waiting for his answer.

Bender's eyes roved over her so slowly and sensuously, Kerri felt as if she'd been caressed. Just as he opened his mouth to answer, Kevin poked his head into the room.

"Ah, good," he said, looking toward Jace. "He's asleep."

Kerri let her breath out with a forlorn little sigh. Reluctantly, she dragged her eyes away from Bender and looked over at Kevin.

"You get a room?" Kevin asked.

"I did," Kerri said.

Kevin nodded his approval. "I spoke with one of the hospital security guards. He's waiting outside the room. He'll stay here with the boy until I get you to the hotel."

"Oh, that's not necessary, Kevin," Kerri said, trying to hide the disappointment in her voice, though she knew before she uttered the words that her objection was futile.

Apparently, Bender sensed it as well, for he stood and headed for the door. "I guess I should be going," he said.

Kerri looked longingly at him, feeling her heart sink. "Where are you going?"

"Home," he said. "I've got patients to see tomorrow, so I guess I should get back to the office."

"Do you think that's wise?" Kerri asked him. "If I'm right about all this, you might be in danger, too."

Bender considered that a moment, then said, "Perhaps you're right. I'll get a hotel room somewhere on the mainland for tonight. My office should be safe enough. I doubt anyone would try anything there. But I'll keep my eyes open. I'll come back here as soon as I'm free."

Kerri cast a disconsolate look at the floor. "Okay," she mumbled, not caring who saw her disappointment.

"Good night, then," Bender said.

Kerri watched him leave, and it felt as if her heart was breaking.

"You falling for that fella, lass?" Kevin asked softly.

Kerri stared at the door, willing it to open, hoping against hope Bender would turn around and come back. "Yeah, Kev. I'm afraid I am," she said wistfully.

Kevin walked over and hooked his arm through hers. "Come on," he said. "Let's get you settled for the night."

With a final worried look at Jace, Kerri let Kevin lead her from the room.

TWENTY-SIX

Kerri stood in front of the window in her room at the Holiday Inn, staring at the hospital across the street. It was only a few minutes past nine o'clock, yet she felt as exhausted and weary as if it were two in the morning. Though most of the windows in the hospital were still lit, Jace's room was dim, its darkness only partially relieved by the meager light drifting in from the hallway outside his door. Kerri assumed Kevin was back there by now—it was only a five-minute walk. She could see him in her mind, sitting in a chair outside Jace's room, tipping it back on its hind legs, chewing on a toothpick, and watching the tall brunette nurse scurry about her business.

Their walk to the hotel had been surprisingly quiet. Kevin said nothing until he saw her to the door of her room, where he deposited her with little ceremony and a warning to stay put and not open the door for anyone until he came by the next morning. He seemed preoccupied, and Kerri wondered if his thoughts were on the brunette nurse or her own situation. *Probably both*, she thought, knowing Kevin.

A knock sounded at the door, and Kerri turned and stared at it, momentarily puzzled. Then she realized Kevin must have come back for some reason, perhaps to tell her something he'd forgotten to say earlier. She crossed the room and was about to open the door when she remembered Kevin's warning. It would be just like him to test her like this. Come back and knock on the door, then yell at her when she opened it. Well, I'll show him, she thought, putting her eye to the peephole. When she saw who was standing on the other side, her heart skipped a beat.

She turned back the dead bolt, undid the chain, and opened the door.

"Hi," Bender said, leaning against the doorjamb and wearing a silly-assed grin.

"I thought you had left."

"That's what I wanted you to think. Or at least that's what I wanted Kevin to think," he said. "I got the distinct impression he wasn't going to have it any other way."

Kerri smiled at him. "I suppose you're right," she said. "Want to come in?"

Bender hesitated, a frown flitting across his face. Kerri's face fell, and a prickly heat washed up over her neck and face. "Oh, I'm sorry," she stammered. "I thought—"

Bender silenced her by placing two fingers against her lips. "I would love to come in," he said, his voice husky. "But I'm not sure I should. The thought of being alone with you, in a hotel room . . ." He glanced past her toward the bed, then returned to give her a slow head-to-toe perusal, his eyes finally settling on her lips. His fingers lightly stroked them, and he let out a sigh that sounded disturbingly close to a moan. Then he seemed to shake himself, blinking hard and pulling his hand away, stuffing it into his jacket pocket. Kerri raked her teeth over her bottom lip, feeling it tingle and tasting the faint saltiness his touch left behind.

"I just wanted to tell you good night," Bender said hoarsely. He cleared his throat with a cough. "And to be careful."

Kerri's eyes danced over his face. There was a pleasantly hollow sensation in her chest, and she felt strangely breathless. "Are you sure?" she asked him, her voice breaking slightly.

"Sure about what?"

Kerri swallowed hard. "That all you want is to say good night." Her eyes locked onto his, and she felt certain he saw her invitation. It was his turn to swallow hard, and Kerri's eyes slid down to his neck, transfixed by the bobbing of his Adam's apple. When she again met his eyes, she saw a hunger there that made her insides quiver. Her lips parted slightly as her breaths turned shallow, and her heart thrashed against her ribs as if it wanted to escape from its bony cage.

Bender's own breathing, she saw, was heavy, almost panting. When he took a step closer, Kerri felt a hot rush of excitement flood her veins.

"No," Bender said with little more than a whisper. "I'm not sure at all." He reached out and pulled her to him, one hand cradling the back of her head. His dark eyes traveled over her hair and face, drinking her in. And then, with an aching slowness, his lips descended. His kiss managed to be both tender and fierce, nibbling tentatively one moment and threatening to devour her in his passionate need the next.

A feeling like hot molten lead spread through Kerri's body, and she pressed herself closer, anxious to feel him against every square inch of her. She felt the hot hardness of him along her belly, and it made her moan with pleasure and need. Bender's hand tightened its grip against her head, and his lips grew more insistent.

"Kerri!"

Bender lunged back away from Kerri so quickly, it made her stagger. Steadying herself, she turned and looked, first with astonishment, then with anger, at Kevin's scowling face.

"Kevin!" she said, breathless with both passion and fury. "What the hell are you doing here?"

Kevin eyed Bender with disdain. "I might ask him the same question," he snarled.

Kerri glanced over at Bender, who was standing there like some schoolboy caught smoking in the boy's room. His erection showed clearly through the front of his jeans, and for some reason, it struck Kerri as comical. A giggle bubbled up from inside her, and she struggled to keep it in, clamping a hand over her mouth and biting her lip.

"I think that's obvious," she said to Kevin, and the giggle managed to work its way loose after all, starting out as a tiny chuckle, then burgeoning into a laugh that shook her whole body. Both men stared at her as if she'd lost her mind, which only made her laugh even harder.

Bender stood there, chewing on the inside of his cheek. With a roll of his eyes and a heavy sigh of resignation, he said, "I'll see you tomorrow." He turned and marched off down the hall as Kerri watched after him, her laughter still threatening. She wanted to call him back but knew it was best to just let it go for now.

"I thought I told you not to open the door to anyone," Kevin grumbled.

Kerri looked at him, trying hard to gain control of

herself. "You did," she managed with a snicker. "I guess I'm just a very naughty girl." With that, her giggles once again took over.

Kevin stared at her, thoroughly befuddled. Then he took a step toward her and thrust her jacket into her arms. "You left this in the boy's room," he grumbled.

"Thanks," Kerri said, still giggling.

Kevin shook his head. "Good night, lass," he muttered. And with that, he too, strode away.

Kerri closed the door behind him. She stood in the middle of the room, her expression of bemusement fading to one of wistful longing, the exhaustion Bender had so thoroughly chased away creeping over her once more. Wearily, she stripped out of her clothes, laid them carefully over the back of a chair, and climbed into bed. Within minutes she was asleep.

Kerri awoke at six the next morning. She showered and dressed, wrinkling her nose as she slipped into the same clothes she had worn the day before. The only makeup she had with her was some lipstick and blush she carried in her purse. After applying them, she frowned at herself in the mirror, disappointed with the results. Though she had slept remarkably well considering all that had happened, her face looked pale and drawn, and tiny dark half-moons had settled in beneath her eyes. Without a blow dryer, her hair hung limp and stringy, accentuating the haggardness of her appearance.

The breakfast she ordered from room service arrived, and she picked at it, her appetite faring no better than her looks. Once she was done, she paced the room, occasionally staring out toward Jace's window, anxious for Kevin to either call or show up. At seven-thirty, she picked up the phone and called the nurse's station on the pediatric floor. The nurse who answered was polite but distracted, obviously busy, judging from the background noise. When Kerri asked for Kevin, she was told he had left the floor an hour earlier, and a different officer was stationed outside Jace's door. Kerri hung up, frustrated. She frowned as she considered her options. She doubted anyone other than Kevin and Bender knew where she was, and after a few more minutes of pacing, she decided to check out of her room and head back over to the hospital. It was a short walk, and surely nothing could happen to her between here and there.

She made the trip without incident, arriving on the pediatric floor a little before eight. After chatting briefly with the nurses, who informed her that Jace had had a restful night and eaten most of his breakfast, Kerri went toward his room. She stopped when she came to the officer posted outside the door, a younger fellow she'd never met before.

"Good morning," Kerri said.

"Hi," the officer said, standing quickly and extending a hand. "I'm Jim Claridge. You must be Dr. Whitaker."

"I am," Kerri said, giving him a brief shake. "How did you know?"

"Kevin described you pretty clearly. Said you might show up over here on your own before he got back."

"Guilty as charged," she said. "Where is Kevin?"

"He had to check on some things, ma'am. Said

he'd be back around nine and if you did come by, to tell you to wait here until he returns."

Kerri's beeper chirped, and she unclipped it from her purse and looked at the number it displayed. "That's my office manager," she told the young officer. "I guess I better call him. Thanks for staying here," she added.

"My pleasure, ma'am," Claridge said, resuming his seat.

Jace was sitting up in bed, the IV gone from his arm, his cheeks rosy. His hands worked busily at his bedspread, wringing one edge of it into a twisted point, while he watched cartoons on the TV mounted on the wall across from him. When he saw Kerri, his eyes brightened.

"Hi!" he said with more enthusiasm than Kerri expected.

"Hi yourself, kiddo. Looks like you're feeling better." She walked over and sat beside him on the bed.

"They took that thing out of my arm," Jace said, pouting at the bandage covering the puncture site.

"I see that," Kerri said. "That's great. You'll be out of here in no time."

"And then I can go in the plane with Mike," he said excitedly, wringing the bedspread even harder.

Kerri was actually encouraged by the return of Jace's hyperactivity, seeing it as a sign of his recovery. Though she did make a mental note to check with the nurses before she left and start him back on his Ritalin before things got too out of control.

Remembering her page, Kerri said, "I need to call Stephen before he has a heart attack, wondering where I am."

Jace rolled his eyes and said, "He's probably playing with his dinosaurs."

"Yep, he probably is." She ruffled Jace's hair, then stood and moved over to sit in the chair next to the bedside stand that held the phone. She dialed the number to her office and waited for Stephen to answer.

"Hi, Stephen," she said.

"Where are you?" he asked, his voice mildly frantic. "You're usually here by now. Is everything okay?"

"Everything is fine, Stephen. Things got a bit crazy last night and I'm running a little late."

"But you are coming in?"

Kerri thought before she answered him. She knew Kevin expected her to stay here until his return, and she started to tell Stephen to cancel all of her patients, telling them she was stricken with the flu or something. But by the light of day, and with Jace's heartening improvement, she began to think her paranoia from the night before was a bit extreme. Besides, she knew her first scheduled patient—Cindy Crandall, a young woman who had attempted suicide a few weeks ago—was still in a dangerous period. It would be a severe dereliction of her duties not to see the woman.

"I'll be there just as quick as I can, Stephen. I'm at the hospital now, so it shouldn't be too long." She glanced at her watch. "I should be able to get there before Cindy Crandall, but if I'm not, tell her to wait. Do me a favor, though, and see how many of the afternoon patients you can reschedule."

There was a brief silence on the other end before Stephen answered with a curious "Okay, boss lady. See you soon."

Kerri hung up, then called for a cab. When she was through, she told Jace she needed to go to the office for a few hours but would be back during lunch to see him again. After leaving the room, she went out to the nurse's station and wrote an order on his chart to restart his Ritalin. As she was handing the chart to one of the nurses, Jim Claridge approached her.

"Are you going somewhere?" he asked her, frowning slightly.

"I need to get to my office, to see a few patients." She saw Claridge open his mouth to object, and she held up one hand to halt him. "I've called for a taxi, and I'll be back at lunchtime. I'll be fine."

"But Kevin was pretty specific about what he wanted you to do, ma'am," Claridge said. "He said that if you showed up here this morning, to make sure you stayed until he got back."

"Well, tell him I'm stubborn and pigheaded. That should come as no surprise to him." With that, she turned and walked away, leaving Claridge frowning after her.

She headed toward the main lobby to wait for her ride, relishing the frenzied activity of the hospital. The corridors bustled with it—people scurrying about, stretchers and wheelchairs rolling along, dietary carts rumbling their way back to the kitchen. The very normalcy of the scene made yesterday's nightmares retreat even further. In their place were memories of Bender's visit to her room—the smoldering look in his eyes, the feel of his lips on hers, the delicious excitement that had raced through her body.

Thus, Kerri was less than pleased when the door to the doctor's lounge opened as she passed, and Nathan stepped out.

"Kerri!" he said, grabbing at her arm. "Where the hell have you been? I called your house all night and never got an answer. I've been worried sick."

His tone was conciliatory, but his eyes flashed with a mix of annoyance and anger. His loud admonishment attracted the attention of a few passersby, and they turned their heads curiously. Embarrassed, Kerri flashed Nathan a scolding look. Not wanting to go into a lengthy explanation that would further deter her arrival at the office, she said in a low voice, "I was here, Nathan. I had a difficult consult that kept me up all night."

Nathan's eyes softened and, thankfully, so did his voice. "Oh," he said. "You should have called me. You know I worry about you."

"Nathan," Kerri said with an exasperated sigh, "I can't be calling you with my every step. I have a life, you know. A life that doesn't revolve around you." *So much for my newfound desire not to hurt him,* Kerri thought when she saw the wounded expression on his face.

Nathan hung his head, the muscles in his jaw twitching. "I know, I know," he mumbled. He raised his eyes to look at her. "It's just that I can't help but—"

"Look, Nathan," Kerri interrupted, glancing at her watch. "I have to run. I've got a cab picking me up out front so I can get to the office." She leaned over and gave him a quick peck on the cheek. "I'll call you later, okay?"

Before he could object, she turned and hurried away, half-expecting him to chase after her. But he didn't. Curious, she looked back just before she went through the double doors leading to the lobby. Nathan was still standing where she'd left him, having been waylaid by Frank Weatherton. The two of them were engaged in a heated discussion punctuated with lots of finger wagging and hand waving, their faces suffused with red. It was a fairly routine sight here at the hospital—Frank Weatherton having managed to piss off everyone on the medical staff at least once. Chuckling to herself, Kerri headed into the lobby to await the arrival of her cab.

It was another drab, gray day, and the dreariness pushed Kerri's momentary lightheartedness away. She began to second-guess her decision to strike out on her own, and the chilling matter of Jeri Sandston's murder nudged its way back to the forefront of her thoughts. She tried to shove it away, wanting desperately to bring back the carefree attitude she'd had just moments ago. But the thoughts kept niggling at her, and with them, their frightening ramifications. She spent most of the taxi ride glancing over her shoulder out the back window, worried someone might be following her.

She found Stephen at his usual post, with the morning paper held out before him and his feet propped up on the desk. He lowered the paper enough to peek at her over its edge, then dropped it on the desk and studied her more closely. "What happened?" he asked.

"Is it that obvious?"

"It is to me. You look like shit, and, if I'm not mistaken, those are the same clothes you were wearing yesterday."

"Thanks for noticing," Kerri said wryly as she hung up her jacket. Stephen turned toward the credenza and poured her a mug of coffee, then carried it over and handed it to her. She accepted it gratefully, wrapping her hands around its warmth and inhaling the aroma before she sipped it. "Thanks," she told him.

"So," Stephen said, his arms folded over his chest,

his head cocked to one side as he eyed her, "you going to tell me what's up or not?"

"Not," Kerri said, walking over to the desk and turning the schedule book around so she could read it. "Cindy will be here any minute. Maybe later." She quickly scanned the names of the patients she had scheduled for the rest of the day. "I don't think any of this afternoon's patients will suffer from being rescheduled," she observed. "Just tell them I'm ill and see if you can slot them in next week some time."

"Okay," Stephen said, his voice sullen.

Kerri knew he was upset with her for not telling him what was wrong, but she felt that the fewer people who were involved at this point, the better.

"If you're going to be out this afternoon, can I take off as well?" Stephen asked, apparently resigned to her reticence. "I have an exam tomorrow night and could use the extra study time. And, there's a study guide I need to pick up at the university bookstore. Since they close at five, it would be nice if I could get there this afternoon."

"Sure," Kerri said, heading toward her office. "That's no problem."

"How's Jace doing?" The question made Kerri pause. She could feel Stephen's eyes boring through her back and knew he suspected Jace was at the heart of what was bothering her.

"Much better, actually," she told him.

"It's got to be tough on a kid to lose both parents that way."

Kerri detected a trace of Stephen's own still-lingering pain, and she turned back toward him, her face filled with sympathy.

"Is he still in the hospital?" Stephen asked.

"He is," she answered, "but he's improving quite nicely and I expect he'll be discharged in the next day or so, if things continue."

"Where will he be going?"

Kerri thought about that a moment. "Well, I'm hoping he'll be coming home with me," she told him. "But I still haven't heard anything from the social worker about the status of my guardianship request."

With all that had happened, she'd completely forgotten about this and made herself a mental note to inquire about it when she got back to the hospital. As she thought about Jace coming to stay with her, she realized she had a lot of groundwork to cover. She would need to make some type of child care arrangements and fix up a room for Jace to sleep in. Knowing how difficult it would be for Jace to make all the necessary adjustments, she was anxious for him to feel at home.

"I kind of wish I hadn't given all of Mandy's toys away to Goodwill," she said with a hint of regret. "Though I suppose there's no reason for the police to keep me from taking some of the ones Jace has at his own house."

"Why don't you give him my dinosaurs?" Stephen suggested. "He really enjoyed playing with them while he was here, and I think I need to update my toy stock anyway."

"What a lovely gesture, Stephen," Kerri said, smiling warmly at him. "That's a great idea. Thank you."

Stephen gave her a nonchalant shrug. "No biggie. Those old reptiles need someone to take care of them."

Kerri could tell Jace had struck a chord in Stephen's heart as well as her own. It occurred to her that she ought to try to bring the two of them together more in the future. Jace and Stephen would be good for each other.

The morning passed by with agonizing slowness, and despite her good intentions, Kerri once again found it difficult to concentrate on her patients. She was glad she'd decided to cancel the afternoon patients; she wouldn't do them, or herself, any good.

When the last patient left at a little after noon, Kerri called Stephen into the office. "Any messages?" she asked.

"Nope. And all the afternoon patients are bumped to next week. You've also got tomorrow morning free, remember. You had that seminar scheduled at the hospital."

"Oh, right," Kerri said. "I'd forgotten about that." Her answer was distracted, as was her mind. She wondered why she hadn't heard from Kevin. *Or Bender for that matter,* she thought with a tinge of disappointment. "Thanks, Stephen."

"Is it okay if I scoot, boss lady?" Stephen asked, glancing at his watch. "If I hurry, I can just catch the next bus for the campus."

Kerri started to tell him that was fine, but then thought of a better idea. "Listen, Stephen, I'm headed up to the hospital, which is right near the bookstore. Why don't you let me drive you up there and drop you off?"

Stephen considered the offer a moment, then shrugged. "Sure, if it's no problem."

"No problem at all," Kerri assured him. She opened her desk drawer and dug her keys out of her purse, tossing them at Stephen. "I need to finish up a few notes here. Why don't you go get my car and I'll meet you downstairs."

Stephen's face brightened. Kerri knew how much he loved to drive whenever he had a chance. Without a car of his own, he was usually dependent on some form of public transit to get around. "Okay, boss lady," he said. "Where are you parked?"

"Under the viaduct, on the waterfront side, right before Marion Street."

"Okey dokey." Stephen tossed the keys into the air, caught them, then turned and left the office. "See you in a few," he yelled back over his shoulder. He started whistling as he went out the door.

Smiling to herself, Kerri finished up the few notes she had to write and prepared to leave. Just as she was about to lock the main office door, she snapped her fingers. "The dinosaurs," she muttered to herself. She went inside, fetched four of the dinosaurs from the collection in Stephen's desk drawer, and stuffed them in her purse. Then she headed downstairs to meet Stephen.

She stood there for over ten minutes before she started to worry. Glancing at her watch, she realized Stephen should have been there by now, even given the vagaries of city traffic along the one-way streets. Perhaps he'd had some trouble getting the car started. She toyed with the idea of heading down to find him, but then figured that if he'd already left the parking area, she would miss him when he did finally arrive at the office. So she decided to wait another five minutes.

She lasted only two. That was when she heard the first of the sirens. The sounds came from at least three different directions but converged just a few blocks away, near Marion Street, near where she'd left her car. Fearing Stephen might have been involved in an accident—after all, he didn't have that much experience behind the wheel—she headed down the street at a rapid clip.

She was two blocks from where her car was parked when she saw and smelled the smoke. A feeling of dread wrapped around her and she started to run.

As she rounded the corner beneath the viaduct, she saw a gathering of people and emergency vehicles: ambulances, fire trucks, and police cars. The scene was eerily reminiscent of the one that had surrounded Jeri Sandston the evening before, and Kerri's sense of dread grew. Staring fearfully at the roiling cloud of thick black smoke rising toward the sky, she hurried toward the edge of the crowd, pushing her way through, ignoring the grunts, groans, and snide remarks of those she shoved out of her way. As she broke through the front-most line of people, she finally saw what had the crowd so enthralled. For a split second, her heart stopped. Then it kicked in again with a thudding pain so severe, so wrenching, she wished it had simply remained still.

Her car—or at least she thought it was her car—was nothing more than a smoldering black ruin. The outside of it was blackened and blistered, the tires melted into shapeless blobs. Two fire trucks were spraying it down with thick streams of water, while paramedics and policemen scurried about. A sickening wave of nausea rose through Kerri when she saw the charred remains of a human being in the front seat.

"Oh, God, no," she muttered in a strangled whisper.

A man standing beside her said, "Yeah, poor guy didn't stand a chance. The thing went up like a dried-out Christmas tree."

"Stephen," Kerri said with whispered anguish.

Hot, stinging tears flooded her eyes and ran down her face. "Oh, God, no . . . not Stephen."

The man beside her turned and stared at her. "Did you know that guy?" he asked.

Kerri ignored him, not that she heard him anyway over the pounding thump of blood rushing through her ears. Numbly, she moved forward, toward the car, toward the policemen and firemen encircling the conflagration. *Maybe it wasn't him,* she thought. *Please, God, don't let it be him.* But a distant part of her mind knew the prayer was futile, knew without a doubt that the hideously charred remains were all that was left of Stephen. Still, she searched the crowd, hoping to see his face staring out from the throng, watching with morbid fascination like everyone else. But as her eyes frantically explored each face, her heart sank. Her body began to shake and tremble, and for a moment, everything turned gray and fuzzy. She knew she was about to pass out.

And then her eyes settled on a face she recognized—or almost recognized. There, on the other side of the car, visible through the wavering heat and smoke, was the same man Kerri had seen in the crowd surrounding Jeri Sandston's crumpled body the evening before. And with a searing flash of memory, Kerri remembered where she knew him from. It was the short, stocky security guard from the Coleman Institute.

Her heart pounded with a force so powerful, she thought it might explode from her chest. Her skin crawled and burned, and though she knew part of it was due to the heat and smoke, she also knew her body was telling her something. At that instant, the guard saw Kerri and their gazes locked. A look of surprise passed over the man's face, followed by a steely, narrow-eyed determination. Slowly, he pushed his way through the crowd, heading toward her.

Kerri spun around and shoved her way back through the crowd, taking off at a sprint down the road beneath the viaduct, then up Marion Street. With no particular destination in mind, operating on nothing more than blind instinct, she pumped her legs as hard as she could up the steep incline. Soon her legs began to ache and complain, and her lungs burned with each gasping breath. Seeing an alleyway that ran off between the buildings to her right, she turned in, taking advantage of the brief flattening of the terrain. She dodged past a truck loaded with boxes of fresh vegetables parked near the back entrance to a restaurant, vaguely aware of the curious stares of the delivery men as she ran past. Moments later, she emerged on Columbia, and once more headed uphill until she reached the corner of First Street. Darting across the street, she ignored the blaring horns of the cars that nearly hit her, and she ran into Pioneer Square, ducking behind the huge totem pole that stood near one end, close to the edge of the trees. With her chest heaving and her body feeling as if it had used the last dregs of its reserves, she peeked out from behind the pole. At first, she thought she was safe, but then she saw the guard come around the corner and head down the other side of First Street, directly across from her, his eyes searching.

She pulled back behind the totem pole, glancing around desperately. Her legs churned as if they had a mind of their own, and panicked, she dashed across the square, toward Yesler Way, trying to keep the trees between her and the guard. Dodging traffic, she crossed the street and ducked into the alcove entrance of a coffee shop on the corner, stopping long enough to risk another look back. The guard stood at the far end of the wrought iron gazebo across the street, earnestly scanning the faces of everyone nearby. Fear slithered through her veins and she lunged out of the alcove and turned down First Street. Half blind with terror, and anxious to put as much distance between herself and the guard as possible, she ran into the street and cut a diagonal swath to the other side, only to instantly regret her action when she saw the sidewalk ahead of her blocked by a crowd of people. Momentarily stymied by this unexpected barrier, she pulled up short and stared at the crowd, her mind reeling. They were gathered at the top of a stairwell, descending the steps in single file and disappearing through a door at the bottom. In a moment, she knew the group would thin enough to let her pass, but she couldn't spare the wait. She turned to cross the street again, back to the other side, when she heard a voice drift toward her from the base of the stairs.

With a flash of memory, Kerri realized what the crowd was. The voice she heard was that of a woman guide ushering the group through a tour of the Underground City—the long-abandoned subterranean section of Seattle. Back in the nineteenth century, because of flooding, fire, and sewer problems, the city had been rebuilt some twenty to thirty feet above the old level, but much of the previous structure still existed in cold, dank tunnels that ran beneath the streets and sidewalks. Kerri had taken the tour herself several years ago, and often saw the tour groups during the day from her office as they made their way from one subterranean level to the next by way of the upper level, real world.

Kerri once more glanced over her shoulder, and seeing no sign of the guard, she made her decision. Melting into the last twenty or so people in the tour group, she followed them down the stairway.

TWENTY-SEVEN

❦

Kerri stepped through the door at the base of the stairs, her face down, trying to look nonchalant in hopes that neither the guide nor the members of the tour group would realize she didn't belong there. Once inside, she mingled with the others at the center of the large room they had entered, keeping a wary eye on the door. Her heart continued to gallop, only starting to slow when the guide finally pulled the huge metal door closed, throwing her hip against it to make sure it latched.

Breathing a sigh of relief, Kerri glanced around the room, trying to recall, from her own tour years ago, which portion they were in. The room was large, with a high ceiling and three thick columns spaced down the middle of its length.

Kerri concentrated on her breathing, trying to slow it down, fearful of hyperventilating. The air in the room was damp and chilly and musty with age, making Kerri think of crypts and catacombs and death. Rubbing her arms for warmth, she tried to focus on the here and now, blocking out the horror of her car and Stephen. She had to think. There would be time to grieve for Stephen later. Now, she had her own safety to worry about. But the image of Stephen's blackened corpse slumped behind the wheel of her car kept pushing its way to the surface, making her panic rise again like a wave building toward shore.

She vaguely recalled this room from years before, but had no idea where this portion of the tour would lead. Except for a narrow dirt border along the wall near the door, the floor was made of slate slabs that had fallen victim to some geological force, so that it was shaped like a giant flattened M—each row of slate slabs angling away from its neighbor and creating an awkward surface to negotiate. There was only one exit from the room, other than the door they had just come through, and it was in the far left corner. Kerri wished the guide would hurry up and move the group along. Standing here, doing nothing, made her feel helpless and vulnerable.

When the group did finally move on, Kerri fell in with the stragglers at the back, trying hard to look like a typical tourist, though she was actually scouting out the area, trying to jog her memory, trying to think of a way out.

They moved through a narrow passageway along a wooden sidewalk that ran down the middle of a dirt-covered floor. To her left was a cinder-block wall; to her right, behind a wooden railing, was a series of small rooms, their interiors dark and sodden and smelling of dirt, rot, and mildew. They were piled high with cast-off junk: discarded furniture, slabs of lumber, piles of bricks, chunks of ragged concrete. Overhead, rusted steel I beams held up the sagging ceiling, and for a moment, Kerri envisioned the whole thing collapsing in an explosion of dust and debris, burying her and the rest of the group. Thick cobwebs hung from the corners and draped the walls. Kerri couldn't believe she hadn't noticed how dismal the place was when she'd taken the tour before. Then it had been a fascinating bit of history; now it was nothing more than a grim reminder of death.

Stephen!

Her mind screamed out his name, and for one heart-stopping moment, she thought her mouth had screamed it as well. But when she saw no one staring at her, she cast her gaze to the floor and shuffled along with the group, struggling to get her mind and emotions under control.

The tour group moved out of the hallway and into a small alcove. Scattered throughout the underground tunnels were overhead skylights, metal grids filled with amethyst-colored glass tiles that formed sections of the sidewalks above. The light filtering down through the one above them now was dim and smoky, its purple hue reminding Kerri of Jace's strange purple light.

Shivering, Kerri thought of Jace, lying unaware and vulnerable in his hospital room. She had to get out of here. If they were after her, then surely Jace was in danger as well. Anxious to get to him, Kerri tapped her foot impatiently as the group dawdled and gawked at the skylight above and the old bank teller cage built into one wall of the alcove.

When they finally moved on, they entered a twisting labyrinth of passageways, eventually opening onto a room even larger than the first. This one was nearly as long as a football field and at least two stories high. Most of the ceiling had fallen, chunks of it lying forlornly on the dirt floor surrounding the narrow boardwalk, but a few of the old tiles remained—yellowed with age, though there were bits of the old scrollwork still visible. Huge, dust-filled cobwebs were everywhere: sheets of it draped along the walls like some Transylvanian wallpaper, clumps of it—some of them as long as three feet—hung brown and heavy, like Spanish moss, from the ceiling rafters.

Along the right side of the room, just a few feet from the boardwalk, crisscrossed two-by-fours formed a barricade to three additional rooms. These, like the others they had passed, had dirt floors and were filled with junk piled, in some places, as high as the ceiling. It was impossible to tell how far back the rooms went. Their depths devoured the meager light coming from the string of bare bulbs hanging above the boardwalk, fading into an inky blackness that seemed to go on forever.

At the farthest end of the main room was a metal stairway, and like a flash, Kerri remembered it from years ago. This was the final leg. At the top of those stairs, just around a bend, was the gift shop. From the gift shop was an exit that would lead her back up to Pioneer Square.

She started to think in earnest now. Somehow, she had to find her way back to the hospital, back to Jace and Kevin and Bender. But what if the guard was still milling about in the streets above? She didn't think he'd seen her come down here, but that didn't mean he wasn't nearby, hanging around, hoping to get some idea of where she'd disappeared to.

Why was he after her? She suspected she knew the answer to that one. Though she wasn't sure exactly what she and Bender had stumbled onto when they visited the Coleman Institute, someone obviously thought they knew something. And they didn't want that something to be known. Both Stephen and Jeri Sandston had already paid for that secrecy with their lives. She,

Bender, and Jace were probably next in line. She had to get help, had to get to Kevin or someone . . . before the Coleman Institute got to her.

The tour group milled ahead, and the first few were climbing the stairs leading to the gift shop. Kerri straggled along, her heart resuming its galloping pace, a fine sheen of sweat breaking out over her body. Slowly, she ascended the stairs, praying God would throw a little luck her way, hoping the guard had disappeared from the streets above. Rounding the corner into the last hallway, she saw the lighted, welcoming warmth of the gift shop. She sucked in a deep breath to brace herself.

And then that breath stuck in her lungs.

Up ahead, standing just past the entrance to the gift shop and studying the faces of the tour group as they meandered through the doorway, was the guard. With a little whimper, Kerri slumped down to keep from being seen over the heads of the other group members. She was trapped. Any moment now, the group would thin out enough for the guard to see her. Panicked, she turned around and headed back the way she had come, back into the bowels of the Underground City. She ran down the stairs, trying to keep her footsteps as light as possible, wincing as they clanked loudly against the metal stairs. The sound turned to a hollow echo as she hit the boardwalk and ran halfway down its length. There she paused, wild with fear, searching about frantically for some way to escape. The vast room was deathly quiet, though the rushing thump of blood coursing through her ears sounded as loud as the crashing surf. Kerri struggled to catch her breath, opening her mouth as wide as she could to minimize the sound, tasting the mix of dirt, age, and decay.

At the top of the stairs she saw a shadow cast against the brick wall. She snapped her mouth shut and held her breath. A pair of man's shoes appeared on the top step.

With a frantic glance around her, Kerri knew she could never reach the next passageway before the man descended far enough to see her. Instead, she ducked between the two-by-four barricade bordering the room immediately to her right and began scrambling over and around the piles of debris. She tried to step carefully, fearful of making noise, but the obstacle course of junk made it almost impossible. The light grew dimmer the farther back she went, making it harder to see the debris on the floor. An endless crevasse of ebony darkness lay ahead of her.

And then the lights went out.

Kerri froze, plunged into a blackness so complete she couldn't see her hand in front of her face. She opened her mouth, trying to breathe as shallowly and noiselessly as she could, listening for any sound. The darkness seemed to close in, squeezing the breath out of her, and panic bubbled up like caustic bile from her gut. She was trapped, and any moment now, the guard would reach out and seize her, dragging her from the trash-ridden room. But then she realized he had to be as blind as she was.

Unless he had a flashlight.

A vision of blinding light spearing through the blackness and pinioning her like some entomologist's bug flashed through her mind. A feeling of helplessness, of loss and defeat, settled over her and she turned around slowly until she faced the huge ballroom, resigned to her fate. Staring into the darkness, she waited for the sudden swath of light to cut through the gloom, finally putting an end to her heart-wrenching fear.

But the light never came. She continued to stare into the oblivion, hoping that, with time, her eyes might adjust some to the darkness. Maybe a few wisps of light from the skylight in the neighboring tunnel would manage to infiltrate the huge room, allowing her to at least see some shadows. But as the minutes ticked by, the thick blackness remained.

Never in her life had she experienced such an immense nothingness, such a total absence of light. For one panicked moment, she wondered if she was dead. Maybe this was what the afterlife was like, sort of an in-between holding stage, before the summoning white light. If there was any truth to those stories about near-death experiences, Kerri wished the light would hurry the hell up.

A noise came from off to her right, back within the recesses of the room. Kerri's head spun toward the sound, and the hair along her arms rose to attention. It couldn't be the guard. There was no way he could have managed to make his way to the back of this room already, even if there was another entrance.

She heard it again—a soft, scurrying sound. And then something warm and soft brushed against her leg.

Kerri's hand clamped over her mouth to hold back the scream housed at the back of her throat. And then she heard another noise—a tiny, almost chirping squeak.

Rats!

She remembered the tour guide's ominous references to the rats who called the Underground City home. The tour groups, of course—though they enjoyed a nervous titter or two—always assumed she was joking.

But Kerri had lived here long enough to know the truth. Several times a year there were stories about the ones who escaped—fat, furry rats who occasionally left their subterranean hideaway for the upper levels where cars, people, and sunshine quickly confused them.

Kerri swallowed down the panic she felt. Okay, so there were rats down here. No big deal. Just furry animals. Harmless.

Easier said than done. Kerri called upon every bit of control and restraint she possessed to keep from hurtling herself forward into the dark . . . into the arms of the guard . . . into the arms of death if need be, just to get away from the rats. But she managed to hold her ground, though a cold sweat enveloped her body, the dampness creating a million crawling sensations along her skin. She stood there in the darkness for what seemed an eternity, her ears tuned to the tiniest noise, her skin keenly aware of every sensation.

And then she heard the man move.

It was a subtle, cautious sound, but unmistakably human. Obviously, his ability to see was no better than her own. Without the use of her eyes, Kerri's ears seemed extra sensitive, and she was able to track the man's movements. He was heading away from her, his gait shuffling and tentative, back toward the stairwell and the doorway leading to the gift shop. Moments later she heard the faint metallic ring of his shoes climbing the stairs. And then an even fainter rush of noise as the door to the gift shop opened and closed.

A thick silence settled in, and Kerri waited several minutes before daring to move. Bent over, using her hands to feel for items blocking her way, she slowly backtracked through the debris, climbing over chunks of concrete and slabs of timbers. Twice, she scraped her legs along the rough edge of something in her path, and moments later she felt the warm trickle of blood as it oozed down her calf. She wondered if rats, like sharks, became incited by the smell of warm blood, and the thought made her move more quickly, with less caution, so that she banged her legs and arms dozens of times before she felt the crisscrossed two-by-fours marking the room's entrance. Seizing the barrier with a tiny whimper of relief, she squeezed through it, shuffling along until her foot knocked up against the raised wooden platform of the boardwalk. Turning in the opposite direction from the gift shop, she felt along the side wall, grimacing as her hands raked through the thick sheets of cobwebs. Taking tiny baby steps, she made slow, but steady, progress.

Gradually, she realized she could see the faintest of shadows around her, and as she turned a corner, she entered the small alcove with the skylight. Though the overhead lights were out here as well, the amethyst tiles let in enough light for her to see by.

Moving with more confidence and speed now that she could see, Kerri followed the wooden platform into the next passageway. As she walked down its length, the meager light gradually faded, until it disappeared altogether as she turned the corner into the room with the crooked floor. Though virtually blind, she moved across the room boldly, spurred on by the knowledge that the door she had originally entered—the doorway to the world above—lay just a few feet away.

The floor's incline was greater than she realized, and she stubbed her toe and nearly fell, her hand brushing against something solid as she flung it out in front of her to break her fall. It was one of the three columns, she realized, and she pulled her body up next to it, practically hugging it as she tried to regain her bearings. Aiming in the direction she thought the door should be, she again moved out, more slowly this time, carefully negotiating the hills and valleys of the cracked, uneven floor, waving her hands in front of her as if they were antennae. Something brushed lightly against her thigh, and she knew almost immediately that it was the rope separating the slate floor from the bordering section of dirt. She tried to pull back, but her forward motion was too great. Her upper body fell forward, and she frantically bicycled her legs to try and catch them up with the rest of her. But the rope held them back and she toppled downward, landing hands first in the dirt with the rope across her midsection. Her purse slid down off her shoulder and landed with a soft *whump* about the same time her left wrist popped painfully. An instant later, there was a scurry of movement and a high-pitched squeal mere inches from her head. Ignoring the pain in her wrist, Kerri shoved herself back over the rope as hard as she could, landing on her haunches, and scrabbling back across the slate floor.

She scrambled to her feet and froze, her ears perked to the continued sounds of tiny feet, her head moving slowly from one side to the other, feeling the pain pulsing from her injured wrist up the length of her arm. Her purse, she realized, was still lying in the dirt where it fell, but she was damned if she was going to go poking around in there to find it. When all had grown quiet once more, she licked her lips, sucked in a steadying lungful of air, and struck out again, angling a little more to the right, keeping her left arm splinted against her waist and using the right one to feel the air

in front of her. When her outstretched hand finally
came into contact with the solid brick of a main wall,
she almost cried with relief. Edging her way along, her
foot eventually bumped up against a hard surface.
Bending down and feeling with her good hand, she
realized she had found the base of the two concrete
steps leading to the landing near the door. Once more
sliding her hand along the wall, she carefully negoti-
ated the steps until she felt the surface of the wall
change from rough-hewn brick to something cold,
smooth and solid. The door!

Frantically, she traced her right hand over the surface until she felt a lock. When she realized it held no
key, she thought she would scream. Then she slid her
hand down a few more inches until she felt a handle
bar. She pushed against it with all of her might, and
the door burst open.

Though the day outside was gray, that little bit of
sunlight, after the blackness below, was blinding.
Kerri stepped through the doorway and stood a
moment in the small alcove at the base of the stairs,
her head several feet below the people walking by
above her. Blinking to try and adjust her eyes to the
sudden assault of light, she slowly climbed the stairs
toward the sidewalk. As she stumbled along, unbal-
anced by her blindness, the shakiness of her legs,
and the pain throbbing through her arm, she failed
to notice the car parked beside the curb. Even when
the door opened and a man stepped out, Kerri didn't
realize anything was amiss. Only when an arm
hooked through hers and dragged her toward the car
did she realize she had walked right into a trap. She
felt something cold press against the side of her neck
and heard a faint hissing sound. And just before

everything went totally gray, just before she was
shoved into the backseat of the car, just before her
briefly burgeoning hope flagged for the last time,
Kerri wondered who would take care of Jace, now
that she was dead.

TWENTY-EIGHT

❧✦❧

The first thing Kerri became aware of was the incredible white-hot pain slicing through her left arm. She was lying on her back, and the surface beneath her felt hard and cold. Moaning, she tried to lift her injured arm, but the pain was too intense. Waiting a moment for the pain to ease some, she opened her eyes.

The light in the room was dim and had an odd, purplish cast to it. The ceiling was gray and blurry, and partially obscured by a large round object hovering a few feet over her head. Squinting, Kerri managed to make out the shape, realizing it was a surgical lamp. It was turned off, the weird purple light coming from long, lavender-colored, fluorescent-type bulbs that hung in rows above it. Kerri thought she must be in a hospital somewhere, but couldn't remember how she got here.

She heard a faint thrumming noise, and her body vibrated gently, as if some giant generator hummed beneath her. Turning her head to one side, she scanned the rest of her surroundings, her brow drawn in a puzzled V. If this was a room in a hospital, it was unlike any she'd seen before. It was small—about twelve feet square—and the walls were windowless and plain. There was no equipment panel, no monitor, no machinery—nothing but the overhead surgical lamp and whatever she was lying on. Gritting her teeth and sucking in a pained hiss of air, she raised herself to a sitting position, dangling her legs over the side and cradling her injured arm in her lap. For a moment, the walls of the room seemed to march toward her in a dizzying spiral, and a zillion tiny lights hovered around her head. She squeezed her eyes closed, shutting out the light swarm and waiting for the dizziness to subside. It did, but with its passing came memories—memories of Stephen, and the guard, and her horrified struggle through the black tunnels of the Underground City. A tiny whimper escaped her lips, and she raised her head and stared around the room with fear, confusion, and sadness.

Not only were there no windows in the room, she couldn't find a door. The walls wrapped around her endlessly, their surface soft and textured, as if they were covered with some kind of felt material. For one crazy moment, Kerri wondered if she'd been committed, locked away in a rubber room at some asylum for the insane. But she quickly chased that idea away. The pain she felt—not just the physical pain, but the fear and emotional anguish as well—was too real, too vivid to be something she'd imagined.

Then a section of the wall slid away with a hiss and Kerri knew she was crazy; she *had* to be—loco, totally whacked, over the edge. Her eyes grew wide with amazement and she gasped.

She recognized the creature at once, both from the picture she'd seen in her psychiatry journal and the descriptions given by Jace and the members of Bender's group. Its body was smooth, not angular, and it glowed with a bluish-white light, as if it were phosphorescent. From head to toe, its skin was unmarred except for a faint crisscrossing of shadowy lines running just beneath the surface. The head was large—at least twice the size of her own—and the eyes were wide and dark and glassy looking, like empty black holes. It had no nose or mouth, but the skin near the chin undulated in an easy rhythm, as if the creature breathed through it.

It took a few steps toward her with a slow, awkward gait, its legs spread apart, its arms hanging in stilted angles by its sides. Behind it, the wall slid back into place with a quiet hiss.

The creature stood just inside the door, and Kerri stared at it, both fascinated and terrified, wondering if it was real or just some figment of her diseased imagination. Her mind felt sluggish and cottony, and she recalled the cold metal object that had been thrust against her neck just before she was shoved into the car. She realized she'd been drugged, and though its effects were wearing off, she was still having trouble seeing clearly. The combination of the drug and the strange lighting made everything seem blurry and indistinct.

The creature moved a few steps closer, and Kerri gaped at it, riveted with shock. It turned slowly as if performing a bizarre dance parody, revealing a flattened ridge running down the length of its head and back, like some spinal vestige. A faint humming emanated from the body, and its skin wavered slightly, as if it had a life all its own. Kerri blinked hard and rubbed at her eyes with her good hand, trying to clear her vision. When she again focused in on the creature, something about the appearance of the skin disturbed her. It looked taut—

thin and fragile, almost as if the creature itself were some giant balloon. There was something about it . . . something familiar, yet troubling.

The creature turned to face her, and Kerri met its unblinking stare with one of her own. Its hands raised up, and Kerri ducked, thinking it was reaching for her. Instead, the hands moved back behind the creature's head. A loud, ripping sound filled the air, and Kerri jumped, her eyes growing even wider. She watched in horror as the skin near the creature's chest and shoulders wrinkled and sloughed, becoming loose and shapeless, just before it dropped into a puddle on the floor at the creature's feet.

A scream surged up through Kerri's throat but died before she could give it birth. Her mouth dropped open and all the blood drained from her face as she stared in total confusion at the creature now standing before her. Her mind spun crazily, trying to assimilate the signals coming from her eyes, but it proved too boggling. She was crazy. This could only be some bizarre nightmare born from her warped and injured psyche.

The creature smiled at Kerri, and she flinched as if she'd been hit.

"It's quite convincing, don't you think?" the creature said.

Kerri gave her head a little shake and tried to swallow, but her saliva had all but disappeared. She spoke, her voice coming out as a mere whisper tinged with disbelief.

"Nathan?"

"I'm afraid so," Nathan said, grinning. "Are you disappointed? Did you think you'd been abducted by aliens like the others?"

Kerri stared at him, trying to think of something else to say, still not convinced she wasn't caught up in some nightmare of her own making. "Nathan?" she repeated.

"My," Nathan said, "you really were convinced, weren't you? But I assure you, it's me. Real, live, and in the flesh." As if to prove his point, he stepped out of the puddle of skin at his feet and walked over to her, caressing her cheek with the back of his hand.

Kerri pulled back from his touch with a look of disgust.

Nathan dropped his hand and frowned at her. "Now, now, is that any way to treat your husband?" he whined, pouting.

Nathan's familiar sniveling finally convinced Kerri that the thing standing before her really was her ex-husband. Fear and astonishment gave way to a mighty surge of anger.

"What the hell are you doing, Nathan? What is . . . that?" she spat out, pointing toward the pile of stuff that had covered him just moments before. "Just what sort of game are you playing here?"

"Now, Kerri," Nathan said with irritating calm, holding his hand up to halt her angry tirade. "Settle down and I'll explain everything."

Kerri forced herself to take a deep, calming breath, though her lips remained grimly set, her eyes afire with fury.

"It's really quite brilliant," Nathan said. "With the use of the right drugs, these specially made suits, and this black lighting," he swept his hand toward the lights overhead, "it becomes quite easy to stage an alien abduction. You believed, and I didn't even use the hallucinogenic on you."

With a look of dawning on her face, Kerri glanced at the lights in the ceiling. Of course. Black lights. That explained the purple light described by Jace. A tornado of thoughts and questions whirled through her mind and she tried desperately to grasp one, to make some sense out of all this. "Why, Nathan? Why would you do this?"

"Come," he said, holding one hand out to her. "Let me show you."

Kerri stared at his proffered hand, debating. Her mind was growing weary of its endless circling. She could make little sense of any of this, and might as well let Nathan have his say. Maybe then she could understand. With a tiny grimace of pain triggered by the gentle jarring of her injured wrist, she slid off the table and stood next to Nathan.

Nathan glanced down at her arm. "That's a nasty sprain," he said. "But I don't think it's broken." His eyes raised up and met hers. "Would you like something for the pain?"

Kerri shook her head. The last thing she wanted was anything that might further cloud her mind. Her arm throbbed painfully, but it helped keep her head clear.

"Come then," Nathan said. He turned and walked toward the wall, and as Kerri followed she could see the outline of a door. It slid open as they approached, and Kerri followed Nathan over the threshold and through a small foyer to yet another door. This one was more conventional, and Nathan pushed it open and held it, allowing Kerri to step past him into the next room.

The brightness, created by rows of normal fluorescents mounted in the ceiling, and accentuated by walls

that were lined with gleaming white tile, was almost
blinding after the dim black light they had just left.
Compared to the first room, this one was cavernous
and filled with an overwhelming array of items. It was
also noisy, thanks to a faint but constant hum created
by the numerous air vents dotting the ceiling. Kerri's
eyes widened with curiosity as she scanned the room.

Situated along the wall directly to her right was a
series of laboratory-type tables covered with various
utensils: beakers, test tubes, pipettes, small bottles of
stain, Bunsen burners, microscopes—obviously some
sort of biology lab. Near the edge of the table closest to
her, a beaker full of liquid agar sat atop a lit burner,
waiting to be poured into the petri dishes stacked
beside it.

At the room's center was a long U-shaped console
with built-in monitors that flashed as thousands of bits
of information scrolled across their screens. Spaced
between the monitors were control panels filled with
knobs, dials, flashing lights, and a dizzying array of
LCD readouts. Four chairs were spread out before the
desktop area, a keyboard in front of each one. All of
the chairs were vacant.

To her left, up against the wall, Kerri saw a large
floor-to-ceiling cabinet made of stainless steel. Four
doors, three feet wide and inset with glass, opened
onto stacked rows of metal racks, each one covered
with dozens of incubating petri dishes. A series of
gauges and monitors were set atop each of the doors,
and Kerri could see that at least one of them measured
the inside temperature, which hovered right at thirty-
seven degrees Centigrade—*body temperature*, Kerri
thought. A matching cabinet was situated farther
down, at the opposite end of the room, and two more

were placed in similar positions along the room's right wall.

Spaced out along the wall between the incubators, were a dozen or so Plexiglas-enclosed workstations, each bearing three portholes along its front and one at each end equipped with gloved arm covers that would enable someone to work on the items inside without exposing them to the outside air.

Though a bit overwhelming, none of what Kerri had seen thus far gave her much pause. She knew she was looking at a high-tech, well-equipped biological lab. But when she moved closer to examine one of the enclosed workstations, she soon realized she had stepped into a chamber of horrors.

Lined up behind the Plexiglas barriers were a number of cylinder-shaped glass containers, some with a capacity she guessed to be around two gallons, others as large as five. All were filled with a tan-colored serous-looking liquid—like a light broth—that bubbled gently, creating a thin cover of white foam at the top. Rows of bottles hung above them, an umbilical of tubing from each one snaking its way to the containers below. Tanks marked OXYGEN sat outside the workstation, and more tubing led from their nozzles to the containers inside. The back wall was filled with gauges, LCD displays, flashing lights, and a series of electrical wires that snaked out, feeding into the containers through large rubber stoppers. As Kerri moved closer, she saw something floating, suspended, inside each of the broth-filled containers. She peered at the one closest to her, and the bubbling broth made the object inside sway nearer to the container's edge. It was a meaty red color, about the size of Kerri's fist, with a shape that made it easily recognizable.

Kerri gasped and drew back, staring into space a moment. Then slowly, reluctantly, she moved her eyes to the next container—bigger than the first—and waited for it to reveal its contents as well. The item contained in this one was much larger—nearly eight inches in length and six in width—its surface reddish-pink like the color of salmon, smooth and glistening, its irregular shape divided into three uneven segments. With a kind of fascinated horror, Kerri moved to the next container, once more identifying the object inside by its distinctive kidney-bean shape.

Stunned, she dragged her eyes from the work-station and turned around to gape at Nathan. "Are those what I think they are?" Kerri asked him.

"I don't know. What do you think they are?" Nathan asked smugly, cocking his head at her.

"I'm not interested in games, Nathan," Kerri snapped. "That first one has a heart in it, the second one looks like a lung, and the third a kidney."

"Ding, ding, ding. You win the prize!"

Kerri stared at him, her face a mixture of pity, fear, and frosty contempt. "Are they human?" she asked, bracing herself for an answer she wasn't sure she wanted to hear.

"Of course they are."

Kerri felt bile burn its way up her throat. She grimaced, as much from the horror of what she was seeing and hearing as from the sour taste filling her mouth.

"It's not what you think," Nathan said, frowning at her. "They didn't come from anyone, at least not directly. We grew them."

Kerri's mouth dropped open. "You *grew* them?" Then, an instant later, "Who grew them? Where are we?"

"You are in the Coleman Institute," Nathan told her. "The fifth floor. The one they wouldn't let you see."

Though Kerri felt a small sense of satisfaction in realizing she had been right all along in her suspicions about the Coleman Institute, she was confused by what she was seeing, unsure of exactly what was going on. "You are growing human organs?" she asked Nathan with a tone of disbelief.

"I suppose saying we grew them is a bit simplistic. In reality, we are regenerating them."

"Regenerating them?"

Nathan nodded. "A most amazing discovery," he said excitedly. "One of our scientists isolated the genetic material key to the regeneration process in starfish and salamanders and found a way to apply it to human cells. The starfish discovery started the whole process, but the isolation of the elements in the salamanders is what made it all possible.

"In a general sense, humans regenerate cells all the time as part of the normal healing process—epithelial cells and corneal cells for example. But differentiated regeneration, the kind that allows salamanders to grow back an amputated limb, bone and all, was something we didn't fully understand. Until now. By combining the proper genetic material with specific human cells and adding in the necessary nutrients and electrical impulses, we can literally grow an organ from a few cells.

"Those containers there," he nodded toward the workstation, "act like a womb of sorts, providing the type of nurturing and stimulating environment necessary for the cells to grow and divide."

Dawning crossed Kerri's face. "And then you can

transplant the fully grown organ into a needy recipient," she surmised. "But what about tissue matches?"

"That's the beauty of this," Nathan said. "By accessing blood donor and hospital records from the general community, we can find the exact tissue type we need and clone the organ specifically for an individual recipient. All we need is a tiny sample of the donor's blood, with enough white cells to do the tissue typing."

"That's the common link," Kerri mumbled, her face furrowed in thought.

"What's that?"

Kerri looked up at Nathan and, for the first time, saw the insanity in his eyes. "Of course," she said. "You have access to the hospital laboratory, and all the blood samples of any patient who ever comes through the doors."

"And the blood bank," Nathan added. "That gives us access to anyone who ever donates blood. In fact, that is our primary source, since the clientele who donate blood tend to be healthier than those who have been treated in a hospital."

"And when you find a match, you steal cell samples from them," Kerri surmised. "From their organs. That's what's been happening to these people. You're stealing their cells."

"Well," Nathan said, rolling his eyes and dismissing her words with a wave of his hand. "Stealing is a rather strong word."

"What the hell do you call it then?" Kerri asked, incredulous.

"They're donating their cells. For a worthy cause."

"Donating implies consent, Nathan. None of these people have any idea what you are doing to them."

"It doesn't hurt them any," Nathan said defensively, scowling.

"How the hell can you say that?" Kerri snapped. "What about Janet Johansen?"

Nathan chewed his lip and looked down at this feet, wearing that little-boy-lost look Kerri knew so well. "She was a heart tissue harvest. They can be . . . difficult."

"Difficult?" Kerri said, aghast. "For God's sake, Nathan. You murdered the woman. Is that your idea of difficult?"

"It wasn't intentional," he pouted.

"That hardly justifies things," Kerri argued, appalled by his justification.

"You don't understand, Kerri. Don't you get it? Can't you see the implications here?"

"No, Nathan, I can't. Jesus Christ! You're violating people in the most ungodly ways! How can you possibly justify this?"

"There aren't nearly enough organs to go around, Kerri. You know that. There are forty thousand people waiting on donor lists right now. There are at least three times that many who can't get on the lists. Every year, some fifty thousand people die waiting for a suitable organ." His eyes looked at her—wide, appealing. "Mandy died waiting."

Kerri reeled back from his words as if she'd been slapped. The mention of Mandy's death made the anger rush out of her, leaving her adrift with her emotions like a sailboat on a windless sea. "What are you saying, Nathan?" she asked, her voice uneasy. "Are you telling me you could have grown a heart for Mandy?"

"And kidneys," he said softly.

Kerri digested this, chewing the inside of her

cheek. "Then why didn't you?" she posed, disgusted with herself for even asking, but helpless not to.

Nathan hung his head again and stared at his feet. "I didn't know about it in time," he muttered. "When Weatherton first approached me—"

"Weatherton? You mean Dr. Weatherton? Frank Weatherton?"

Nathan peered up at her and nodded. "By the time he realized Mandy's condition and brought me into the fold, it was too late. She died before her organs were fully grown."

Kerri's emotions churned. Confusion, anger, sadness, disgust, and—dare she admit to it?—self-pity. Mandy might have been saved. The thought made her heart ache with loss and her face tighten in agony. Nathan was right about one thing. This discovery carried far-reaching implications for the future of medicine. It might have been too late for Mandy, but the hope it held out for thousands of others was staggering. Yet, what Nathan and Weatherton were doing was wrong. Not the organ cloning itself, but rather their methods.

"Nathan, why all this alien crap? Why make these people think they've been abducted?"

"It's simple, really," Nathan said with a shrug. "We needed some way to explain the markings left behind from the tissue harvests. This whole alien-abduction thing has been growing, yet is still looked upon with a fair amount of skepticism and disbelief. Making the donors think they've been abducted not only explains the markings, it assures us a certain amount of security. For the most part, the donors are reluctant to say anything, fearful of public derision. Those who do speak up are ridiculed, their mental stability questioned. This whole alien thing has become so popular, it seemed like the perfect setup."

"Who gets the organs?" Kerri asked him.

"Anyone who can pay," Nathan said simply.

"You're *selling* them?"

"Of course," Nathan answered, looking insulted. "How do you expect us to pay for all this?"

"What about the usual routes for research, Nathan? Government funding, grants, that sort of thing?"

Nathan waved away her suggestion. "Even if the government was willing to allow this research to go on, it would take years to get past the ethics committees, and then there would be no guarantee of willing donors. This way, we avoid the wait, control the supply and demand, and make a nice little profit to boot."

"This is sick, Nathan," Kerri said. "You can't really believe you can get away with this."

"Oh, but we have gotten away with it," Nathan said with a smirk. "That's the beauty of it. Once we identify our potential donors, we examine their health histories to determine the best candidate. A few days before the scheduled harvest, we send a phony utility man out to the house and rig up some tanks of concentrated carbon monoxide. When the time comes, our harvest team goes out in the middle of the night wearing night goggles and black clothing so they won't be seen. One member of the team is an expert locksmith, so access is never a problem. When they reach the house, they first trigger the tanks to release just enough gas into the house to render the occupants unconscious. Once they are inside the house, they put on the alien suits and go to work.

"Those suits are a stroke of genius in themselves,

made from a resin we extract from tube worms. The resulting material is not only thin, lightweight, and impermeable, it has a biological component to it, so its texture is not unlike skin. They are self contained units equipped with cooling channels, transmitters and receivers that allow our workers to communicate with one another, and a complete respirator system that filters out the carbon monoxide. Of course, they also provide the necessary visual impressions. Combine that with the hallucinogenic we give the donors, and you've got some disturbing memories and images. The crews operate with portable black lights, which not only provide sufficient light to work from without attracting undue attention, they also trigger a chemical in the resin that creates a phosphorescent glow in the suits. Then, just to make sure the donor's memories are vivid enough and believable, we use a virtual reality helmet that's been programmed with staged scenes from our supposed spaceship surgical suite—the room you were in before. Hidden in the walls in there are some holographic units and cameras. All in all, the whole setup works quite well."

Nathan paused, and frowned. "Until the mess at the Johansen house, everything went along flawlessly. We never meant for the woman to die. We thought we had things covered up when we packed up her stuff to make it look as if she had left. Then those damned divers had to go and find her body."

"You killed Thad Johansen, didn't you?" Kerri asked him. She braced herself for the answer, knowing what it would be, but taking no satisfaction in the fact that her theory had been all too right.

"It was necessary," Nathan said simply. "If the woman's body hadn't shown up, everything would have been fine. But with the cops looking into things, it became necessary to provide some, shall we say, *closure*, to the whole thing. Planting the rope in Johansen's garage and then making it look as if he did himself in out of remorse was rather brilliant, don't you think?" He ignored Kerri's look of pure disgust. "Though I'm still confused about how the kid managed to see anything," he said thoughtfully. "We doped him up along with his father."

"You doped them? With what?"

"Phenobarbital," Nathan answered, pointing a finger at his jugular vein. "With an air injector. Generally, we give them just enough to knock them out for a few hours."

"Ritalin," Kerri muttered.

"What?"

"Ritalin. Jace is hyperactive. He was taking Ritalin. The Ritalin would have acted as an antagonist with the phenobarbital. That's why it didn't work."

"Of course," Nathan said, his face brightening. He bestowed a prideful smile on Kerri. "You see, you're a natural for this kind of work."

"You're crazy, Nathan," Kerri said, her anger flaring at his suggestion. "You, and Weatherton, and anyone else who's involved with this crap. You're nothing but a bunch of criminals. Despicable. The lowest of the scum that crawls the earth."

"Don't say that, Kerri," Nathan warned, his face darkening. "You need to understand. You need to buy into this." His words were slow and measured; the muscles in his cheeks twitched with tension. "It's only because I've convinced them you'll be willing to work with us that they are giving you a second chance. They wanted to kill you, you know. Hell, they already tried. I went ballistic when I found out. It's damned fortunate you weren't in your car when it exploded."

Kerri felt as if Nathan had plunged a dagger directly into her heart. The agony of it made her squeeze her eyes closed and take a sharp, shuddering breath. "Stephen," she whimpered. "You killed Stephen."

"I'm sorry about that," Nathan said, managing to sound somewhat remorseful. "Though perhaps it's just as well. It bought you another chance, Kerri. It bought *us* another chance."

Kerri opened her eyes and shot Nathan a look of pure hatred. "No way, Nathan. This is sick. You are sick." She shoved him aside and strode toward a door on the far side of the room.

"Kerri, please," Nathan called after her. "You have to listen to me."

Kerri ignored him. When she reached the door, she slammed her palm against the button on the wall beside it, waiting as it slid wide with a gentle hiss. Beyond was a small foyer, an airlock similar to the one she'd encountered during her tour with Letitia Miller. She marched into it and headed for the next door, only to be brought up short when it opened and she found herself staring into the face of Frank Weatherton. He was holding a gun aimed at her head. On either side of him stood two men: the security guards she and Bender had encountered the last time they were here.

Weatherton entered the foyer with the two men moving in concert beside him. The door behind him hissed closed.

"I told you she wouldn't understand, Palmer," he said, glancing over Kerri's shoulder. His eyes moved back to Kerri's face and he shook his head with disappointment. "It's rather a shame, Kerri. I always liked you, you know." His eyes raked up and down her body—a quick, raping assessment.

"I really hate having to kill you," he said with a heavy sigh. "It's so hard to find good, attractive physicians these days."

TWENTY-NINE

Kerri took a few steps back, only to bump into Nathan. She glared at Weatherton.

"I should have known you'd be mixed up in something this sick," she said with contempt. "You always did have a penchant for doing and saying the wrong thing."

Weatherton gave her a tolerant smile. "It's unfortunate you don't understand what we've achieved here, Dr. Whitaker."

"Oh, I understand it all too well," Kerri snapped. "You're using people, taking advantage of them for your own personal gain. Something you've always excelled at."

Weatherton shook his head and sighed. "No one is harmed by what we do, Kerri. In fact, the organ recipients have achieved incredible benefits that might not otherwise be available. The fact that we make a little money off the venture is beside the point." He punctuated the statement with a dismissing wave of his gun.

"You're playing God, Frank. Doling out organs to the highest bidder. Not exactly fair, do you think?"

Weatherton shrugged. "We have costs. They must be recouped somehow."

"What about the cost to those you victimize?"

Kerri shot back. "Who is going to recoup the lives of Thad and Janet Johansen?"

"As with any area in medicine, there are losses," Weatherton said, his voice growing impatient. "You know that."

Kerri shook her head in disbelief. "You're crazy," she muttered. "What you've discovered here is nothing short of miraculous. But to use it for your own warped purposes this way is insane."

Weatherton's face suffused with red as his eyes drew down to a steely glint, making Kerri wonder if she had gone too far. "Is it insane to want to give people another chance at life?" Weatherton asked, his voice rising in challenge. "Is it insane to want financial independence? Is it insane to want to get out from under the wrath and control of a filthy rich bitch wife and establish an identity of my own in the world?"

"Is that what this is all about?" Kerri asked, incredulous. "You're killing and abusing people for financial gain because you're pussy whipped?" She knew she was pushing him, but she found the whole thing so appalling, she was powerless to stop. Besides, if she was going to die anyway, she might as well go out zinging a few well-placed barbs at the murderous bastard who had created this nightmare.

Weatherton's face turned furious. "Andrew!" he barked, looking over at the bald security guard. "You and Thompson get her the hell out of here. I don't care what you do with her, just make sure we are in no way connected."

Kerri's face paled as Thompson's barrel chest loomed in front of her face. Andrew grabbed her right arm and she shook him off angrily. "Don't you touch me," she said, seething with anger.

Weatherton chuckled. "You are a feisty one, Whitaker. It's a shame you're so stubborn. You can make it easy on yourself, or difficult. It's your choice."

Kerri spun around and cast an appealing glance toward Nathan. "Don't let them do this."

Nathan hung his head a moment, then looked up at Kerri with an expression of sad resignation. "Don't you see, Kerri? It's for the better. The needs of the many outweigh the needs of the few. Now no one has to suffer what we went through when we lost Mandy. Think of all the lives that can be saved. Think of all the anguish and human suffering we can prevent."

Kerri stared at him with pity. "Nathan," she said softly, "I know Mandy's death was hard. I didn't realize until now just how much it affected you . . . how much it affected us. And you're right about all the lives that can be saved through this process. But not like this. These people are murderers, can't you see that? Now they're going to kill me. Will my death make the loss of Mandy any easier?" She saw a look of indecision fly across Nathan's face and she held her breath, trying to keep her own expresssion impassive. Her only hope—and it was a slim one, she realized—was to get Nathan on her side.

Nathan studied her, weighing the conviction of her words. After a moment, he flashed her a smile that was both pathetic and childlike. He looked past her toward Weatherton. "Look, Frank, give me a little more time here. I think she'll come around. If I can just—"

His words were cut off as a look of astonishment crossed his face. His mouth formed a tiny O, and an exhalation of air that sounded disturbingly like a sigh of relief passed his lips. An instant later, Kerri's eyes grew wide with shock as she saw a small hole open on his forehead, a tiny trickle of blood meandering toward the bridge of his nose. Then, with a hard, solid thump, Nathan crumpled into a heap on the floor. Stunned, Kerri whirled around and saw Weatherton holding his gun at arm's length, its muzzle still pointed in Nathan's direction. The acrid smell of gunpowder filled the air.

"He was a pain in the ass," Weatherton scowled, slowly dropping his arm to his side. "You're better off without him anyway."

A cold wave of terror rose up from Kerri's bowels, making her feel dizzy and nauseated. Her arms twitched with barely contained energy, the fingers opening and closing spasmodically. She wanted to leap at Weatherton and claw his eyes out, rip his hair out by its roots. But some still-functioning part of her rational mind told her all she would get for her efforts was a bullet through the brain, just like Nathan. For one frightening second, she considered that possibility, and didn't find it all that horrible. At least with death, she would be at peace.

Then she remembered Jace. He had no one left. He needed her. Now was no time to get selfishly suicidal. She struggled to shake off her melancholy and control the panic that seized her, trying to clear her mind in hopes of finding some way out of this mess.

"Get her out of here," Weatherton muttered, waving his gun toward the door behind him. He punched at the button on the wall and the door slid open.

Kerri's mind searched frantically for something she could do or say to turn things around. But one look at Weatherton's cold dead eyes told her it was futile. Her shoulders sagged as the hope drained out of her.

Thompson's hand settled on the back of her neck with a viselike grip and steered her toward the door.

Defeated and resigned, Kerri shuffled along meekly, her eyes downcast as she passed Weatherton and entered the hallway. She knew this was her death march, and some distant part of her mind struggled against the apathy that had overtaken her. But her will to fight was gone. She felt tired, weary of the whole damned mess. Idly, she wondered how they would kill her. Hopefully, it would be quick and painless; she was no hero when it came to suffering.

Thompson and Andrew escorted her to the far end of the hallway where there was a single elevator. Andrew slid his keycard into the slot beside the door. As they waited for the car to arrive, Kerri gazed longingly out the window to her right, at the oceanfront below, realizing this would likely be her last glimpse of its powerful beauty. It filled her with a terrible sadness that rapidly gave way to anger—anger over her helplessness, anger with the people whose misguided intentions had led them to greed and moral corruption, anger at a world that held innumerable dangers and hurts. The anger was somehow bracing, and she straightened her shoulders, momentarily shored by a renewed sense of hope. There had to be a way out of all this. *Think*, she told herself. *Don't give up yet, not as long as you're still alive.*

A chime sounded, and the elevator door slid open. Kerri stared into the car for a frozen moment, once again thinking she must be losing her mind. Standing in the elevator were Kevin and Bender.

With a suddenness that made Kerri yelp, Kevin charged out of the elevator like a bull moose, his head lowered, throwing himself against Andrew and pushing him back down the hall. "Get Kerri out of here!" he yelled back over his shoulder.

Bender stepped out of the elevator and reached for Kerri to pull her inside. But Thompson, at first stunned into immobility by Kevin's actions, quickly came to his senses. His arm snaked around Kerri's neck, his other hand pulled out a gun and held it to her head. Bender froze where he was.

Kevin and Andrew rolled around on the floor, grunting and groaning as they struggled with each other. Kerri stifled a scream when she saw Andrew's hand come up toward Kevin's head holding a gun. Kevin saw it and grabbed Andrew's wrist, slamming his hand onto the floor. The gun flew from Andrew's grasp, skittering across the floor past Bender's feet and sliding into the elevator just as the door started to close. Bender made the tiniest flicker of movement toward it, and Kerri felt Thompson jerk his gun away from her head and aim it at Bender.

"Noooo!" she screamed. She reached up with her hands and yanked Thompson's arm down as hard as she could. The gun fired. From one corner of her eye, Kerri saw Bender lunge for the other weapon, but the elevator door slid closed before he could reach it, shutting the gun inside.

"Shit!" Thompson yelled. Kerri tried to move out of his grasp, but his grip only tightened. Once more Thompson trained the gun on Bender, and Kerri knew their time had run out. Her mind screamed in denial and she squeezed her eyes shut, waiting for the end.

But nothing happened. Slowly, she opened her eyes, relieved to see Bender still alive, standing near the wall. His eyes were fixed on Kevin and Andrew, his face blanched white. Gradually, Kerri realized there was no longer any commotion coming from the direction of the other two men. She looked over to where they lay, and felt her heart crawl into her throat.

Andrew was lying on top of Kevin, perfectly still. A tiny circle of blood surrounded the ragged hole in Andrew's shirt where a bullet had entered his back. Kerri realized that when she had yanked Thompson's arm, she'd unwittingly sent the bullet in Kevin and Andrew's direction. Kevin lay beneath Andrew's body, his face beaded with perspiration and twisted in agony. With a great will of effort, he tried to roll to his right side. Andrew's body slid off, and Kerri saw the gaping hole in Andrew's stomach. A loop of intestine protruded through the man's shirt, and Kerri clamped her hand over her mouth, afraid she was going to be sick.

Then her eyes saw the bloodied mess on Kevin's shirt. At first she thought it was Andrew's blood. But now she could see the ragged tears in Kevin's shirt, the torn flesh beneath oozing a steady stream of blood. Apparently, the bullet had gone clear through Andrew, fragmenting and expanding as it tore through tissue and bone, exiting on the other side and striking Kevin where he lay beneath him. Kevin's hands clutched at his belly, his face riveted in agony. He tried to rise up from the floor but couldn't even lift his head. Then his eyes rolled back and his whole body went limp.

A cry of anguish escaped from Kerri's lips.

"You!" Thompson yelled at Bender. He gestured back down the hallway toward the lab with a nod of his head. "Move it!"

Bender did as he was told, moving slowly past Kerri as Thompson held the gun trained on him. Thompson grabbed Kerri's shoulder and spun her around, then shoved her in the same direction. She stumbled, managing to regain her balance before she fell. Bender reached out to steady her, and got a punch to his gut from Thompson as his reward. Bender doubled over in pain, his breath coming out in a loud *whoomph*.

Thompson's gaze shifted toward Kerri with a look of cold fury that made her blood turn to ice. "Move it, sister," he growled. Shooting him back a look of pure venom, Kerri helped Bender straighten up, wrapping her arm around his waist as they moved back down the hallway.

They entered the laboratory, and Kerri saw Frank Weatherton standing in front of the computer console, studying the multiple readouts on the screens before him with an expression of smug satisfaction. Nathan's body still lay on the floor, a widening pool of darkening blood surrounding him. Though Kerri no longer loved him, and had even loathed him at times over the past year, the sight of him lying there, discarded like some bothersome piece of trash, infuriated her.

"You are a murdering, sick son of a bitch, Frank," she seethed. "You'll never get away with this."

Weatherton looked up at them, his face briefly registering his surprise. Then his expression changed to one of amusement. "I've always admired your spirit, Kerri," he said dryly. "Misplaced though it may be." His eyes shifted to Thompson, and all traces of humor disappeared. "I see we have company," Weatherton said. "What happened?"

"We had some trouble," Thompson said in his deep rumbling voice. "This one," he indicated Bender, "and another guy came up in the elevator. The other guy took one look at us and charged out of the elevator like some lunatic. Caught us completely by surprise. He and Andrew have both been shot. Dead or dying," he added.

Weatherton's face drew into a thoughtful frown. "This won't do," he said with a sigh, gazing down at Nathan. "All these bodies to dispose of." Then his face brightened. "However, there is an up side to this. Let's bring them all in here and we can harvest the organs. An extra added bonus," he said gleefully. His eyes moved to Bender. "I must say, I'm glad to see you, Dr. Bender. Now we can kill two birds, so to speak, with one stone."

Bender's eyebrows arched in surprise. "You know who I am," he said.

"Of course," Weatherton said. "I make it my business to know everything that goes on here. I reviewed the tapes of your prior visit. Rather ingenious, I might add, posing as an investor the way you did. Of course, if we'd been successful in tapping the phone in Kerri's office, we might have discovered your little deception sooner. It was unfortunate Kerri interrupted my man. The cops were watching the office a little too closely after that, forcing us to settle for tapping her home phone instead. We knew as soon as we saw that drawing the kid did that there might be trouble."

"You took the drawing." Kerri said. "Didn't you?"

Weatherton shrugged. "A foolish move, taking the thing," he said. "Trust me, my man was properly chastised. If you hadn't interfered with his next visit, the picture would have miraculously reappeared."

Kerri said nothing, she merely glared at the man.

Weatherton reached inside his suit coat and pulled out his own gun. He aimed it at Bender's face. I think we'll give you and Kerri a personalized tour of our special surgical suite," he said. "I'm sure the two of you will make excellent organ donors as well. If you cooperate and go without a fuss, I'll see to it that you're

dead before we take them. Otherwise, I'll strap you
down and rip them from your body while you're still
awake." He flashed them a grin of malicious glee, as if
the prospect of gouging out their organs like some
priest in an ancient Aztec ceremony was immensely
appealing.

Thompson grabbed Kerri's arm and yanked her in
the direction of the surgical room. His gun jabbed
painfully into her spine. "Move it," he said.

Kerri obeyed, moving toward the back of the lab,
her head hung in misery. A heavy blanket of despon-
dency settled over her. How had everything gone so
wrong? She couldn't believe these murderous bastards
were going to get away with this. Yet what could she
do? With each step she took, she knew she was moving
closer and closer to her own grave. Her eyes cast about
wildly, her mind spun as she tried to think of some way
out of this. There had to be a way! She refused to give
up without a fight.

Her eyes settled on the laboratory table at the
back of the room, and an idea sprung into her head.
Quickly, her mind raced through the scenario, weighing the pros and cons, trying to determine all of the
things that might go wrong. And, unfortunately, there
were plenty of them. Thompson was right on her
heels, the gun aimed at her midsection. More than
likely, his reflexes would make him pull the trigger
and she'd be dead in a flash. But they were dead anyway if she didn't do anything. Thompson was right
handed. Maybe, if she ducked to the left, the bullet
would miss her. She glanced toward the huge incubating oven along the wall to her right and saw the room
reflected in the glass. Bender was behind Thompson,
with Weatherton bringing up the rear. Kerri prayed

Bender would be on his toes and quick to react, or everything would be lost.

They were nearing the lab table and Kerri sucked in a deep breath, locking in her nerve. It was now or never.

She came down cockeyed on her left foot, twisting her ankle out of her shoe, and faking a stumble. Her left hand grabbed the corner of the lab table to catch herself, and she winced as spears of pain shot up from her injured wrist and along her arm. Her right hand reached out with lightning speed and closed around the beaker full of hot agar sitting on the burner.

The heat from the glass seared her palm and she yelled out in agony, fighting against the reflex to pull back from the pain and let the beaker go. Wheeling around, she flung the beaker's contents into Thompson's face, the glass container itself following a split second later. Thompson screamed in agony and clutched at his face, while the beaker fell to the floor, shattering into hundreds of tiny shards. Thompson's gun went off, just as Kerri had thought it would, but the bullet fired harmlessly into the acoustic ceiling tile. Thompson clawed at his face, reeling around, howling like a wounded beast.

Bender, as Kerri had prayed, was quick to react. He spun around, his arm knocking Weatherton's gun-toting hand aside. Weatherton also pulled the trigger reflexively, and the bullet winged across the room, hitting the valve on one of the oxygen tanks beside a work station. It ricocheted off with a metallic whine, but not before dislodging the tubing that led from the valve into the workstation. The reverberant hiss of oxygen emptying into the air filled the room.

Weatherton's reactions were quicker than Kerri

had hoped. He dodged from beneath Bender's swinging fist, falling into a crouched position. The gun swung back toward Bender, and in an instant Kerri knew Bender was as good as dead. She let out a screaming, "Nooooo!" and lunged toward Weatherton. He saw her motion from the corner of his eye and it distracted him for the split second Bender needed. Bender's foot swung out, connecting solidly against Weatherton's hand. A shot fired before the gun went skittering across the floor, bringing Kerri's headlong lunge to an abrupt halt. A split second later, the exterior of one of the workstations shattered.

Weatherton dove after the gun, sliding along the floor like a baseball player going for home base. Bender went after him, his efforts impeded by Thompson's writhing body, which was now prostrate on the floor, his face beginning to blister from the agar clinging to his skin like hot wax. Kerri lunged after Weatherton as well, but was still several feet away when she saw his hand close around the gun. He rolled onto his back, aiming it squarely at Bender's chest.

Another shot rang out and Kerri screamed. Her eyes riveted on Bender, who had stopped in his tracks so suddenly Kerri knew he must have been hit. She waited for him to slump to the floor, but he simply stood there, his eyes blinking in disbelief and confusion. Frantic, Kerri searched his body, trying to find the wound, but she could see no blood, no holes, no nothing. Puzzled, she looked over at Weatherton, her eyes widening with horror when she saw the pulsing fountain of blood arcing from a hole in his neck. Weatherton's eyes were glazed, the color of his skin nearly matching the stark pallor of the white-tiled wall behind him.

Still confused, Kerri caught a glimpse of movement from over near the console. She turned and stared in shock a moment before her mind registered what her eyes were seeing. At the far end of the console, nearly doubled over as one hand clutched at his blood-soaked shirt, beads of sweat dripping off his face, stood Kevin. He held a gun in his other hand, his arm trembling wildly, wavering in the air a moment before it fell heavily to his side. With a tiny moan, he slumped against the edge of the desk.

Kerri rushed over to him, followed closely by Bender. They positioned themselves on either side of him, each draping one of Kevin's arms over their shoulders. With silent communication, they heaved Kevin off the console and started dragging him toward the door. Struggling beneath his weight, they made their way out of the lab and down the hallway to the elevator. There they paused, staring at the closed elevator door with the keycard mechanism beside it.

"Kevin has a keycard in one of his pockets," Bender told Kerri. "Let's set him down here against the wall."

They eased Kevin onto the floor and Kerri knelt in front of him, her eyes fearful. He was still alive—she could see the pulse in his neck fluttering—but she knew he had to get medical attention soon. With a grimace, she pulled back the blood-soaked edges of his jacket and searched through the pockets on his right side. Bender did the same on the left.

"Here it is," Kerri said, pulling the card out. She stood and shoved it into the slot beside the door, breathing a sigh of relief when she heard the whine of the elevator's motor. Resuming her post at Kevin's side, she looked at his ravaged belly with tears in her eyes.

Then she stared up at the elevator door. "Hurry," she whispered. "Please, hurry."

Back in the laboratory, Frank Weatherton lay inches away from death. The blood spewing from his neck had weakened him and he was barely conscious. His oxygen-starved brain struggled against the black void that tugged at it, functioning on a level a mere hair above survival. Thompson, the agar on his face having cooled enough to give him some control over his senses, staggered to his feet and moved toward his boss. Weatherton's mind, long past rational thought, saw nothing more than a body lurching toward him. In a last reflexive effort to survive, he raised his gun a foot or so into the air. But he lacked the motor control necessary to bring his arm around and aim at his pursuer. With his last dying spasm, his finger tightened on the trigger, sending a bullet winging across the room, where it lodged in the rear wall of the shattered workstation, pulverizing the flimsy barrier and shredding the electrical wires that ran in a maze behind it. Blue-white sparks lit the air, connecting with the pure oxygen that had been steadily feeding from the nearby tank. With a roar like a freight train, a huge fireball erupted, decimating everything within a twenty-foot radius. It instantly fried Thompson and Weatherton, then rolled across the lab, hungry for more fuel. It filled the room, licking at the walls and ceiling, melting the other workstations, feeding on oxygen released from the other tanks as tubing connections burned away. More sparks flew as flames consumed the console, the intense heat molding the computer casings into lumps of misshapen plastic. The flames rolled across the laboratory tables, melting away the plastic pipe that fed the still-burning Bunsen burner, allowing a steady stream of gas into the room, fueling the flames even higher. An overhead sprinkler system kicked on, but the fire was so hot, so rabid in its pursuit, that the water hissed into steam almost as soon as it left the sprinkler heads.

Back at the elevator, the car finally arrived. Kerri held the door open while Bender grabbed Kevin beneath his arms and dragged him inside. Once Bender had Kevin's upper body well into the car, he eased Kevin's head to the floor, then stepped back into the hallway to get his legs. It was then he heard a strange roaring noise coming from the direction of the lab. He turned and looked down the hallway, his eyes widening when he saw the door to the airlock heave and buckle. A fire alarm went off.

Grabbing Kevin's feet, Bender shoved them into the elevator, throwing himself in as well and nearly doubling Kevin back on top of himself. Struggling to his knees, Bender reached up and yanked Kerri inside, then frantically jabbed at the buttons on the elevator control panel until the door began to slide closed.

A loud boom echoed through the air, rattling the walls, the floor, and the elevator car. The rubber bumper that ran down the side of the elevator door was inches away from settling into its groove in the wall when a second explosion sounded, followed by a roar like the engine on a jet plane. In the tiny crack of space left, Kerri saw the door to the airlock blow off its hinges and hurtle down the hallway toward them. Behind it, was a huge ball of rolling flames. Kerri screamed and covered her head with her hands.

The airlock door hit the elevator, denting the metal. Though the elevator door was completely closed now, the heat of the fire outside quickly made its way into the car. With the walls and ceiling of the elevator snapping and crackling, the car lurched as it began its slow descent.

Inside, Kerri and Bender sat silent and frozen with tension, their eyes focused on the descending numbers overhead, praying they would reach the bottom before the maelstrom above made the car malfunction and plunge them to their deaths.

Another explosion echoed from above, and the elevator car rocked violently, making Kerri gasp and brace herself against the wall. But the car continued downward, and Kerri muttered a brief prayer of thanks when the number one appeared overhead and both the front and back doors to the elevator slid open with a mockingly gentle ding.

Bender reached over and pulled a red button on the control panel, locking the door in the open position. The rear door of the elevator opened onto a loading dock, the front faced the lobby. A frantic crowd of employees rushed through the lobby, which had already filled with thick, black smoke. Yet another explosion rocked through the building, and a shower of glass and flaming debris rained down on the loading dock.

"This way," Bender said, heading into the lobby. He ran over to the security desk, snagged a wheeled chair, and hollered to two nearby men for help.

Kerri stood inside the elevator car, her face pinched with worry when she saw that Kevin's breathing had grown more shallow. The elevator shaft overhead creaked and groaned, and she worried the inferno above was working its way toward them. Bender shoved the chair inside the car and, with the help of the two men, hoisted Kevin into it. They quickly pulled the chair out of the elevator, moving across the lobby with Kerri close behind. Seconds later, a terrible roar descended from above and the whole ceiling of the elevator exploded, flames shooting out from above and around the car.

The smoke was much thicker now, making it difficult both to see and breathe. As soon as they pushed through the main door to the outside, Kerri gulped the fresh air greedily. She followed the men as they dragged Kevin's chair to a distant part of the parking lot. There, panting from their efforts, they leaned against the chain-link fence circling the property and stared back at the building. The windows on the upper floor blew out with a shower of exploding glass, and white-hot flames licked along the wall. Off in the distance, they heard the sound of approaching sirens. Stunned and bewildered, the growing throng of people who exited the building gathered in small groups in the parking lot, staring in disbelief at the conflagration.

Kerri knelt down in front of Kevin's chair, staring up at his pale, drawn face with tear-filled eyes. Bender pushed himself away from the fence and came around to join her.

"Kevin?" Kerri whispered. "Kevin? Can you hear me? You've got to hang on, Kev. Please. For me." She rolled her eyes heavenward, uttering a prayer, begging God to spare this man who meant so much to her.

As if in answer, Kevin's eyes fluttered open. He looked down at Kerri's soot-smeared, tear-streaked face and managed a weak smile.

"Help is on the way, Kev," Kerri said, her voice catching with emotion. "Just hang on, okay?"

Kevin didn't answer her. Instead, his eyes rolled up and focused on Bender a moment, then they dropped back to Kerri. "I tried to get him to stay at the hospital," he whispered, the effort showing on his face. "But he would have none of it."

"True enough," Bender agreed. "I don't listen too well."

"Stubborn as a mule," Kevin muttered, rolling his eyes. "You two will make a perfect couple."

And then he passed out.

EPILOGUE

Kerri dragged the last pile of books off her desk and gingerly placed them into a box. Fortunately, the damage she sustained to her left wrist had been only a sprain, and it was now fully healed. But her right palm was still tender in spots, and she flexed the hand a few times to ease the stiffness left behind by the second-degree burns she sustained when she grabbed the hot beaker of agar. Several weeks' worth of dressings, ointments, and therapy had done much to heal it, but the doctors told her it would be months before the tenderness disappeared. Staring at the fiery red scar tissue, she couldn't help but be reminded of Stephen's horrible death, and tears filled her eyes.

With an expression of weary sadness, she gazed around her empty office, stripped bare of all but the desk, the chair, and the empty bookshelves. The decision to close it down had proven surprisingly easy. She had no regrets, though she did suffer a few pangs of guilt as she referred her patients to other practitioners in the area. Still, she knew it would be better in the long run for everyone involved. She had a lot of personal healing to do before she would be able to help anyone else. And this office, with its memories of Stephen, was simply too painful a reminder.

Favoring her right hand, she picked up the box of books and carried it out to the waiting room, where she stacked it among the others piled near the door, awaiting the arrival of the movers. Finished, but somehow reluctant to leave the office for the final time, she turned and looked at Stephen's desk.

Six weeks had passed since his senseless death, and still it angered her greatly. Her fondness for Stephen had grown deep over the years. The sharing of their personal losses had created a bond that went far beyond that of employer and employee, or even friend to friend. She had loved Stephen like a brother and, in fact, was the closest thing he had to family. Hence, it had fallen to her to arrange his funeral, a task she found to be taxing and oddly relieving. She was both surprised and touched by the number of his fellow students who came to the ceremony. Their immense support and caring served to validate all she'd done to make Stephen's life better. Though the bitterness remained—and likely would for a long time to come—it was tempered by this brief glimpse into the life she had helped Stephen to mold.

On the second day after Stephen's death, as Kerri hovered near Kevin's bed praying for his recovery, a police officer came by to return her purse. A maintenance worker had found it lying in the dirt where she'd dropped it in the Underground City. She opened it, intending to check and make sure all its contents were intact, and there, on the top, were Stephen's dinosaurs. The pain she felt at the sight of those simple toys tore her breath away. Not since Mandy's death had she felt so devastated. A few days later, she arranged for Stephen to be buried in a plot beside Mandy. She considered giving the dinosaurs to Jace, as had been

Stephen's intent. But she couldn't bear to do it. In the end, she carried them out to Stephen's grave, placing them atop the freshly turned dirt, and instructing T-rex to watch over him.

Now, with tears flooding her eyes, she stared at the desk where Stephen had sat so many mornings, hiding behind his newspaper. So vivid were her memories, she swore she could smell the coffee brewing on the credenza behind him and hear the faint rustle of his newspaper as he haphazardly folded it and tossed it onto the desk. She stared a moment at the vision of his smiling face, his warm brown eyes. With an empty ache in her heart, she whispered a last good-bye. Stephen's vision faded away, and blinking away her tears, she grabbed her jacket and left the office, locking the door behind her.

It was a sunny day, but bitterly cold, the wind whipping in off the sound carrying along a frigid moisture that drilled right through Kerri's skin, chilling the bones beneath. Huddled inside her jacket, she hiked the few blocks to the parking garage where she'd left her rental car. After driving out and paying the man at the gate, she turned and headed uptown.

Half an hour later, she was pulling into the parking lot of the hospital, preparing to visit Kevin in his room on the eighth floor. His recovery had been long and hard. The bullet fragments had torn through his gut, mincing intestines and taking a nick out of one kidney. The blood loss he suffered was tremendous, and by the time the helicopter got him to the hospital, the doctors gave him a less than 10 percent chance for survival. During the first few days, he lay in a coma, balancing on a precipice between this world and the next. Kerri stayed by his side—watching, waiting, praying—leaving only long enough to make periodic visits to Jace down on pediatrics, or short runs home to tend to Shadow, take a shower, and change her clothes. Her worry was compounded by the guilt she felt, knowing it was her actions that had led to Kevin's getting shot in the first place.

On the third day, Kevin's doctors felt he was stable enough for surgery, and they did what they could to repair his ravaged gut. But still he remained unresponsive, hooked up to a frightening array of tubes, wires, and monitors.

On the fifth day, Jace was released from the hospital, and Kerri left her self-imposed post as Kevin's guardian to take the boy home with her. At first, she feared they would deny her guardian request. The investigation into the fiasco at the Coleman Institute and Kerri's proximity to those involved left the police and most of the hospital staff eyeing her warily. But as the story unfolded, it became clear that Kerri's involvement was above suspicion.

On the day of Stephen's death, Bender had arrived at the hospital to find Kevin pacing the hall outside Jace's room. Despite the worried, frantic look on his face, Kevin had tried to deny there was anything wrong. But Bender sensed otherwise, and when no one could provide any answers as to Kerri's whereabouts, he started pushing Kevin for some answers. Finally, Kevin filled him in on what he knew.

After Kerri's revelations in the hospital cafeteria the night before, Kevin became concerned for her safety. In addition to getting her to stay at the Holiday Inn for the night, he also assigned round-the-clock officers to watch her. Unbeknownst to Kerri, she had someone tailing her from the moment she left the

Holiday Inn the following morning. Unfortunately, when Kerri ran from the guard at the scene of Stephen's death, she managed to lose her tail as well. When the officer assigned realized it was Kerri's car that had been destroyed, he knew the danger was all too real.

The officer immediately tracked Kevin down and filled him in on what happened. Unable to find Kerri, Kevin waited at the hospital, figuring Kerri would try to come back there out of concern for Jace, or at least beep him to let him know what had happened and where she was. But after an hour or so of restless waiting, he made the decision to head for the Coleman Institute. Bender made a complete pest of himself until Kevin finally agreed to let him come along. On the way, Bender filled Kevin in on more of the details of his and Kerri's prior visit, and they decided to start their look around on the mysterious fifth floor. When they arrived at the institute, Kevin flashed his badge at the receptionist behind the security desk, and she gave him a keycard that would allow him access to the fifth floor. Though she wanted him to wait until she could find someone to escort him, Kevin refused. He and Bender went up in the elevator alone.

Once the facts of the case became clear, Kerri's request for temporary guardianship of Jace was approved, primarily because Jace became hysterical whenever anyone suggested otherwise. But the approval came with a caveat. If she hoped to turn her guardianship into something more permanent, Kerri was going to have to demonstrate her ability to provide a secure and stable home environment for the child.

It was this, most of all, that led to her decision to close down the practice. It didn't take Kerri long to realize that the rigors of trying to keep her practice going, of trying to balance the work hours and the long commute with Jace's care and schedule, would be impractical. Besides, without Stephen, she had little desire to keep the practice open.

She had saved up enough money over the years to allow her to take a few months off without working. She reasoned she and Jace would need the time together to sort things out and establish some type of routine. When she found out Nathan still had her listed as the beneficiary on his life insurance, it gave her the resources to expand that free time to nearly a year. By then, she decided, she and Jace would have a chance to settle down and be well along the way in the healing process required to overcome the terrible emotional wounds haunting them both. Maybe then, she would consider returning to practice somewhere on a part-time basis.

Bender had offered her a partnership in his own practice, but she declined. Bellingham was no closer to where she lived than Seattle. Besides, she wasn't sure she wanted to return to work in a private practice anywhere. It was then that Bender offered to give up his practice as well, offering Kerri a partnership in his life instead, by repeating his proposal of marriage. She had considered his offer, but in the end, she stalled him. Her feelings for Bender ran deep, and there was little doubt in her mind she would eventually say yes. But for now, she felt the need to take things more slowly, to focus the bulk of her time and energy on Jace. Bender understood that, and pressured her no further. He sold his practice to another psychiatrist in the area, and though he still saw some of his patients—those who had the most difficulty making the transition to a new doctor—he spent less and less time there. In the interim, he followed through on a dream he'd had for years, and set up a commuter air service to shuttle people back and forth from the islands to the mainland.

He also insinuated himself into the daily aspects of Jace and Kerri's lives. He invited them out to his house on San Juan Island, where Jace was delighted to discover Bender owned several horses, including a gentle Shetland pony named Sugar. The look of sheer joy on Jace's face as he sat tall in the saddle, riding Sugar at a slow lope around Bender's small corral, made Kerri's love for Bender grow even deeper.

Over the past few weeks, Jace and Bender had grown quite close. Kerri found herself even feeling a little jealous at times when Jace confided things to Bender that he didn't share with her. But she could also see how good they were for each other. Jace brought out a side of Bender Kerri hadn't seen before—a playful, childlike quality she found rather endearing. And though Jace still had his periods of melancholy from time to time, his recovery had been nothing short of amazing. A large part of that, she knew, was thanks to Bender's influence. When Kerri enrolled Jace in a school in Port Townsend, she hoped he would escape some of the notoriety surrounding his parents' deaths. At first, he adapted well, catching up with the studies with little difficulty and making a few new friends. But news of who he was and what had happened eventually leaked out. Bender spent long hours with Jace, talking him through the brief flurry of taunts and teasing that came from his fellow classmates, until Jace was able to tolerate them with a stoic indifference that soon made the kids lose interest.

Today, while Kerri packed up the last of her office and paid a visit to Kevin, Bender and Jace were out on the flight Bender had promised. Kerri could easily imagine the expression of delight and excitement on Jace's face as they flew out over the ocean, hopping between the islands, looking for deer on the runways. Jace's anticipatory excitement the past few days had made him so restless, Kerri feared she would have to up his dose of Ritalin. But they managed without doing so.

As she rode the hospital elevator to the eighth floor, Kerri's thoughts shifted back to Kevin. He had given her quite a scare. His coma lasted for almost three weeks, and when he did finally come around, there were complications from infections that required additional surgery. Now, six weeks later, he was finally well on the road to recovery, though he was weak as a kitten and had lost a tremendous amount of weight.

As she entered his room, she made a mental effort to shove aside the depression that had seized her in the office and forced a smile onto her face. The smile became more genuine when she saw Kevin sitting up in bed, a half-chewed toothpick hanging out one side of his mouth, wearing what Kerri could only describe as a shit-eating grin. Sitting beside him, with one hand lying casually on his arm, was the brunette nurse from Peds who had caught his eye several weeks ago. Though Kevin still looked pale and gaunt, there was a familiar sparkle in his blue eyes that Kerri hadn't seen for a long time.

"Well, well," Kevin said when he saw Kerri enter the room. "If it isn't the one-woman IRA."

Kerri blushed. Kevin's frequent teasing about her

heroic efforts at the Coleman Institute were a source of continual embarrassment for her.

"You seem to be doing well," she said, with a pointed look at the brunette nurse.

"Feeling pretty spry today, lass, I must admit. Of course, Suzanne here might have something to do with that," he said with a wink.

Suzanne turned to Kerri. "Is he always this full of blarney?" she asked.

"You have no idea," Kerri said, shaking her head.

"Well," Suzanne said, glancing at her watch, "it's time for my shift to start. I'll stop by later during my dinner break and see how you're doing." With that, she rose, gave Kevin a quick peck on the cheek, and left the room.

"Looks like things are getting serious here," Kerri teased once Suzanne was gone.

Kevin shrugged, as noncommittal as ever.

Kerri sighed and shook her head. She moved over and took the chair Suzanne had vacated. "So, what's the latest word from the doctors?"

"Well, you'll be happy to know I'm to be discharged in a couple of days. Got some physical therapy ahead of me, but Suzanne has promised to help me with that."

"I see," Kerri said, grinning broadly. Then, in a more serious tone she said, "I suppose you've heard they indicted the owners of the Coleman Institute, as well as Arthur Cavanaugh, Letitia Miller, and a few of the other officers. Most of the employees were exonerated. Seems Weatherton had a handful of trusted employees who were in the loop and knew what was going on. The majority of those people out there didn't have a clue."

Kevin nodded. "I just hope the bastards get what's coming to them," he said. "Unfortunately, all of the records of what was going on out there were destroyed in the fire. It's going to be tricky to prove their guilt. The way they had things set up, all the owners need to do is claim ignorance of what was really going on. All we can prove at this point is that they were silent partners in the venture."

"What about the diary they found in Jeri Sandston's apartment?"

"Unfortunately, the only people she named were Weatherton, Cavanaugh, and that Miller woman."

Kerri found herself feeling a certain satisfaction that Letitia Miller was one of the ones who would probably be convicted. She was also startled at the relief she felt over Nathan's name being left out of the overall scheme. Though he was no less guilty than Weatherton and the others, she knew his involvement was the result of a temporary form of insanity, brought on by the tremendous grief he experienced with Mandy's death. That grief drove him over the edge, robbing him of the morals and beliefs she knew he had once ascribed to. His motivation, at least in the beginning, had arisen from his desire to save their daughter's life. The fact that he failed had to have been devastating for him.

At times, Kerri wondered what her own decision would have been had Weatherton approached her instead of Nathan. Would she have been willing to sacrifice Mandy's life for her own beliefs about what was right? The answer was murky at best, and it left her with a tremendous burden of guilt over all that had happened. That, and the fact that her own self-pity and grief after Mandy's death had made her blind to

Nathan's despair. Many times she replayed that final scene in the lab, wondering if the outcome might have been different had she set aside her own self-righteous indignation.

"The worst part," she said to Kevin, voicing some of her thoughts, "is the loss of the research papers detailing the technique they used for cloning the organs. When you consider the potential of something like that, if it's used properly, it seems such a terrible waste."

"Someone else will find a way," Kevin said with confidence. "It may take awhile, but it will happen."

"I suppose you're right."

Kevin studied her face a moment, then asked, "So how's the boy doing?"

"Amazingly well," Kerri told him. "He and Bender are out flying today."

"They seem to get on well, those two," Kevin said, still eyeing her closely.

"They do," Kerri agreed.

"So, when are you going to go ahead and marry this guy?"

Kerri arched her eyebrows in surprise. "Why, Kevin, you sound as if you're in a hurry to see me get hitched here."

Kevin shrugged, plucked the toothpick from his mouth and casually tossed it onto the stand beside his bed. "He's okay," he said.

"Just okay?"

"Well, what do you want me to say, lass. The man helped save my life."

"And mine," she reminded him.

"Yeah, so he's okay," Kevin said, pouting.

"You just have a hard time admitting anyone is good enough for me, Kevin."

"I'm just looking out for ya, lass. Promised your father on his death bed that I would."

"I know, Kev," Kerri said, giving his arm an affectionate squeeze. "And you've done a fine job of it." Seeing she had embarrassed him, Kerri glanced at her watch and stood. "I need to get going. Jace will be home soon. Can I get you anything before I leave?"

"No thanks. I'm fine."

"You try and behave yourself, okay?" She bent down and kissed him on the forehead. "And don't you ever scare me like this again, you understand?"

Kevin gave her a snappy salute. She turned away, shaking her head and heading for the door.

"Lass?" Kevin called after her.

Kerri turned back toward him. "Yes?"

"If I were you, I'd snatch that shrink fella up quick, before he gets away."

Kerri smiled at him. "I might just do that," she said. Then, feeling better than she had in weeks, she headed home to her new family.